CUT LIKE WOUND

Praise for *Cut Like Wound*

'Nair captures the seedy side of shiny new India vividly, and Inspector Gowda—with his weary self-knowledge; his secret, wistfully aspirational biker tattoo; his stagnating marriage and his confusion when an old flame re-enters his life—is a welcome addition to the ranks of flawed-but-lovable fictional cops.'

The Guardian

'I loved this book and was constantly gripped. Truly astounding writing.'

Peter James, author of *Dead Simple* and *Looking Good Dead*

'Nair weaves a fast-paced, engrossing tale of suspense ... This is not an old-fashioned whodunit. And therein lies the strength of *Cut Like Wound.* It is not just a story of another smart cop on the trail of another serial killer. It is more a story that explores the mind of a killer, even tempts the reader to sympathise. All the time, without letting go of the fact that Gowda is the true protagonist.'

India Today

'*Cut Like Wound*, set in Bangalore, is a racy page-turner. But it is also a commentary on a society, a people, a way of life, love, longing, identity and loneliness'

The Hindu

'The plotting is tight, the setting is familiar to Indian readers and the characters are riveting. The Trainspottiest side of Edinburgh couldn't have hosted *Cut Like Wound*'s startling scenes of ritual worship or its lively transgenders. Even the venal corporator is believable.'

Hindustan Times

'The murder is well plotted with the requisite smoke and mirrors to keep the reader guessing. *Cut Like Wound* sets a gripping pace.'

The Deccan Chronicle

'This book [is] consistently interesting as a commentary on the lives of the sexually marginalised, on the blurring of gender expectations, and the emotional baggage carried by both men and women in a world of role-playing and self-presentation.'

The Sunday Guardian

'[Those] who enjoy international settings will surely enjoy the well-drawn tension between modern and traditional Indian culture, Gowda's steady confidence and the heady immersion in Bangalore's hidden recesses.'

Booklist

'[A] startling debut crime novel.'

Sunday Times

'The psychological thriller is soaked in the sights and smells of Bengaluru and introduces quite a few interesting characters, including the hero, Inspector Borei Gowda. As usual, Nair's writing is lucid which makes the reading light and quick.'

Verve

'In *Cut Like Wound*, Nair retains that same earthiness, in a dramatically different genre. The unglamorously named

Inspector Borei Gowda literally pops out of the pages at you, and by the finish, is so lifelike that you have his entire appearance and personality mentally mapped out ... The story is an honest yet uncomfortably raw exposé of the underbelly of contemporary Indian life.'

Khaleej Times

'Gowda's first case delights—and sometimes shocks—the senses and is a very welcome addition to the still frustratingly small ration of Indian crime fiction now appearing in Britain.'

Morning Star

'Anita Nair has successfully leavened the standard mystery novel with her own brand of character-driven narrative.'

New Internationalist

'[This] is a fine crime novel.'

Crime Chronicles

'*Cut Like Wound* is a fresh mystery.'

The Mystery Gazette

'Excellent, and hopefully, start of a series of novels featuring Borei Gowda.'

Afternoon Despatch & Courier

CUT LIKE WOUND

A BOREI GOWDA NOVEL

ANITA NAIR

HarperCollins *Publishers* India

First published in India by HarperCollins *Publishers* 2012
4th Floor, Tower A, Building No. 10, DLF Cyber City, DLF Phase II,
Gurugram, Haryana – 122002
www.harpercollins.co.in

This edition published 2023

2 4 6 8 10 9 7 5 3 1

P-ISBN: 978-93-5029-380-5
E-ISBN: 978-93-5029-559-5

Typeset in 10.5/13.9 Stempel Garamond
by Jojy Philip

Printed and bound at
Nutech Print Services - India

FSC
www.fsc.org
MIX
Paper from responsible sources
FSC® C143748

This book is printed on FSC® certified paper
which ensures responsible forest management.

For Sunil,
big brother, best friend and partner in crime from Day 1

'Flora, what makes up a man? That's the question to ask. Well, apparently something within me had asked and I wonder, how sane am I? Yes, yes, I talk sane at times, but without warning, something else emerges like the shadow but more concealed and deadly. What is the trigger? Yes, that's the question…'

—*The Shoemaker*, Flora Rheta Schreiber

MONDAY, 1 AUGUST

9.14 p.m.

It wasn't the first time. But it always felt like the first time as he stood in front of the mirror, uncertain, undecided, on the brink of something monumental. On the bare marble counter was a make-up kit. He ran his finger along the marble to check for dust. Only when he was satisfied that it was clean did he touch the quilted cover of the lid. The satin shirred under his fingers. Something leapt in him, a wave of pure delight that was enough to set him off.

A giggle emerged. A snickering sound of pure joy, girlish glee and unfettered excitement.

He switched on the series of light bulbs that circled the mirror. The electrician had stared when he had asked for the light bulbs to be placed so. The electrician's assistant had sniggered and asked his boss, 'Why does he want so many lights? Who does he think he is? Rajinikant? Is he going to put make-up on?'

But he had set his heart on it after seeing it in a film. And so he had frowned and said in his coldest voice, 'If you don't know how to, I can always find someone else.'

That had settled it.

In the mirror, he gazed at himself just once. Fleetingly. Then it was time. He opened the kit and started working quickly with a practised hand. The concealer to cover the shadows on his chin and around his mouth. The foundation, the fine creamy talc to smoothen the complexion, eyes enhanced with the kohl pencil, and a twirl of the mascara brush on the eyelashes for the wide-eyed look. He wet the tip of his finger with Vaseline and traced his eyebrows. A pat of blush and then carefully he outlined his lips with a lip pencil and filled it with a deep pink lipstick. He pressed his lips together and applied a coat of gloss. Glistening lips smiled shyly at the reflection in the mirror.

He took a tissue from a box and carefully wiped the counter. Marble was like skin, it showed up how it was used. He crumpled the tissue into a ball and flicked it into the bin. Then he stepped out of the track pants he was wearing and hung it from a hook behind the door. He averted his eyes as he slid off his briefs and, making a moue of his lips, tossed it into the basket that held the T-shirt he had been wearing.

Naked and wearing just his painted face, he walked out of the bathroom. Then he paused and went back again to the dressing table. He opened a drawer in which were six vials of the finest attar.

He opened the stoppers one by one and sniffed at the mouth of the perfume vial. Nag Champa. Raat Shanthi. Roah al Oudh. Shamama. Moulshree. And his favourite, Jannat ul firdous.

He chose Shamama. Tonight he would be a garden of flowers. A complex scent would herald his arrival and trail his footsteps.

The last door of the walk-in wardrobe was locked. Only he had access to it. He hummed under his breath as he opened the door. Green, green, tonight he felt like wearing green, he told himself as he pulled out a shimmery green chiffon sari.

From one of the drawers, he pulled out a pale-green petticoat and blouse. Then, with a smile, a padded bra and the matching panty. He was still humming as he adjusted the blouse and pinned the sari so it hung low, showing off his waist and his navel piercing. He touched the topaz in his navel. A frisson of excitement unfurled in him.

From the shelf on top, he chose a wig of waist-length hair. He placed it on his head and, as he looked into the mirror, something about the way his eyelids drooped told him who he wanted to be tonight.

With elaborate care he arranged himself so he was the woman from a Ravi Varma painting, fresh from a bath. He brought his hands to his chin and laced his fingers so the tip of the forefinger of the right hand touched the edge of his lower lip.

Hair to her knees, loose and flowing. The sari clasped between fingers, an attempt to cover herself but hinting at the nakedness of her breasts. The fullness of flesh. Shy, yet seeking more. All woman.

He laid out the earrings. He always wore the same pair. Old-fashioned pearl earrings with hooks so he didn't have to fumble with screws. He clipped a necklace around his neck and slid glass bangles on both wrists. The tinkle of green glass as he lifted the hem of the sari and stepped into two-inch-high green-and-beige sandals made him smile again.

No matter how busy he was, he always found the time to go shopping for clothes, accessories, cosmetics and perfumes. The sales assistants presumed it was for the woman in his life and they would exchange glances as he took forever to decide. Once, one of them had said, almost enviously, 'She must be very special, this woman you are shopping for ...

most men who come here just pick the first thing they see and leave ... but you...'

He had nodded. 'She is the most important person in my life!'

In the mirror, he saw himself as the woman the goddess wished him to be.

The goddess spoke every Friday. The goddess whispered in his ear what he should do. Ten days ago, the goddess had said it was all very well that he liked to dress up as a woman in the privacy of his home, but it was time for him to step out into the world as Bhuvana. It was time to take control. He had obeyed.

For the first time, though, the goddess had appeared on her own this afternoon. He had dozed off after lunch. He woke up to her whispering his name. She was sitting at the foot of his bed. For a moment, he saw her and then she disappeared. All that was left was a smell of camphor in the room and her incessant whisper in his ear: Tonight you must be Bhuvana. Tonight you will be Bhuvana. As Bhuvana, you will walk the streets. Will you or won't you?

'I will, I will, Amma,' he had whispered, overwhelmed at the vision.

She had left him then, but the fragrance of camphor still hung over the room. A reminder that she was there and was keeping tabs on him.

Now he was the woman he wished to be and he knew again that wave of pure delight. I am she! I am her! I am the most beautiful woman I know.

It was Bhuvana who stuck a hand on her hip and pouted her lips at him.

It was Bhuvana who placed the tip of her finger against her glossy lip and murmured, Tonight, tonight...

And it was Bhuvana who took his hand and led him into that secret place in his head where he was queen of the night, draped in sheer chiffon, with the lustre of those exquisite pearls tantalizing everyone.

Bhuvana, who knew how to make it all possible.

A gentle knock on the door brought him out of his reverie. A voice murmured, 'Are you ready? We have to go now.'

He smiled at the woman in the mirror. Bhuvana smiled back and blew him a kiss. Tonight, all would be well. Tonight, she would have her fill.

'Yes,' he called out. 'I am done.'

Then, turning to the woman in the mirror, he said almost coyly, 'Let's go, Bhuvana!'

Bhuvana giggled.

9.51 p.m.

'Go home, Liaquat,' one of the vendors said quietly. 'Go home, son.'

Liaquat shook his head. 'No, I don't want to go home. I don't want to go home alone,' he hissed. 'Leave me, bhai jaan. You don't know how I feel ... All day I stayed in the house by myself. I fasted too, bhai jaan ... Allah knows how I did it ... I summoned every ounce of willpower and didn't touch even a drop of water. But who am I doing it for? What's the point?'

The vendor exhaled loudly. It was the first day of Ramzan and Mohammed and his wife too had kept the fast. Only the little ones had been fed. 'Why do you do it, Abba?' Tasneem, his girl, had asked him.

'Because Allah wants us to,' he had said. The truth was

they did it for their children. So Allah's dua would shower down on the little ones.

Soon everyone would come out of their homes after the Iftar meal. Through the night they would wander the streets, picking up a treat here, a bargain there ... Many things were bought for the year ahead. Saeed's daughter was buying her wedding clothes and accessories though the nikah was four months away. He had heard that the rent for a pushcart this year during the Ramzan month had gone up to Rs 15,000. But it would be worth it, Yusuf, one of the men, had told him. They would make a clear profit!

Mohammed had his spot and stand all year round in the same place. And the Ramzan business would spill over to where he was. He smiled. Everyone profited during this month. So would he.

It was late in the night but the Shivaji Nagar bus stand area was simmering with activity. On Saturday nights the streets were more alive than they were during the weekdays. And this was the first night of Ramzan. A certain excitement resonated through the alleys and lanes.

The vendors had their carts edged along the roads, which buzzed with life. The smell of meat cooking on charcoal mingled with the aroma of samosas being fried in giant vats of hissing oil. Chopped onions and coriander leaves, pakodas and jalebis, strings of marigold and jasmine buds, rotting garbage and cow dung. The high notes of attar. The animal scent of sweat and unwashed bodies.

Men of all sizes and shapes trawled the alleys. Some seeking a hot kebab to sink their teeth into; some seeking a laugh, a suleimani in a glass and a smoke. Men returning home from work. Policemen on the beat. Autorickshaw drivers and labourers. Whores. Eunuchs. Urchins. Beggars. Tourists. Regulars.

A composite cloud of a thousand fragrances and desires in that shadowed underbelly of the city.

Mohammed pummelled the dough for the roomali roti. 'Stay by my side and help me with these. We'll go home when I am done. You can stay with us tonight. Shama will be pleased to see you. She's cooked some haleem. You like that, don't you?'

Liaquat swallowed. He hated being alone. He was tempted by the thought of spending the night in Mohammed Bhai's house. Shama-bi would serve him food that tasted of his mother's cooking. Not the rubbish Mohammed and the other vendors dished up to feed these fools who came to Shivaji Nagar looking for what they thought was Muslim cuisine.

He would sleep in the hall with the children. He would sing songs and tell jokes and make them laugh. Everyone thought he was a scream. Most of all, his big-bearded Razak.

He thought of how those fierce eyes softened when they fell upon him. Of how gentle his caresses were as he turned him over and murmured into his ear, 'My Leila. The sweetness of my Leila ... you make me forget it all.'

A deep pang of longing seared through him.

'No one calls me Leila any more,' he said. 'Ever since my Razak mia...'

'He'll be back soon,' Mohammed said quietly. 'Go home,' he urged again, seeing Liaquat's dilated pupils. The boy had been shooting up again. Allah knew what he would get up to in a little while.

'See that...' he said, his eyes following the two police constables ambling lazily down the road, 'the thollas are out in full force tonight. If they catch you…' Then unable to help himself, he demanded, 'Why do you get into this state? Why do you do it, Liaquat? It's not good for you…'

'What state?' Liaquat shrieked. 'Don't lecture me. I am fine. Do you hear me? I am fine. I am horny. I want to get fucked. That's what I want. That's the state I am in,' he said, rising and weaving his way through the stalls.

'I want to fuck … I want to fuck all night…' He laughed as he slid into the shadows. His white kurta pajama cut a swath through the darkness.

Mohammed turned back to his skewers of chicken cubes. In the distance he could hear Liaquat's falsetto shrill, 'Tonight … Leila will fuck all night tonight!'

10.04 p.m.

They had set out together and she had to wait for almost half an hour for a moment to escape her companions' gaze, which dogged her every gesture and step. She didn't particularly want to be with them but the one she called Akka wouldn't allow it any other way. 'You have to be careful. We have to be careful. If someone saw you…'Akka said.

She hadn't responded to Akka's words of caution. But resentment simmered within her. It was like being four all over again. When her mother would take her to see the sights at the trade fair but she wasn't allowed to touch a thing. 'It has a price attached to it,' her mother would say. 'If it breaks, how do we pay for it?'

Everything has a price attached to it, she knew. But now she could afford it. It was hers if she wanted it. Anything and everything she wanted.

Akka touched her elbow. 'I am not so sure you should take such risks!'

She tossed her head with the hauteur only beautiful women can affect and get away with. The pearl in her earring swung against her cheek. 'Don't I need some fun too?'

Her mouth curled in an almost wolfish way as she turned away. Akka thought she knew all her secrets. But the best secret of all, she kept close to her heart. No one knew. No one knew how powerful it made her feel. She giggled. Akka shot her a look, but said nothing.

The market that had sprung up for Ramzan was on the other side. Akka wouldn't let them go that way. 'They won't like it,' she said. 'Why invite trouble to sit in our laps?' she told one of the others who claimed the bargains were better there.

'Besides, even our best customers will pretend they don't know us. It's their holy month. And they bring their families with them to see the shops ... We'll stay here near the bus stand and go towards Cubbon Road. The others will be there as well,' Akka said, leading them in that direction.

The crowds pressed against her as she and her companions wove their way through. She felt a hand caress her waist and cup her arse. She leaned into the caress but it was over even before it had begun. Leaving her feel used. Dirty. Dirty. Dirty.

A nerve snapped. A pulse throbbed. She saw Akka sneak a look at her. But she didn't let any of what she felt show on her face. And when the moment arrived, as they all stood near a bangle vendor, flirting with him, trying on bangles, scouting for prospects, she slipped away.

She felt him follow her down the dark alleyway. She swung her hips, leading him on. He knew. He knew what she could offer him. She smiled and suddenly paused. She turned her head to smile at him. Her smile froze. There was another man following him. A man who laughed when he caught her eye.

'Go away,' she snarled.

The interloper laughed. A high, shrill laugh. 'He thinks you are a woman.'

Tears welled up in her eyes. Then she pulled herself together and said through clenched teeth, 'Why do you say that? I am a woman, can't you see?'

The interloper giggled. 'In which case, I am the prime minister of India.'

He tapped the puzzled man on his shoulder. 'She's not a woman. She's a chhakka ... Didn't you see a group of them near the bus stand?'

The man's face fell. Disgust replaced lust. He walked towards her and scrutinized her carefully. 'He's right. You are a fucking eunuch.'

The interloped smirked. 'But if that's what you like ... Mia, come to me, I can do better...'

The man hawked and spat on the street. 'Fuck off. I don't want you sucking my cock either. As for you,' he turned to her, 'I am not desperate enough to fuck a man in woman's clothes. Go find some fool who'll be taken in by this...' He gestured at the fullness of her bosom and the curve of her hip. He flicked a pearl drop with a forefinger, watching it swing like a pendulum. 'Nice earrings, but you know something, they don't suit you. You are not pretty enough ... or woman enough to wear them.'

She stared at her feet where the blob of saliva had come to rest. She heard his footsteps as he hurried from the alley. She was nothing. She was filth. She was scum. She had been so happy this evening and then...

She raised her eyes and saw the mocking expression on the other man's face. If only this fucking cocksucker hadn't followed her. If only ... As the rage gathered in her, she forgot all about who she was.

She hurled herself forward and sank her fist into the fool's belly. He bent over double with the impact, the pain, the breath knocked out of him, and as he tried to find his feet, his hands flailed in the air, grabbing for anything they could find to support him. It was her loosely woven plait of hair that he clutched at. The wig came away in his hand.

His eyes widened as he saw who stood before him. The face, even under all the layers of make-up, was one he recognized. Through pain and disbelief, he felt a grin stretch his lips. 'I don't believe this ... you ... it's you...'

She flicked the small switchblade she kept in her bra and held it to his throat. 'Quiet,' she said coldly.

He stared at her, suddenly afraid. 'Let me go.' He fell to his knees. 'I won't tell anyone ... I promise by everything I hold precious. I won't. You must believe me ... please.'

She hummed under her breath as she moved behind him, still holding the knife to his throat. He heard the snap of a bag open and shut. What was she doing?

Then the steel edge of the blade no longer pressed against his throat. He relaxed his clenched muscles. But before he could turn his head to look at her, he felt something descend on the back of his head.

He felt his skull crack. He screamed. Through the blinding pain, he felt something tighten around his throat.

'No, no,' he whispered, trying to snap the string, and felt a million particles of glass pierce his hands. Flashes of light burnt his eyelids and hissing serpents filled his ears. He felt unable to resist any more.

'Are you here?' Akka called out as she entered the mouth of the cul-de-sac. The elderly eunuch was shocked into silence by what she saw. The man on his knees and she standing behind him with her disguise in disarray. As Akka watched, the man crumpled to the floor. He hadn't even felt the string cut the skin of his throat and press down into his jugular vein.

Akka saw her take a tissue from her bag and wipe her fingers clean. She threw it on his face. The line of blood on his throat grew with every beat of his heart.

Akka ran towards her.

She didn't speak for a while.

'He recognized me. I had no option but this...' she said in an even voice.

Akka felt a chill seep into her. Who was this person who stood before her?

'Anyway, he is just a lowlife. No one's going to miss him. So don't waste your emotion on him,' she said, arranging her hair carefully. 'Give me your mobile.' She opened her palm out to Akka.

Akka handed it over silently and watched as she pressed a few keys.

'It's me,' she said. 'I've left a thing in the alley near Siddiq's garage. Deal with it. No leftovers.'

Akka's eyes darted to the man on the floor. But he was still alive...

'Let's go,' she said, handing the phone back to Akka.

As they turned into the street ahead, she suddenly stopped. She turned and walked briskly back to where he lay on the ground. She bent over and peered at him for a moment. Then she stood up and kicked him on his face with the heel of her sandal. 'Scum,' she muttered as the pointed tip split the skin on his cheek.

11.42 p.m.

Samuel rubbed the cuff of his biking jacket across his eyes. He was tired and sleepy as he rode his bike home. It had begun to drizzle. A fine stinging rain. What kind of a life was this where a man had to ride thirty kilometres across the city in the middle of a wet night after a whole evening of watching models cavort in their underwear and society types toss free alcohol down their throats?

How they wooed him. All of them. The models, the hosts, the sponsors, the party goers, the gatecrashers; Sam here, Sam there, Sam this, Sam that ... Sammy, Sammy ... and then they would want to see the frames he had shot, what they looked like as they held their pert poses with pasted-on smiles ...

It disgusted him, this job he did as a photographer of the society pages for the *Bangalore Messenger*. Some days at least. Most days it was just a job, and one he was good at. He knew how to capture the right poses and intersperse the familiar faces with new ones. And he knew who was who. So he aimed his camera at the butterflies, leaving the moths and caterpillars for the photographers from the rival papers.

'You have the eye,' his editor said. 'You are good. You don't miss a thing. That's why the readers prefer our page three to the others'!'

This was still better than working for the news pages as he had once. Prowling outside the house where a child had been mauled and torn to death by a tiger during a visit to Bannerghatta National Park. Crowding at the gates of Golden Palms for a glimpse of a Bollywood actor when he arrived for his nuptials. Sneaking on a politician's tryst with a TV actress. On the day he was asked to get an unusual shot of the grieving family of a former Miss India who had killed herself, he decided to make the move. It had shamed him that he had to prey on people's vulnerabilities and privacy to fill space. He preferred to capture images of people pretending to have a good time rather than impinge on naked emotion.

Samuel thought of his bed longingly as he turned from the airport road into Sathanur Cross.

Another eighteen kilometres and he would be home. The wind had an edge to it. The fine drizzle had turned into a steady rain, but Samuel felt hot under his collar. He had had too much to drink. He shouldn't have while he was on an assignment. Now Samuel felt his evening's excess curdle in his gut and rise upwards as he rode down the desolate road. He pulled over to the side of the road, retching. From the corner of his eye, he saw a Scorpio with Tamil Nadu number plates drive away. But a fresh rush of vomit hurled itself up his throat, obliterating all thought...

He wiped his mouth with a piece of crumpled tissue he found in his pocket. Then he sat on the kerb, letting the rain wash over him. He hoped a Hoysala wouldn't drive by. It would be a bloody nuisance to explain to the police that he'd had too much to drink and have to flash his press card for instant immunity from the breath analyser.

Then, through the rain, across the road in the eucalyptus grove, he saw a movement. A tongue of flame crawling. A flash of white at ground level. Samuel rubbed his eyes and stood up. Then he ran across the road, instinctively picking up his camera, a Nikon D700.

A man lay in the ditch at the edge of the grove. Or what was left of a man. From the charred mess of flesh and cloth emerged a low moan.

Samuel's hands dropped to his side in horror. What had happened here? What should he do?

Unable to help himself, he raised the camera and clicked.

11.51 p.m.

The night made it seem less unreal. Nights are the same everywhere, he thought. Only up there in the skies, the stars are different.

For fifteen years he had lived in another hemisphere. Different constellations had watched over him, his destiny cast by unfamiliar stars. Michael Hunt, Anglo-Indian by birth, Australian by choice, leaned back in his Meru cab and wondered at the conjoining of two stars from two different hemispheres that had brought him back to Bangalore.

'It's much better by daylight,' the cab driver said. 'Bangalore is a very hi-tech city. Have you heard of Infosys? We have big IT companies – Wipro, Dell, IBM … and Kingfisher beer!'

Michael smiled. 'I know,' he said.

'Your second visit?' The cab driver saw his skin and assumed he was a foreigner. No touch of the tar brush for Michael, former inhabitant of Whitefield and Lingarajapuram.

'I grew up here,' he said quietly in English and then again in Kannada, '*Nanu illi beldhidhuu.*'

The cab driver gulped and peered at him curiously in the rear-view mirror. He opened his mouth to speak and then changed his mind. Michael knew his words had had the desired effect. He shut his eyes to still the conversation. It had begun raining. He would have liked to roll down the windows and feel the breeze bring in the rain. Would it feel the same? Or would the rain in Bangalore have changed too?

The cab turned off the airport road. The new airport road. He hadn't been to this new airport ever and thought of the old one longingly. That had been more in tune with the India he had grown up in and remembered. Michael opened his eyes and sought familiar landmarks. He was certain that his friends and he had explored these small roads a long time ago. But he couldn't recognize a thing.

'Where does this lead to?' he asked.

'Kothanur, and then to Hennur, and from there to Outer Ring Road,' the driver said. 'If we go straight ahead, we can go into the city via Lingarajapuram. But we'll take a left and continue towards Whitefield.'

Michael nodded. One day he would go to Lingarajapuram. One day, when he had summoned the strength for it. For now they would go to Whitefield, where his grandaunt's house waited. A house he could sell or keep, or do with as he pleased. Michael felt a great weariness descend over him. At his age, he ought to be making retirement plans and not having to consider new possibilities in life. But Becky, childhood sweetheart, wife of twenty-three years, had slipped out of his life and all that was left were memories, remorse, sorrow, anger, and the looming question: Where do I begin?

He had done this once before, when he migrated to Australia at thirty-three. How could any man be expected to do it all over again? Where was he to find the energy, the drive, the need?

Up ahead in the distance, through the windshield, he saw a man step onto the road and wave his arms. The man's arms moved furiously, seeking attention, calling for help...

'It is dangerous to stop at this time of the night,' the cab driver said.

Michael didn't speak. The cab driver knew best. Suddenly he spotted the bike.

'No, no … stop the car,' he said. 'Something is wrong.'

WEDNESDAY, 3 AUGUST

Borei Gowda peered at the general diary. In the time he had been away, the station must have been bustling. Two cases of burglary. A domestic squabble. An accidental drowning of a child. A homicide.

His head hurt. There was a pounding at the back of his head like a 4-stroke Royal Enfield engine. Only, this one had a faulty tappet setting. The dhuk-dhuk note increased by the minute and then suddenly became something else.

Gowda pressed the sides of his forehead with his fingers. Harder, harder, hoping the pressure on his temples would stem the pounding. Why had he drunk all that whisky last night? He should have stuck to his regular drink. Old Monk Rum with Coke and a twist of lime. With rum, no matter how much he drank, he never had a hangover. Whisky offered no such assurances the morning after.

He wished he could go back home and lie in a dark room. He wished his wife would sit by his side and massage Tiger Balm on his forehead with fingertips that were soft but sure. He wished she were the kind of wife whose silkiness of flesh he could turn and nuzzle his head into.

Gowda's wife Mamtha lived in Hassan. He had organized her transfer there when they found a seat for their son in the DGA Medical College in Hassan a year ago. They had to pay five lakh rupees as capitation fee. This, despite the minister's recommendation and a majority of Gowdas on the management committee. To leave Roshan there on his own wasn't advisable, his wife had said. The boy had a predilection for getting into trouble. So Gowda called in yet another favour, and his wife was now the doctor at one of the ESI hospitals. Roshan lived with his mother and until he graduated, Gowda was going to have to be on his own, except when he could get away to visit them. Or, when Mamtha was inclined to take a few days off and come to Bangalore. But she was increasingly reluctant to do so, saying it bored her to stay at home doing nothing while Gowda was away all day. It was better if he came to Hassan, she insisted.

It was always hard coming back to a silent home after being with his family. By reaching much later than he had intended to, he had lost one more day of earned leave and had also failed to fit himself within the rhythm of a working day. If he had gone to the station house, it would have swept him into its coils and made sure that the minutes and seconds of that first day were accounted for. Pending files, briefings, bickering, paperwork, phone calls – it was only when a man had none of these to hinge his day to that he realized the worth of a working day.

Gowda had pottered around in his house from five in the evening, wondering what he ought to do. There was something disquieting about being at home early in the evening. He switched on the TV and channel-surfed. None of the shows held his interest. Nor did the pile of magazines on the coffee table. What did people do at this hour anyway?

So it had seemed like a good idea when Nagaraj called. 'Two of my friends are in town and we are going out for dinner. Why don't you join us?'

Gowda had hesitated. Then he thought of the long evening stretching ahead. In a couple of days he would settle down, but the first night was the worst. That was when loneliness gnawed at him with piranha teeth. If he stayed at home he would drink on his own. Drink himself senseless. This way he would drink less, he had decided.

'God knows how long this place will be here,' Nagaraj had laughed as they parked outside the new Nandhini restaurant near Kothanur.

The Outer Ring Road and some of the main thoroughfares in the city outskirts were speckled with places such as this. Supposedly restaurants that families might want to eat at but more often filled with groups of middle-aged men getting drunk to their eyeballs as they discussed politics, mistresses, real estate and religion.

Gowda had looked around him carelessly, taking in the nature of the custom. Nagaraj and his friends belonged here along with the little Japanese bridge that ran over a blue-tiled artificial stream, the cluster of gazebos, the low-wattage lighting, the potted palms, the gingham tablecloths already splotched with turmeric and grease stains, and the overriding smell of curry. What the fuck am I doing in a place like this? he had thought. It had 'This Way to Alcoholics Anonymous' written all over it. And yet, what else was there for him to do? For that matter, who was he to sneer at Nagaraj and his friends? Just because he knew better didn't make him any different or superior.

Gowda reached across and rang the bell. One of the constables rushed in.

'Bring me some tea,' Gowda said, and as the man turned to go, he added, 'and increase the speed of the fan. Is it hanging there as an ornament to look at? Who turned the regulator all the way down?'

'I was on leave yesterday, sir,' PC Byrappa mumbled. It was obvious Gowda was in one of his moods.

Gowda waved him away and sank his head into his hands. The constable's shiftiness had reminded him of someone. Suddenly he knew. Roshan. The moment you asked the boy something, he would produce a disclaimer. I don't know; I wasn't there; no one told me…

The faulty 4-stroke engine pounding in Gowda's head shifted to his temples and accelerated its rhythm.

Gowda didn't know what to make of his son. The boy had alternated between surliness and an eagerness to please. Gowda hadn't known how to be with him. Aloof father or buddy daddy. In the end he had been neither and chosen to behave as if he were a guest just visiting. There and not there. *Hello, how are you? How is college? Have you seen any good movies?*

Hard work, this parenting, he told himself as he stared at the stack of files on his table. And for what? The little fucker won't even give me the time of the day when he's a hotshot doctor somewhere. But he was a father and fathers can't absolve themselves of their responsibilities even if they know what lies ahead.

Neither can you absolve yourself of what you need to do now, Inspector Gowda, he told himself as his eyes paused on the mazhar report on the homicide at Horamavu.

Gowda read through the case diary. The homicide had

taken place almost two weeks ago; in fact, on the very Friday night he left Bangalore. There seemed to be no obvious intent. There was evidence of sexual activity but somewhere between sex and that final placement of the victim on the back seat of the Tata Sierra, he had been bludgeoned and strangled to death.

The deceased was a middle-aged man who had owned a medium-sized pharmacy. Preliminary investigation had revealed that he had no business enemies or pressing debts, no illicit liaisons or association with any underworld dons. He was just an ordinary man who had probably sought sex outside his marital bed and had to pay for it with his life. In fact, the only extraordinary thing about his life may have been the manner in which he died.

Gowda tried to recreate the crime in his head. The pharmacist in the back seat with the woman. He is so busy getting a blow job that he doesn't realize that another person has sneaked into the car through the hatch. A hammer or something similar is used to strike the pharmacist on his head. He is strangled quickly but just as they get ready to strip him of his possessions, they are interrupted and so the murderer and his accomplice flee the spot without taking anything.

The deceased had on his person Rs 10,000 in cash and an iPhone. He had been wearing a diamond ring, a four-sovereign gold chain and an expensive watch.

Gowda pressed the bell. SI Santosh walked in and saluted.

'What is this manja thread reference to the ligature used?' he asked in greeting, pretending not to notice that the man who stood before him was a perfect stranger.

'Sir?' The sub-inspector's eyes widened.

'You are SI Santosh, aren't you?' Gowda said, peering at

the badge pinned on his chest. Thank god, this one was a man. With his predecessor, a woman inspector, Gowda had without thinking stared at her chest to read her name and felt her eyes blaze on him.

'Sir?' she had barked. *You haven't heard of sexual harassment, have you?* the fire in her eyes demanded.

He had looked away, embarrassed. He had been petrified of the repercussions. For the next three months he had managed to avoid her till she was transferred to a station in south Bangalore.

'Sir.'

The young man's strident voice cracked his reverie. Gowda gave himself a mental shake.

'Well, explain this to me.' He jabbed at the file. 'Case number 84/2011. The homicide at Horamavu. The pharmacy shop owner Kothandaraman. I thought the cause of death was strangulation.'

The young man straightened. He began by clearing his throat, but catching Gowda's impatient glare, hurried on to recite almost word perfect the contents of the case diary.

Gowda's eyes narrowed. 'Do you think I can't read? I said, explain. Are you saying a manja thread was used as the ligature? But a manja thread would snap. So it couldn't have been a manja thread!'

The sub-inspector swallowed. A convulsive sound that made Gowda want to reach out and strangle him. Did he naturally attract fools? Or was it a conspiracy by the department to shunt the foolish and inept into his care?

'Sir,' SI Santosh began, having found his voice again, 'the post-mortem report showed the ligature used was a string. From the tissue discolouration, the forensics department...'

A bark of laughter erupted from Gowda. 'Forensics

department!' He shook his head. 'The only man who counts in the forensics lab is Dr Shastri.'

Santosh turned the pages of the file and said, 'This is signed by a Dr Shastri.'

'In which case, go on...' Gowda said, leaning back.

Santosh cleared his throat again. 'From the tissue discolouration, the forensics department thinks it to be a one-cm-thick string. The kind masons use at building sites to mark straight lines. But there were cuts on the victim's hands as he tried to resist. Particles of glass were found in the cuts and in the throat wounds. In fact, there were cut-like wounds on the neck. It seems the string had been coated with glass in the manner manja threads are. So the ligature worked as a blade as well. It severed as it strangled.'

'What have you discovered? Any possible motives? Business rivalry? Family feuds? Anything like that?'

'No, sir, his son said he couldn't understand it at all. The ACP thinks it is a robbery that went wrong.'

Gowda nodded. Somewhere deep within, he knew this would be one of the cases that was destined to be a C report. For lack of evidence it would stay in the pending file for months, years, and then be forgotten. Only in the dead man's home would they remember how one horrific Friday night, he had been slaughtered for no apparent reason, and ask themselves, 'Why?'

Gowda closed the file and asked, 'Who found him?'

'That was the strange thing, sir. His family, of course, was worried when he didn't come home as usual and didn't respond to their calls. They went to the medical shop but it was shut. A tailor across the road apparently saw him leave at about nine p.m. At about two in the morning, the son received a call saying his father was dead. The boy was frightened and called his uncle who lived next door. At about five in the morning, a milkman noticed a car parked in Horamavu near the lake. He peered inside the car but couldn't see anything. He tapped on the car window but there was no response. That's when he came here. Head Constable Gajendra was there when they broke open the car window.'

Gowda looked into the middle distance to signify end of conversation.

'Sir, there's something else that's come up,' SI Santosh said.

'What? One more of those land disputes?'

'No,' Santosh said, unable to hide the excitement in his voice. 'A hospital report has come in of a man admitted last night. He was badly beaten up and then someone, or a group, tried to burn him alive. But because of the rain last night the fire must have died out, so he was still alive when he was found. It happened in the eucalyptus grove a little before Kannur. He was taken to JJ Hospital near Kothanur. That was the nearest hospital. Apparently, one of the witnesses insisted.'

Gowda sighed. 'Shouldn't it be taken up by the Yelehanka police station?' he asked, unable to hide his irritation. It seemed to him that more and more police stations were showing less interest in investigating offences. All they wanted was the power of the uniform.

'It comes under our jurisdiction. Fortunately for us, there are two eyewitnesses, three in fact. But the man died before regaining consciousness. The medico-legal report showed some complications. I have already signed for the body to be moved to the mortuary. This is our case, sir.'

The boy was almost puffing with pride. Us. City Police. One of these days he would discover for himself the slimy stench of criminal investigation. I'd like to see how he feels about 'us' a year down the line, Gowda thought.

He pulled open a drawer in the table and took out a strip of Brufen. He popped out two of the tablets, threw them down his throat and drank deeply from a bottle of water.

Santosh looked at the seated man, studying him feature by feature. So this was Borei Gowda. A little over six feet tall and with what was once a big-boned muscular frame. But fat had come to pad what was once muscle, so he looked soft in the middle, blurred at the edges. Gowda's greying hair was cut regulation short, lending a certain distinctiveness to what would otherwise have been a composite blandness of features. Eyes that were neither big nor small. A straight nose. A clean-shaven jaw with a cleft in the chin. Once, Borei Gowda must have been a striking figure. Now it seemed as if the air had gone out of him and his body had crumpled to its current stance of poor muscle tone and wilted ideals.

Santosh tightened his gut and squared his shoulders unconsciously.

Gowda felt Santosh's eyes on him.

'What?' he snapped.

'Shouldn't we go to the scene of the crime, sir?'

'Should we?' Gowda asked querulously.

'Sir?' Santosh's horrified tone rattled Gowda.

The boy was way too earnest. It was time to treat him to a reality check.

'Let's go,' Gowda said, rising and pulling his Aviator shades on.

'I didn't mean to rush you, sir. But if we leave it too late, the crime scene will be contaminated,' Santosh sought to explain, trying to keep abreast with Gowda.

Gowda didn't speak for a moment. The fool thought

he was bloody Sherlock Holmes and Inspector Madhukar Zende rolled into one.

'How long have you been in service?' he asked carefully.

'Three months; two weeks in this station. I asked for this posting, sir.'

Gowda looked at him. 'Why?'

'I wanted to work with you. I have heard so much about you. I know I can learn a lot from you.' He paused and then added slowly, 'And, sir, I am a Gowda too.'

Gowda felt his mouth curl. 'And you think that will make a difference?'

'I just want you to know that you can be assured of my complete loyalty. We are from the same caste, after all.' Santosh tried to gauge Gowda's reaction but his eyes were hidden behind his sunglasses and his silence gave away nothing of what he felt about Santosh's troth of allegiance.

'Santosh Gowdare, why did you join the police force?' Gowda asked as they walked towards the jeep.

'I always wanted to. So I did my BSc in Forensic Sciences from Karnataka Science College, Dharwad.'

'You mean to say you didn't want to be an engineer or a doctor?'

'Like everyone else, I too had those as my first choices, sir. I wrote both the engineering and medical entrance exams but didn't get the necessary marks. Then I decided that I would focus on becoming a police officer.'

'You still haven't told me why, Santosh Gowdare,' Gowda murmured softly.

The young man flushed. Was his senior officer mocking him, he wondered. Why did he insist on calling him by his caste name and with a suffix of respect attached to it? He had done only as Head Constable Muni Reddy at his previous posting had advised him to.

He ran his fingers through his hair and said, 'I wanted to do something meaningful. I didn't want to be stuck in a job doing the same thing day after day. At the end of each day, I wanted to feel that I had done something worthy.'

'You could have done that as a teacher,' Gowda said.

'No, sir, I want more than that.'

Gowda saw the glitter of excitement in the young man's eyes, the fervour to do good in his stance and gait, the smooth, shaven cheeks and the precision of his movements. The innocence of the uncorrupted mind; the naivety of youth. Gowda felt a pang of regret. Once, Gowda had been that young man, seeking to protect the weak and needy, aching to scourge the world of its evils. Where had it all gone?

Gowda felt a great fatigue descend on him. That's all he needed now. A bloody do-good bigot. Well, he'll learn soon enough, Gowda told himself as he watched the young man talk to PC David, the driver.

'Where's Gajendra?' Gowda snarled

'Coming, sir!' The head constable rushed out of the station house and got into the back of the Bolero along with Santosh. Gowda slid into the front seat and slammed the door shut.

As they waited at the traffic light, Gowda felt the heat of the day press down upon him. The din of traffic and the blare of horns, the dust, the hangover that refused to lift … Gowda's gaze swooped on the reflection of Santosh in the rear-view mirror. Something made him want to wipe away the smugness in Santosh's profile as he sat lost in thought. His face hardened.

He turned and asked, 'Tell me something. Have you seen the body?'

Santosh almost leapt out of his seat. Then, struggling to find composure in a split second, he mouthed, 'Sir?'

The young man's puzzlement irked Gowda even further.

'Is that a yes or a no?' he drawled in a voice that was silky smooth.

Gajendra turned pale. This was how it always was when Gowda's mean streak surfaced. A silkiness of tone that, instead of underplaying the viciousness, only heightened it. He felt a great sympathy for Santosh. Older, hardened men were known to have sniffled when Gowda chose to turn silky.

'Yes sir, I mean, no sir, I haven't seen the body yet,' Santosh fumbled, thinking he had never felt so intimidated in his life. 'I thought it could wait. Whereas the crime scene...' His words trailed off as he caught Gowda's expression.

'So that's what you think,' Gowda said and then, turning his head to the driver, he muttered, 'mortuary.'

Santosh opened his mouth as if to say something. Then he checked himself. Gowda saw him pull a small notebook from his pocket and flip through it surreptitiously.

'What is it? What's troubling you?' Gowda asked slowly.

Santosh licked his lips. How had they got so dry?

'No, sir, nothing sir. But the crime scene...'

Gowda sighed. 'If you insist, we can go to the crime scene now. But has it occurred to you that it rained all night? And do you realize how many people would have walked all over the eucalyptus grove by now? Some of them may have even shat on what is your scene of crime! That's what you'll find there – a pile of shit! We will discover a lot more from the post-mortem than the scene of crime.'

Santosh didn't speak. He looked down at his hands. It

seemed to him that no matter what he did, he just couldn't seem to please Gowda. And he had so wanted to be part of Gowda's team.

'Look, we will get to the crime scene sometime later in the day, we have to. It's part of the procedure. We will have to do a house-to-house, question nearby homes or shops to find out if anyone saw anything, noticed any suspicious movements, but trust me, this will be more conclusive,' Gajendra whispered in Santosh's ear.

Santosh had heard about Borei Gowda at the Meenakshipalaya police station in Bangalore Rural where he had been posted first.

The head constable was a man called Muni Reddy, who took it upon himself to educate Santosh when he protested about certain laxities at the station house.

Muni Reddy looked at him carefully as if sizing him up. 'Please don't be offended, sir. But you are a young man, and I have been around for a while. You must forget all that they taught you in the police college. Out on the streets, it is a different world altogether.'

Santosh had listened to him, unsure whether to be amused or irritated. 'Are you saying I have to turn into a criminal to be able to deal with criminals?'

Muni Reddy twirled the end of his moustache, deep in thought, and said suddenly, 'Ever since you arrived here, I have been wondering why you seem so familiar. Now I know who you remind me of. Borei Gowda!'

'Who?'

'Borei Gowda. He was posted here as SI a long time ago, when this was an outpost station. He was like you. Earnest and wet behind his ears. He thought the police had a duty to protect the people.' Muni Reddy shook his head incredulously at the mere thought.

'Why? Don't you think that's what we are here for?' Santosh said as he watched Muni Reddy ladle sagu onto his plate.

Meenakshipalaya was a village that had turned into a little town when a Japanese car company set up a factory nearby. Santosh had rented a small house near the police station, where he lived alone.

Muni Reddy had taken to dropping in on him and some days he brought along a tiffin carrier of home-cooked food. 'You must miss home cooking; eating out every day must have turned your taste buds deader than a dead rat's tail,' he offered in explanation the first time, when Santosh had protested.

Soon the mealtimes had turned into sermons on the Diktats of Life according to Muni Reddy, which Santosh had no option but to endure. Muni Reddy's wife was a splendid cook and if the food came at a price – Muni Reddy's life lessons – he would stomach that as well.

Muni Reddy put the spoon back into the dish and said, 'We protect people when they come to us; we don't go out looking for trouble to save them from.'

'You mean to say that we will watch someone commit a crime and get away with it simply because no one filed a complaint. How can you be like that, Muni Reddy?'

The head constable shook his head ruefully. 'That's exactly what Borei Gowda would say. And he wouldn't listen to me, either. Look what happened to him!'

Santosh pondered if he should question Muni Reddy on Borei Gowda, whoever he was. But would it be construed as gossiping about a senior officer with a junior? Santosh stuffed a piece of puri into his mouth before the curious streak in him overwhelmed prudence.

But Muni Reddy was not a man to be silenced. 'The thing is, I have never seen an officer like Borei Gowda. He was fearless and intelligent. Do you know what it means for a policeman to have both those qualities? It is a terrible combination, if you ask me. It means he becomes unstoppable. It means he goes looking for trouble. That's why I want you to listen to me carefully. I've been wearing this uniform for twenty-five years now. I can see when an officer will go places and when he will be shuttled from one station to another like a lost soul seeking salvation.'

For the next few weeks, Santosh tried to trace Borei Gowda's service record. At the Meenakshipalaya police station, it seemed there had been a golden era for a period of seventeen months. The crime rate had fallen drastically. Known defaulters were kept under surveillance. A murder case had been solved. And then suddenly Borei Gowda had been sent to the traffic desk. From star officer he had been condemned to a posting where he was little more than a clerk.

'What happened, Muni Reddy?' Santosh demanded.

The older man looked away. 'Why are you digging up the past? What is going to change?'

Santosh drew himself to his full height, schooled his features to forbidding grimness and snapped, 'As your superior officer, I command you to tell me exactly what happened, without leaving out any detail.'

Muni Reddy sighed. 'It was a little past nine in the morning when Ramesh Rao, who worked at the State Bank of Mysore, came to the station. His eyes darted all over the station. I could see it was the first time he had entered a police station and he seemed guilty. Why do people look guilty when they enter a police station even if they have done nothing wrong?'

Santosh sniffed impatiently. 'Don't digress ... tell me what happened.'

'Apparently, the night before, the bank clerk had heard some noises in his neighbour's home. He had thought they were quarrelling. They did that a lot. But in the morning when their maid came to his house and told Mrs Bank Clerk that no one was opening the door, the two of them went across. The neighbour's scooter was parked outside. All the windows were shut. But through a slit in the curtain, Ramesh Rao could see the furniture had been turned over.

'Gowda drove the jeep himself to the house and in less than half an hour had the door broken down. It was as Ramesh Rao had said. The house was a mess. Furniture lay scattered, and pans were strewn around. In a bedroom on the ground floor, Shankar, the husband, lay unconscious. He had been bludgeoned on his head and there was a small pool of blood. Upstairs, Suma, the wife, was found dead. Her nightie lay in shreds around her and her throat had been slit.

'By the time Shankar was discharged from the hospital and Suma's post-mortem report arrived, Gowda had solved the crime. He merely needed the medical reports to validate his findings. Shankar had murdered his wife and made it seem like an intruder had attacked and incapacitated him, and then raped and killed his wife.

'In the case diary, Gowda's preliminary findings were categorically recorded: A ladder was found propped against the balcony that opened from the bedroom upstairs. As it had rained the previous night, footprints were clearly visible. However, there were no footprints leading to the ladder. Instead, the footprints led to the back door. The gash on

Shankar's forehead seemed to be self-inflicted rather than caused by an intruder's weapon. No weapon or heavy object that could cause such an injury was found anywhere in the premises or surrounding area. Neither jewellery nor money was stolen from the house.'

'But how did he know the husband did it?' Santosh was incredulous.

Muni Reddy smiled. 'Gowda found a small trace of blood on the door jamb of the puja room. It matched Shankar's blood type. He saw that a pair of rubber slippers had been left under the tap near the back door. Shankar's slippers. The post-mortem report showed evidence of sexual activity. Shankar had had sex with his wife that night. They found a trace of semen in the lungi he was wearing and a couple of his pubic hair in one of the shreds of the nightie the wife had worn. Gowda had sent that to the forensic lab.

'The post-mortem report also revealed that Suma had had sleeping pills that night. Shankar had slit her throat when she was asleep, torn her blouse and petticoat to suggest force had been used but there were no bruises of any sort that should have been there.

'Then he threw the furniture around and hit his head on the door jamb to make it seem like he had been attacked. The doctor's report showed that it wasn't a major injury. Shankar had taken three sleeping pills himself so he would be found unconscious. And groggy when consciousness returned, just as someone with a head injury would be. He had thought of everything.

'It was an open-and-shut case. Shankar confessed and the case went to trial.

'And Gowda felt he was infallible. He was Huli Gowda. Tiger Gowda. That was his mistake.

'He heard of a group of underage girls being held in a little house in Shanthi Colony. I was part of the raid and we booked two men under 366/366A/376/349 IPC and Section 2, 3, 4, 5, 7 Immoral Traffic Prevention Act. One of them was a minister's cousin and the other, the underworld don Kolar Naga's brother-in-law.

'Gowda could do nothing but watch helplessly as the case became a no-case. In his haste he had forgotten to get a warrant issued. Suddenly he became the one who had broken the law by trespassing. The underage girls disappeared from the shelter they had been taken to. There were no records to mark their admittance there. The register had been tampered with as well. Gowda was shunted off to traffic and that was the beginning of the end. He got into trouble there as well and eventually, five years later, he was moved to Bowring Hospital station. The huli was reduced to an ili. A hospital rat at that.

'He has had twelve transfers so far and has been bypassed for promotion. Which is why he is still only inspector. And there is a joke about him. They call him B report Gowda. Gowda, whose cases come to nothing.'

Muni Reddy shrugged. Santosh looked at his desk, unable to meet the older man's eye. He was being cautioned, he realized.

What was this path he had chosen for himself? Would he too become another B report Gowda? The tiger who became a rat. But Santosh had made up his mind. His brother, who was an author of some repute and the editor of a Kannada weekly, knew whom to call. There was always a cousin or an uncle or the friend of a friend who could be prevailed upon to pull strings.

When Santosh's transfer orders to Gowda's station

arrived, Muni Reddy said thoughtfully, 'He is not an easy man to work with. But thank God, you have one thing going for you. You belong to the Gowda caste too, don't you? He will watch out for you, I am sure.'

Gowda smoked a cigarette and watched while Santosh threw up his breakfast. The young man was retching as if to evacuate every trace of what he'd had to look at. When he straightened, wan and glassy-eyed, Gajendra offered him a bottle of water.

Santosh thrust it away furiously. 'He knew, didn't he?' he snarled.

Gowda frowned. 'You smell of vomit. Clean yourself up before you get into the jeep with me.'

Santosh grabbed the bottle and splashed water over his face and into his mouth. Somewhere in his chest a sob of outrage gathered. Who the fuck did Gowda think he was? That *boli maga*!

'I thought you said you had been in service for three months. How do you expect me to know that you hadn't seen a corpse yet?' Gowda offered.

Santosh stared at him. It was the closest to an apology he would ever get, he realized.

'He has seen corpses, sir, but nothing like this,' Gajendra said carefully. The young fool would worsen the situation by saying something silly. Especially now that Gowda seemed to be exhibiting a slight trace of remorse. Gowda didn't like to feel remorseful, Gajendra knew.

'Third-degree burns can be hard on the eye,' Gowda said, confirming Gajendra's reading.

Santosh raised his head, unable to believe what he had heard. Could anyone be so callous? So unmoved by the nature of the horrific death? That was a man once. Hard on the eye! 'Think of what he must have suffered,' he whispered, feeling a chill down his spine.

'Third-degree burns are not painful, you didn't know, did you? What did they teach you at Mysore? All the nerves would have been damaged so they wouldn't have been able to relay any pain signals to the brain.' Gowda lit up yet another cigarette. 'In fact, he would have lost all sensation in the first thirty seconds or so...'

Santosh felt bile rise up his throat. 'Stop,' he screamed. When the jeep ground to a halt, he tumbled out, retching. This time, when Gajendra offered him a bottle, he didn't say anything.

'The next time, you won't be so affected,' Gowda said when Santosh was back in the Bolero.

'After a few times, you won't even blink an eyelid. It's all part of the learning curve of being an investigating officer.'

PC David shot Santosh a look of pity, but didn't speak. He was only a driver but he was attuned to the tenets of police dharma: don't get involved in what doesn't concern you. He started the vehicle and glanced at Gowda's face. But Gowda was deep in thought.

The throbbing in his temples increased as the day sped by. All he wanted to do was get into bed and pull the covers over his head. He knew that he should stay on in the station house and tackle the mountain of paperwork that had grown on his table in his absence. But at a little past six, he had PC David drop him home.

He pulled the curtains across the windows so it was dark and quiet. And then, like a wounded animal retreating into its burrow to lick its wounds, he crawled into bed and passed out.

When Gowda woke up, it was almost eight. The headache was gone and had been replaced by a dreadful lassitude. He lay on his bed in the dark room and felt the emptiness of the house and his life gnaw at him. Until, unable to bear the nipping teeth of his own thoughts, he stumbled out of bed into the bathroom.

He turned the shower on, hoping that, in his absence, the God of Blocked Showers may have decided to step in with a miracle. The shower hissed to life, spluttered and stopped. Gowda sighed. Obviously the God of Blocked Showers had bypassed him again. He would have to call a plumber one day very soon.

Gowda filled a bucket with water and splashed sleep and inertia out of himself.

He padded naked into his bedroom and looked at himself in the full-length mirror. He ran his fingers through his greying chest hair and tugged at them absently. He didn't much like how he looked. The sag in the belly. The hint of grey in his pubic hair. The flaccid penis that seemed content to stay flaccid most of the time, to Mamtha's immense relief, he thought. Even the texture of his skin seemed to have changed.

In the movies, policemen his age looked distinguished if they were good cops. Or, were fat and feckless if they were the bad ones. His eyes narrowed as he appraised himself in the mirror. The truth was he looked neither. He just looked fucked.

Then he turned and felt the first sight of pleasure at his own body. On his right bicep was his first act of impulse in many years. A three-inch-high, five-inch-wide tattoo. A wheel with wings.

Gowda had never thought that he would get a tattoo done but, some months ago at the Bullet mechanic's shop, he had seen a young man with a giant tattoo of a bike on his back. The string vest he wore covered most of it, but it was visible enough to trigger Gowda's interest. Kumar, the mechanic, had seen Gowda's eyes return to the body art again and again. 'Sir, there is a tattoo place here in Kammanahalli. Just two streets away. He is the best in Bangalore, I am told. You should get one too ... a small one!'

On a whim, Gowda had walked to the tattoo studio. The tattoo artist had seen the hesitation in Gowda's gaze and gait; this would be a convert worth having, he decided. Besides, it was a quiet afternoon and he had all the time to pander to this man who was clearly a policeman. He had never had a policeman's skin to work on before. He opened his album and showed Gowda the various designs he could create. Only one of them excited Gowda. He looked at it for a long time.

'Great choice, sir,' the tattoo artist said. 'It is actually a compound symbol that indicates the kind of speed one needs to be airborne ...'

Gowda nodded.

'Do you like bikes?'

'Kumar sent me here.'

The tattoo artist smiled. 'Ah, so you must have seen what I did for Freddie ... that took several hours and multiple sittings.'

'How long will this take?'

'About three hours max and it will cost about seven thousand five hundred rupees. Though for you, I would do it for five K.'

'Why?' Gowda frowned.

'I am a biker too. I have an old Bullet that Kumar fixed for me ... and Kumar doesn't send me clients ever. So you must be someone special.'

Gowda watched as the stencil was placed on his arm. When it was done, the tattoo artist bound his arm and gave him a whole list of do's and don'ts. 'You can take the bandage off after an hour and no wetting or bathing for the next twelve hours,' he said, walking him to the door.

The tattoo made Gowda feel special. It was not about the symbol of a bike as much as the freedom it suggested. An open road, the song of the wind, the thump of the engine, the dream of a lifetime to keep going without ever pausing.

He traced the wings on the wheel with the tip of his finger. It still filled him with awe that he had actually gone ahead and done it. Mamtha wouldn't approve, he knew. So he kept it a secret. He had made sure his arms were covered when he was with her, wearing a T-shirt even to bed.

He looked at it one final time. Then he dressed and walked into the kitchen.

He looked around him. The counters were bare except for four bottles of water that stood in a row. One bottle of water stood on his bedside table. In the fridge were four plastic boxes and a bowl. The ceramic bowl held curd that had turned firm without souring. One of the two plastic boxes held potatoes and peas cooked precisely the way he liked them. The other held a small portion of chilli chicken he had brought back from the restaurant the night before. His wife couldn't have done better, he thought wryly, pulling out the containers of rasam and rice. He poured the rasam into a steel saucepan and put it on the stove. He stood watching the rasam simmer.

Shanthi, the maid, knew his habits and tastes. She knew

how he preferred his coffee and where he liked his newspaper kept every morning. She sorted his clothes and sewed on missing buttons. She laid out his handkerchief and socks every day and replenished the toiletries in the bathroom. She told him what groceries were needed every month and shopped for the vegetables and meat herself. She said little and glided through the rooms, an apparition taking care of his needs without reproach or complaint. In fact, other than sleeping with him, Shanthi had slipped into the role of wife with a casual ease that saddened rather than pleased him.

It occurred to him that his marriage couldn't amount to much if he scarcely missed his wife.

The ping of the microwave.

Rasam and rice, Gowda thought as he toyed with his food, must be the loneliest dinner written in the destiny of any man. A meal you ate because anything else was too much of an effort. A culinary straw you clung to because the familiar taste and aroma, its suggestion of heat and spice evoked memories of a time when your mother stood at your elbow making sure you had everything you wanted. As it slid down your throat, you knew a strange pang: if there was someone else across the table, there would be accompaniments – pickles, vegetables and conversation. Not this silence, broken only by the sound of the metal bracelet of his watch clanging against the rim of the steel plate.

Gowda put the plate into the sink and ran water over it. He stared at the lone plate in the sink and the saucepan in which he had heated the rasam, and the plastic box that had held the rice. He had never felt this alone before. At almost fifty, he had nothing to look back upon. Not even a real memory to clutch at.

From the first floor that was let out to a young couple

and their dog, he could hear the dog's nails as it scratched at a corner of the room.

Gowda paused as he wiped his hands on a towel. He knew what he would do. He would get a dog. Not a silly fluffy yappy dog that his wife may approve of, but a proper dog with a loud bark. He would call Guru at the Dog Squad for his advice. Suddenly Gowda grinned. Maybe they had a retired inspector dog he could bring home. It was a thought. Two police officers past their prime, seeking consolation in each other's company.

Gowda walked into the living room and rifled through his CDs. He chose a Mukesh CD and slid it into the music system.

He lit a cigarette and sank into a cane chair in the veranda. His house was the only one on that road. On either side and opposite were empty plots. A line of silver oaks demarcated each plot from the other. At first the developer had kept the plots spruced up for customer visits. But when the recession happened and people were laid off, the bottom fell out of the real estate market and the developer stopped bothering about cutting the grass and trimming the casuarina that lined the roads. Weeds took over. Shrubs grew and trees spread their branches, fearing neither the electricity department's routine lopping off of branches nor the ruthless home builders who sought to fill every square inch of land they had paid for with brick and mortar. Some days it occurred to Gowda that he lived in the middle of a forest. He woke to bird calls, and when it rained, the frog chorus croaked all through the night.

Four years ago, when Gowda broached his plan to build a home in Greenview Residency, Mamtha had been appalled. She had hated the thought of moving from Gowda's family home in 5th Block Jayanagar. After Shimoga, where Mamtha had grown up, Jayanagar had been everything she had imagined Bangalore to be. You stepped out of your home into a bustling street of shops and people. And yet, it was like what Shimoga had been. There was Suma Coffee Works, where she could buy the coffee-chicory blend she liked. There was Shenoy's, where she could buy her choice of condiments and short eats; and a sweetshop that sold the best obattus and chirotis. Brahmins Café and MTR were nearby. Mamtha had loved it there. It was also convenient for her as she was posted at the Vanivilas hospital in Chamarajpet, which was only a fifteen-minute drive away.

After living in south Bangalore, the thought of moving across the city into the wastelands of north Bangalore worried her.

'It's just the other side of the city. Why are you behaving as if I'm suggesting we move to Outer Mongolia?' Gowda said.

'It may well be for me,' she snapped. 'What do I know about that part of Bangalore?'

'The new airport's coming up there,' he said, clutching at any straw.

'And how many times do I go to the airport?'

Gowda had retreated behind his newspaper. He had seen his father do this with great effect when his mother was spoiling for a fight. Behind the newspaper, he held his breath, wondering if she would tear it out of his hands. But Mamtha was not given to such outbursts of emotion. She stared at him and walked away.

She had sulked for the next few weeks but Gowda pretended not to see her distress and went ahead with his plans. The developer had given him a whopping discount on the market rate.

'This is all I can afford,' Gowda had tried to placate his wife every now and then as the house took shape. 'At this price we'd get a hole in a wall somewhere else, but here we have a plot that is five thousand square feet. We can even have a garden!'

Mamtha glared at him. 'Did I ever ask you for a garden? For that matter, do you know the difference between a mango and a turnip?' She turned on her side and went to sleep.

Gowda had come to love the quiet and so when the first truck load of stone arrived two years ago for a plot at the end of the road, he felt as if his private space was being intruded upon.

But Mamtha had welcomed the thought of neighbours. 'About time!' she had said. 'It will be nice to have some people and noise instead of the cheep-cheep of birds all day.'

Gowda hadn't spoken.

Despite Gowda's daily glowering at the construction workers, the new house had been built and an elaborate housewarming ceremony held. Gowda and Mamtha had attended the puja, one reluctantly and the other compensating with an overdose of effusiveness. But after a few months the owners were transferred to Mumbai. Gowda had watched the movers' truck arrive with a grin and, when they left, he had walked around with a light step.

Mamtha hadn't said much, but when Roshan's medical seat at Hassan came up, she had broached the idea of a move. Gowda had refused to even consider the thought. And then Mamtha played her ace. Someone needed to keep an eye on Roshan, she didn't trust him to be on his own. She would have the hospital find her a house right in the heart of Hassan.

'Maybe when you are here on your own, you will be

ready to consider moving away from this wilderness,' she had said as she packed.

Gowda didn't think he could live anywhere else. He liked it too much here. But he had to buckle in and let the first floor out when Mamtha insisted. 'We've sunk everything we had into this house and Roshan's medical admission,' she said. 'They are a young couple and will be no trouble. And I'll know that if you need any help, there will be someone around.'

Night had settled in and from the first floor, he could hear sounds of muted conversation. His tenants were back from wherever they had gone to. Had Mamtha and he ever behaved like newlyweds? He had been busy using up all his energy being angry with the system and she had her nose in her medical books. By the time his anger had run its course and she had become a qualified doctor, the baby had arrived. Suddenly they were parents worrying about inoculations and school admissions.

He heard the man say something and the woman laugh. They laughed a lot, those two. Had they, he and Mamtha, ever laughed like that? he wondered.

Gowda turned his head and watched the phone as it vibrated on the glass table. He picked it up and peered at the screen.

It was SI Santosh. Gowda felt his mouth stretch in a grim line of its own volition. What now?

Santosh could barely keep the excitement out of his voice as the words tumbled out. 'Sir, I picked up the post-mortem report from the mortuary just now.'

'And?'

'Shall I read it out to you, sir?' Before Gowda could tell him to save it for the next morning, Santosh began, 'More than eighty per cent of the body surface is burnt. The trunk and anterior abdominal wall are almost completely burnt. The line of redness, the blisters with serous fluid, the presence of acid mucopolysacharides and enzymes all indicate that he was alive when burnt. And, sir, the pathologist has also stated that either kerosene or petrol was used to start the fire since the burns had a sooty blackening and a very characteristic odour.'

Gowda grunted impatiently. 'We knew that's what would show up. So what was the need to call me at this hour? Tell me, what has got you all worked up?'

'Sir, around the neck there are ligature marks, but it is a cut-like wound extending into the jugular.'

Gowda sat up. 'And?'

'Glass particles were found in the wound and under his fingernails. A manja-coated ligature was used. Again. And, sir, similar lacerations on the face like the one mentioned in the Horamavu homicide.'

Gowda felt a prickling down his spine. A flaring of life. Perhaps it wasn't over till it was over.

THURSDAY, 4 AUGUST

Gowda rode his Royal Enfield Bullet to the station house earlier than usual. It wasn't much of a place, but in the last five years he had grown attached to this rented building that stood in a quarter-acre plot on the outskirts of Neelagubbi village.

Land had been earmarked for a permanent station house, tenders from building contractors had been invited, and one day it would eventually get built. But until then, this green-washed building with its small poky rooms and rented furniture was Gowda's fiefdom.

In the summer, when water dried up in the lake, a stench rose up from the slimy mud. And in the evenings, giant swarms of mosquitoes would descend on every living creature in the station house. Head Constable Gajendra would order a constable to fill a bandli with eucalyptus leaves and burn them so smoke would drive those 'bloody bastards' away.

'We are all going to die of dengue fever,' he would remark darkly every summer. 'We should move from here, sir.'

'It's only mosquitoes,' Gowda would murmur, swatting one against his arm.

'Mosquitoes,' Gajendra would retort, 'do not care if you are a policeman or a pimp. They want blood to fill their bloody bellies. Like our corrupt politicians. No one is above or below their bloodsucking.'

But once the rains fell, the swamp would turn into a lake beside which migratory birds descended to nest and breed. Gowda liked to walk to the edge of the fence that overlooked the lake and gaze at the expanse of water. Some evenings, he would ask for a chair to be brought to his favourite spot under a mango tree near the fence. He would sit there and gaze at the yellow and pink crocus lilies dotting the grassy verges along the lake's edge, the green-winged teals and the common coot gliding past, the movement of the breeze as it passed through the clumps of bulrushes. It was the closest Gowda came to acknowledging the presence of content in his life.

A clap of thunder. A drop of rain fell on Gowda's face when he peered at the sky. In the dull grey light, the station house was even more bleak. When the monsoon was over, he would have it painted white, he told himself. Even if he had to call in a favour or two.

By the time Gowda parked his bike, it was drizzling. He swore under his breath and rushed towards the station house, holding a hand over his head.

'Sir, no one told me to pick you up. I was going to come at the usual time.' PC David rushed to his side.

Gowda waved him away. The post-mortem report had preyed on his mind all night and he had woken up early, unable to go back to sleep. He had decided to come in and read the post-mortem report himself. He was certain that there would be something more to it than what Santosh had chanced upon.

A constable brought him a small plastic beaker of tea.

Gowda took a sip and opened the file.

He turned a page and threw the file back on the table. SI Santosh, who had been hovering, rushed to his side.

'Come along,' Gowda said, without any preamble.

Santosh glowered at him. I am not a bloody dog, he thought. But something about Gowda's expression silenced him.

As the vehicle turned out of the gate of the police station, PC David asked, 'Where to, sir?'

Gowda narrowed his eyes. 'Whitefield. I want to see this M. Hunt.'

'Shouldn't we have him brought to the station?' Santosh asked.

'We could. But that's where we go wrong. No one likes to enter a police station. Witnesses tend to clam up, sometimes even go hostile. It's better to talk to them in familiar surroundings.'

Gowda saw that Santosh wasn't entirely convinced. He sighed. What was wrong with him? He had thought he would let the boy profit from his experience but it was obvious that the silly idiot thought otherwise.

'You don't have to come with me if you don't want to. You can go back to the station and catch up on your reading…'

Santosh looked at him to see if Gowda was sneering. But the big bland face was marked by no sign of malice or slyness.

'No, sir, I am fine. I would like to go with you.'

Gowda grunted.

A little later, he opened a pack of India Kings. 'Do you smoke?' he asked.

Santosh shook his head. 'No.'

'Good for you,' Gowda conceded. He cupped the flame as he held the match to the cigarette. Then he peered at Santosh. 'What about alcohol?'

'I don't drink, sir.'

'And you believe in God, I suppose?'

Santosh nodded. 'I never leave home without saying my prayers. I chant the Hanuman mantra every day. With God on my side, I know that nothing will go wrong.'

'So the poor bastard we saw yesterday must have forgotten to say his prayers that night, eh?'

Santosh didn't speak. Was Gowda naturally obnoxious or did he have to work hard at it? he wondered.

Michael leaned forward and planted his feet firmly on the ground. The rocking chair stopped. He stared into the middle distance, unable to decide what to do next.

'Would you like some tea?' the woman asked from the doorway.

'No,' he said shortly. Then, as if to apologize for his brusqueness, he mumbled, 'Would you get me a glass of water with some ice in it?'

Seeing the incomprehension in her eyes, Michael smiled. She hadn't even realized that he was being rude to her. He switched to Tamil. He hadn't spoken Tamil in a long time, but once he began he discovered that he could do it without too much of an effort.

Holding the glass of water that he didn't want, Michael leaned back and set the chair rocking again. It had been almost dawn when he finally reached Aunty Maggie's home. Narsamma had opened the door asking, 'Sir, shall I bring some tea?'

Michael shook his head. He didn't want tea. He'd had at least three cups of watery over-sugared tea at the hospital.

He had just about gone to sleep when there was a knock on the door. 'Sir, breakfast,' Narsamma said from the doorway.

Narsamma was relentless. At regular intervals she appeared at his elbow offering him food. For lunch, he had been served ball curry and yellow rice, and the Captain Chicken curry 'just like Missy amma taught me to make'.

When he poured himself a drink in the evening, she arrived bearing a tray on which was a plate of crispy meat strips.

'What's this?'

'Ding Ding. Missy amma always said how much you like it. And for dinner I have made pork vindaloo.'

Michael groaned at the thought of more bloody Anglo-Indian food. Why did she think that he was hankering for it?

The truth was he wanted none of this. Neither the house nor the responsibility that had been thrust upon him to provide for Narsamma, whom he seemed to have inherited along with the house. And to top it all, he was now a prima facie witness in what looked like a murder case. That was all he needed.

Michael Hunt groaned.

The woman appeared at his elbow. 'Do you have a headache, sir? Shall I bring you a Saridon? And some tea?'

Michael made an attempt to smile. 'I am fine,' he said and closed his eyes.

Fuck off. Just get the fuck out of here. Leave me alone.

A fan whirred quietly. An old GEC fan that Uncle John had fixed when they had built the house. Everything in the house was old. The furniture and the floors, the doors and the dishes, and Aunty Maggie had preserved it all in mint condition until she died.

'It's for you all,' she had said, when Michael visited her just two days before Becky and he left for Australia. 'Child, I'll keep it for you all. Just in case ...'

'Uff, men, what do you think the old bat's implying, men?' Becky had fumed. 'Why she saying just in case? Putting all negative thoughts in your head, one after one!'

Michael bit his lip. He knew what Aunty Maggie meant and he also knew Becky wouldn't care to hear it.

He looked away and said, 'Becky, we have to stop talking like we do at home. It's going to be hard enough making a new life in Melbourne. We don't want the people there thinking we are struggling with our English!'

Becky taught science at the primary level at Francis Xavier School. She was sometimes called to step in when the English teacher was away, and every year she MC-ed the concert day. But when Becky and Michael were together, she slipped into the patois they spoke at home. Michael did too. Queen's English was what they kept for strangers and the outside world.

Becky took a hanky from her clutch and mopped the beads of sweat on her forehead. Michael smelt the eau de cologne on her hanky and a wave of feeling suffused him. When they were in Australia, all of this would change. All that was familiar and all that was his world would cease to be.

What on earth was he thinking, moving bag and baggage across the world? Who knew what lay ahead there!

'I believe you are bloody worried, Michael?' Becky said. 'I believe you are thinking how we will manage when we are in Australia?'

Michael pulled out a pack of cigarettes. He looked at the pack of Wills Flake, suddenly stricken. 'I am going to have to find a brand I like there. Even that will change.'

'Why you fearing change, men? We are together. You, me and the boys.'

Michael nodded and took her hand in his. She leaned towards him and kissed his cheek.

Michael lit his cigarette and walked into Aunty Maggie's kitchen where he had promised to fix a broken window latch. Becky wiped the frown off her face and went to help Aunty Maggie change the curtains. 'Who is going to do all this for you when we are in Australia, Aunty Maggie? I tell you, find a young girl to live with you here. That way, there will be someone to clean your dekchis and bartans and you won't be all alone and we won't worry about you. That's all Michael thinks of: Aunty Maggie all alone in that bloody big house in the boondocks...!'

Michael heard Becky from the kitchen. She was a good

woman but she was stubborn. She had been the one who wanted to leave India. And Michael did what she wanted.

When Michael was twenty-three, he had met Becky at a dance at the Catholic Club. That night he saw his father get drunk and humiliate himself and all of them. He saw his mother wring her hands at first and then match a drink with every jibe his father hurled her way. All of this was routine. As were the growing stains of perspiration on the blue polyester silk dress his mother wore, the louche slack of his father's jaw, the arguments when they reached home, the stench of vomit and sweat, the embarrassment, the silence the morning after. And Michael was determined even more than ever to join the army, the navy, the railways, anything that would put a distance between him and this hell called home.

Until his eyes alighted on Becky, sitting on a morah. Her brown hair fell like a sheath, her sweetness was wrapped in a buttercup yellow dress and her clear grey eyes sparkled with fun and hope. Her father wore a proper suit that fitted him and her mother wore a grey silk dress with a long string of pearls round her neck. They sat together, exchanging smiles and small talk. And Michael had a moment of epiphany. This was what he wanted. To escape his own grimy, sordid life, and be part of that charmed circle. To be them.

Without her, Michael was nothing. Becky defined who he was.

But now, without Becky, he had to define himself all over again.

Through the morass of memories he had sunk into, Michael heard the sound of a 4-wheel drive coming to a stop under the porch.

Narsamma had said that a real estate developer had been calling every day after Aunty Maggie died. 'He wants to build flats here,' she had said.

'I don't want to meet anybody,' he said now, as she hurried to his side.

'No, no, you have to come!' Her eyes were wide as saucers in her bony face. 'It's the police. The police is here.'

Michael untangled himself from his thoughts. They were here to take his statement, he realized. The young man must have died then. He felt a pang of something akin to regret. He didn't know the man to grieve for him. But no one deserved to die as he had.

Michael walked into the living room where a policeman waited. From the two stars on his lapel, Michael knew he was a sub-inspector. Had he come on his own? Then he saw a burly figure standing in the porch, smoking.

'Good morning, Inspector,' Michael said, stretching his hand out.

'Good morning. I am SI Santosh,' the young man replied, reaching for Michael's hand.

Someone ought to teach him how to shake hands. What did they teach them in the police college these days?

'Is that your colleague out there?' Michael asked, gesturing for him to sit down.

'That's Inspector Gowda,' Santosh said in a low voice. 'He has more than twenty years of experience. I am new to the service. He'll be the one talking to you.'

Michael felt the young man's eyes on him.

Suddenly Santosh asked, 'Sir, you are native of which country?'

'India. I grew up here in Bangalore but have been living in Australia for the last fifteen years.' And then, unable to resist a spark of mischief, Michael put on his most innocent expression and asked, '*Matthe Neenu? Yaav ooru nendhuu?*'

Santosh stumbled as he caught his foot on the edge of the carpet. The white man had just said in chaste Kannada, 'And you? Where are you from?'

Michael tried to hide his smile. He was beginning to enjoy this. First the cab driver. Now the young cop. He looked at Santosh carefully. Inexperienced. Nervous. And clumsy too. The senior man seemed to have got the boy worked up in knots. He looked at the man in the porch. Was he a bully who got his kicks out of intimidating people? Michael sighed. He wasn't looking forward to this at all.

Michael stepped out into the porch and cleared his throat. 'Good morning, Inspector. Why don't you come in? I smoke myself, so I have no objections to anyone smoking in here...'

The man turned and Michael saw his gaze turn incredulous. 'How do we know each other?' they seemed to demand.

Did he know him? He did look very familiar. Something about the way he cocked his head, and the eyes. The pieces fell into place and Michael stepped forward with a little laugh. 'I don't believe this ... Mudde, it's you.'

'Bloody hell, you are M. Hunt! Macha, someone told me you were in Australia, what are you doing here?'

Santosh perched at the edge of the sofa. Then, giving in, he sank back, only to discover the seat of the sofa had sucked him in so he was trapped with his chin almost touching his knees. He tried to hoist himself up but the sofa held him fast. A line of sweat broke out on his brow. Inspector Gowda would think nothing of laughing aloud at the sight of him. Like a turtle on its back trying to right itself.

That was all he needed now. First the white man speaking Kannada. And now this. Then he heard laughter and saw the most amazing sight of his boss and the foreigner clasp each other like long-lost friends. Did they know each other from their youth? Were they friends, perhaps? Only, Santosh couldn't imagine Gowda ever having had a youth or a friend.

Gowda seemed to have been born with an expression that hovered between weary, tetchy and surly on the odometer of expressions. For that matter, he hadn't in the course of the last twenty-six hours seen Gowda smile once. Pleasantly. As if he meant it.

And such was Santosh's shock at seeing Gowda smile that he found himself on his feet again, escaping the clutch of the malevolent sofa that had been so determined to make him look foolish and ineffectual.

'Look at you, Bob,' Michael said, holding his friend at arm's length.

'Look at you, Macha,' Gowda retorted, a boyish grin erasing the years from his face.

Bob. Macha. Boy speak. From those years in college when every boy, mate or acquaintance was a Bob or a Macha. When had Gowda used it last? It was all yaar and dude these days. His son couldn't seem to speak a sentence to his friends without placing a dude in it somewhere.

'We are two middle-aged men now. You have a paunch and I have lost most of my hair.' Michael smiled. 'Did you ever think this is how we would be in our forties?'

'Almost fifty. I'll be fifty in November.' Gowda smiled back at him.

'And to think that we should meet like this. Bloody destiny, Bob.' Michael found his carefully cultivated accent dropping in a moment.

Gowda straightened. 'Destiny! Is that what you call it? You know why we are here, don't you?'

Michael nodded. 'Mudde,' he began.

Gowda winced and then smiled. He'd been called Mudde Gowda at college. For a while he had been the star of the basketball court, his lean, lanky frame cutting through the defenders and slicing the air as he leapt. Shooting baskets with an ease that forever after would be his early morning dream. The lift, the heave, that amazing grace.

'It's all that bloody ragi mudde he's been fed as a child,' someone had overheard the visiting college captain muttering. And the name had stuck. Mudde Gowda. Ball Gowda. Gowda with the balls to grab the ball.

'It was the most horrible thing I ever saw, Bob, and I thought I had seen it all in my years of service in the fire brigade in Melbourne.' Michael's voice drifted away as he stepped back in time to the roadside near the grove.

'We have to do this formally. I think I should ask my colleague to take your statement,' Gowda said softly.

'When do we meet?'

'Anytime you want. Just give me a shout,' Gowda replied.

Gowda's phone rang. Michael's eyebrows rose at the ring tone. '*Kabhi kabhi...*' a song that Gowda had made an anthem in those college years when his world had revolved around two things: the basketball court and Urmila.

Every day after college, Gowda and his gang, including Michael, would walk down to Breeze on Brigade Road. The jukebox there was a point to congregate around and each of them had his own favourite. Michael had Neil Diamond's

'*Cracklin Rosie*' and '*Song sung blue*', Satish ABBA's '*Dancing queen*', Imitiaz Boney M's '*Rasputin*'. And every day Gowda would complain about jukeboxes that pandered to colonial tastes and forgot that Indians may want to listen to Indian music.

'Like what,' Satish asked one evening.

'"*Kabhi kabhi*", what else,' Imitiaz laughed.

'Don't you tire of hearing that song, Mudde,' Michael asked curiously.

'Bugger off, guys,' Gowda said with remarkable calm. You couldn't rile Gowda those days, no matter how hard you tried.

Later, Gowda would peel himself from the gang and go to the restaurant on the first floor of Nilgiris where Urmila would be waiting for him.

Gowda, Michael thought, had forsaken both basketball and Urmila but perhaps not...

'You know she's back in Bangalore, don't you?' he murmured.

Gowda stiffened. Then he affected a casual ease into his flesh and voice. 'Who?'

'Urmila. Are you telling me you've forgotten her?'

'I haven't. It's been a long time ... But how do you know?'

'Facebook.' Michael grinned. 'We discovered each other on it...'

'Oh!' Gowda said, too ashamed to admit that he had heard about Facebook but didn't know how it worked. Everyone he knew seemed to treat their computer like a slave, a pet, a companion, a minion that made life easier. Computers and he were on nodding acquaintance at best.

'You are not on Facebook, are you?' Michael asked suddenly.

'I don't have the time…' Gowda put on his official voice, a bite with each syllable, then paused. What the fuck was he doing? This was his friend. Not a subordinate or an accused. 'I am a bloody dinosaur,' he said quietly. 'It's like the world changed when I wasn't looking and I don't know where to begin to comprehend the change. I don't even know what this thing called Facebook is.'

Into the silence that followed Gowda's declaration, Santosh walked in and said, 'Sir, the station called…'

Gowda turned to him, eager to escape. 'You'd better take his statement.'

At home that night, Gowda sat in the veranda. He had studiously avoided pouring himself a drink. He could hear laughter from above. What did they laugh about so much?

He rose and went to put on the stereo. Last night's CD was still in it. As if on cue, the strains of Mukesh singing '*Kabhi kabhi*' floated into the veranda and filled his head. Something lodged in his chest. He tried very hard not to think of her but Michael had brought it all back. He had been nineteen when he first met Urmila … He shook his head, trying to dispel his thoughts, when suddenly another laugh rang through the air.

The ensuing silence filled Gowda with disquiet. That's it, Gowda decided. He would get a dog, whether Mamtha agreed or not.

Gowda laughed aloud, imagining the expression on Michael's face when he told him, 'Meet Inspector Roby. He was top dog in the narcotics department.'

Michael would seize on the pun immediately.

God, how he missed all of that. The asinine word games that Michael and he had played during their college years.

The fools in this life he led now wouldn't recognize a pun if it stood before them with a tea cosy on its head, waving its arms...

All these years it hadn't mattered that he inhabited a different world from the one he had envisioned for himself. But this evening, ever since the meeting with Michael, it was as if everything about him and his life had been held up for scrutiny and found wanting.

His phone burst into song. Gowda frowned. He glanced at his watch. It was one of his informers from the time he had been in the Crime Branch. What was he calling about so late at night?

'Tell me,' he murmured into the phone.

'Sir, Gowda sir...' The voice was hesitant. Unsure.

'What is it, Mohammed? Go on...'

FRIDAY, 5 AUGUST

By now Gowda had worked out every moment to perfection in his head. The corner was important. It couldn't be just any corner of any room. The corner had to be flanked by two cupboards. Preferably the olive-green steel Godrejs. Or even a grey metal filing cabinet. The purpose was to create an alcove in which the man would be forced to crouch with no room to escape.

Then there were the boots with spikes. Sturdy black leather boots polished to a gleam, with dagger points for spikes. When he slipped the boots on, they would hug his feet and ankles, so when he stretched his leg and kicked the creature in the corner, he would feel the impact at the back of his skull.

The impact of all eighty-three kilograms of him slamming into a spot. The crunch of metal against bone. The shredding of skin and laceration of flesh. Kick. Kick. Kick. Till it screamed for mercy.

Gowda tried hard not to slouch, and allowed his pet fantasy free rein. This time the man in the corner had a face. Assistant Commissioner of Police Vidyaprasad. IPS Cadre.

Gowda had known a few fine IPS officers in his time. But ACP Vidyaprasad was not someone Gowda could summon any deference for, let alone admiration or respect. The man was a bloody joke. And what added to Gowda's ire was the thought that this fool was so much younger than him, with not even half the experience Gowda had in the field. And yet the ACP talked down to Gowda as if he were a recalcitrant child who needed to be made to toe the line.

'What's this I hear about you going to meet the witness in his house?' the ACP snapped. The senior officer had summoned Gowda to his office for his monthly quota of advice, recrimination and threats.

'Why? Is something wrong with that? I have always seen that a witness is less guarded in his own environment.'

'Sir.'

'What?' Gowda asked carefully.

'When you talk to me, you need to say sir. Do I have to remind you that I am your senior officer?'

'Oh!'An image swam into Gowda's mind: the howl of pain from the ACP's smashed mouth as Gowda's boots slammed into his ribs once again. It offered a soupcon of comfort that would allow him to mouth the hated 'sir'. With a devilish gleam in his eye, Gowda murmured, 'Sir, if that's all, sir, may I, sir, leave now, sir?'

The ACP frowned. Was he being ridiculed? Gowda was a problem. Always had been. The man was a good police officer. If only he would stick to procedures and established police practices. Instead, he made it hard for himself and the department by choosing to do as he saw fit. Surely the man should know by now when he ought to back off.

The wireless crackled. The ACP cocked an ear. Gowda sighed.

'What about that burns case? Don't waste too much of the department's time on that, do you hear me? Close it as quickly as you can. There's no need to waste the department's time or money on scum.' The ACP flicked the case sheet in front of him and peered at the name. 'You don't even have a name for him, I see. This lowlife is of no consequence, alive or dead.'

'A man was murdered. Whether he's a lowlife or not shouldn't matter,' Gowda spoke quietly.

'That's precisely it. He is ... no, was lowlife.'

'That's beside the point.'

The ACP's eyes narrowed. 'You know, as I do, that it's going to be a C report. We have nothing to take it forward with. Not even a missing person's complaint. What I am pointing out to you, if you want to know, is the likelihood of the DCP coming down on me. I don't want to have to answer for your squandering of time and resources. Besides, it's Ganesh Chaturthi soon. Do you realize that half of Bangalore is going to descend on the lakes near your station house to immerse their Ganeshas?'

Gowda thought of the giant painted Ganeshas; pink torso-ed, with painted-on gold jewellery and green robes, mounted on a truck and led through the roads with much singing and dancing to the lakes in his station zone. Ganeshas who would dissolve into a heap of mud and carcinogens, killing the fish and polluting the water. For which he was to stand guard and aid the process. Gowda grimaced.

'I want you to concentrate on law and order for that week when the Ganesha immersion begins.'

'It's almost a month away…' Gowda murmured.

'Well then, there's Independence Day coming up … And there's some information on illegal betting in your jurisdiction area. There's a great deal you need to do, Gowda.'

Gowda stared into the middle distance. On the wall behind the ACP's chair were a few framed photographs. The national leaders at their benevolent best. 'I've been meaning to ask you something,' Gowda said suddenly.

'What?' The ACP tried to fathom Gowda's expression.

'Why do you have these photographs here?'

The ACP counted to ten under his breath. 'Go, Gowda, just leave, will you?'

When Gowda was out of the room, the ACP pulled out a strip of Deanxit and popped one. How could any man get under his skin with such little effort?

Gowda glanced at his watch. He had asked Mohammed to meet him at Chandrika, at the junction of Cunningham Road and Millers Road. No one would recognize Mohammed there. Or him for that matter. He smiled as he thought of the expression on the ACP's face. He had known his question would have the ACP foaming at the mouth. And that he would be asked to leave.

No one looked kindly on informers, not even their own families. And Mohammed was scared that if he was discovered, the wrath of the powers that controlled Shivaji Nagar would descend not just on him but on his biwi and their children. And so, when it had seemed that the ACP was going to keep him there all morning, Gowda had known it was time to speed things up. He grinned, thinking of the play of emotions on the ACP's face as he walked out of the room.

Gowda saw Mohammed enter the restaurant. He stood by the cash counter, his eyes darting this way and that, swooping on each face and discarding. In the twelve years of their association, Gowda and Mohammed had met only five times, and each time they had spent barely fifteen minutes together. Gowda sipped his coffee and waited. Mohammed would eventually spot him. A few minutes later, Mohammed stood at his table. 'Sir, I didn't recognize…'

'Sit down, Mohammed.'

The vendor hesitated, then, seeing the impatience in Gowda's eyes, he pulled out a chair and perched on it gingerly.

'When did he go missing,' Gowda asked quietly.

A waited sidled up to their table.

'What will you have?' Gowda asked.

'Nothing.' Mohammed shook his head.

'Get him a badam milk. You like that, don't you?' Gowda said.

'I…'

'Our badam milk is very good,' the boy said, shoving his pencil behind his ear. 'Nothing to eat?'

Gowda wanted to box his ears. 'Just get the drink,' he growled.

Mohammed looked down on his hands that rested on the table top. 'Sir, I am fasting … it's Ramzan.'

Gowda nodded. 'That's fine. I'll drink it. So, when did this boy go missing?'

'I saw Liaquat on Monday night. It was late. I asked him to go home with me. He had been shooting up. The boy seemed unhinged. I was afraid he would get into trouble ... he hasn't come home yet.'

Gowda nodded. 'But that's not all, is it?'

'Someone said they saw him go into the lane near Siddiq's Garage. It is a small lane with a dead end. I don't even know why I went there. But I did, and I found this.' Mohammed laid out a silver talisman on a black thread. 'This is his. I got it blessed by the mullah at the dargah near my home in Bijapur. Liaquat's from there. That's why I feel responsible for him. He's only nineteen.'

Gowda touched the talisman thoughtfully. 'You'll have to come with me. A body has been found. A young boy, of about that age. No one's come forward to claim it. I hope it's not your Liaquat but we need to start somewhere.'

Mohammed put his head in his hands.

'Walk up Millers Road near the Carmel College ground. I'll pick you up from there.'

Mohammed didn't speak. He couldn't. His face was ashen. His lower lip wobbled as he sought to bring some control to his emotions. 'Why, sir?' he whispered after a while. 'Why would anyone do this?'

Gowda shrugged. 'Are you sure this is Liaquat?'

Mohammed nodded. 'Liaquat had a sixth finger on his left hand. It was attached to his thumb. There was an extra toe on his left foot too. And he was the same height and build as this...' He gestured to the nearly charred corpse laid out in the mortuary.

'No one has come forward to claim the body,' Gowda said quietly.

'No one will,' Mohammed mumbled. 'Liaquat's an orphan and Razak's in jail.'

'Who? Chicken Razak?'

Mohammed looked away. 'Hmm...' His voice dipped again. 'Liaquat was Razak's frooter.'

Gowda frowned. Razak's catamite. That changed things. Was this part of a gang war? The homicide showed all indications of it, right down to the manner in which they had tried to dispose of the body. Yet, somewhere in Gowda niggled a worm of disquiet. What about the manja string? And Kothandaraman, the other victim – what could he have had to do with rowdy gangs? Twenty-four years of police experience had honed his instincts to follow a hunch when he had one. In this case and Kothandaraman's, that was all he had to go on.

'What happens if no one claims the body?' Mohammed asked suddenly.

'It will be sent to the crematorium.' Gowda sighed.

'Would I be able to claim the body?' Mohammed looked up at Gowda. 'We are from the same village. He's a Muslim, sir. He has to be buried according to our customs. It is against our religion for the body to be cremated. We have to bury the body quickly, before it is night. That is what our religion says we must do.'

Nineteen. A boy. His son was the same age. What if it had been Roshan? How would he have borne it? Gowda shuddered. 'You'll have to claim some kinship. Tell everyone he's your uncle's son and I'll take care of the rest. The attendant here is a Muslim. I'll have him wrap the body in a white cloth so you can do the ghusl without having to take the kafan off.'

Gowda took out his wallet and pulled out two thousand-rupee notes. 'I know this will not be enough but this is all I have with me now.'

Mohammed's eyes filled. 'You are a good man, Gowda sir. Our religion teaches us to take care of orphans. We are promised the companionship of the Prophet in jannat. But that you should do this…'

'Do you think there are separate heavens for Hindus and Muslims, Mohammed?'

'I have embarrassed you,' Mohammed said quietly. 'I just want you to know that God, yours or mine, wherever he is, in my heaven or yours, will remember this. Like he will not spare the devil who did this to Liaquat. Liaquat was a rascal. He was silly and unscrupulous at times. But he was a boy. No one deserves to die like he has. Were they men or beasts?'

Gowda patted the man on his shoulder.

'Someone will have to tell Razak,' Mohammed said, as they finished the formalities.

Gowda ran his fingers through his hair. 'I will have that organized, Mohammed,' he said on a whim. 'Ask around, will you? See if anyone remembers anything from that night.'

He watched as Mohammed and the remains of what was once Liaquat drove away in the hearse.

Gowda felt a strange desolation wash over him.

He glanced at his watch. It was almost four. Santosh would be back with the photographer's statement. Not that either his or Michael's statements were going to provide any leads.

Gowda scrolled down the contacts in his phone.

'Ashok,' he barked. 'I want you to look up something for me.'

'How about a hello first?' Ashok's indignation bristled through.

'Hello, Ashok. How are you? How are the babies and the missus? What about your grandmother? Oh, and I forgot, her cow? How's the postman, and the vegetable vendor?'

'Gowda, give it a rest.' Ashok sighed. 'What do you want?'

'Tell me everything you know and can find out about Chicken Razak.'

'He's in jail. Why?'

'The truth is, Ashok, I don't know. I may be wasting your time and mine. But until I have the information you can give me, I won't know…'

'Next week then.'

'No, tomorrow,' Gowda retorted.

'What?' Ashok yelped.

'Will be there at four. See you then,' Gowda said and walked to his motorbike.

He stood looking at it with a small smile. When nothing seemed to go right, when everything else failed, when he felt old and wrung out, looking at his bullet brought him succour. God, how he loved this bike!

The world could keep its Harleys and R1 Yamahas. It was only the Bullet that did it for him. Make him feel as if it were an extension of himself. From the smooth curve of the petrol tank to the unflinching tiger-eye lamp that threw light into nooks and corners of the alleyways to the beast-like growl of the 500cc engine producing 41.3Nm of torque.

When Gowda prowled his way through the city on the Bullet, its distinct thump, the Bullet sound, resounded through his very being, flooding him with power, strength and with the unassailable knowledge that this was who he was: rugged, unrestrained and not afraid to go forth.

Her thighs brushed against his knees as she found her way to her place two seats away from his. His eyes trailed her. Even in the darkness of the movie theatre, she knew. A frisson of excitement. A heartbeat that slipped. All her womanly instincts told her that a pair of eyes was following her, fondling her ... Bhuvana smiled her secret smile of knowing.

She sat in the almost straight-backed theatre seat and placed her hands on the wooden armrests. A musty smell suffused the theatre and the dialogues were muffled as they emerged from the speakers. But no one would complain. The people who patronized Kalinga theatre would continue to come there even if the place smelt like a urinal in a public bus stand. Such was its pull.

The theatre was only half full. Mostly men, with a few women randomly scattered. She pulled the dupatta around her neck and adjusted it so that it fell over her right shoulder, covering her breasts and revealing a bit of her hair so her profile would be that much more striking. On her face was a half smile. She knew she looked like the singer in the Ravi Varma painting. Not the one in the centre, holding the tanpura, but the woman at the far left: mysterious, alluring, with an enigmatic expression in her eyes.

Monday had been a disaster. She had been so hopeful when she set out that evening. But it had all gone horribly wrong and Akka's disapproval had dogged her every step home and as she wiped her face clean of make-up.

Akka watched as Bhuvana faded out and was replaced by a man in the mirror.

'I suggest you don't go out for a few weeks,' she said.

It was the man who nodded, pretending to agree.

'You really can't take chances like this,' Akka added.

He nodded again. It was best to let Akka believe that Bhuvana wasn't going to emerge for a few days.

Akka would be furious if she knew Bhuvana had slipped out again. She bit on the fleshy pad of her thumb to stop the giggle from emerging. Bhuvana had a mind of her own. And Bhuvana did exactly what she wanted.

She touched her earlobe. It was a new earring with rubies in it. She missed the pearl earrings. But she had lost one of the pair. Perhaps in that scuffle in the alley or somewhere else. Or it may have fallen off on its own. The hook hadn't been long enough to take the weight of the pearl. She would have that earring replicated. To feel again the cool touch of the pearl against her skin when she moved her head. She held her head pertly, seeing in her mind how it would be when her pearl earring adorned her ears again.

She gave him fifteen minutes. It was a low-budget flesh flick. The plot seldom changed. The horny sister-in-law. The desperate housewife. The untouched schoolgirl. The film pandered to the average fantasy of the average Indian man. If you wait your turn, everything you want will come to you. The epics taught you this, so did the movie changes at Kalinga theatre.

In fifteen minutes, the bits would start appearing. Inserts of hard porn. When the first bit came on, she stared at the screen in disgust. How could these louts here be turned on by this? The mechanical sucking and fucking; the moaning, groaning and slurping ... her stomach turned.

All around her, as if on cue, the louts had begun their groping and fumbling. What was she doing here, she thought as she saw the man across the aisle fumble at the crotch of the man sitting next to him. They were strangers. She knew that. They had walked in separately along with her. Bloody homo cocksuckers.

Two nights ago the goddess had appeared in her dream and said it was time to begin. Friday was assigned as the chosen day when she would have to wait for the goddess's call and follow instructions on where to go. No more stepping out on other days of the week, the goddess had warned, that doesn't seem to have the desired effect. For the rest, listen to your inner voice, she had said.

But when the goddess spoke to her, she had to heed what was asked of her. This was where the goddess had asked her to go. And so she had slipped out of the house and brought herself here.

But this theatre that seemed to be filled with rutting animals, why had the goddess sent her here?

As she rose and walked past the row of seats, a hand pulled her back. 'What's the hurry?' he asked. 'Where are you going?'

A bird rose within her chest. A fluttering of wings in her ears. The tang of an expensive aftershave. Her mouth went dry.

'I…' she stuttered.

'Don't go, please,' he said.

The plea in his voice, the softness of his skin, held her back. As she gazed into his eyes, she knew why the goddess had led her to Kalinga theatre. For it is in a pond of black mud that the lotus blooms.

SATURDAY, 6 AUGUST

Gowda woke up to the insistent ringing of the doorbell. He shoved his feet into a pair of slippers and walked to the door, rubbing sleep out of his eyes. He glanced at the clock. Quarter to six. Which bastard was it? Waking him up at this unearthly hour?

Roshan stood on the veranda, punching keys on his mobile. Gowda frowned. 'What are you doing here? And can't you let go of that bloody phone for once!'

'Wow! When did you get that done?'

Roshan's eyes lit on Gowda's tattoo.

Gowda looked at his arm self-consciously. He had worn a sleeveless vest to bed. 'Er ... some months ago...'

'But why didn't you tell Mummy or me? Man, I can't believe my father's got a biker tattoo done. Cool!'

Roshan grinned at his father and walked past him. 'Are you alone?' he asked, his eyes taking in the fastidiously clean living room.

'Are you on a fact-finding mission for your mother? Well, you can tell her that I was frolicking with half a dozen ... Forget it. Do you want some tea?'

The boy nodded as he dropped into the sofa and settled his feet on the coffee table. Gowda opened his mouth to tell him to get his fucking feet off the table and then held himself back. This was his son. He had as much right to be here as he himself did.

As he spooned the tea dust into the boiling water, Gowda was stricken by a thought. Was this what the police force did even to ordinary nondescript men? Turn them into tyrants zealously guarding their fiefdom with abuse and violence.

Gowda was quiet as he sipped his tea. In a span of fifteen minutes, Roshan had turned the order of the room into chaos. His rucksack lay on the floor, its contents spilling out. His sneakers and a pair of balled-up socks were by the door. The magazines on the table were strewn and Roshan's jacket sat in a heap on a chair. The boy was rifling through the stack of CDs and had it all messed up.

'What's ... this?' Gowda began, then held himself back. What was with him? Was he turning into an old woman? Soon he would be ironing his newspaper...

The dog, yes the dog, he would have to get the dog. That would teach him to ease up.

'Yes, Appa?' Roshan looked up. 'You were saying something.'

Gowda ruffled the boy's hair. 'Nothing,' he said, feeling a forgotten streak of gentleness, or was it tenderness, as his fingers slid through his son's hair.

'Shanthi will be here by seven. Tell her what you would like for breakfast. She's a good cook.'

Roshan looked at him curiously. 'I know, Appa. I used to live here,' he said, smiling.

'Yes, you did,' Gowda said in a quiet sort of voice. 'I'm going back to bed. You should too.'

Roshan nodded as he pulled out the CD and inserted another one.

Gowda couldn't sleep. Roshan's every step boomed in his ears. He could hear the boy shuffling his feet ... then a dull thud as the rucksack hit the bed ... buttons snapped, the screech of the zip on his fly ... a sigh, a tuneless humming, the stream of urine as it hit the toilet bowl ... was the boy actually making a zigzag as he peed? ... The rumbling of his stomach at the lack of food ... air travelling through the nostrils into the trachea down into the thoracic cavity, and the rise and fall of the diaphragm, the swelling and diminishing of the lungs as the alveoli gathered each breath ... I can't be hearing this. It's all in my imagination.

Or was it, a discomfiting thought rose to the surface of his mind, that he resented the intrusion? The sharing of space even if it was his son.

Gowda pulled the sheet over his head.

How long would the boy stay?

He groaned as he thought he heard Roshan shut his eyes as he fell asleep.

No, no, I must remember he's my son and I his father. I can't resent his being here. What's wrong with me?

Gowda was reading through Samuel the photographer's statement when Mohammed called.

'I hope I am not disturbing you, sir.'

'No, Mohammed, tell me. I know you wouldn't call without a reason,' Gowda said as his eyes stalled on a line. *A Scorpio with Tamil Nadu registration reversed and drove away as I stopped.*

'The mortuary attendant gave me a small package. He said it came from the hospital. Liaquat's possessions, or what's left of it. There is a flat little gold leaf that he wore on a thread around his ... lower waist. It was a love token from Razak. And there is a pearl earring. A rather large pearl. It looks expensive. It made me wonder what Liaquat had been up to.'

'I'll call you in about an hour. Will you bring it to Jeweller

Street? That's not too far from where you are...' Gowda said, thumbing through his phone book to call a jeweller acquaintance.

Gowda watched Narayan Rao's face as he wiped the pearl with a soft cloth and examined it. It reminded him of his mother and their trips to the vegetable shop when he was a boy. Her eyes would narrow and flare in turns, her mouth would purse into a line as she hefted the brinjal and snapped the tail off a runner bean. Look, I know exactly what I am doing, that's what it was all about. It hit Gowda how much he missed her and how little he thought about her any more...

'It is the real thing, a South Sea pearl.'

'How do you know it's real?' It puzzled Gowda, this secret sense that jewellers and women possessed to distinguish the fake from the real, the ripeness of mangoes and the age of gold and ridge gourds...

'You said it was in a fire. It had burn marks on it which went away when I rubbed it with a cloth. If you rub it against your teeth, you'll feel it's gritty. A fake one would be smooth,' the jeweller said, offering him the pearl.

Gowda looked at it for a moment and put it into a pouch. God knows how many places it had been rubbed against. He most certainly wasn't going to put it in his mouth.

'One of this size must have cost at least eight thousand rupees. Add to that the gold of the chain and hook. About four thousand. Altogether, with the making charge, about twenty-five thousand rupees at least for a pair,' the jeweller said as Gowda rose.

Gowda stared. 'That expensive!'

Narayan Rao nodded. 'Not too many people would spend that kind of money on pearls. Resale value is almost nil, you see. And the workmanship is unusual. I think it's been copied from an antique design. See how the pearl has been fitted here.' The jeweller pointed to a detail.

Gowda grunted, more for effect. He could spot no difference between this one and the forty others on display in the shop. 'Would you be able to tell who made it and if it was made here in Bangalore?' Gowda asked carefully, not wanting to give anything away.

'I could ask around. Better still, I'll ask my goldsmith. He knows everyone here in Jeweller Street and beyond.' Narayan Rao smiled.

Gowda put the pouch back on the velvet tray. The jeweller took the pearl earring out and held it to the light. 'She is a beauty.'

As he put the earring back into the pouch, Narayan Rao said, 'If you put a real pearl in a glass of water and hold it up on a night when there is a full moon, it will reflect the moon. Pearls look best in moonlight. Did you know?' The jeweller stroked the pearl through the pouch with the tip of his finger as if it were a woman's cheek. 'On a full moon night, such pearls in a woman's ears would turn even an ugly crone into an apsara.'

Gowda's mobile burst into song. It was Santosh.

'Sir, where are you? The ACP's been calling for you. And there is a package that's come for you from Inspector Ashok. And—'

Gowda cut the call with a brusque, 'I'll call you back.'

Pieces of a jigsaw heaped around him: Liaquat. A pearl earring. Chicken Razak, known defaulter and current jailbird. An SUV with a Tamil Nadu number plate. A middle-aged pharmacist. And the only connecting link was a string. A string coated with fine glass dust.

Where did it all lead to?

It was a narrow street intersected on either side by two main thoroughfares: Seppings Road on one side and OPH road on the other.

Once, it had been a slum strewn with shops that dealt in scrap. The real gujri was Stephens Square, but this had become a gujri of the gujri. They called it Gujri Gunta – the second-hand hole. Gujri Gunta dealt in everything from nuts and bolts to automobile spare parts to old newspapers and other raddi – plastic bottles, dented aluminium vessels, broken flashlights.

Here and there, on the street, were doorways. Not many knew what lay behind them. Narrow corridors opening into small square courtyards, around which were a warren of two-room tenements. The people living there had learnt to make do. Clotheslines were strung in the courtyard and there were a couple of brick stoves, so each household could make its own hot water to take to the two bathrooms that had to serve the entire populace of eight households. When it rained, the road turned into a stream of fast-flowing dirty brown water in which garbage floated. To open the main door of the house was dangerous then. There was no knowing what would float in. An old tyre or a single chappal or a dead bandicoot.

Then, in the late 1990s, the cleansing began. The slums were demolished overnight and the riffraff removed. The character of the street changed. One side of the street became a line of tenement shops that had nothing to do with scrap. A tyre retreading shop, a warehouse, a welding unit, a carpenter, a teashop, a rice wholesaler. The other side became houses. But the name stayed Gujri Gunta and it was here that Corporator Ravikumar had decided to build himself the home of his dreams.

The corporator's eyes followed the man's as they darted around his house.

He saw the man taking in the marble floors, the tinkling fountain, the gargantuan chandelier, the gilt-edged mirrors. He saw his gaze wander through the open door of the room that was located to the left of the courtyard, the heavy swag of silk that draped its windows, the leather sofas, the glass-topped coffee table and the gigantic brass lamp – the trappings of a man who has money and knows how to make more of it.

He sensed the man assessing the opulence, the grandeur. It was precisely the reaction he had hoped to elicit when he built the house. Right from the compound wall which stood eight feet high with shards of glass embedded on the top and two lines of barbed wire thereafter, to the sweeping curve of steps that led to the main door and an enclosed veranda that ran the breadth of the building. Every aspect of the house had a reason for being the way it was.

Both sides of the staircase were flanked by two wings – house within house, each independent with its own private entrances and kitchen. No one needed to know who came and went at either end.

The staircase was at the end of an imposing courtyard, one end of which was occupied by a lone throne-like chair. It was here the corporator received his guests.

A waterfall trickled merrily in one corner, into a pool where fish swam in circles. Sometimes, in the middle of a discussion, the corporator would rise from his chair and take a handful of fish food to scatter into the pond. He would stand there watching his fish feed while the discussion trembled and hung precariously in midair.

Upstairs was the corporator's private domain. Half of it was his personal space. The other section was his office. A long hall that could seat two hundred people if required. Stacked against the wall of the office room, as it was called, were a row of folding steel chairs. Anyone who came in would have to unfold a chair and make a seat for himself if asked to sit down. It immediately put the person at a disadvantage.

Right now, all that the room held was a chair and a table with a sea of phones on it. None of the phones except the black and red ones worked. The rest were mute witnesses to the corporator's dealings. The office room too had its private staircase so that people could come and go without entering the main house.

He saw the man's eyes fix on Tiger.

The corporator reached across and stroked Tiger's head. The dog turned its head and licked his fingers. The man's eyes almost popped out as the corporator hefted the gold chain around the dog's neck. A flat chain almost an inch wide.

'It's not gold, if that's what you are thinking. It's just gold-plated,' the corporator said.

The man didn't speak.

The corporator continued to stroke the dog's head absent-mindedly. 'I am only a corporator. Do you know there are one hundred and ninety-eight wards in Bangalore and I am corporator of only one ... So don't start assuming things about me! You have to realize that I am your representative. A simple man who has simple tastes. A man of the people.'

The corporator's expression dared the man to contradict him with word or gesture. The man bowed his head and murmured, 'I know, Anna. Which is why I am here. You are one of us. Only you will be able to help me.'

The corporator had a name but no one called him by it. He was anna. Big brother. The omnipotent, omnipresent ruler of the ward he had claimed for his own. He was anna to his siblings and henchmen. And he was anna to the people who had voted for him and to the supplicants who sought him out with pleading eyes and open palms. What need for a name then?

The corporator tilted his chin at Chikka, who stood by him.

Brother, stooge, voice of the corporator when he was not inclined to speak, Chikka asked, 'What is your problem?'

The man took a deep breath. 'I bought a little house in Obaidullah Street, 3rd Cross, off Shivaji Nagar Road. It's a few streets away from the mosque. Razak has been living there for the last ten years. No one told me this…'

'Chicken Razak?'

The man nodded. Chikka hissed in annoyance. Tiger scratched himself. The corporator maintained a bland expression. 'So?' he asked finally.

'He refused to vacate when I asked him to. He just laughed in my face. I sank everything I had into the house. The pagadi on the house we live in will expire next month. Where do I take my family when we have to vacate the house we live in now?'

'Isn't he in jail?' Chikka asked.

'But his frooter lives there.'

'Who?' Chikka asked.

'Liaquat. Calls himself Leila.'

'If he's Leila, aren't you man enough to throw him out?'

'I can't do it alone,' the man said. 'And no one will go with me. Razak may be in jail but his pals are outside and if Razak is annoyed, they will not spare me or my family.'

The corporator waved his hand lazily in dismissal. The light caught the diamond solitaire on his finger. It pleased him to see that arc of light. He moved his hand again. Enjoy and dismiss. Dismiss and enjoy. Whatever it was, with a toss of the wrist, he could make the world turn.

'Go now,' Chikka said, reading his brother's gesture. 'Anna will do what he can.'

The man continued to stand.

'What is it now?' Chikka asked.

'When will I be able to get my house back?'

Chikka merely stared at him. The man paled. Then he left quietly.

The corporator stood up. In a few minutes it would be time for him to leave for a visit around his ward. He wondered if he had time for a bath.

'What are you going to do?' Chikka asked.

'I am going to have a bath.'

'No, what will you do about him?'

'Is he useful?'

'He works in the PWD. A lowly clerk, but he may come in useful. There's no telling...'

'Then we take care of it,' the corporator murmured. 'Our contacts are what brought us here. Where's King Kong?'

Chikka grimaced, thinking of the ape-like creature who doubled as driver and bodyguard for Anna.

'He's washing the car.'

'He's going to strip the shine off my new car with all that washing. Bloody monkey!' the corporator grumbled.

Chikka smiled. 'He treats the car as if it were his pet ... You should have a word with him.'

The corporator stretched. 'Whatever one may say of him, he is loyal. If I ask him to shoot himself for me, he'll do it. That's rare, that kind of unconditional loyalty.'

'Are you saying I am not loyal enough, Anna?' Chikka's face tightened.

'You are my brother. You are expected to be loyal. But he's an outsider, an employee ... enough of this! Now make a list of what's happening in my ward. What I should know about when I get there.'

The corporator walked up the staircase. The left wing that stretched three thousand square feet was all his. No one was allowed to enter it unless accompanied by one of the ladies. It was here that the corporator bathed, dressed, slept and plotted the many schemes that made him richer and more powerful by the day. The rest of the house, all two thousand square feet of it, was where everyone else lived. His brother, visiting relatives from Vellore and Ambur in Tamil Nadu, the staff, the ladies. Even Tiger had a room of his own, with a teak bed and a silver water bowl.

Each time the corporator had to don his public face, he felt a little dirty. Tainted by the stench of fear and weakness he was asked to alleviate. It was like climbing into a closed car with an unwashed and drunk driver.

'Anna,' Chikka said from the foot of the staircase.

'What?'

'We have to leave in half an hour's time.'

'Says who?'

'The meeting is fixed for eleven a.m. The traffic...'

'Let them wait. I need to bath first.'

'Yes, Anna,' Chikka murmured.

The corporator paused and looked down.

'Chikka,' he said, 'tell Akka to send Rupali and Leena up to my room.'

Chikka stood at the foot of the staircase, marvelling yet again at the mind that had conjured up this house. It is a strange house and we are a strange household, he thought as he stepped into the left wing that housed the ladies whenever they came by.

A flurry of voices met him at the door. He winced. He ought to have been used to it by now. But after four years, he still found that simpering note in a male baritone hard to stomach.

'Akka,' he called from the doorway.

'Akka is not here,' one of them called out.

Chikka stepped into the room.

'Look who's here!' Nalini tittered. 'Our very own Chikka Master! And what can we do for you?'

Chikka pretended not to hear the mockery flung at him. He was no one's master and would never be. No one took him seriously. Not even these bloody eunuchs, he thought.

He had been a tiny baby, premature and weak, and so his mother took to calling him her Chikka. The little one. The name stuck. When Chikka stopped growing at five feet, no one gave it much thought. He would have his growth spurt later, everyone said. But Chikka stayed five feet tall. Neither a real dwarf, who might at least have got a government job under the handicapped quota, nor a proper grown man.

Even Anna treated him like a pet rather than a man. 'My Chikka has more brains in his little finger than all the scientists at IISc,' Anna said, ruffling Chikka's hair with the careless hand he stroked Tiger's head with. 'Go on, ask Chikka how much is 1298765.35 x 409878?'

When the health inspector the corporator was talking to blinked uncomprehendingly, the corporator urged, 'Go on, ask him!'

Obediently the man asked, 'How much is it?'

And Chikka, who knew what was expected of him, murmured, '532335344127.3.'

'See.' The corporator gleamed, holding up his mobile to show the answer. 'He did that in his head in less than three seconds. My Chikka is amazing!'

Chikka felt a quiet rage gather in him. He and Tiger were no different. Tiger shook hands and he did mental math. They were both performing animals.

'As are you bitches,' Chikka said under his breath, gazing at the eunuchs.

'Anna wants Rupali and Leena to go up to him,' he said in a flat voice.

'What about me?' Nalini demanded. 'It's my turn today.'

'No, it's my turn,' Meena whined.

'Listen, I don't have time for this. You'd better not keep him waiting,' Chikka said, turning to leave.

'If Anna doesn't want us, we could keep you company,' Nalini offered coyly, playing with her plait.

Chikka's gaze hardened. He looked at the tall muscular creature in front of him. The square jaw and straight nose. No matter how long her hair grew or how many hormone shots she took, it was impossible to hide the fact that Nalini had been born a man.

'I don't think so,' he said.

Nalini made a face. 'Not up to your exacting standards, are we? For a short man, you have a very big ego.'

Chikka felt his fingers gather into a fist. 'At least I know I am a man. You? What are you?'

Gowda kicked off his shoes and slid his feet into a pair of flip-flops he kept under the table. He loosened his belt and opened a couple of his shirt buttons. When Gowda needed to work, constraint of any sort fettered his thought process. Santosh watched him, more appalled than amused. What if the ACP walked in without prior information? Or, what if an MLA or even a corporator came in?

Gowda felt the young man's eyes trail his every move. 'Is something bothering you?' he asked.

'Sir ... yes sir ... no sir,' Santosh stuttered. Then, summoning his courage, he said, 'Your uniform...'

Gowda narrowed his eyes. There it came again. Censure from seniors. Disapproval from juniors. No one gauged a policeman by how keen his mind was. The stars on his epaulettes and the shine on his shoes were what mattered.

'*He shall appear at all times in police dress and accoutrements and shall always be neat and clean in appearance.* We do that so we look trim and fit and vested with authority in our dealings with the public. The police manual doesn't mention that I should at all times button my collar and cinch the belt until it cuts into my belly.' Gowda flicked the pages of the file Ashok had sent him.

'For now I want you to assist me. Not police how I wear my uniform.'

Santosh flushed. At the police academy, he had been called promising, dynamic and intelligent. Gowda made him feel like a foolish old woman. One day, one day, he promised himself.

Two hours later, when they raised their heads, Gowda looked at Santosh.

'So?' his eyes asked.

'I...' Santosh began, then quelled his words, afraid he would have his head bitten off.

'What? Say it...'

'I don't think Razak has anything to do with the Liaquat murder. His enemies are not gang lords. He's just a petty case rowdy!'

'We say homicide. Not murder. That's a constable's language.'

Santosh swallowed.

'But that apart, you are right. Razak was a dead end. So, Sub-inspector Santosh, we are back to square one. Think, think ... I am sure you will see something I have missed. You have it in you...'

The words of praise were a shower of rose petals. Santosh felt the caress of a million pink lips on his upturned face and then like a slap of cold water he heard Gowda say, 'That is, if you stick to police matters and not silly things like how many buttons of my shirt are open.'

Santosh's brother, the author, called it the most Indian of traits: the penultimate paragraph of condemnation. As though we are unable to allow undivided praise for anything without adding an 'if only' clause. It was a congenital fault among Indians, his brother claimed. At this moment, Santosh was inclined to agree.

Gowda went home early. He would call in for a pizza, he decided. A new pizza place had opened on Hennur Road and was making home deliveries this far. He didn't particularly care for pizza himself, finding it too doughy and bland, but

Roshan would wolf it down as if he hadn't seen food for a week.

As the vehicle turned in through the gate, Gowda saw that his Bullet had been moved. He frowned.

He rang the doorbell. From within he could hear the din of a heavy metal band trying to raise their dead ancestors.

'Should I wait, sir?' PC David asked, trying to hide his curiosity at the noise that boomed and spilled over into the front yard.

Gowda shook his head. 'No, you can go back.'

Gowda fished out his key and stuck it into the keyhole. But the door was latched from within. He hammered on the door. There was no response.

Gowda walked around the house and peered through the window into Roshan's room. The boy had brought the stereo into his room. And he was prancing around in his underwear, head banging!

He tapped on the window. Once. Twice. He felt his irritation compound into rage. He had to tap on the window several times before Roshan noticed his father staring at him.

Gowda didn't know what triggered it off – the frustration he felt at not knowing what to do next on the manja thread case, the irritation at being locked out of his own house, annoyance at seeing that his Bullet had been used by the boy without even a cursory 'if I may', his blocked sinuses, his growling belly, the thought of yet another pointless evening stretching ahead, the emptiness of his bed, the tedium of an everyday that seemed relentless – all of it sent his blood pressure soaring and smashed the last vestige of control.

When Roshan opened the door, Gowda reached across and slapped him, snarling, 'When are you going back?'

SUNDAY, 7 AUGUST

Gowda stared at the head of foam in his glass. He raised his eyes and looked across the table at Michael. 'I can't believe I said that to my son,' he said despondently. 'What kind of a father am I?'

Michael toyed with the coaster on which the beer mugs had been placed. 'Don't be so hard on yourself, Bob,' he said quietly. 'Our fathers said as much to us. If not the same words, something similar. We put it out of our minds, didn't we?'

Gowda nodded. His father and he had a turbulent relationship. Nothing he did ever seemed to please his father. Basketball, his friends, the science forum, his plans to join the Indian Police Service. All through his student years he had felt the weight of his father's disapproving gaze and once, the bite of his belt. His father wanted him to write a bank test and join the State Bank of India or Canara Bank. 'You will have an organized life,' he had said each time Gowda talked about his dreams for himself as an IPS officer.

Gowda enrolled for his postgraduate degree and prepared for the Civil Services exam. He failed his first attempt. He got as far as the interview in his second attempt but failed again.

In the end, Gowda succumbed to his father's expectations for him. After his post-graduation, he never touched a basketball again. He wrote the bank test and passed.

Three years later, bank clerk Gowda had a rude awakening. A college mate walked into the bank and was surprised to see Gowda in the teller's cage. 'So they finally put you behind bars, Gowda.' The girl giggled, running her fingers along the mesh of the cage. 'And I always thought you would be the one putting people behind bars!'

Gowda flushed. He counted out her money carefully, daubing his finger on the wet sponge.

That evening, Gowda went looking for a place to start basketball practice again. He didn't tell anyone about his plans but when the next Karnataka state recruitment notifications were published, Gowda wrote the test.

Gowda announced his new avatar in life only after everything was in place. 'I have joined the Karnataka police,' he announced in the middle of dinner, tearing a piece of akki roti and dipping it into a small bowl of koli saaru. He was prepared to battle this through. It was his life, after all.

His father looked up from the spinach mossoppu he insisted on every night as an accompaniment to rice, roti or mudde and murmured, 'You always wanted to be a policeman, didn't you? But why did you leave it so late? You have lost out on so many years of service now.'

'When do you start?' his mother asked, placing an akki roti on his plate and ladling some more of the chicken curry into his bowl.

Gowda was baffled. He had expected fireworks and recrimination from his father; much hand wringing and crying from his mother. And here they were, calm as a firmly set pot of curd and as unruffled by his change of career.

'You don't mind?' he asked, trying to make sense of his father's quiet acceptance.

'Why should I?' His father's eyebrows rose. 'This is a government job too, with an assured pension. And you will have the kind of power no bank employee can even dream of. Besides, Nagendra is already in the SBI, so we can be sure of bank loans if we need any.'

His mother smiled. 'You must take a photograph of yourself in full uniform ... I want to send it to your aunt in Pune.'

Gowda shook his head. Three fucking years of his life wasted in a bloody bank and he had thought he had done it to make them happy. And they seemed just as pleased at the thought of a police officer son.

There was no knowing what parents really expected of you. He had told himself he wouldn't be that sort of a father. One you had to make allowances for, be patient with, even forgive.

Gowda grimaced and drank deeply.

Michael smiled. 'I hardly see my sons, you know, Borei. So enjoy your boy's presence while he is at home. Once he leaves, he is gone...'

'Your boys?' Gowda asked.

Michael's mouth tightened into a line. 'One is in New Zealand. The other's in Melbourne where I am. But he may as well be in New Zealand. I saw them last when Becky died.'

Gowda nodded. He searched his mind for something they could talk about without it touching a nerve, a still healing wound. This catching-up business wasn't so easy. Too much time had lapsed. They were two different men whose lives had taken different trajectories.

'Do you remember that place, Variety, on Residency road, where we used to go?' Gowda asked suddenly, seizing on a subject that was guaranteed to trigger reminiscence and merriment.

Michael smiled. The cheapest beer in town. And rum that burnt a trail as it went down your throat and was guaranteed to get you drunk very quickly. It was the greatest lure for any student. Gowda, Michael and a few others had been regulars. Weekend regulars, they would have been quick to clarify.

Life then had been structured around their haunts. Every hour and day had its own specific texture and rhythm. Gathering at noon at Mamu's canteen, which was housed in a small tile-roofed shop beyond the men's loo at St Joseph's, and crunching on mutton samosas. Afternoons in Ayah Park at Rest House Crescent, dubbed as Ganja Park. Sitting in a giant cement pipe that was part of the park's play space for kids and smoking grass.

Heading to Rex Theatre on Brigade Road to the slot machine games parlour between its two gates. Catching an English movie at Blue Diamond. And then ambling to Bascos, which had cabaret shows. Gaping at the black-and-white photographs of the dancers in the glass case – Ruby, Suzy, Lily...

'Remember the one time we took Urmila to Bascos?' Michael grinned.

Gowda's face smoothened into an expressionless mask.

Urmila had demanded that she be taken along. And she had hated that Gowda gaped as much as the other boys. Her snide remarks had only made them laugh harder.

Michael frowned. 'She said she tried calling you a few times. But you didn't take the call.'

Gowda shrugged. 'Did she? Sometimes I ignore numbers I don't recognize. It is usually some bank or credit card company asking if I want a loan.'

Michael gulped down his beer and poured himself a glass from the pitcher. 'Well, here's her number,' he said, pulling out a paper from his wallet.

Gowda took the scrap of paper and let it lie on the table.

'Call her, Mudde. C'mon, call her. We were all friends

once, remember! What happened between the two of you is so far back…'

Gowda punched in the number with great reluctance. Something leaden sat in the pit of his stomach.

The phone at the other end rang six times before a woman's voice murmured a 'hello'.

Gowda's heart stilled. She sounded the same after twenty-seven years.

'Hello, who is this,' she asked and then, 'Borei, is that you? Do you know I have been trying to reach you for the last two days?'

'Hello, Urmila,' he said softly.

'Ask her to join us,' Michael mouthed from across the table.

'Michael and I are at Pecos. Do you know the pub? It's the one on Rest House Road…'

Gowda gestured to Michael. 'She can't come,' he mouthed.

'Sure, I understand. Tomorrow? I am not sure … Let me call you.' Gowda clicked shut his phone. 'There, satisfied?' he asked Michael.

Michael peered into his beer mug gravely. 'What's the harm in meeting her? You were inseparable once.'

'Once.' Gowda's face was grim. Once was the operative word.

It was almost half past one when Gowda rode into the two-storeyed family house on 7th Main, Jayanagar 5th Block.

As he parked his bike, he saw the two coconut trees were laden with coconuts ready for picking. He shrugged; it wasn't his business any more. He had severed ties with this house and its demands. Now he could just be a guest here.

Gowda paused. Was this how Roshan felt when he was home? As if he no longer felt any ties to the place he had once called home? Gowda felt a physical jolt of pain at the thought.

When Roshan was a baby and even as a young toddler, Gowda would often cradle his sleeping son to his chest. And he would feel a fierce love, a great tenderness suffuse him. He would bend and nuzzle his son's cheek and feel tears swell in his eyes at the milky sweet smell of his child's skin. He would do anything to keep his son from harm's way. Destroy anything that threatened his child. He would do everything he could for Roshan, he had sworn then. This was the child he had slapped. He flinched, thinking of how Roshan had reeled from the force of the slap.

'What are you doing? Who are you frowning at?' Nagendra asked from the doorway.

Gowda smiled at his brother. A thin watery smile as he sought to compose his emotions.

'I thought I heard your bike,' Nagendra said, looking at his brother carefully. 'Are you all right?'

Gowda nodded.

'The coconuts need to be plucked,' he said. 'Do you want me to send someone?'

Nagendra cocked his head ruefully. 'It would be good if you did. Meena can't seem to find anyone. As it is, she keeps threatening to chop the jackfruit tree down.' He added, 'It's not the same without you at home, Borei.'

Gowda's eyes flicked through the living room as he walked to the dining room. It was a little more than a month since he had visited. The TV and its cabinet had gone and instead there was a huge wall-mounted one. And there were new curtains.

Nagendra saw Gowda's eyes settle on the TV. 'The old one was giving trouble,' he said. 'There was a good exchange offer. And then Meena thought the old curtains needed to be changed. They were beginning to look tatty.'

Gowda smiled, trying hard to not show how unsettled he felt by the changes. 'Good decision.' He cocked his head. 'I've been thinking of getting an LCD TV too, but with Mamtha and Roshan at Hassan, it seems pointless to invest so much money in a new TV.'

'Aren't you coming in for lunch?' his sister-in-law called out.

'You are late,' his father grumbled as Gowda pulled a chair out and sat himself at the dining table. Lunch was in progress.

'I thought you were not coming,' his sister-in-law said, setting a plate before him.

Gowda said nothing but ladled the bisibele bath into his plate. His brother pushed a bowl of tomato and onion raita towards him. Gowda smiled gratefully and bit into a crisp.

'How is Roshan?' his father asked.

'He is here. He arrived yesterday morning,' Gowda said.

'Why didn't you bring him then?' Meena asked.

'Take it easy ... the boy must have things to do on his own,' his brother said. 'He is not four years old to be dragged everywhere his parents go.'

Gowda shot his brother a grateful look. How could he tell them that through the night Roshan's hurt face had kept slipping into his mind. He had skulked out of the house early, asking Shanthi to stay back to make sure Roshan had everything he needed.

'I would like to have seen my grandson but it is all "take it easy" these days,' their father growled. 'That is the problem with your generation. Everywhere you go, everyone is taking it easy. The clerk at the bank would rather stand out and smoke while we pensioners wait. The doctor at the hospital is talking on his mobile phone while checking my BP ... when I protest, they tell me: Aja, take it easy! The world is going to the dogs all because of this "take it easy" policy. And the two of you aren't any better. Look at the coconut tree outside! And the state of this house...'

The brothers exchanged a glance. How was it that their seventy-nine-year-old father could still make them feel like incompetent eleven-year-olds?

And I do precisely the same to Roshan, Gowda thought, a stab of remorse twisting in him.

The household settled into its Sunday afternoon routine once lunch was eaten and the dishes cleared up. His father hobbled to his bedroom downstairs for a nap. His brother went up to his room to read the newspaper, he said. His sister-in-law went to the living room and switched on the TV for the afternoon movie. And Gowda found his way back to his room which his nephew had claimed for his own until he went away to BITS Pilani.

A cupboard still held Gowda's books and some of his certificates from college. He lay on the bed and stared at the ceiling. He should have asked Roshan to come along, he thought. But he had been unable to meet his son's eyes all evening. He shuddered. What had he been thinking of? How different was he from his father?

His father had come home in a rage. Someone had told him that he had spotted Borei at Bascos. His father had unclasped his belt and lashed out at Borei, who hadn't even realized what he was being belted for. 'You badvaa raascal, what were you doing at that place?'

'What place?' Borei had said again and again as the belt cut into his skin. He hadn't known what to think, what to feel, except a deep sense of hurt. Why was his father doing this to him? What had he done that was so wrong?

Roshan had had the same expression on his face, Gowda thought with a great sense of shame.

He would apologize to Roshan, he decided. He would ask his forgiveness for his brutishness. For being such a lousy, miserable failure of a father.

At some point, Gowda slid into a deep sleep. It was almost five when he woke, his mouth dry and parched. He sat up and stared around him, disoriented. Where was he? Then he saw the familiar cupboard and it came back to him.

Gowda went to the bathroom, sluiced his face with water, combed his hair and stepped back into the room. He opened the cupboard and peered inside. The zoology text was where he had kept it. And inside the brown paper cover was a photograph he had placed there twenty-seven years ago. He slid it out of its hiding place and looked at it.

Urmila, just before they separated. He pushed the photograph into its place and took the book with him. Then he took the photo out again and placed it in his wallet and put the book back. What am I doing? he asked himself. He had a case to solve. Two homicides that seemed to have nothing in common and yet seemed to be linked. What could connect the middle-aged medical shop owner Kothandaraman and that young male prostitute Liaquat? And he had a young son back home, a teenage son he had slapped the previous day. What am I doing? he asked himself again.

He could hear the hum of conversation. His sister-in-law called out to him, 'Borei, your coffee's turning cold!'

Across the table, Borei Gowda watched his family drink their Sunday coffee and crunch their nippattu. In a little while, his father would start playing the kirtanas of the Kannada composers he favoured – Purandara Dasa and Vyasatirtha. His sister-in-law and brother would set out to a bhajan meeting they went to most Sundays. He felt removed from them and what their lives entailed. This was his family but they may as well be strangers, he thought. They haven't once asked me how I am or what it is I am doing these days. And yet, if I skip a visit, they will be angry, hurt even.

Gowda mumbled his goodbyes and started his Bullet. At least in its saddle he felt as if he belonged.

From within the house, he could hear the stereo burst into his father's favourite album *Daasara Padagalu*, Rajkumar Bharathi singing '*Krishna nee Begane Baro*'.

Gowda fled.

Chikka sat in the front seat beside King Kong. Not that Anna had asked him to. But he sensed that this evening that was how the corporator wished it, all of the back seat to himself. If there had been others in the car, Chikka would have sat with him.

The car was new; the corporator had bought it only a few weeks ago. The inside of the car had that new car smell. Add to it the rose fragrance of the car freshener, the two incense sticks that had been lit and the little garland of jasmine buds that had been draped around the little gold Ganesha who sat on the dashboard. And add to that the cologne the corporator seemed to have washed himself with and the fumes of the body spray King Kong had drenched himself with. Chikka felt bile rush up his throat; if he didn't open the window, he would throw up any moment now.

At the traffic light, Chikka had King Kong slide down the tinted windows. 'I need to buy a newspaper,' he said, gulping in air and hoping some of the fug in the car would clear.

Chikka took one long breath as the window went up again.

'What's in the newspaper?' the corporator asked.

'Someone said there's a report on a corporator from south Bangalore. I wanted to see what it said,' Chikka said, turning around. 'They are doing a series on corporators. "Know your corporator." That's what it's called.' Chikka tried to gauge his brother's expression. 'It will be your turn one of these days,' he added softly.

'Tell me what it said.' The corporator glanced at his watch. 'There's something I want to see on Palace Cross Road. A place has come up for sale. Do you remember the apartments Amma used to work in? A first-floor apartment there is on the market ... King Kong, we'll go there before we head to the town hall.'

Chikka swallowed. He felt a bead of sweat run down his forehead.

'Anna,' Chikka began, 'the meeting...'

'No, Chikka, I need to see this place. The meeting can wait. Do you think they will start at six p.m. on the dot? Useless fellows, each one of them. It will be at least seven before everyone gets there ... You haven't heard a word of what I said, Chikka,' the corporator said. 'What are you thinking about?'

'Nothing,' Chikka murmured.

'You can't be thinking of nothing.' The corporator's

voice was petulant. 'What about the dog menace problem the fools will bring up when we go into the ward meeting next week?'

'What dog menace?'

'What's with you, Chikka?'

Chikka felt King Kong's glance linger on him. King Kong didn't speak much but he didn't miss a thing. His narrow eyes swooped on everything around Anna and gauged it for any potential threat to Anna's well-being.

Chikka snapped, 'What are you staring at me for?'

'Don't snap at him. He can see as I do that your mind is elsewhere,' the corporator growled from the rear.

Chikka shook himself out of the strange apathy that seemed to have coiled around him. 'I'm sorry, Anna,' he said quietly. 'I have a headache ... we have to be careful with this dog business. The animal rights people can be a nuisance. The best thing to do would be to rope them in. Perhaps we can get one of them to go with us to the meeting.'

The corporator beamed. 'I like that.' Then he narrowed his eyes. 'I don't want any bad press about this. There's always some nosy journalist who's trying to climb to the top. How people want to move up in life is their business, but I won't allow anyone to step on my back to reach where they want to.'

Chikka was silent. He saw King Kong look straight ahead. He knew what the man was thinking. Chikka was thinking the same.

When the corporator was elected, one of the newspapers had carried a story about him. His years as a garbage collector, his job at the gujri, his association with the gangs and his sudden affluence. The journalist had even found out that he had once been called Caddie Ravi. And had raked up the story of Caddie Ravi and Jackie Kumar.

It had begun as a friendship between two boys. One of whom wielded a car jack to great effect. And the other was apprenticed as a caddie at the Bangalore Golf Club under Ijas Mamu, his father's friend, who assured them that there was nothing better in life than caddying. 'All those rich men wouldn't be able to play golf without us. That is real power. To help them decide if it should be a number eight iron or a number two iron.'

Anna hadn't known better till the day a golf ball flew across the fence and cracked a scooterist's head. The next day he hid a ball in his bag. Later, in the one-room tenement that was home, he pushed it into a cloth bag and swung it against the wall and saw the wall splinter. This was real power, he decided. Not placing a wedge in some bored rich man's hand…

He showed his new weapon to Jackie Kumar, his best friend. Jackie Kumar was two years younger but he had been out on the streets since he was nine. Jackie approved and took him along on his next assignment. He gave him a name too – Caddie Ravi.

They had a routine. Caddie Ravi stunned his victims with one swing of the golf ball in a sock. This allowed him greater economy of movement than a cloth bag, and a harder impact. It was a move he had learnt on the greens. Not a flick of the wrist but a full swing of the arm as if he were wielding a number six iron at the skull of the victim. As the ball struck bone, he saw in his mind the splintering of the wall. He felt the outer layer of the skull cave in, the fracturing of the inner layer into two or more pieces. Jackie Kumar would do the rest, which was kitchen work really. But it was he who struck the first blow.

Trouble began when Anna wanted to move on to irons. Jackie Kumar wouldn't let him. 'Do you realize that the police still haven't figured out what your weapon is? Once you use an iron, they'll know. And do you think they won't track you down? How many people have access to golf clubs?'

Anna relented. At first. Then he used an iron. He had his favourite. The sand wedge. Anna wiped the sole of the wedge carefully with a handkerchief he found in the victim's pocket. 'See this,' he said, running his finger around the end of the wedge head, 'it is angled in such a way that it will slide through mud, coarse grass and, of course, sand, lifting the ball off the ground in one smooth motion, and because there's a lot more material here, it is heavier and the impact is that much more ... beauty, isn't she?'

Jackie didn't reply. He stared at the victim on the ground, wondering if there was anything left for him to do.

'I told you not to,' he said, trying hard not to show his displeasure.

Anna saw that Jackie Kumar was displeased. But he had known the note of triumph when the iron struck the victim's skull, felt the power of perfect impact. A single arc from shoulder to wrist to club, slicing through the air. Thwack. So he did it again.

When the police sprung him, Anna directed them to Jackie Kumar.

'You are still underage, a minor, you'll get sent into a delinquent home. I will go to prison. You understand, don't you?' Anna had been nineteen then.

But Jackie Kumar didn't and he never forgave Anna either. There had been no direct confrontations, but they were not friends any more. Anna had moved on to politics while

Jackie Kumar remained a man of the streets. But with every new triumph prised from beneath Anna's nose, Jackie felt he was inching his way towards him. Anna didn't retaliate. He would bide his time. That was the other thing he had learnt on the golf course: patience. And how essential it was.

But most of that had become a matter of memory. Until the journalist decided to build his story around it.

'Caddie to Corporator' was the headline. It was a rag of a newspaper that survived on the scurrilous stories it published. No one was spared. And the corporator was merely one among the many whose past had been raked through. But someone at the press had called Anna to let him know. Anna had made a few phone calls. The entire print run was bought and burnt. And the journalist had an accident. He would never walk again.

'I'll make sure that a press report is released by the animal rights group,' Chikka said.

'A favourable one,' said the corporator. 'No point otherwise. And make sure they know how much of a dog lover I am.'

'Yes, of course.'

'What about that PWD man's problems?' Chikka asked in the silence that had crept into the car.

The corporator didn't hide his irritation. 'Now you tell me...'

'But, Anna, I reminded you last evening.'

'When?' The corporator frowned.

'Just after dinner, when you were with the chha...' Chikka almost bit his tongue and then hastened to add, 'Chandini, Rupali and Nandini.'

The corporator leaned back into the plush comfort of his car and mumbled, 'What do you have against them? I know what you were about to say. You were going to call them chhakkas, right? The girls tell me all about the way you abuse them. Behind their backs. It hurts them.'

'They are not girls, Anna.' Chikka's mouth was grim. 'They are bloody eunuchs; freaks of nature!'

'Well, let me tell you if you have forgotten that when the Station Muthu gang left me beaten to a pulp outside Byppanahalli railway station, it was a freak of nature who saved my life. So many people walked past me and they walked away without even stopping to check if I was alive or dead. One of those freaks took me home, brought a doctor, nursed me till I could sit up. None of this you see would exist if a bloody chhakka, as you call them, hadn't...'

Chikka turned, hands folded in penitence. 'Did I say anything about Akka? But the rest of them ... they give you a bad name.'

'Do I care?'

'And can you trust them not to blabber about us?' Chikka asked quietly. He wondered how much King Kong understood. He was a Bihari with only a smattering of Kannada. Chikka and the corporator spoke in Tamil. Nonetheless...

'They won't. They fear the wrath of the goddess as much as they fear me. And they know I can summon the goddess if I choose. Enough about this.'

'The PWD man...' Chikka reminded him.

But the corporator had closed his eyes. 'Later, Chikka, later,' he said.

As if on cue, King Kong put the music on.

MONDAY, 8 AUGUST

He looked around him carefully. It was just as he had expected it to be. The deep leather sofas and the chrome and leather bar stools. Gleaming floors and glass counters displaying cakes that seemed to be made of shaving foam mostly. The smell of coffee, and smart young men and women in smart clothes bustling around, taking orders, serving customers. With complete ease and absolute control.

SI Santosh looked around and bit down on his lip. How did one get to be like that? Was it an urban phenomenon or were you born with the knowledge that the only reason the world existed was to make your life better?

SI Santosh looked at the menu card one of those young gods had left on his table with a smile and a deft flick of his wrist. He blanched. A coffee cost one hundred and fifty-nine rupees. He could buy his whole month's supply of freshly ground coffee blended with twenty per cent chicory for that money. What kind of people came to coffee shops like this?

His eyes darted around the premises. A hum of voices rose above the music. Music that resonated with a certain tempo to suggest youthful vivaciousness. Music the like of which SI Santosh had never heard before. Music that the girls in their cropped tops and balloon pants, the boys in skinny fitted T-shirts and ears studded with strange devices masquerading as earrings, must understand and even enjoy. If Gowda made him feel foolish, being here swamped him with a sense of inadequacy.

He had walked into the coffee shop on a whim. He had gone to the commissioner's office on an errand. On his way back, he had decided to take in a few sights. He was unfamiliar with Bangalore still, except for what he had seen in the movies. On M.G. Road, which seemed to have grown a spine on which soon the metro rail would run, he saw a coffee shop and was lured in by its glass and chic.

The parking attendant had instantly recognized that he was a policeman even though he was in mufti. A place had been magically found for his bike. But in here, it was as if he was invisible. He thought of snapping his fingers at one of the young gods and booming, 'Hey, waiter!'

As he raised his hand, a young man appeared at his elbow. 'Ready to order, sir?'

SI Santosh's eyes trawled the menu once again. 'It's all so expensive,' he said, unable to help himself.

'All our outlets have the same prices,' the waiter said, trying to hide his smile. 'If you prefer something cheaper, there's the India Coffee House in Church Street, it's just a few minutes from here…' he added quietly.

SI Santosh didn't like that. His eyes flicked over the young man, trying to read a veiled insult in those innocuous words. 'I know where Church Street is. No, that's fine, give me a hazelnut…' he said, sticking his finger at the item on the menu. How did one say 'frappe'?

'One hazelnut frappe coming up,' the waiter said.

Santosh grimaced, wondering what would appear before him.

'Would you like any extra topping? Raspberry? Or chocolate? Or whipped cream?'

'No, just what I ordered. And a glass of water.'

'Plain or mineral?'

One more choice. What was it about urban life that demanded you make a choice every minute, every day?

'Plain,' he said, and stared down at his fingertips.

'Hello sir,' a voice said from nearby. SI Santosh looked up. From an adjacent table, Samuel smiled at him.

As he watched, the photographer rose and came to his table. He drew a chair out and seated himself. SI Santosh wasn't too sure about the man's familiarity with him. He was a police officer after all.

'How is the case coming along?' the photographer asked.

SI Santosh wondered if he should tell him that both Gowda and he seemed to be walking into one cul-de-sac after another. That, in all probability, it would stay an unsolved case. There was no one out there baying for the blood of Liaquat's killer. But SI Santosh swallowed his frustration and said with as much gravity as he could muster, 'The investigation is under way. We should make a breakthrough very soon.'

The photographer smiled as the waiter brought a tall glass with an intricately convoluted plastic straw and a tall spoon.

SI Santosh stared at the straw. Did he drink his hazelnut frappe through the straw? Or did he strip the drink of the straw and use the spoon instead? Oh, why the hell hadn't he taken the waiter's advice and gone to India Coffee House?

The photographer reached forward to draw the straw out. 'May I?'

SI Santosh shrugged.

'My daughter loves these things. I pick them up whenever I can,' he said in explanation, wiping the straw clean with a tissue. Then, suddenly struck by a thought, he said, 'It's not very often you see a policeman in a place like this!'

'I am on duty,' SI Santosh spoke carefully, digging the spoon into what seemed like a glassful of ice. And for this, Rs 159.

'Yes, I know about it too,' the photographer murmured.

SI Santosh's eyes widened.

'They come here claiming to be students, but they're ruthless bastards. Each one of them,' Samuel said.

What on earth was the fool talking about? SI Santosh took a sip of his drink and crunched noisily on a cube of ice.

'But they won't come here. This is too conspicuous. I have heard about a couple of places closer to your station. I would go there,' the photographer added. Then, pulling a pad out of his pocket, he scribbled a few words and pushed it towards SI Santosh.

The policeman gaped at the words. Gamal. Nirvana.

'Cafés. One's on A Cross in HRBR Layout and the other's on Eighty Feet Road. A lot of them gather there,' Samuel said, rising to leave. Then he paused. 'That burn victim could have been involved for all you know. Have you thought on those lines?'

SI Santosh threw him a look that he had seen Gowda cast his way every few hours: don't teach granny to suck eggs, etc. 'Like I said, the investigation is still on,' he said, signifying end of discussion. Another trick he had picked up from Gowda.

At the traffic light, SI Santosh watched appalled as a eunuch wove her way through the traffic towards him. Tapping at a car window, clinging to the bar of an autorickshaw, blowing a kiss at a man on a bike, muttering to another, who was driving a little open van packed with trays of eggs. Two other eunuchs were swiftly working the traffic before the lights changed and their captive prey fled.

No, I won't allow them to terrorize me, no, I won't let them embarrass me; no, I won't open my wallet and give them a tenner just so they will go away, a voice screamed in SI Santosh's head. What was this city, he asked himself for the hundredth time, that spawned such ignominy in the sixty seconds it took a light to change? Young men wearing a tie and rubber chappals selling jigsaw puzzles, ear buds and boxes of tissues with a mindless line of sales chat. Small children with whiskers drawn on their faces, turning somersaults through an iron hoop...

In the little town where he had grown up, there had been life at the street corners. But nothing like this. There too were flower sellers and fruit vendors, beggars with maimed limbs and dead eyes, but this was something else. The desperation of a child turning cartwheels for money rather than for the sheer fun of it; the wretchedness of the salesmen whose ties flapped in the breeze with a certain hopelessness; the rage of the eunuchs who, without a single word spoken, demanded that the city pay for who and what they had become.

The truth was the city was beginning to scare him. The truth was his job was beginning to feel like it was beyond him. The truth was SI Santosh wanted to lay his head in his amma's lap and howl. In the wake of that desolation, as the lights changed, SI Santosh took a forbidden U-turn amidst the screeching of traffic and the angry voices of people manning them. Somewhere in this locality was Gamal. In there he would discover what Samuel had hinted at. And with that he hoped to find his faith again: the belief that had brought him this far that the world would allow itself to be righted. That all was not lost even in this cold, heartless city.

What SI Santosh did discover at Gamal was the sight of Gowda's Bullet in the parking lot. Did he know about the goings-on here? Santosh stood by Gowda's bike, uncertain.

Should he go in? Would Gowda be livid that he had walked into the middle of an investigation?

A small ball of rebellion turned in Santosh's heart. He should have been told if Gowda was doing some undercover work. And this was a bloody café. Anyone could go in. C'mon, SI Santosh, his inner voice, which in these few days had acquired the timbre and countenance of Gowda, murmured with a sneer, where are your balls? Do you have any goolies or do they fill your Y fronts only for show? C'mon, make a move.

SI Santosh adjusted his trousers. The bloody thing had rucked up between his bum again. Get some new trousers, the Gowda voice hissed, ones that fit.

He walked into Gamal through the glass doors that were kept permanently open. The deeply satisfying aroma of coffee and something sweet met him and drew him in. Santosh's eyes widened. In its shadowed interior, amidst several young couples, Indian and foreign, Gowda sat with a woman.

Gowda stirred the spoon round and round. He felt her eyes on him, taking stock. The coffee sloshed against the rim of the cup. Gowda took a sip. But it may have been hot water for all he could taste. Again the slow stirring, the need to do something as the silence and the years gone by stretched between them. She hadn't waited for him to text her as he had said he would. Instead, she had called him. He had agreed to meet her at a café that was only twenty minutes away from the station.

'Fantastic,' she had said. 'I need to go to a couple of places in your neighbourhood. So I can combine it with this.'

He had grunted in reply. It was only when the call was over that he realized he had been holding his breath.

He tried to read her expression. What did she see? A

middle-aged policeman of no particular significance. The college athlete gone to seed, the slackness of muscles and a burgeoning belly. He wasn't even a spectacular wreck. An ordinary man with little charm and even sparser conversation. It was this, the image of his very ordinariness in his own head that made him demand, 'Do you still wipe the leaves of your plants?'

Her eyes widened. Her lips twitched.

'What?' he growled. 'Did I say something funny?'

'I see you after, what is it, twenty-seven years, and this is what you want to know? Do I still wipe the leaves of my plants? I do, Borei, I do…' Urmila laughed.

'You haven't changed one bit, Borei.' Urmila shook her head in wry resignation.

'Would you have preferred it if I had changed? Become another person entirely?' Gowda asked quietly.

She looked at him carefully. 'Still so defensive, Borei … why would you think I want you changed? When Michael called me and said he had met you, do you know what I asked him?'

Gowda examined his fingernails. He knew she wanted him to ask 'what?' Something stilled his tongue. That damn cussedness of yours is going to slam every door in your face, his father had repeatedly warned him.

'I asked him if I would recognize you if I saw you now. I asked him if you had changed. Especially given your profession. But somewhere in me I wanted to believe that you would be the same. You would be the Borei I once knew. And fell in love with.'

Gowda felt his heart hammer in his chest. How easily she spoke the L-word. When had he used it last? He felt all of nineteen again. He raised his eyes to hers.

'I was so young then; so spineless and so wanting everyone's approval. Do you still hold it against me? The shoddy manner in which I treated you, the carelessness with which I broke up with you ... it has haunted me every day. Through my marriage and later, when my husband and I ... I thought my sins were catching up with me.'

'Enough,' Gowda said. 'I survived. I am all right. You don't have to put yourself through any of this guilt thinking you ruined my life. You didn't.'

I did it on my own: Gowda suppressed that last thought.

'Are you happy with how your life has turned out?' she asked.

He shrugged. 'I have no complaints.'

'No regrets either?'

Gowda took a deep breath. 'What is it you want to know, Urmila?'

He saw her lip tremble. Her fingers tore at the napkin.

'If you are asking whether I missed you these last many years, I didn't.'

'Borei, I...'

'No,' he said softly. 'Let me finish. Suddenly, out of nothing, a pang would seize me. It would clutch at me with iron fingers and I would wonder where you were, how you were, and if our lives would have been different if we were together.'

She continued to tear the napkin to shreds.

'Are you disappointed?' he asked.

She shook her head. 'A little. I had imagined you nursing this eternal flame of longing for me. But I am relieved too. That your life didn't pause because of me.'

Gowda smiled. A mirthless smile that didn't even hint at

how often the iron fist squeezed his being. Seeing her had only exacerbated that pang of: If only…

'Your family?' she asked.

'My wife is a doctor. She's in Hassan. I have a son, Roshan. He is a medical student. And you? Do you have any children?'

'No.' She shook her head. 'We didn't. My husband didn't want any. He was very insistent.'

Gowda saw the lines of defeat that striated her face. He ached to reach forward and smoothen them away.

'I'm glad I picked up the phone and called you this morning,' she said candidly. 'Would you have?'

Gowda spread his hands out. 'I'm glad you did too. I wouldn't have. I would have been too afraid to. We are not who we once were. What if you were standoffish … what if you were dismissive?' His eyes bored into hers.

She reached out and took his hand in hers. 'Dismissive? I have thought of you every single day after we…'

Suddenly Gowda, SI Santosh saw, pulled his giant paw out of the woman's clasp and ran out of the room with a speed that belied his size, leaving SI Santosh surprised and Urmila aghast.

His heart, it seemed, had lodged in his mouth, threatening to fall out with every step he took. His breath heaved, pumping his chest out farther and farther. In his head a swarm of bees buzzed, banging against the wall of his eyes, clouding his vision, seeking to escape his ears in a whoosh of heat. But Gowda continued to run, trying to gauge which way his son and the African man had fled.

He hadn't known where to look when Urmila took his

hand in hers. Perhaps that was why his gaze had flitted around the café nervously; was anyone watching them? Two middle-aged fools holding hands in broad daylight while somewhere in the background Dire Straits sang '*So far away*'.

Perhaps it was an occupational hazard. The police eye. A cold clinical eye turning everything in its path and around it for a hint of suspicious behaviour. An eye of doubt forever.

Perhaps it was just the male gaze. The congenital habit of the male species. Darting this way and that, checking out two in the bush despite having one in hand.

Or perhaps it was that thing called happenstance.

That his eyes should land on what seemed a familiar profile. Roshan. At first, he felt a surge of panic. Had Roshan seen him with Urmila? Then he saw that his son was engrossed in whatever he was doing with the African man. His son appeared to be pleading, while the other man looked unmoved despite the desperation, the fervour, the abject need. The man licked his lips, leaned back and crossed his arms, distancing himself, and as he did so, his eyes locked with Gowda's. A flicker. A recognition. Criminals and policemen have that. An innate ability to spot each other in a crowd.

He stood up hastily. After a moment's hesitation, he grabbed Roshan's arm and almost dragged him away. And the silly fool, Roshan, went without even protesting. And as Urmila continued to speak about god knows what, Gowda had pulled his hand from hers. There was no time for polite niceties and excuse-mes. He went after them. Only to see them breaking into a sprint the moment they were out of the glass doors.

Gowda followed them to the end of the street. But they

had had a head start; they were young and racing to get away. They disappeared into a by-lane, leaving Gowda breathless and furious at his own lack of form. And an overwhelming sense of dread: what was Roshan up to?

Gowda stood bent over in the middle of the road, clutching his knees and sucking in large mouthfuls of air. As the blood slowly retreated to his veins and arteries instead of threatening to erupt from the top of his head in a spray, he realized that Santosh was at his side, asking, 'Sir, sir, what happened? Are you all right? Why were you chasing the boys?'

Gowda straightened slowly. 'What are you doing here?'

Had the fool seen him with Urmila? Had he recognized Roshan? Panic buttons beeped at the back of Gowda's still buzzing head. Then from somewhere he dredged up the voice of authority and barked, 'I'll tell you in a bit. Wait here.'

But Urmila had already left and paid for her coffee so he would know that she was furious. Gowda sighed. Nothing had changed, it seemed. This had been customary behaviour back when they were together too. He paid for his coffee, ignoring the curious glances, and went out to where Santosh waited, eager and expectant.

He should call Urmila, he knew. He should explain. And then what? They would have to go back to whatever it was she had been trying to tell him. It had felt good to see her again, hear her, feel the warmth and softness of her skin against his. A part of him yearned to revive all that they had had. Another part, the greater part, balked at the very thought. He had slept around, yes, he had done that. There had been a college lecturer for a while and a hotel receptionist. Affairs that had involved sex and some chit-chat but nothing of consequence had ever been shared. It had meant little more than an appeasement of a physical need. And he never had to deal with either guilt or remorse. But this? Urmila would never be a random fuck. She would need more. Did he have it in him to give her what she expected? And even as Gowda was wondering what to do about Urmila, his phone burst into '*Kabhi kabhi*'. Damn. The first thing he would do was change the bloody ringtone that had landed him here.

'Yes,' he said into the phone. An alertness, a pulling in of gut, a reining of emotion … the furious rhythm of a ticking mind.

As Santosh watched, he saw the muddled, flustered-looking Gowda of a moment ago metamorphose into something else. Gowda snapped the phone shut and looked at Santosh. 'There's been yet another murder. A young man. They fished him out of Yellamma Lake. His throat has been slit too.'

It was almost midnight when Gowda reached home.

Santosh and he had driven to the mortuary first. 'Tomorrow, we'll go to Yellamma Lake. I haven't been there in years. I just need to see the place again,' Gowda explained to Santosh who, he could see, was itching to go to the crime scene. 'But first I need to see the body. I need to make sure the MO is the same as the previous ones. One quick look and then I need to get back. I have something to attend to,' Gowda said, eyes narrowing.

In the end, the evening had dwindled to nothing as various tiers of procedure were dealt with. Apparently, the boy was a Haryana joint secretary's son and the father had received a call two nights ago that his son was dead. The father had dismissed it as a prank call. He had spoken to his son only that evening. But when his son hadn't called for two days, the man began to worry. A missing person's case was registered. The boy had been identified by the driving licence in his wallet.

Suddenly, the bureaucracy of two states had swung into action. Gowda watched helplessly, unable to hurry things up.

Roshan was pretending to be asleep. But Gowda, tired, hungry and furious, wasn't going to let that stop him. Nor the thought that the peace he had negotiated last night with an apology had lasted a mere twenty-fours. He opened the door and clicked the light on. The boy's eyes were shut tight. Too tight.

'I know you are awake,' Gowda said, walking to the side of the bed. 'Get up.'

Roshan sat up, blinking furiously.

'Who was he? And what were you doing with him?'

'What are you talking about?' the boy demanded, matching his father's belligerence with wounded indignation.

'Stop pretending, Roshan. I saw you. I saw you at Gamal with an African man.'

'Osagie,' Roshan mumbled.

'What?'

'That's his name. It means God Sent in Nigerian.'

Gowda picked up Roshan's wallet from the bedside table and opened it. 'What are you doing, Appa?' Roshan asked.

'Looking for drugs ... what do you think?' Gowda ground out between clenched teeth.

'In which case, why don't you frisk me as well,' Roshan said, standing up with his arms aloft.

Gowda stared at him. Roshan met his gaze evenly. The boy was as tall as he was, if not taller.

Gowda threw the wallet down on the bed with a sigh. 'So, what were you doing with God Sent?'

'Nothing, Appa. He is a friend's friend and we were talking ... you know, things,' the boy said defensively.

'In which case, why did he run when he saw me?'

The boy bit his lip. 'There's some trouble with his visa. There was no time to reason with him. He just grabbed my arm and I ran with him, not knowing why. Later, I did tell him that I would have introduced him to you. But he is scared, Appa. They put all of their savings ... everything ... to come here and study and to be deported means the end.' Roshan's voice faded out.

Gowda sat heavily on the bed. 'You are either a practised liar or an incredibly naive idiot. I am going to give you the benefit of doubt and accept what you say. The café's been under surveillance as a place where drugs are bought and sold. You don't want to get involved in that. If you are sensible, you will understand that it is your life you are toying with.'

Gowda rose and walked to the door.

'Appa,' the boy asked carefully, 'who was that woman with you?'

Gowda halted. Trading time. You don't tell Amma about this and I won't tell her about what I saw. That settled it. The boy was up to something.

'Urmila. We were in college together. She's visiting Bangalore,' Gowda said quietly.

TUESDAY, 9 AUGUST

ACP Vidyaprasad frowned. SI Santosh looked at his watch haplessly. The other officers shifted in their seats, each creak voicing their impatience. 'Where is Gowda?' the ACP growled. 'Didn't you come in together?' He turned his ire on Santosh.

'No, sir, he said he would come on his own,' Santosh mumbled. Where had Gowda gone? 'He'll be here any moment, sir,' he added. A placatory afterthought of sorts.

Voices outside. Santosh relaxed. The deep voice was unmistakably Gowda's. The door opened. Santosh stared in surprise. Gowda had the DCP with him. Deputy Commissioner of Police Sainuddin Mirza. The only man in our entire police force who has any brains and ethics to match, Gowda had explained to Santosh.

The ACP's mouth tightened. This was a meeting he had called. What was the DCP (Crime) doing here? And he hadn't known that Gowda and the DCP were chaddi yaar! The ACP stood up, as did the other officers, saluting briskly.

The DCP nodded. 'So officers, we seem to have a peculiar situation on our hands.'

'That's why I thought we had to call the CCB in,' the ACP began. 'With their experience...'

The DCP nodded at the two men seated at the farther corner of the briefing room.

'So, Stanley,' the DCP asked, 'do you think we have a serial murderer on our hands? Gowda seems to think so...'

ACP Stanley Sagayaraj cleared his throat. 'That's my preliminary thought too, sir. But until...'

ACP Vidyaprasad butted in before ACP Stanley Sagayaraj could finish his thought, 'That's exactly my point. Three murders in three parts of the city. One a middle-aged, middle-class man. Another a lowlife from Shivaji Nagar. And the last one, a BPO employee from Haryana. Nothing to suggest a pattern. In fact, the second homicide died of burns. We are clutching at straws.'

'That's how most investigations begin. With a whiff of suspicion and a mere straw to clutch at,' Gowda murmured, tapping a pencil on the table impatiently.

ACP Stanley Sagayaraj's mouth twitched. Santosh stared at his hands. He felt a hollow in the pit of his stomach. Why did Gowda do this to himself?

The DCP glared at him. Sometimes, he thought, Gowda's mouth had to be taped. There was no knowing what he would say. He was a liability to the department ... the pity was that the fool didn't realize his own potential. DCP Mirza had never seen an officer with a finer instinct or acumen when it came to investigation.

'Sir, with due respect, this is India. We don't have serial murderers here. Gowda is being fanciful,' the ACP said, pretending to ignore Gowda's laconic aside.

Gowda looked up. 'Are you saying that serial murderers like Auto Shankar, Surender Koli, Umesh Reddy were the figments of someone's sick imagination?'

ACP Vidyaprasad sniffed. 'Oh, them! Anyway, even if there is a serial murderer at work here, I think the CCB is in a better position to investigate it than we are.' He threw a glance at Gowda's face as he pronounced his verdict. He waited to see disappointment shadow it. But all Gowda did was stifle a yawn behind his palm. A vein throbbed in ACP Vidyaprasad's temple. He thought he was going to pop an artery. 'Gowda's station is not equipped to handle criminal investigation of this sort,' he added.

Not even the DCP could deny that.

Gowda was a thorn in the side. A pain in the ass. Not just to ACP Vidyaprasad, but an entire group of officers, all of whom had collectively worked to place Gowda in his rat hole of a station.

The DCP laced his palms and said nothing for a moment. 'That's true. But I think it would be short-sighted of us to not include Gowda in the investigation. We're all here because of a connection he has made about what could have been perceived as three random murders. Here is what I suggest. Stanley and his team can start independent investigations. And Gowda will also work on the case. Our need here is to catch the criminal. Whether it is a series of random murders or whether we have a serial murderer is besides the point ... I hope you understand that, ACP Vidyaprasad.'

The man flushed.

'Perhaps Inspector Gowda can share his thoughts with us,' Stanley said quietly.

'Good,' the DCP said, standing up. 'Keep me informed. I want to know every single development.'

The DCP watched Gowda and Santosh walk out with the CCB team. The ACP sidled up to him.

'Sir, I really don't see the need to bring Gowda in,' he began.

'I didn't bring him in. He was the IO on two of the three cases. Giving it to the CCB entirely would demoralize him. The officers need to be encouraged, not discouraged.'

'All that's fine, sir.' The ACP's mouth twisted into a line. 'But Gowda on his own...'

'Why? Where are you going?'

'I am on leave for ten days starting next Thursday, sir.'

'Well, cancel it then. Whatever it is can wait,' the DCP said, collecting his cell phone from the table.

The ACP sighed. 'Yes, sir,' he said. The DCP was a pompous prick and the ACP had no intention of antagonizing him. But if the DCP thought he was going to cancel his foreign holiday ... He would get a medical certificate stating he had the bird flu, kill his mother-in-law off, plead a family emergency, whatever.

The ACP pulled out his pad and looked at his list. He still had to buy a few things for his holiday. One of the real estate developers had put the holiday together for him and his wife. Five days in Bangkok, three in Singapore. 'Everything's taken care of, sir. Air tickets, airport transfer, hotel,' the real estate developer had said, handing over an envelope. '... and this is to buy some chocolates,' he had added. And then with a coy smile, 'My man will take you to some interesting places when your wife is resting.'

The ACP patted his list. He was determined to have his 'happy ending' no matter what the DCP said.

'So tell me,' Stanley said, leaning back and crossing his arms.

Santosh held his breath. Would Gowda explode? He didn't take very kindly to being patronized and the CCB man was talking to Gowda as if he were a fractious child who had to be placated.

Gowda glared at him. Then his mouth twitched. 'I like that "perhaps Inspector Gowda can share his thoughts with us". Where did you learn to speak like that?'

A burst of laughter. 'I could see that our ACP sir can't stand your guts. I wanted to fuel the fire some more...'

Santosh's gaze darted between the two men. So they knew each other and presumably were friends. That made the next step simpler. Santosh heaved a sigh of relief. He was beginning to feel like Gowda's elderly spinster aunt to whom Gowda's well-being had been entrusted. Constantly fretting about him and worrying about what he would do next.

'ACP Stanley Sagayaraj was my senior at college. And my basketball captain for two years,' Gowda murmured to Santosh as he walked to the table.

Santosh studied Stanley Sagayaraj. He wasn't as tall as Gowda but he had looked after himself better. His jet-black skin had a sheen to it, and he had the body of someone who worked out regularly.

Gowda sat across from the CCB man and pulled out his notes. 'SI Santosh,' he said, 'did a thorough search of both the CCRB and the SCRB for some indication of who else may have used the MO, but came up with nothing.'

Santosh thought of the hours spent peering at the City Crime Record Bureau and the State Crime Record Bureau. It had been frustrating, but that was the first time Gowda had brought him into the investigation procedure. And so he had sat at the computer, sorting through countless files for some clue as to whether the modus operandi had a precedent. A blow on the head to stun the victim, then the ligature encrusted with glass to sever as it strangled. Santosh had tried every permutation and combination possible. A single MO, two separate MOs, but the records failed to throw up any leads.

Stanley nodded. 'So, this is a new boy on the prowl.'

Gowda shook his head. 'There is something else…'

Santosh stared. What did Gowda mean?

'Among the possessions that were found on Liaquat, there was a pearl earring.'

Stanley leaned forward. 'And...'

'All three victims this far, Kothandaraman the pharmacist, Liaquat, and Roopesh who was fished out of the lake, were all killed in the same way. They were all healthy males who could have put up a fight, but none of them did. There was clear evidence that Kothandaraman had had sexual intercourse. Traces of semen were found. It was impossible to determine if Roopesh had sex. You can imagine the state the body after almost three days in water. But something tells me that he too had sexual intercourse. Liaquat was not an intended victim. He probably walked in on something he was not meant to see and was rid of for that reason. What if the killer was not alone? What if he worked with an associate? A woman?'

WEDNESDAY, 10 AUGUST

Gowda let the ice clink. Whisky sloshed against the sides of the tumbler. He peered at his drink, the golden brown veering to cinnamon at the heart. Or was it a trick of the light?

Music played, and here and there in the room were clusters of fat candles. Everyone seemed to know everyone.

A couple sat on a sofa, deep in conversation about their children at foreign universities. Another group stood near French windows opened to let the night breeze in, and discussed microbreweries and Cat Stevens. And yet another group sat on the cane furniture in the veranda and discussed the wine club dinner they had all attended a week ago. Laughter, muted conversation, expensive fragrances, the swish of silk and linen, the sparkle of diamonds. What was he doing here? And with a woman like Urmila?

He had thought Urmila would never speak to him again, but she had called earlier in the day and spoken to him as if they had parted under perfectly normal circumstances the last time. 'I am having a small dinner party this evening ... just a few friends ... in fact, I decided just this morning. I have asked Michael to come as well. Will you join us, Borei?' she said.

He had thought it churlish to make an excuse. Especially when she was being so gracious.

'Borei, are you all right?' Urmila stood at his side.

He smiled foolishly, shrugged and mumbled, 'I was just enjoying the colour of the whisky.'

She smiled back. 'Perfect! One should look first. Then smell it. Try and assimilate the hues of a single drop before you let your mouth savour it. That's how your taste buds will learn to match colour with aroma with taste to distinguish one whisky from the other. I do wish you hadn't added ice to your single malt. It's sacrilege...'

Gowda stared at her. What the fuck did she mean, an irate voice in his head demanded. A whisky was a whisky and if she wanted to know the truth, he preferred rum any day. Suddenly, he felt a great yearning to be with someone like Mamtha. She didn't know the difference between a mural and a frieze, and wouldn't know a single malt if it bit her on the nose, but she was everything Gowda knew. Every mutinous, grumpy square inch of her was familiar territory.

But another, less belligerent but more stern voice spoke up: You are doing it again, Borei ... you are screwing up. All these years, twenty-seven fucking years, you kept her in a secret place in your heart and carried it with you everywhere you went, to the police training college and into the station precincts; to your bedroom and into your conjugal bed; into those secret silent moments you grabbed for yourself; into noisy processions on the road and gruesome murder scenes ... She was your oasis of calm through every waking moment and now you want to screw it up again with your boorish policeman behaviour, your prickly defensiveness. Borei, Borei, what are you thinking of?

Urmila touched his elbow. 'What are you thinking of?'

Gowda started. 'Nothing,' he said. 'Urmila, about the other evening, I have to explain...'

She turned her head. 'I shouldn't have. I embarrassed you...'

'No, Urmila, you didn't. It was...' Gowda groped for words. 'I had always hoped that one day you and I...'

'Borei, don't...'

'No, you have to hear me out. At the café, I saw my son.'

He saw her eyes widen. He hastened to explain. 'What worried me was that he was with a foreigner. An African. That café's been under surveillance. It's one of the places foreigners and students frequent. A perfect place for drug dealing. So when the African man spotted me, he fled, taking Roshan with him. And I had to chase after them. You understand now, don't you, Urmila. It wasn't you...'

A smile tugged at the corner of her lips. Gowda wanted to lean forward and kiss the smile. Touch the bloom in her skin and press his weary eyes against her still unlined cheek. She had aged well. For a woman who was nearly fifty, she could pass for someone in her early forties. Gowda thought of his wife. Mamtha was younger, but she had elderly stamped all over her: the stringy grey hair scraped back into a little bun at the nape of her neck, her starched cotton saris and her old-woman leather bag; her line of a mouth and the faded laughter in her eyes.

Gowda sighed. Mamtha made him feel tired. Urmila, she made him feel young again. She made him feel that he could still do things; that somehow life hadn't passed him by.

'Did you speak to your son?'

Gowda nodded.

'And?' Urmila persisted.

'Some rubbish about the man with him called Osagie which means God Sent in Nigerian having overstayed his visa, etc. And so being a fugitive in the eyes of Indian law,' Gowda said slowly.

'But you don't believe him,' Urmila probed carefully.

Gowda took a swallow of his whisky. He shook his head. 'No, I don't.'

Gowda remembered the shock of discovering a weed pouch rolled up carefully in a T-shirt. In it was a little stash of marijuana and another of hash. Linked to the shock was relief. At least he wasn't into the hard stuff. Yet.

'And…'

'And I dare not confront him. Confrontation leads to either–or situations. And you can't do that with the people you love.'

'Is that why, Borei, all those years ago, you…' Urmila began and then suddenly there was someone else standing by their side.

'Quit kitchi-cooing to each other,' Michael burst in.

'Do you realize that you have only talked to each other all evening?'

Gowda and Urmila looked at each other. What had she been about to say? He would never know now.

'So, how is Lady Deviah liking Bangalore now?' Michael asked, a teasing lilt entering his tone.

'Lady?' Gowda's eyebrows rose.

Urmila flushed. 'My husband was knighted some years ago. Since we are not legally divorced, I am still Lady Deviah.'

'I didn't know,' Gowda said quietly. His heart sat in the pit of his belly. Lady Deviah.

Urmila gazed at him. A silent yearning crept into her eyes; her fingers fumbled as she played with her rings. There is so much you don't know. But would you even want to listen if I were to tell you?

Michael looked at the play of emotions on their faces. He cleared his throat noisily. Had he made a mistake by bringing these two together again? Uff men, such a meddling bugger you are, Becky used to say. All the time doing one damn thing you shouldn't and look no, where it has led to!

Michael felt overwhelmed by the weight of emotion. His and theirs. For a past that seemed to have been spent with no means of making amends now.

'I have to go,' Gowda said suddenly. 'It's a weekday…'

'But you just got here.' Urmila touched his sleeve. I can only presume so much, the gesture said. I cannot ask more even if I want to. For you are a married man. And I am Lady Deviah.

'Another ten minutes, that's all I ask,' she said.

Gowda nodded and was rewarded by a smile that snarled his gut. What am I doing? he asked himself. My career is going nowhere, my wife is a stranger, my son is probably a drug addict, and here I am falling in love again. Do I really need this in my life now?

'No, you don't,' Michael said.

'What?' Gowda growled.

'I said you don't have to rush. You can stay another ten minutes.'

THURSDAY, 11 AUGUST

Gowda stared at the screen of his mobile. He had just selected 'Create message', and the blankness of the space was a taunt.

He put the phone on the table and leaned forward, clenching the edge of the table. The phone beeped. He picked it up and saw one new message. Urmila. She had written: *Thank you for attending my do last night. Do you think that one day it may be possible for us to finish a conversation?* ☺

Gowda's heart raced. A smile hung at the corner of his lips. He felt like he was nineteen years old. His fingers felt all thumbs as he pressed 'Reply'. Roshan had said that was the way to text. With thumbs, and not as he did, meticulously and methodically pressing the keys with his index finger. *Yes*, he texted. *You choose the day, time and place and I promise not to run away this time.*

He imagined the message flying through the air and across the city into her lap. He imagined the expression in her eyes. Something in him quickened.

His phone lit up. '*This evening at my house. 8 p.m.* ☺'

'*Will be there*,' he texted back.

'*Can't wait*,' she wrote.

'*Likewise*,' he texted and felt a foolish grin settle on his face. Fuck! What had he gone and done?

Santosh walked in and almost convulsed in shock at the sight of the taciturn Gowda staring at his phone with a soppy smile. Must be one of those vulgar jokes. He couldn't think of anything else that would induce laughter in Gowda.

'Good morning, sir.' Santosh saluted.

Gowda raised his eyes and in that split second Santosh saw Gowda settle into his habitual demeanour of 'what now?'.

'The photographer is here, sir.'

Gowda frowned. 'Which photographer is this?'

'Samuel, sir. The witness in the Liaquat case.'

'What does he want? Can't you deal with it?'

'No, sir, he wants to see you. There are two others with him. Ladies, sir.'

Gowda nodded. 'Send them in,' he said and opened a file. He heard them troop in but kept his eyes resolutely on the pages in the file. Suddenly, it struck him that he was doing exactly what the ACP did to him when he was summoned to his room. Pretend to be engrossed in a file. Subtext 1: Look, I don't have the time for whatever it is you have come for. Subtext 2: Duty comes first. Only then, you and your problems.

Gowda slapped shut the file and gestured for them to sit. Again, he saw the ACP possess him. Why couldn't he smile and be pleasant? Say, do sit down, make yourselves comfortable, whatever. Instead, it had to be that lordly wave of sweeping condescension: You may sit, but that doesn't mean a thing.

Gowda willed his face into a smile. 'Yes, how can I help you?'

'Sir, this is Prabha,' the photographer said, gesturing to the grey-haired woman on his left. She had the face of someone who had survived much and wore her battle scars as a pennant that proclaimed: don't mess with me.

'And this is Ananya.' Samuel smiled, indicating the young woman.

Pretty, but she was too tall and her face too angular for Gowda's taste. And there was something else about her that Gowda couldn't put his finger upon. He had seen Santosh's eyes linger on her as he had ushered them in.

'Thank you for seeing us,' Samuel said.

Gowda reached beneath the table and pressed a buzzer. A constable came in. 'Some coffee? Or juice?'

The photographer smiled. 'Thank you, sir, but we just had breakfast.'

'No, no, you must have something.' He turned to the constable. 'Juice. And some of that cake.'

Gowda leaned back in his chair. He really should get rid of the towel he draped the back of his chair with.

'Sir, we are having a photography exhibition at Ananda, the artists' retreat near Gubbi. The proceeds of any sale we make will go to fund our NGO that was set up to help transgenders.'

Gowda chewed his lip. 'Do they need help?' He moved a paperweight this way and that. 'Have you seen the menace they are at traffic lights? We receive so many complaints!'

The photographer looked at Ananya.

'Ours isn't an easy life, sir,' Ananya said.

The paperweight fell to the floor with a crash. Gowda stared at the girl; no she wasn't a girl, but she wasn't a boy either. But you wouldn't know. Who would have thought that she was a eunuch?

'You...' Gowda began hesitantly.

'Yes, I am a transgender. I was fortunate that an indulgent grandmother brought me up, educated me and let me be. I was teased, but mostly it wasn't unbearable. But so many of us know only ridicule. And then, because there is no other option, we become sex workers; eventually we die of disease or degradation. We don't have the solace of clutching to a dream called the happily-ever-after that even the poorest of Indians may dream about. Governments can change, wars will be fought, our GDP may grow, our scientists can conquer space, our lives alone remain untouched. Nobody wants us. Nobody even considers us. Like our sexuality, we are there and not there.' Ananya's earnestness caught at Gowda's throat, even though he knew that it was the practiced speech of someone who had said this many times before.

'So, sir,' Samuel piped up, 'we would be very grateful if you could inaugurate the exhibition.'

Gowda flushed. 'Why me? I am just an inspector. You should call an artist, or a social worker, or some celebrity.'

'What we want is acceptance. Not to be showcased for a week. Someone like you would bring that first stamp of acceptance. Your coming to the show and inaugurating it will send a message to the common man. We are not dangerous. We are human too,' Ananya spoke up before Samuel butted in.

Gowda nodded. She, er ... Ananya had a point. On a whim, he said, 'I'd like to bring along a friend, Lady Deviah.'

Ananya smiled. 'Actually it was Urmila who suggested that we invite you.'

Gowda wondered if his mouth had fallen open again. 'You know her…' he offered weakly.

'She is one of the trustees,' Samuel said.

'In which case…' Gowda smiled. 'I'll be happy to. When is the inauguration?'

'Tomorrow at six thirty p.m. Shall we send a car to pick you up?'

'No, no, I'll drive myself,' Gowda said.

When they left, Santosh bustled in. 'What did they want?'

'They came to invite me for a photo exhibition. It's tomorrow at six thirty p.m. You should come too,' Gowda said carefully.

The young man's eyes lit up. 'Certainly, sir. I have always been interested in photography,' he gushed.

Gowda felt his mouth curl. The fool had fallen for Ananya. What would he do when he discovered who she really was?

Gowda rubbed his eyes and looked at his watch. It was almost half past six.

Roshan walked out of his room and stopped in his tracks, surprised to see his father. 'What are you doing here?' he asked, nonplussed.

'I do happen to live here…' Gowda raised his eyes to his son.

'You are never home this early,' the boy mumbled.

Gowda sighed. There, he was doing it again. In a gentler voice, he explained, 'I know, but I had some work to do and the station was bustling with petty cases and the incessant ringing of the station phone and mobiles.'

Roshan nodded.

Then he peered at his father slyly. 'Are you going out this evening?'

Gowda stared. 'Why?'

'I have to go out ... I am meeting some of my school friends and I didn't want you to think I would be at home.'

Gowda tried not to show the relief flare in his eyes. 'No, that's fine. I have some things to do as well.'

'Will you be late?'

'Will you, Roshan?'Gowda answered with a question.

'By eleven...' Roshan shrugged.

'I should be home by then too. Don't latch the main door. You have your key, don't you?' Gowda said, placing the files back on the table and rising.

He had come home early with the post-mortem reports of all three deaths. Stanley had ensured that a copy of Roopesh's post-mortem had reached the station by lunchtime. Gowda had needed to be on his own to find what he knew would be that one vital link that would take this case forward.

Only Kothandaraman's body had been available for them to draw clear conclusions of a violent strangulation. In Liaquat's case, the strangler hadn't completed the job and so Liaquat had survived only to die of burns rather than strangulation. And Roopesh's body had already entered a state of decomposition when it had been found. Was he, as the ACP said, clutching at straws?

But what of that one fact staring him in the face – the glass encrusted ligature? The MO linked the murders. What else? Think, think, Gowda. The words swam in front of his eyes.

Had anyone thought of doing a DNA match? He groaned. That should have been the first thing to do. No doubt Stanley would get there eventually. But why wait until then?

He drew his phone out and called Stanley.

'What are you thinking about?' Urmila asked as he sipped his drink wordlessly.

'Oh, what?' Gowda said, startled out of his reverie. He looked at her as though he didn't recognize her.

'Have you talked to Roshan?' she asked.

He shrugged. 'No.'

'You must, Borei. You have to deal with it. It won't go away because you don't talk about it.'

How could he tell her about the slap? The very thought of it filled him with a deep sense of shame. Gowda clinked the ice in his glass. Pale cubes of melting ice.

'Shall I fix you another and will you then tell me what's wrong?' Urmila leaned forward and took the glass from his hand.

He watched her go towards the bar counter in a corner of her living room and unscrew a bottle. 'The same, right?' she called out.

He rose and walked towards her. 'I'm sorry I am not a great companion this evening … the case has me all twisted up inside.'

She poured herself a small whisky and took both glasses to the veranda. 'Let's sit here,' she said. 'It's a beautiful night.'

Something within Gowda froze. What next? She would put on ghazals now, he thought. As he stood there, she glided past him, suffusing him in a wave of expensive perfume. Melon and mandarin oranges, jasmine, lily of the valley, sandalwood and incense. All of it in one scent that rode up his nostrils and left him feeling that he had walked into a dream.

The music preceded her. She put off the stronger overhead lamps, leaving only the table lamps on. 'This is better. Less like an interrogation room!' She cocked her head and stood there, looking at him. Then she reached out and took his hand in hers. 'Borei, you still are such a pussycat.' She laughed and led him into the veranda.

She dropped into a cane chair without letting go of his hand and so he had no option but to lower himself into a cane pouffe placed at her side.

'You haven't asked me about my husband,' she said quietly.

Gowda's mouth went dry. He had studiously avoided the subject.

'He...' Gowda began, not knowing what he should say next. 'I ... I didn't want to embarrass you,' he said finally.

'He turned our marriage into an embarrassment with his serial philandering. But when he took up with a woman in the neighbourhood, I felt ... I couldn't bear to see the pity in the eyes of our friends.' Her smile was bitter.

Gowda took a sip of his drink. In the silence, the whisky slipping down his throat made a distinct sound.

'Will you go back?' he wanted to ask. 'Do you want to go back?' In a day they had assembled the basis of a relationship. Text messages and calls that punctuated the day. Random meetings which were not allowed to have even the slightest whiff of an assignation. But through it all, there had been an undercurrent of 'this has to go somewhere'.

And it seemed that the moment had come.

'Borei,' she said, her voice dropping, 'do you ever think of what our lives would have been like if we hadn't broken up?'

He looked at her, wondering if he should be honest or say what she wanted to hear. All his life, the dilemma had burdened him. His inability to speak the right words instead of the biting truth. But it seemed that Urmila wanted no answers from him tonight. She was content to merely speak her thoughts.

'Sometimes I think it's best that we went our ways when we did. We are two different people now and the people we have become – mature, calmer – will allow us to enjoy each other better.' Her voice acquired a dreaminess that strangled his every thought.

'I...' he began. Whatever it was she was suggesting, how could it be? He was married; he had a son; he had his responsibilities. Unlike her, he was not a free being.

'Ssh ... Borei.' She put a finger on his lips. 'Hear me out, please. I don't want to take anything from your life. I don't want Borei the husband or father.'

She took her finger away and said, 'I don't want what you have given Mamtha or Roshan. I want us to live in a parallel universe. You and I, no strings attached. No fangs, no claws, no blood, no tears, no hurt. But I want a long-term relationship. One that's all about laughter, stars, dreams, life ... You there for me, and I there for you. But without hurting anyone else in the picture. I think we can, my Borei, I think we can.'

Gowda felt his breath snag in his throat. For once you can have your cake and eat it too, a little voice whispered. A voice that resembled the ACP's in that it bore the timbre of corruption. But then young Santosh's incredulous tone overrode it with a 'Sir, but it still is adultery...'

Gowda squirmed. His eyes that never ceased searching any room he sat in, fell on a coffee-table book on the table. A big glossy book, and on its cover was the painting of a woman juggler. But what caught his eye was the earring she wore.

Urmila whispered, 'Am I asking too much of you?'

Gowda stood up. 'No, you are not. But you need to give me some time to allow this to grow...' He paused, and then unable to help himself, he asked, 'May I borrow this book? I promise to return it in a day or two.'

She looked at him wordlessly as if she couldn't believe her ears.

'We are meeting tomorrow, aren't we?' he asked, stricken by the expression on her face.

'Do you really want to? I am not so sure.'

'You know I do.'

She looked away.

He saw her trying to feign a nonchalance she didn't feel. She didn't see the complexity of the situation. All she knew was she had been rejected again.

He reached for her, unable to help himself. 'I can't bear to leave you looking like this.'

FRIDAY, 12 AUGUST

Chikka smoothed the page down with the tip of his index finger. Again and again, as if the glossy photo plate in the book had been irrevocably crumpled.

The page was smooth, the man noticed. It was as if he were stroking a small animal. A cat or a squirrel, perhaps. The absent-minded, mechanical stroking with the tip of the middle finger got on his nerves. The man cleared his throat.

'How much longer will he take?' he said, not bothering to hide his irritation at having been kept waiting for almost forty-five minutes.

The stroking stopped. Chikka's eyes settled on the

man's face briefly. He looked away. 'I said he cannot be interrupted.'

'Well, you'd better interrupt him as I really can't wait any longer. I work for the government, not your brother,' the man snapped, rising from the chair in his rage.

'My brother is the government.' Chikka's voice rasped.

The man flinched. He walked to the window. These bloody bastards. They knew they had him by his balls. They knew that he needed them more than they needed him. A son whose admission at DGS Engineering College had to be paid for. A daughter who had found a place at the IIM but whose fees had to be paid. A house that needed renovation. The slum clearance board official had needs that weren't commensurate with his salary. In a moment of frustration, he had acquiesced. A few signatures here, a few papers that went missing. A file that rose to the top of the pile.

'You are not doing anything wrong,' the corporator had reassured him. 'All you are doing is looking away, moving the place of a file, organizing a few signatures, throwing some paper into the waste basket … tell me, don't you do this anyway, every day?'

Ramachandra, who in his twenty-six years of government service had restricted his criminal doings to petty pilfering – taking home some pencils and erasers – saw the expectant faces of his children and wife. They depended on him, but what had he ever done for them beyond the usual? Here was his chance to make things better for them. Here was his chance to be truly Ramachandra – the benefactor.

'No one will know,' the corporator had added. 'If there is an enquiry, what will they discover? Nothing. Negligence at the most. And what will they do to you then? A suspension at the most. And I am there to make that go away.'

Ramachandra complied. He did everything as he had always done; only, now he was rewarded for it.

The next time, it needed a little more effort, but he was given a bigger reward. Ramachandra's family looked at him with greater respect. But corruption is like the worm in a mango, he soon discovered. It waits there unseen but boring with its rabid jaws the flesh of your soul, the juices of your life. A rot that taints the very breath from within. Ramachandra saw how his colleagues eyed him; the diminishing of the deference in the corporator's gaze. The worm gnawed and gnawed…

He turned to Chikka. 'I managed before the two of you entered my lives. I will again if I have to. So go and ask your brother to stop whatever it is he is doing and see me.'

Chikka put the book down. He rose and went out.

It was a big room. Long, rather than broad. And the doors to it stretched the breadth of the room. Teakwood frames were inlaid with intricate carvings of what was claimed to be fake ivory, but which Chikka knew for a fact was ivory. When it came to what Anna wanted, he had his sources, legal and illegal. The twin doors, gigantic beasts of doors, were embellished with brass strips. Two heavy brass rings hung from the middle of each door and the threshold was plated with brass. The doorway resembled that of a temple, which was exactly how Anna wanted it.

Chikka pushed the doors but they were latched from inside. From within he could hear the chanting. Chikka glanced at his watch. The puja had taken longer than it should have.

He tapped gently on the door. One of the eunuchs opened it. 'Come in, quickly,' Rupali said.

Chikka swallowed and stepped across the raised threshold. Would Anna be angry, he wondered. Would Anna's wrath blaze and burn, for every Friday Anna became Angala Parameshwari, the goddess of wrath.

Anger has no friends. Anger only has acolytes. Slavish creatures that feed the seed of rage with their daily obeisance of resentment and bitterness; hurt and betrayal; deprivation and wounds to the soul. Anna knew all about anger.

Anna made his acquaintance first with anger when he was a baby. He saw with his fierce baby eyes his drunk of a father slap his mother around. He felt her wince and shrink with each blow and kick. He felt her nuzzle him closer to her breast, but as the slapping grew in intensity, her nipple slipped out of his mouth. He shrieked his anger. She wept her pain. When he began to walk, he found a face for anger.

They lived in a little hamlet, Maruthupati, a few minutes away from the Mayannur temple. Every Friday evening his mother took him to the temple, trudging through a cremation ground. It would live forever in Anna's mind. The reddish-tinged twilight skies, the cawing of crows as night fell, the feel of the hard ground beneath his bare feet as they walked through giant clouds of billowing smoke from the still burning funeral pyres, the stinging in his eye, the smell and taste of smoke incense and wood, and underlying it all, the stench of charring flesh.

Anna learnt to negotiate his way through the pyres as he learnt to be unmoved by the anguish and sorrow that hung over each death. In the temple was Angala Parameshwari, the goddess who demanded angry tributes. Anna saw there the face his mother wore as she cuffed him under his chin or slapped his calves. He saw how anger made his mother strong and how the timid creature turned into a powerful goddess who matched her husband's violence with screams and blows that petrified him. Anger would not allow her to be kicked around any more. Anger was her weapon and it was this secret weapon she bequeathed him.

Every Friday, his mother retreated into herself. She would wash her hair and let it flow down her back. The turmeric paste she applied on her face before her bath emphasized her eyes which she outlined with 'maie'. She would bring out the red sari she wore only on Fridays. These were the colours of anger: Yellow, black, red. From her would waft the fragrance of camphor and incense, and the bitterness of dreams turned to ash.

She would place the bronze statue she had of the goddess on a wooden pedestal. Then she would dress the statue as she had dressed herself. She would adorn the goddess with flowers and light a lamp. And slowly her lips would part and words would form:

Om sri maha kalikayai namah
Kreem hum hleem
Kreem kreem jatt vaha
Kreem kreem kreem kreem kreem kreem svaha

As the frenzy and fervour of the chant grew, her voice would rise in a rhythm that stoked some strange fire within. Slowly her body would begin to gyrate, the bunches of neem leaves she held in her hands swirling as she sang:

Sooranai vadhikai wanda samariye
Soolam eduthe aadiya angakaliye

Anna would cower by the doorway, watching his mother metamorphose into a woman who invoked the goddess in her with strange words, rhythms and a manic frenzy – howling and screaming as she spun wildly.

When his mother was in her trance, she ceased to be the woman he called Amma and snuggled up to in his sleep.

He trembled in fright, watching her every move.

Who was this woman who stood before the goddess and ate the meat she had cooked early at dawn, chewing on each morsel, sucking on the bones and drinking deep of the pot of arrack? Who was this creature who raised into the air a chicken, its feet tied, to slit its throat and let the blood drip on her? Over her hair, her face, her chest and back; rivulets of warm blood that turned her into a horrifying monotone of anger appeased. When the blood ceased to flow, she would curl into a deep sleep from which she would awaken only some hours later.

Anna would sit there wondering about this woman who seemed to have created a ritual of her own. Who had taught her this? His mother could barely read. But the words she spoke were weighed with knowledge as with an inbuilt rhythm. Every syllable was exact, precise and loud. This from a woman whose speaking voice was like that of a sparrow.

When Anna was eight, he asked his mother, 'How, Amma? What happens to you?'

His mother smiled. Anna saw in that smile a secret. 'Ma Kali Amma lives in each one of us. When it is time for her to emerge, she will. And then she will demand you worship her in the way she wants you to. She will tell you what she expects of you. The tribute you pay her may horrify everyone else, but if it appeases her, that is all you should think of. And she will then bestow on you all you wish for. She will make her weapon yours. Anger. That is her weapon. For those of us who have nothing, anger is our only blessing.'

Anna learnt about anger when a year later his father dragged his mother, his baby brother and sisters to Bangalore. He had been offered a job as a watchman. 'And you can work as a maid somewhere,' his father said, opening the door to their one-room tenement in a slum near Shivaji Nagar.

Anna had looked around and wondered how they would all fit in. After the warmth of the sun in the fields of Maruthupati, the air in Bangalore chilled him, causing little shivers to run down his legs. Why had Appa brought them here? This little hole of a house and the crowds of strangers bustling around. Why had Appa done this to them? And thus Anna stumbled upon the anger in himself.

Soon anger and he were on first-name basis; soul mates. And, as his powers grew, nurtured and fed by anger, the goddess made her demand for tribute.

Chikka, who had seen their mother turn into a frenzied, fierce creature, had hoped that with her death, all of it would cease. But here was Anna now, seeking to be the repository of the goddess. Anna, who said the goddess expected him to invoke her in the guise of a woman. And that to help him arrive at his full powers, he would have to be surrounded by a bevy of eunuchs. For in the hermaphrodite exist both he and she, and in the coming together of man and woman is Shakti. The goddess at her fiercest.

What could Chikka tell Anna, who only did what he wanted to? Chikka had learnt young that with power came an arrogance that didn't like to be questioned.

Now Chikka waited, leaning against the wall, as Anna dressed in a sari and with braided false hair stood with hands stretched out, palms wide open. One of the eunuchs placed a piece of camphor on each of his palms and lit them with a lamp. With blazing hands, he circled the goddess, three times around. Chikka flinched at the thought of the searing heat but Anna wouldn't use a plate. If he did, the plate would absorb all the divine powers and Anna wanted it all for himself.

Chikka looked at his watch surreptitiously. A few more minutes and Anna would be done. Fortunately, this was only the weekly puja and not the amavasya one. That went on for hours and Anna took a long while to emerge from the trance.

Then Chikka heard a gasp and turned around.

Ramachandra stood at the door, gaping. His eyes were wide open and his mouth parted in shock.

In an instant, the eunuchs surrounded Anna so it was hard to discern who was who. Seething with rage, Chikka grabbed Ramachandra by his elbow and dragged him away.

'Who the fuck asked you to come in here?' he hissed.

Pale and trembling, the man stuttered, 'I ... I...'

'Forget what you saw here. Do you understand? If you breathe even a syllable of what you saw here, you'll regret it,' Chikka bit out.

'I ... the corporator...' The man began to make amends.

'The corporator's not here. He is at the Muthayalamma Devi temple on Seppings Road. What you saw is a family ritual. But we don't like strangers intruding or talking about it.'

Ramachandra swallowed. He knew he had seen the corporator dressed as a woman. He knew the corporator's brother was lying. But he dared not contradict him.

'I suggest you come back tomorrow at three p.m. Anna will see you then,' Chikka said, opening the door.

Chikka stood by the doorway, watching the man leave.

'Did he see me?' Anna asked softly. Chikka jumped.

He turned around. 'I am not sure. I said you were at the Muthayalamma temple.'

The corporator licked his lips. 'Do you think he believed you?'

Chikka didn't speak. What could he say? He dropped his gaze till he heard Anna leave the room. He wondered: what next?

Gowda was combing his hair when his phone beeped. Again. A flurry of text messages between U and him. In less than twelve hours he had taken to calling her U, so even you became U. It was a little conceit that U seemed to delight in, as he did her G. They were creating a little parallel universe of their own and, for the first time in many years, Gowda let thoughts of work slide to some lower realm.

What colour shirt are you wearing?

Navy blue. And U?

A lemon yellow sari.

Lovely. Have U left already?

No, G. Just about to. Ready to leave?

In a few minutes.

Gowda saw his son reflected in the mirror. He pocketed his phone almost surreptitiously.

'Was that Amma?' Roshan asked. 'I heard your phone beep. I thought you were texting each other.'

Gowda put down the comb. 'No, just some work-related texts. Besides, you know your mother texts only if she needs something.'

'Where are you going? You are all dressed up.' Roshan leaned against the door.

Gowda frowned. Did the boy suspect something? The

only thing to do was intimidate him into silence. 'Who's the policeman here? You or I? What's with all this curiosity?'

Roshan shrugged. 'I've never seen you looking so smart, Appa.'

Roshan's smile made Gowda flush.

'Thanks,' Gowda said, trying to hide his pleasure. 'I've been invited to inaugurate a photography exhibition.' On an impulse, he added, 'Do you want to come along?'

Roshan straightened. 'I'd like to, but are you sure?'

Something about the boy's tone squeezed Gowda's insides. The longing. The fear. The thought that his father saw him only as an irritant, an intrusion. Had he ruined his relationship with his child for ever?

'Yes, of course, I wouldn't ask otherwise. You have three minutes to put on a clean shirt and run a comb through your hair,' Gowda said, gently propelling Roshan towards his room.

In the car, Gowda kept an eye on the boy. In turn, he realized the boy was watching him. As he adjusted the rear-view mirror, changed gears and fiddled with the radio, he felt Roshan's eyes tag his every move. We are like two fighters sizing each other up, Gowda thought. Despite our differences, my father and I were never like this. So when did I become this tyrant? Or rather, how did you let this happen, G? Urmila, who seemed to have taken permanent residence in his head, queried. If you don't do something to heal the rift, the time will pass and it will be too late.

'I usually play Hindi songs when I am in the car. But if there's something else you would rather listen to...' Gowda offered. A small bridge of understanding towards something more concrete.

'No, it's fine. I'll listen to whatever you like,' Roshan said.

'So what does that friend of yours, Osagie, do?' Gowda asked.

'He's doing an MBA,' Roshan said. Then, as if on an impulse, he added, 'It really is a hard life for the African students here, Appa. No one will give them houses to rent. They get turned away if they go to clubs or discos ... We are as racist as anyone else.'

'I am not sure if it's racism,' Gowda said.

Roshan turned around. 'What else do you call it?'

'Some of them deal in drugs. But you don't know who is doing what ... so people tend to be cautious with everyone. Once a place is known as a spot where drugs can be bought, it brings with it a whole caboodle of other issues. That's what it is.'

Silence stretched between them as Gowda turned into the main road. An airport cab whizzed by. Gowda swerved, muttering 'motherfucker' under his breath. From the corner of his eye he saw a grin of pure delight splice the boy's face.

'These arseholes ought to be hauled up and fined,' Gowda said, feeling the boy's smile some more.

Gowda's phone beeped. His fingers itched to draw it out from his pocket and read the text. He knew it must be her, asking where he was.

'Don't you want to read the message?' Roshan asked.

'Not when I am driving,' Gowda mumbled. He hadn't had the time to warn her that Roshan would be with him.

'When are you going back?' Gowda asked.

He saw the boy's face fall. Gowda touched his elbow. 'I was wondering if you will be here long enough for me to give you some driving lessons.'

Gowda hadn't realized that there was such a place located in his station precincts. Twenty acres of trees with paths that beckoned you to stop and explore. As he parked, Samuel came to the car, his face beaming. 'Hello, sir,' he said, his gaze shifting to Roshan as he stepped out of the car.

'This is my son Roshan,' Gowda said, putting his arm around him. 'He's a medical student.'

Samuel led the way to the building where the exhibition was being held.

'This is a really lovely place, but will you get people to come here to view the photographs? It's a little out of the way,' Gowda said as his eyes took in all that was around him. 'Maybe the Alliance Francaise or the Chitrakala Parishat?'

'Lady Deviah said the same thing,' Samuel said with a smile. 'In fact, she's speaking to a couple of galleries. But sir, I am a page-three photographer. I've seen what these art events are like. And I fear that what we want to say will be lost. Everyone is so busy sipping their wine, posing for pictures and networking.'

Urmila appeared before them. Gowda felt his heart skip a beat. Gathering himself, he put his hand out and said, 'Good evening, Urmila.'

She stared at his palm for a split second, took it in hers and murmured, 'Good evening, Borei.'

Gowda turned to include Roshan. 'This is my son Roshan. And Roshan, this is Urmila. We were classmates at Joseph's.'

Roshan smiled. 'I saw you the other day at the café.'

Gowda swallowed. Urmila flushed. As if sensing the tension, Samuel moved towards him. 'Roshan, let me introduce you to the others.'

Gowda and Urmila stood there, looking at each other,

but the guests were beginning to trickle in and it was time for Gowda to be chief guest, light the lamp and speak a few words.

What did he say? Gowda couldn't remember. He had written down a little speech and memorized it. Had he parroted the words? Or had he said something else? Urmila had seemed moved and so did the others.

It had been easy enough to find the words, to sound as if he meant it, especially after he had seen the group of transgenders cowering at the back of the room. So afraid to come forward and be among the rest of the invitees. So certain that ridicule would be meted out to them if they did. So wanting to belong, but so definite that they would not be allowed to. Gowda had felt outraged to see the trepidation in their eyes and how they shrunk within themselves.

After an initial viewing, Gowda walked about, lingering before each photograph. He felt Urmila come to stand at his side. 'Borei, you haven't changed at all. You don't know how ridiculously pleased I am about that,' she murmured.

Gowda continued to stare at a photograph. 'Why would I have changed?'

'You are a police officer now.'

'So…' Gowda turned, amazed that she could be so affected by stereotypes.

'You don't expect much sensitivity from a policeman!' She smiled.

'Or is that you don't expect sensitivity from me?' Gowda asked quietly.

He saw her stiffen. 'Don't twist my words, Borei, please.'

Gowda took a deep breath and moved to the next photograph.

'So which one do you like the most?' he asked, trying to slash the tension that had crept between them.

He saw her clench her jaw as if to still her words. 'Come with me,' she said. 'It's an amazing shot; Ravi says he shot it in Shivaji Nagar market some days ago in available light. It's stunning.'

It was a photograph that defied all rules of light, focus and framing in the conventional sense. It was a photograph of a group of eunuchs at a bangle seller, each one of them only partially visible. But what drew the eye and made it linger was the untainted joy that emanated from them. For a moment they were free of the demons of their own making and the world's and so they stood there, radiating girlish delight at choosing glass bangles; the pleasure of seeing them slide onto their wrists, the clink of glass against glass as one of them held up her wrists. The light caught the glee and the nakedness of their dreams in their eyes.

And the light caught some more. A curve of a cheek as it leaned forward to touch a roll of bangles. And an earring that dangled into the frame. A beautiful pearl-drop earring.

Gowda's breath snagged in his throat.

She told herself she had to stop. She told herself she had already crossed the threshold of danger and would arouse suspicion. She needed to get a grip on herself. But how could she? She couldn't help it, like she couldn't resist the caress of the pearl against her skin. She swung her face a little so the jhumkas bobbed gently against her cheek, jhumkas with little shimmery pearls until her pearl earrings were ready.

A week after the earring had been misplaced, she had found a jeweller who had promised to replicate the earring for her.

Akka had made a face when she asked her to take the earring to the jeweller. 'Take King Kong with you so the jeweller doesn't mess around,' she had told Akka. 'And tell him I need it in ten days' time.'

'Do you think I can't handle the jeweller? I don't need anyone to go with me ... anyway, what's so special about that earring?' Akka had grumbled.

The elderly eunuch disliked King Kong and he, Akka. Each felt the other had usurped the other's place.

'Just do as I ask, Akka,' she said, allowing a trace of steel to enter her voice. How could anyone understand what those earrings did for her?

They were standing at a crossroad near Infantry Road. Akka sidled up to her and said again, 'I don't like this. I don't like you being here ... it is dangerous.'

She sniffed. A little girlish sniff. 'Don't you get tired of saying this to me, Akka? I am tired of hearing it!'

'You don't realize ... we have nothing to lose! But you are not like us,' Akka murmured.

She raised an eyebrow. 'That's true! I am not like you or the rest of them.'

'Since you have such contempt for us,' Akka began.

She touched Akka's elbow. 'That was uncalled for. I'm sorry. But why do they have to flaunt themselves? It only makes them a joke, a sick repulsive joke. You are not like that!'

Akka looked away. 'I was once like them ... we cannot help ourselves. We do not know who we are. And so we exaggerate in the only way we can. But you ... you are not like us. You don't have to be like us.'

She stared into a pool of darkness beyond Akka. 'I cannot help it any more than they can. Why won't you allow me that?'

They stood there side by side, watching the flurry of traffic. It was a few minutes past nine. The beat police weren't out on the prowl yet. Anyway, the policemen wouldn't trouble them unless they solicited blatantly. They had been dealt with. It was all part of a process and if you knew how to, you could survive working the street. That was lesson number 1 of the street – every man has a price.

A young man stepped out of one of the small restaurants. He stood at the entrance, hands on his hips, looking speculatively at the street. She saw how his T-shirt clung to his chest. She saw the corded muscles of his throat and the swell of his biceps. She saw how his jeans hinted at the tightness of his haunches and the bulge of his groin. She thought of how his breath would reek of garlic, onion and the spice of the biriyani he must have just eaten.

She watched him walk to the paan shop and buy a paan. She saw how his hand reached into the back pocket of his jeans to pull out a wallet. The slow thumbing of notes, the return of wallet into pocket, and the stuffing of paan into his mouth. His lips parting, the gleam of his teeth, his tongue receiving the betel-leaf pouch ... she could taste it now. The sweetness of his saliva honeyed by the gulkhand in the paan, flavoured by the betel-leaf juice. His jaws moved as he chewed. That strong jaw chiselled almost out of sandstone. Firm, but soft. In the pit of her belly, there was a leap of longing. She swallowed. She adjusted her sari, ignored Akka's imploring gaze and walked towards him.

The young man had walked a little further down. There was a row of shops housed in an old building with colonnades and arches. He stood by a pillar, waiting. What was he waiting for, she wondered. A friend? A whore? I can be both, she told him in her head.

She went to stand on the other side of the pillar. A smile tugged at the corner of her heart, the curve of her mouth. How had it come about that once again she found herself located within one of the paintings she loved? She saw him lean forward to look at her. She touched the pearl strings around her neck and draped the edge of her pallu over her right shoulder so it flowed into the crook of her right elbow. She leaned against the pillar so her jhumkas were visible.

She folded her hanky into four and let it unfurl, a pale pink flower that she toyed with as she felt him assess her. It felt so right, this moment, almost as if it were destined. This old-fashioned shop front, the man by the pillar, and she on the other side. *The Stolen Interview*. That was what Ravi Varma had called the painting. Why stolen, she had always wondered. But now she knew. She was there to steal his time, his soul. She smiled, lifted her gaze and let her eyes sneak a look at him.

Their eyes met. She dropped her gaze and played with her hanky flower.

'Are you waiting for someone?' he asked.

'My brother,' she said, allowing a trace of shyness to touch her voice.

'It's not safe for a girl to stand here by herself,' he said. 'Rather irresponsible of your brother!'

'He's not really my brother. He's a distant cousin and I am new to Bangalore, so when he offered to pick me up and drop me at my hostel, I...' The words flowed. She liked this little story about herself.

'You stay at a hostel?' His voice quickened.

She smiled secretly. All men were the same. All they needed was a thread to latch on to. All they needed was a crack in the door to wedge their foot into.

'Yes, it is a hostel for working women. Near Banaswadi,' she murmured softly.

'You know what, I'm going that side. Would you like me to drop you?'

She looked at him with her eyes wide open. More shock than surprise, she told herself. Oh, how she enjoyed this! Playing them like an instrument. And how easily they allowed her to play them. 'No, it's all right. I'll wait for my brother,' she said softly, moving away ever so slightly from the pillar, as though she wanted to distance herself from his preposterous suggestion.

'It's really not safe for you to stand here. This is Bangalore. Not ... where do you come from?'

'Haveri,' she said, mouthing the first name that came to her.

'That explains it! Bangalore girls wouldn't be this naive. And this isn't a safe part of the city.' He paused. 'And someone as attractive as you...'

She felt him look sidelong at her to see if his compliment had registered. A small smile. That was all he would need to pursue his suit. That was all she should allow him. Or he'd think she was easy ... and that she wasn't.

'My name is Sanjay. I came to Bangalore about six months ago from Tumkur. There's only fifty kilometres between here and there but it could very well be another planet. That's why I am concerned...' he said carefully. 'So listen to me and let me drop you. I live near Ramamurthy Nagar, so it's not all that far from you. In fact, it's on my way,' he lied.

He came to the other side of the pillar, to where she stood.

He was even more perfect up close, she thought, and then remembered to say, 'But my brother!'

'Call him on his mobile and tell him that you found your own way to the hostel,' he said. 'Come, my bike's parked there!'

'You have a bike?' She was surprised.

'Yes, that's the first thing I did when I got here. Took a bike loan and got this beauty.'

She touched her hair. Then took the end of the sari and draped it over her hair. That should hold it in place.

They walked to the bike. She watched as he started the bike. Through the visor of his helmet, he said, 'C'mon, get on the bike! Are you afraid? You have been on a bike before, haven't you?'

She nodded and perched sideways on the pillion.

'No, sit properly. And you'd better hold me. You don't look like you are used to sitting on bikes.'

She held his shoulder with her palm. A touch-you-touch-you-not sort of a grip. He sighed, but didn't say anything.

Soon they were in the thick of traffic. He talked to her all the way. Words the wind whipped out of his mouth. Words that lost a syllable in the din of traffic. For all she could hear was her hammering heart. It didn't matter what he said; the pressure of his body against hers felt like heaven. What was he doing to her? Giving in to impulse, she wrapped her arm around his waist.

He turned his head and murmured, 'That's better!'

She knew that he would stop. That he would find a pretext of some sort to take her into a quiet place. That he would then move in on her. All men were the same. She preferred them to be the same. That way, there were no surprises.

But he didn't stop.

At Banaswadi, she helped him find the street where the hostel was located. Some months ago she had helped a distant relative find a place here. So it wasn't hard to lie when he wanted to know what they ate for breakfast and the closing time, how many inmates to a room and if there was hot water.

He took her number and gave her his. He said they must meet again and elicited a promise from her that she would call. He looked at her carefully one last time and touched her cheek with the tip of his finger. He waited for her to enter the gate. And then, on his large noisy bike, he drove away into the darkness.

She walked back into the quiet street. She felt bereft and alone. Then, further ahead, she spotted a man. She felt his gaze on her. A hungry gaze she knew she could appease.

She stood by the side of the road, knowing he would come to her.

She thought of what would happen next. The frantic unravelling of clothes and inhibitions, the glorious need, a desperate need to caress and pummel, rake skin with nails and nip flesh with teeth. She would offer it all, her mouth, her tongue, every orifice and crevice for him to plunder and fill, so the clamour in her head would cease, so there would be stillness thereafter. The deafening thunder of stillness that would allow her to forget.

SATURDAY, 13 AUGUST

Santosh tried not to stare. So this was the Crime Branch office. It wasn't all that much. He had expected something more grand. Something imposing, significant and representative of the importance of the work its inmates did.

A careless coat of pale-blue colourwash had been slapped on at some distant point in time, but the damp had worked its way through the plaster and paint so that large splotches of grey coloured the walls of the hallway and the staircase. A heap of broken chairs, tables with their Formica tops peeling, and old sofas were piled into a corner of the room that opened from the staircase. Beyond this was the Serious Crime Division, a hive of rooms with flimsy partitions made of plywood and glass.

ACP Stanley Sagayaraj's room was a vast improvement. The senior man had a vast granite-topped table, a Dell PC that was still wreathed in its plastic cover on a side table, and several glass-fronted, locked cupboards of books. Santosh's eyes darted over the spines. Police diaries, *Law of Arms & Explosives*, *Indian Penal Code*, *Criminal Procedure Code*, *Criminal Law Journal*, *Criminal Major Acts*, *Criminal Minor Acts* and, incongruously, *The Book of Indian Birds*. On the walls, which seemed to have been painted more recently, were three framed pictures of birds.

'I was a keen birdwatcher once.' ACP Stanley Sagayaraj's voice didn't hide the amusement he felt at Santosh's careful gathering of details. 'I don't have the time for it any more.'

He gestured to the two men to sit down.

Gowda pulled a chair out and sat down while Santosh wondered if he should sit in the same line as Gowda or in the next line of chairs behind Gowda. What was the protocol when it came to these things?

'Sit down, Santosh, what are you dithering about? The view is the same no matter where you sit,' Gowda said impatiently, gesturing to a chair next to him.

'My team's been busy,' ACP Stanley Sagayaraj said, pulling out the case diary. 'Roopesh, the BPO employee, had told his roommate he was going for a movie that evening. In his wallet, we found a bill from Empire on Mosque Road. The nearest theatre is Kalinga, which as we all know is a pick-up place. So in all probability he went for the evening show with one express purpose. To get laid.'

Santosh dropped his eyes. Gowda's and Stanley's eyes met in amusement at Santosh's discomfiture.

'So they checked at the theatre. The ticket checker remembers him. He was alone and had asked the ticket checker if he could move from the seat he was allotted. The parking boy, who remembered him as well, said he drove away on a Kinetic Honda with a woman. Roopesh had apparently entrusted his helmet to the boy and promised to tip him when he collected it. By the way, the scooter hasn't been found. We have sent out an alert. So I am inclined to agree with you. Perhaps this is a team working together. A woman who is the bait and a man who is the actual killer. We'll know for certain when the DNA tests arrive.'

Gowda nodded. 'There's something else. Do you remember the earring I mentioned? The one that was found on Liaquat. I had it sized, appraised, etc., by a jeweller. Last evening I was invited to a photo exhibition and one of the photographs was of a group of eu ... er ... transgenders. An evening shot set somewhere in one of the by-lanes of Shivaji Nagar.'

'I saw you looking at it for a very long time and wondered...' Santosh said.

'Well, it was a very interesting photograph, but that wasn't the reason. One of the eunuchs had a similar earring. I am not completely certain though, so I've asked them to forward me a copy of the photograph.'

'Have you thought of rounding up the eunuchs and questioning them?' Stanley asked, looking at the photographs of the victims again.

'I was going to get that done,' Gowda said.

'Sir, we could ask them to come to the station this afternoon,' Santosh butted in.

Stanley and Gowda exchanged a look. 'He's new, isn't he?' Stanley asked sotto voce.

Gowda smiled. 'Give him a break, how does he know what they can be like! No, Santosh, we go to them. Bringing them into the station would be like, what's that idiom? Bringing a bull into a china shop. Except this would be several bulls who would think nothing of breaking up things, stripping their clothes off and rolling on the ground. So, Santosh, we go to them. In fact, I want you to do it. Take Head Constable Gajendra with you when you go for the questioning. He is an experienced man.'

Gowda's phone beeped as they stepped out of the Crime Branch office. He glanced at the screen, his face tightening.

Gowda didn't speak much as the police vehicle drove back to the station. Santosh tried to read his face but apart from the grim set of his features, it was hard to decipher anything. What could be wrong? Santosh wondered. With a tiny mental shudder he decided it might be best to stay clear of Gowda for the rest of the day.

A little past lunchtime, Gowda called for PC David to drop him home.

The house was empty. Gowda had waited for Roshan to step out. He stood at the doorway of his son's room for a moment. Then he went in and opened Roshan's rucksack. He rummaged through it briskly. There was nothing there. The weed pouch was empty. The grass and hash had been smoked up.

Gowda sat on the bed. Had Roshan gone out to score some more? What would come next? Speed. Angel Dust. E... Gowda chewed on his lip thoughtfully.

The address had been patchy. A door number in Kelesanahalli. Gowda rode his Bullet into the dirt roads that led off the main road. The house was in the middle of a chikkoo grove. A two-storeyed house with peeling paint. An old Maruti van was parked outside and a couple of 100cc bikes.

A few hens scratched in the dirt outside the house and a cat sat sunning itself on a wall. As Gowda rode in through the gates, he saw an old woman go into the house. That would be the landlord's mother.

Gowda parked his bike and went up the staircase to the first floor. He rang the bell.

Osagie himself opened the door. He looked terrified at the sight of a man in uniform at his doorstep. He hastened to shut the door but Gowda held it back firmly. They looked at each other till Osagie dropped his gaze.

He stepped back and said, 'I ... we...'

'I can do this standing here or I can come in and do it without your landlord wondering what is going on,' Gowda said in an even voice.

Osagie opened the door wider and beckoned Gowda to follow him.

Gowda looked around him carefully. The room smelt warm and sweet, of something organic and of food cooking. The curtains were drawn against the afternoon light. Or were they seeking to protect themselves from prying eyes? His eyes drifted to the African masks on a wall. A gigantic bronze plate sat on a table. A window sill was adorned with a row of brass animals. Otherwise it was just another living room with a few chairs and a small rug on the floor.

A young African woman came in from an inner room. She was wearing a white T-shirt, against which her breasts thrust, and a pair of tiny shorts. She had a bandana wound around her frizzy hair and she held a towel in her hand. She was saying something but stopped when she saw Gowda.

'So this is Adesuwa, your wife?' Gowda said.

Osagie and Adesuwa glanced at each other. It was Osagie who spoke. 'Who are you? What do you want?'

'I am Gowda. Inspector Borei Gowda.'

'We have done nothing wrong.' The woman's voice was shrill.

'Ade,' Osagie's deep treacley voice halted his wife's denial of guilt.

Gowda took a deep breath. 'I want the two of you to listen to me. I had you looked up...'

Adesuwa opened her mouth to speak.

'Don't,' Gowda said, fixing his gaze on her. 'Don't interrupt me.'

He turned to Osagie. 'Both your wife and you are being watched. One of these days you will make a mistake and the vice squad will pounce on you. But that is not why I am here. What concerns me is your association with my son. I want you to stay clear of my son Roshan. And I want you to tell your friends and associates to stay clear of him. Neither you nor they will sell him any drugs. Do you understand what I am saying?

'I know that your wife's visa has run out. I am not even getting into that. But if I discover that you have continued to associate with my son and have sold him drugs, it won't take me very long to have your wife deported. And then to round up your friends, associates, anyone you have met in the course of your stay here. I will make it impossible for you to live here. I hope I have made myself clear.'

He went down the stairs briskly. There was no certainty that Roshan wouldn't find another supplier. But he had to do this for himself as much as for Roshan. It was what a father did: watch out for his son.

He called early that morning. But she didn't take the call. He texted her. But she didn't respond. She wasn't Bhuvana then. But at night, she sat in her room and laid out a skin to crawl into. She became Bhuvana, the name she had given him; she became the woman the two of them so wanted her to be.

She pressed the key ever so gently. He picked up on the third ring.

'Bhuvana?' his voice asked urgently.

'Yes, it's me, Sanjay.' She said his name as if it were an endearment.

'I tried calling you this morning. I texted you. You didn't respond to either. I really was worried. I was going to turn up at your hostel tomorrow.'

A conflagration of feelings. Her fingers gripped the phone tightly.

'Bhuvana, you've gone silent,' he asked.

'I can't talk or text when I am at work,' she said. 'They don't like any of us using our mobile phones. And I'm new there. So…'

'I understand.' His voice softened. 'But you can text a word or two in the lunch break. You have one, don't you?'

She took a deep breath. 'I will try,' she said. 'This is the best time though.'

'Shall I come tomorrow to your hostel? It's a Sunday. You won't be working, will you? We could go for a coffee and tiffin. Do you like masala dosas? I know some really nice places…'

'No, no,' she cut in. 'My brother, I mean, my cousin was really annoyed when I left last evening without waiting for him. He's going to pick me up every evening, he said. And I have to go to their home tomorrow. I am to spend the night there. Monday is a holiday…'

'Oh yes, Independence Day. I forgot,' he muttered. Then, after a pause, 'Is this cousin married?'

She smiled at herself in the mirror. 'No, and…'

'And he sees you as his would-be.' Sanjay's voice was harsh with resentment.

She nodded. In the mirror she saw the girl she had become. Tremulous creature, but so needing to let him know that he was all she wanted. 'He's behaving as if I am … But,' she paused, knowing he would seize on that pause.

'But you don't like him?'

'I don't,' she said in a small voice. 'He's a short man. You know how short men are! But it's not that he is short or has curly hair and sometimes a squint. What I don't like is the way he is. So full of himself. So full of pride.'

He sniggered. 'Most short men are. As if to make up for the lack of inches.'

'So you see...' she murmured.

'Shall I come to your hostel on Tuesday then?'

She caught her breath in a little gasp. In the mirror, she was the girl flustered. Eyes wide, lips parted, her fingers fluttering to her mouth.

'No, no, you mustn't ... He has spies everywhere. They'll tell him. And he's dangerous!'

'What, that little peanut?' He laughed aloud. 'You really think I would be afraid.'

She could imagine him flexing his muscles. She felt a wave of tenderness. He was a little boy after all.

'Please, you mustn't underestimate him. He has connections. He knows all kinds of people. I won't talk to you again if you take silly risks.' The woman in the mirror pouted.

'Fine. But how am I to see you?'

She put her hand on her hip. Decisive girl. 'I'll call you. Maybe on Friday evening next week. He said he is busy most Friday evenings. Which is why he was late yesterday.'

'Does peanut have a name? I don't like you referring to him as though he is your bloody husband.'

She giggled. 'Chikka,' she said.

'Perfect for a peanut. Chikka!'

He told her of his day. She told him of her imagined day. They progressed to endearments and jokes. Then he sang her a song. She held the phone to her ear and forgot about all that life tormented her with.

She was still smiling when she put down the phone.

'Who were you talking to?'Akka demanded from the door.

Shutters came down in her eyes.

'No one,' he said, reverting to being who he was.

Akka stood there looking at him. 'You will get hurt,' the elderly eunuch said. 'You know you will. Then why?'

'How can I help myself?' he asked. He placed the phone down on the dressing table and leaned towards the mirror. In there was the girl Sanjay had fallen in love with. In there was Bhuvana, who had tossed caution to the winds and made a gift of her heart.

SUNDAY, 14 AUGUST

Roshan watched his father chew his breakfast thoughtfully. 'What's wrong, Appa?' he asked.

Gowda looked up from his plate of idli-sambar and said nothing.

Roshan's face fell. 'Is it me, Appa? Have I done something wrong?'

'No, no...' Gowda shook himself out of his reverie to answer his son. 'Nothing to do with you, Roshan. Just troubled by a case I am working on.'

And the fact that this thing with Urmila was getting a little too hot to handle. It was like holding a hot potato. He didn't want to let go, but it would burn his fingers if he didn't.

Gowda saw Roshan's face clear and felt something akin

to guilt wash over him. At what he had done to turn his son into this fragile creature so afraid of his censure and so needy of his approval.

'Appa, the driving lessons,' Roshan said. 'Can we postpone it for the next time? I have to go back later today.'

Gowda had forgotten all about the offer he had made Roshan. He closed his eyes in an attempt to pull himself together. What am I? If I were to draw up a chart about myself, what would it say? Lousy cop. Lousy father. Lousy husband. Lousy lover...

'Appa, you are not upset, are you? But my classes start on Tuesday and I need a day to organize things,' Roshan added, seeing his father's face cloud.

Gowda reached across and patted his son's hand. 'When you come back next time, we'll start. You just need a couple of hours behind the wheel and you'll be fine. It's simple. Any fool can do it. It's no rocket science.'

His reward: the light in the boy's eyes.

'Appa, I'm sure you will be able to crack the case,' Roshan said, clasping his father's fingers.

Gowda looked away. How easy it was to be loved if only one could learn to show love. Was that where he went wrong? Keeping it all locked within?

He had been right to not confront Roshan. Perhaps when their relationship was on a stronger plane, he would. But until then, he would pretend he didn't know that Roshan smoked up.

'I used to smoke grass in college,' Gowda said suddenly. 'My friends and I did an occasional joint.'

Roshan frowned.

'But I knew when to stop. I didn't want it to take over my life.'

'Why are you telling me this?' Roshan asked carefully.

Gowda shrugged. 'I don't know. I just felt like I should.'

When his mobile rang, Gowda reached for it gratefully. When his mind churned, and the debris from his past and dilemmas of his present turned into a whirling frothing mass, the call of work was an escape from making sense of his life. From needing to address the mistakes and perhaps mend them. Gowda knew it was cowardice, but he didn't want to go down that path. One day he would. For now, he barked into the phone. 'Yes Santosh, tell me…'

Roshan watched his father's expression change from his habitual blandness to incredulous horror.

'Yes, of course,' Gowda murmured. 'I'll come right away.'

Roshan spooned a dollop of chutney onto his plate. 'So you have to go?' he asked, as his father put down his mobile phone.

Gowda nodded. 'What time is your bus?'

'I'll find one at the KSRTC bus stand. I think there is a bus every hour to Hassan. So don't worry. I'll find my way home.'

Gowda flinched. Home. The boy saw Hassan as home. And not this house where his father was. 'Oh,' he said quietly.

Probably realizing what he had said, Roshan smiled and added, 'I'll come back home when I have a three-day weekend. Will you give me driving lessons then?'

Gowda stood up. He walked towards the boy and squeezed his shoulder. 'I will. Now you take care. And study … and come back soon.'

Roshan stood up and hugged his father. Gowda was startled by the unexpected hug. He didn't speak but hugged him back.

Gowda's phone beeped. He sensed it was Urmila. She had taken to texting him early.

'Do you need any money?' Gowda asked. Then, opening his wallet, he pulled out a 500-rupee note and gave it to the boy. 'Buy a book or some music...' he said. Please not any dope. Please. Please.

Gowda stepped outside the house and checked his message. *GM darling, r we meeting 2da?* she had asked.

GM U, will let you know, he texted furiously. His text language wasn't as adept as hers. Until Urmila, he had used texts rarely. He watched the text float away and looked up. Roshan was watching from the door. He swallowed and swung his leg over his Bullet. He turned on the ignition and the dthuk dthuk sound filled the silence that stretched between father and son.

Santosh had called to say that the control room had reported a murder at Dodda Banaswadi. A young man with a slit throat. 'I thought you should know. Maybe it has some connection to our case,' Santosh had said, unable to hide his excitement.

At the station, Santosh was waiting.

'We'll go on my bike,' Gowda said. 'There's a spare helmet in the station. Ask Byrappa. He'll know where it is.'

Santosh pulled the helmet on and perched on the Bullet. After his 150cc bike, this felt like sitting on a horse. A sound, sturdy horse that wouldn't miss a step. No matter how bad the roads were or how the traffic pressed upon them.

There was a crowd gathered outside the house. Two police vehicles and a posse of policemen were keeping it under control. The wireless in one of the Boleros crackled.

Gowda parked the bike and the two men walked towards the group. One of the policemen saw the three stars and the red-and-blue ribbon on the outer edge of Gowda's shoulder straps and nudged the others. They sprang to attention, saluting. Santosh felt a flush of pride. No matter what he may think of Gowda, the man had a certain presence.

'Sir, Inspector Lakshman's there,' the constable said. 'Upstairs. At the crime scene.'

Gowda nodded at the constable and unlatched the gate. It opened with a long drawn out creak. A bike was parked to the side of the house and a flight of stairs led up to the first floor. Gowda climbed the stairs. Halfway up, he turned to Santosh and gestured for him to follow.

'The upstairs portion was designated for tenants. For a small family,' the landlord was explaining as Gowda arrived. He was sitting on a chair, ashen-faced, still unable to believe that a murder had been committed even as he and his family had eaten their dinner, watched TV and gone to sleep downstairs. 'And Kiran was a good boy. His uncle's a friend of mine and so I didn't worry too much that he was a bachelor. He was well-mannered, god-fearing, and no habits … if you know what I mean,' he added. 'I don't understand. I don't understand who could have done this to him. And why?'

Gowda looked around. The first floor was a large terrace on which two rooms had been built with a provision to build further. A few potted plants stood on the side of the terrace that faced the road. To the rear was a clothesline from which hung three T-shirts, a shirt, a pair of trousers, two undies and a towel. There was a tap, beneath which was placed a plastic bucket.

A coir doormat sat outside the door. WELCOME, it said. As Gowda watched, Santosh walked towards the door.

'Don't,' Gowda called out.

'Sir?' Santosh stared.

'Don't wipe your feet on the mat,' Gowda muttered.

'I wouldn't have, sir,' Santosh said slowly. 'I know you think I am an idiot, but even I am not that much of an idiot.'

Gowda didn't speak, but had the grace to look ashamed when Santosh stepped back and waited for him to walk into the crime scene first.

The room showed no signs of struggle. Books on the table. A helmet on a rack. A pile of ironed clothes with an electric iron still plugged in. The small kitchenette had a few vessels and a row of jars with some essentials. The gas stove had been wiped clean and a kitchen cloth had been draped over the counter to dry out.

There was a small built-in wardrobe. Gowda used a handkerchief to hold the handle as he opened the door. He examined each shelf methodically. A stack of shirts and trousers in one, and on another a couple of sweaters. The third shelf held sheets, pillow cases and towels. Placed on the bottom shelf was a pair of black shoes. The other section of the wardrobe had a hanging rail and a small shelf above it. The rail had a few hangers from which hung a couple of shirts and a pair of jeans. There was a camera on the rack above and a shirt box. Gowda pulled out the shirt box. A small pile of porn magazines sat in it.

Gowda's eyes shifted to the victim. His sneakers were thrown to the left of the bed, his trousers and underwear were another puddle of colour, suggesting that he had taken everything off in a hurry. His shirt lay half across the bed as though he had pulled it off in a rush. The young man sitting on the chair was naked except for his socks.

His throat had been slit. But, as with Kothandaraman, he exhibited just about every classic sign consistent with strangulation by ligature. Eyes open, distended eyeballs, dilated pupils, signs of haemorrhage in the cornea and skin around the eyelids, forehead and face; the protruding tongue that was almost dark brown while the lips were blue. Some signs of bleeding from the nose and ears and bloody froth from the mouth. There was a well-defined ligature mark on the neck at an oblique angle. Bruises and abrasions and a deep cut-like wound where the ligature had cut into the skin. The hands were clenched and his penis was semi-erect. He had peed and shat himself in that final moment.

And once again, there it was, the wound on the cheek. Skin tattered, tissue ground into, the bone broken. Around the edges of the wound, the skin was broken and irregular. In fact, apart from the raw smell of putrefaction and the contorted features of the young man which bespoke an expression of shock, horror and the knowledge of impending death, the rest of the room was perhaps as he had always kept it.

Investigating Officer Inspector Lakshman looked up and sprang to attention.

Gowda nodded. 'I have had two murders in my station precincts in the last one month. Same mode of death as this one. We thought we would take a look if you don't mind,' he said, including Santosh in his inquiry.

Santosh stepped forward. Gowda was making amends, he realized.

Inspector Lakshman too had once passed through that great university of real-life police science called Gowda's tutelage. Before Gowda had chewed him up alive, Inspector Lakshman had been transferred. So he looked at Santosh with a great deal of sympathy, and some envy. You might want to smash Gowda's face with a blunt object, but you couldn't help admire the man. He turned investigation into a fine art and there were times such as this when he wished he had spent more time with Gowda. He would have learnt how exactly to go forward.

'What do you think?' Gowda asked carefully. He didn't expect much from an arselicker like Lakshman but you never knew. He may have tired of rimming his way up the ladder.

'I have already informed the ACP, sir,' Lakshman said, indicating he still hadn't.

Gowda's mouth twisted into a line. 'The CCB will be here too ... so what is your reading this far?'

From the corner of his eye, he saw Santosh put on a pair of gloves and do a spiral search. Good, the boy had imbibed some of what he had told him. 'Never ever start your search for evidence in a haphazard manner. There is a method even to that. When I am alone or when I know that I have to do it before the rest of the circus turns up, I do the inward spiral.'

'I don't actually understand, sir,' Lakshman admitted. There was no point trying to put on a face with Gowda. He would realize in a matter of minutes how clueless he was. And that was the thing. There was no evidence of any sort to even form a preliminary opinion. Everything was in place and even the victim seemed at rest, almost as if he hadn't known until the last moment what was happening to him.

Santosh checked the windows. They were all shut from within except the ventilator in the bathroom. There was only one door through which to enter the room and that had been shut as well until the police broke it down. So the assailant had entered the room with the victim's knowledge and left the crime spot after pulling the door shut.

At first, the landlord had thought Kiran was unwell. He had heard the bike come in two nights ago at about 10 p.m. So he knew Kiran had returned home. On Saturday morning, the bike had stayed in its place. It was his wife who first thought something was amiss. A day later, the milk sachets lay where they had been left. When her husband sat down for breakfast, she mentioned it to him. He called the young man. They could hear the mobile ring upstairs. The landlord went up and rang the bell. There was no response. Meanwhile, a boy called Suraj whom Kiran had introduced as his colleague came by. He had a worried expression. Someone had called him two nights ago saying Kiran was dead. Suraj had laughed it off. Kiran and he had been at the gym together that evening. But he had been trying to call Kiran since yesterday evening, he said, and Kiran wasn't picking up the phone.

The landlord was terrified now. He hammered on the door and hollered. But there was still no response. That's when he called the police.

'Where do we go from here, sir?' asked Lakshman.

'Let's see what the post-mortem comes up with. Meanwhile, let me know what you discover about the victim. Look at the calls made on his phone, talk to his friends and get a sense of his routine, ask around and corroborate when and where he was last seen alive. Seen, not heard … And talk to this Suraj right away. See if you can trace the number that the call came from. That's going to be vital!'

The corporator stared at his fingernails thoughtfully. Tiger sat at his feet, looking up at his master with an equally thoughtful expression. Both man and dog had something on their mind that required someone else to make a move, Chikka thought from his customary perch on the courtyard ledge. He sighed. He would have to do it.

Chikka stood up. 'Come, Tiger,' he said, walking to the door. Tiger shot his master a look of reproach and followed Chikka. He stood by the open door and then stepped out. A dog's got to do what a dog's got to do.

Chikka thought he knew how Tiger felt. A Chikka's got to do what a Chikka has to do.

'Anna,' he said from the door, 'what's troubling you?'

The corporator's eyes rose and met his brother's gaze. 'Remember the PWD clerk Shivappa who wanted our help to retrieve his house? He's been talking to Jackie Kumar. If he didn't work in the planning department, I would have thought, good riddance. But he will know about the city projects as and when the files come up for clearance and I need that information to use, to sell … I don't need to tell you this. I should have sorted it out, but I had other things on my mind. If Jackie Kumar has him in his book, our entry into that section is closed. I should have remembered that Jackie Kumar has been looking to make things difficult for me ever since we fell out.'

'What do you want me to do?' Chikka asked quietly.

'Take a few of the boys and go to the house. Throw out Chicken Razak's keep and his belongings. Lock the door and bring the key to me. And call the PWD clerk over this evening. I want him drooling gratitude all over my feet. Next week, we'll call in our favour.'

The corporator rose from his chair and went to the door. Tiger whined from outside. He let the dog in and patted its head gently.

'You really love this dog, don't you?' Chikka said.

The corporator smiled. 'With him, I know where I am.'

Chikka frowned. 'Are you saying you don't trust me?'

The corporator held his brother at arm's length and smiled. 'You, I trust. But it is foolish to trust anyone else. Life is all about learning to barter. You just need to know who needs what to make them do your bidding. Tomorrow, if someone else comes and offers them the same at better terms, they will go to them. My Tiger will too. He will wag his tail and eat their meat. But he will not give anything back. His love and loyalty are mine. I prefer dogs to people.'

Chikka didn't speak.

'One other thing. Ramachandra, the slum board officer, needs to be dealt with,' the corporator said abruptly, his tone hardening.

Chikka stared. 'Has he been babbling?' he asked.

'Not yet. But I don't trust him. When he came to see me yesterday, his manner had changed. There is a certain cockiness. Almost as if he has a bargaining chip. Almost as if he thinks he can control me...'

Chikka drew closer. 'Did he say anything to you?'

'Not really. But when I wanted him to pull out a letter from a file, he made excuses. They are talking of clearing up the slums near the East Station and I wanted to see what the recommendations were. Once, all I had to do was mention the letter and it would have been done...'

Chikka watched his brother go back to his chair. Tiger followed and sat on his haunches. Chikka watched his brother tug the dog's ears gently. Tiger rubbed his snout against the corporator's hand, demanding more of the playful attention. The corporator smiled and scratched the dog's neck.

'He has a dog,' the corporator said. 'A little white bag of fur. A silly, yapping, spoilt creature. They tie a red ribbon around its neck. Apparently, the daughter is devoted to it. Slit its throat.'

'What?' Chikka asked.

'They went to Mysore last night and will be back only late tonight. There is a live-in maid, but the dog is usually out in the front yard.'

'How do you know all this, Anna?' Chikka was incredulous.

'I make it my business to know. Slit the dog's throat and leave it for him to find. Tell him the dog barked too much. Tell him the dog's barking reached me this far and hurt my ears. Tell him this is how we deal with dogs that don't know how to keep their mouths shut. Tell him that...' The corporator rose. 'I am going to have my bath,' he said.

Chikka swallowed. More and more, his brother worried him. More and more, he felt his brother turning into something he didn't even want to recognize.

They took the Scorpio that evening. Anna insisted. 'Take that villain vehicle,' he said with a laugh. 'Intimidation is the key to what you wish to achieve when you are out on the streets.'

Chikka, King Kong and the three men Anna had trained to be his fists and feet, now that he couldn't personally make house calls swinging the sand wedge. Each one had his favourite weapon – switchblade, screwdriver, machete, cycle chain. And Chikka had his revolver. Anna insisted that he carry it when he went out with the boys.

The dog was by the gate. Darting this way and that with little high-pitched barks when man, machine, or even a leaf wafted across its line of vision. The door was closed, and no one was in the front yard. Chikka watched as Raghu opened the gate and threw a kebab on the ground. The dog's eyes glittered at the sight of meat. As it fell upon the meat, in one swift motion King Kong grabbed the little dog by the scruff of its neck and, with the other, ran the edge of his switchblade across its throat. The dog struggled and then stilled. King Kong dropped the dead dog, took the note from his pocket and tied it to the dog's paw carefully with the red ribbon from around its neck. It had taken less than three minutes and on that quiet street, hidden by the high compound wall, no one had seen or heard a thing. Not that they cared. Anna would take care of everything.

'Where to next?' Raghu asked, as he got into the car.

'Shivaji Nagar,' King Kong said.

Chikka didn't speak. The only reason he was here was because Anna felt the men would start thinking too much of themselves if they were sent alone on a mission. 'The trick is to make them believe that they cannot function without us.'

Did these men at night ever think about the texture of their day, Chikka wondered. Did it ever come to them that these random acts of cruelty were perpetrated against someone they didn't even know?

The house was locked. Chikka frowned.

'Break the lock. Get rid of everything in there and put a new lock in its place. Tell the neighbours that the landlord has sold it to someone else and that Chicken Razak and his catamite have been evicted,' Chikka said.

The men stepped out together, muttering under their

breath. 'Any street thug can do this,' Swami said. 'Why did Anna send us?'

'Something to do with Jackie Kumar. It's a message of sorts to him. Don't mess in my terrain, etc.,' Raghu explained.

A man walking by stopped. He stared as Anna's men heaped a few things on the road. A chair. A bed. A TV and a few clothes. Someone brought a can of petrol and sloshed it over the heap. A match was lit and flung onto the things. The heap erupted into a blazing fire in moments. King Kong and Swami stood around, watching the fire crackling, while Raghu poked at the flames with a stick.

The man watched the fire throw up little sparks with a hiss and splutter. Flecks of ash danced through the air and floated away as King Kong inserted a big bright steel lock into the padlock.

And then they all piled into the mean-looking SUV and drove away.

TUESDAY, 16 AUGUST

Gowda was certain others were plotting this diagram. Nevertheless, he had to do it.

'What are you doing, sir?' Santosh asked. He saw the graph on the table and Gowda's meticulous markings on it.

'The PM report estimated the time of death at about eleven p.m. and the landlord heard the bike at ten. The stomach contents and extent of digestion indicate that the meal was eaten at about nine thirty p.m., which means somewhere in the radius of ten kilometres is where the meal was eaten. Either the victim ate dinner with the assailant or met with the person on his way home. So what we need to do is methodically search this entire area.' Gowda indicated the radial lines drawn from the scene of crime.

Santosh stared at the diagram and said carefully, 'Sir, we can reduce this by at least five kilometres on each line. The brakes of his bike are faulty so he can't have been driving very fast. I checked it on our way back.'

Gowda looked at him and smiled. 'Well then ... There is one major problem though. It's not technically our area, but I want you to draw up a chart and put all our constables to cover this locality. You realize, don't you, that we don't have much time...'

Gowda stretched as far as his arms would go and yawned. He had been up since three in the morning, dwelling over the case. Somewhere in his mind he knew for certain that there was a link between the dead Kothandaraman, the burnt-alive Liaquat, Roopesh fished out of Yellamma Lake and now Kiran. All four had their throats slit with ligatures that had manja on it. Each one's skull had revealed a depressed fracture. A signature fracture that resembled in its pattern the weapon that had caused it. A heavy weapon with a small striking surface. The outer table had been driven into the diploe and the inner table had fractured irregularly. Suddenly he was struck by a thought.

'Do you have a calendar, Santosh?' he asked.

'I have a card.' Santosh pulled out a small date card from his wallet.

Gowda peered at it. 'Do you see something?' he said.

'All the murders except the assault on Liaquat took place on Friday.' Santosh's voice shook with excitement.

'Santosh, I want you to find out if there have been other murders in the last six months, on Fridays. We already know there is no history of this MO. But look for slit throats. Maybe the weapon has been changed. And one other thing. All the victims were male. That narrows it down further, don't you think?' Gowda spoke as he made notes on the back of the paper.

Santosh took the calendar back and slid it into his wallet. His first murder investigation and it seemed they were already on track.

'Have you started questioning the eunuchs yet?' Gowda asked.

'I have asked Head Constable Gajendra to do it, sir. I'll check with him,' Santosh said.

'You mean it's not been done. You mean you didn't do it ... I thought I asked you to handle this, Santosh. If I thought Gajendra could have, I wouldn't have asked you to.'

The sternness in Gowda's tone chilled Santosh. For a moment there, he had relaxed his guard. Gowda was treating him as an equal. But no, he was back to being the halfwit assistant who had to be told what he could and couldn't do.

Gowda's mobile rang, and Santosh used the opportunity to escape before more of Gowda's wrath descended on his due-for-a-haircut head.

Gowda put down his mobile thoughtfully. This was a new twist. He leaned forward and rang the bell. 'Ask Santosh to come in,' he told the constable who had answered his bell.

Santosh hurried back in. Constable Byrappa had warned him that Gowda's face resembled that of someone who had bit into grit in a mouthful of rice. Santosh couldn't even imagine what such a face would be like, but he didn't want to take any chances. Not with Gowda.

'Sir,' he said.

Gowda looked thoughtful, almost agonized. Was this how one looked when you bit into grit in a mouthful of rice? Santosh asked himself. He wasn't certain. Constable Byrappa ought to be writing novels instead of mazhar reports, he decided.

'One of my informers just called me. Apparently, a group of men were at Liaquat's house. They threw out his possessions, burnt them, locked up the house and left.'

Santosh leaned forward in excitement. 'Does he know who they were?'

Gowda nodded. 'Corporator Ravikumar. Though I can't understand the connection at all...'

Santosh waited for Gowda to finish his sentence.

'I think we should pay the corporator a visit,' Gowda said.

'I was just going to suggest that,' Santosh offered, unable to help himself.

'You mustn't hesitate. A good police officer would never do that. So, tell me, what's on your mind?'

And have my head bitten off, Santosh thought bitterly. He was beginning to think that Gowda suffered from a personality disorder.

The compound wall ran almost the length of the entire road, a high wall washed in a sandstone hue. The top of it was embedded with shards of glass over which two lines of barbed wire stretched. Gowda's jaw clenched when they were kept waiting at the tall black gates.

'Bloody upstart,' Gowda growled. 'Who the fuck does he think he is? The bloody governor?'

The watchman opened the gates reluctantly. PC David glared at him. 'Can't you see it is a police vehicle?' he demanded. 'Hurry up!'

The man shrugged. 'Anna has a lot of enemies. It's my duty to make sure that all and sundry don't go in.'

In response, PC David pressed the accelerator down and raced through the gates towards the house.

Santosh's mouth fell open. 'Sir,' he whispered, 'how can a corporator build a house like this? It's so...'

'Ghastly,' Gowda supplied helpfully. 'Monstrous? Nauseating?'

'It's so big,' Santosh said. 'As big as the Mysore Palace!'

'Not as big, but almost...' Gowda grinned as the police vehicle pulled up outside the house.

'Even the gates are like the palace gates. How can a corporator have this kind of money?' Santosh murmured.

'Welcome to the world of politics,' Gowda rumbled. 'In a survey conducted last year, Karnataka was declared the fourth most corrupt state in the country.'

'I can see why,' Santosh said grimly, his eyes falling on the line of cars parked by the side of the house. He thought of his father, one-time corporator in the municipality of Londa. A little, frail man who wore his principles like his hand-spun clothes, with fierce pride; a Gandhian who eschewed personal gain in favour of public welfare. Santosh and his siblings had borne the brunt of those Gandhian tenets. Would he have been here, sitting in a police uniform, if his father had been built on the lines of Corporator Ravikumar? Perhaps not. Who knows what he would have become?

A group of men stood huddled on one side of the house. One of them, an apelike man with arms that curved in towards his body and a wide barrel chest, went in quietly as soon as they saw the police jeep. By the time Gowda and Santosh climbed the steps to the main door, it was flung open by the corporator himself.

'Please come in,' the corporator said in his most cordial voice. 'What brings you here, Borei Gowda? Ah, I forget.' He struck his palm on his forehead in a theatrical gesture of reproof. 'You are in uniform ... so what can I do for you, Inspector?'

Santosh felt his jaw slip a fraction of an inch. So Gowda and the corporator already knew each other.

The corporator turned his gaze on Santosh. He looked at him, up and down, and dismissed him as inconsequential.

Turning on his heel, he led the way into a room so hung with heavily embroidered drapes that Santosh felt all air escape his lungs. The floors gleamed. On the walls were giant paintings in gilded frames. A woman talking to a swan. A group of singers. Santosh felt his mouth fall open as a shiny black Labrador wearing what seemed like a gold dinner plate trotted over to sniff at them.

'His father, Romeo, was an inspector in the dog squad,' the corporator said in a bland voice. 'Perhaps he senses a connection.'

Gowda smiled. 'If he's anything like his father, he can't be very happy here. Romeo was at his best when it came to sniffing out criminals.'

Santosh looked at Gowda in admiration. Wasn't the man scared of anybody?

The corporator flushed. 'What can I do for you, Inspector?'

He sat down in a chair that looked like a throne and waved to Gowda and Santosh to perch on the black leather sofas.

A young man, slight and short, with curly hair and a hint of a squint in one eye, appeared. Diamonds glinted at his earlobes. Gowda felt an instant dislike for him. Thank god Roshan hadn't got any piercings done yet. The sight of men wearing earrings made him want to gag. With the young man was the ape who had slipped in to inform the corporator of their arrival. A servant followed, carrying a tray. Santosh saw it was silver, on which were two silver glasses brimming with buttermilk.

'The milk is from my dairy. So the buttermilk is exceptional,' the corporator said, reverting to an affability that had disappeared for a brief while.

'This is my brother Ramesh,' the corporator said. He didn't bother introducing the other man. But his role was obvious when he placed himself beside the corporator's chair, arms folded and legs planted in a stance that suggested, 'here is a being I will guard with my last breath'.

Gowda's glance flicked over him with interest. But he didn't speak. Instead, he took the glass of buttermilk and gestured for Santosh to do the same.

'Yesterday afternoon your people went to Liaquat's house in Obaidullah Street,' Gowda said, ignoring all polite niceties.

The corporator stared at him uncomprehendingly.

'It's not Liaquat's house. Chicken Razak lived there. Liaquat was his frooter,' the corporator's brother said.

'Frooter?' Santosh asked, unable to help himself.

'His catamite,' Gowda murmured.

'What?' Santosh asked again.

'Never mind. I'll explain it to you later.' Gowda felt a great urge to pinch Santosh, like Mamtha used to pinch Roshan when he wouldn't shut up and continued to ask embarrassing questions at important gatherings.

'Your colleague's new, I see.' The corporator smiled.

'Liaquat was murdered some weeks ago. His throat was slit; he was taken to the outskirts of the city and burnt. Probably to get rid of the body, but he was still alive when he was found,' Gowda said.

The corporator and his brother exchanged glances. 'What does that have to do with us?'

'Exactly! What were your men doing in his house?'

The corporator took a deep breath. But it was the younger brother who spoke up. 'Anna knows nothing about what happened.'

The corporator put his hand on his brother's arm and said, 'Inspector Gowda, I would have expected you to have done your homework before you came here. Chicken Razak only rented the house. It was sold to Shivappa, a PWD clerk. But Liaquat wouldn't move out, no matter what. Shivappa even found him another place. I told Shivappa I would look into it, but I see that my brother has been hasty.' The corporator paused and closed his eyes for a moment. 'I don't even know what this Liaquat looks like.'

'Neither do I,' said Ramesh. 'Sir, in fact, I went along to ensure there was no trouble. Didn't your informer tell you that? All the men did was to break open the lock and empty the house out.'

Gowda nodded. 'In a murder investigation, we can't afford to not check on the smallest detail.'

'This is the first I have heard of Liaquat's murder. You realize, don't you, that Liaquat was a male whore. With Razak in jail, he must have got desperate...' With a slow smile, the corporator added, 'Would you like me to make some enquiries? My reach far exceeds yours.'

Gowda frowned. 'That won't be necessary.'

The corporator rose. Gowda and Santosh followed. Gowda paused. 'As a corporator, you should know that you cannot take the law in your hands. The man you mentioned should have gone to the police, who would have taken care of it.'

The corporator smiled. 'Indeed, and I didn't take the law into my hands. I will, of course, speak to my brother about this and make sure it doesn't happen again. But both you and I know that Shivappa wouldn't have been able to afford police intervention. I don't ask for much, except loyalty. Most people can afford that. By the way, you don't need to come all this way if you have any more queries. Just call me,' he said.

'Sir, but that was a criminal offence. To break into a locked house! We could have hauled up the brother for that,' Santosh muttered as they walked to the jeep.

Gowda nodded. 'Yes, we could have. But he would have been out on bail even before you and I got back to the station.'

Santosh turned to look at the house.

'I don't believe him. He knows a lot more than he is letting on,' Gowda said, as they drove back.

'He is rather strange. That house and the dog; and the bodyguard. Did you see he's got a gaggle of eunuchs there? Did you see them? They went in by a separate entrance ... it's like something out of a movie,' Santosh murmured as Gowda stared at him wordlessly.

'And, sir,' he added, slowly, 'there was a Scorpio parked by the side of the house. It had Tamil Nadu number plates.'

WEDNESDAY, 17 AUGUST

Gowda made a gopuram of his hands. The wall on the left threw up shadows and, on an impulse, Gowda made a fist of one hand and stuck his thumb between his middle and ring fingers. Next, he laid his palms on top of each other and moved his thumbs and little fingers this way and that.

Santosh peered over the stable doors and wondered what Gowda was doing. The wall was alive with shadows. Was that a man's face? Now it was a fish…

Gowda looked up and spotted Santosh.

'What are you doing, lurking there?' he called out.

Santosh opened the door and stepped in. 'Er… what were you doing, sir?'

'I was thinking,' Gowda said, trying not to sound self-conscious. What must the fool have thought as his fingers formed shadows? 'What did you think I was doing?'

Santosh flushed.

'Here,' Gowda said, pushing the coffee-table book of Ravi Varma paintings towards the younger man, 'take a look at this. Something about it is very familiar to me but I can't put my finger on it.'

Santosh leaned forward and gazed down at the cover. The juggling woman. He stared at it intently. Then, slowly, carefully, he flipped the cover to look at the inner colour plates.

'Sir, some of these paintings… I've seen them too…' he began as his fingers turned page after page. Suddenly he looked up and said, 'I know. It was in the corporator's house. In that rather grand room we sat in… some of these were hung there…'

Gowda's eyes lit up. 'Fantastic, Santosh! That's where I thought I saw them too, but I wanted to make doubly sure…'

Santosh's face glowed with pleasure. When he was being pleasant, there was no one quite like Borei Gowda.

'There's something else,' Gowda said, his voice lowering. He took a set of keys from his top drawer and threw it at Santosh.

Santosh watched the bunch of keys fly towards his face, stepped back and caught it neatly.

'Played cricket, did you?' Gowda smiled.

'I was in the college team.' Santosh grinned.

'Good. Now open the cupboard,' he said, pointing to a regulation grey-painted steel cupboard in the corner. 'On the top shelf is a blue shoebox. You will find in it an earring in a ziploc bag.'

Santosh rifled through the contents of the shoebox. 'This?' he asked, holding up a pearl earring.

'Now look at this painting again,' Gowda said, turning the leaves of the book to one of a woman suckling a child.

Santosh's eyes almost leapt out of their sockets. He didn't know what to look at. The bare breasts or the earring, which was an exact replica of the one the woman wore in her ear. 'But, how?'

'Precisely. That's what got my attention too. This was found on Liaquat's body. Probably fell off in a tussle. We know that Liaquat was homosexual…' Gowda saw Santosh's mouth twist. 'What? You don't like the word?' he asked.

'It's not just the word. The thought of those freaks…'

'Sit down, Santosh,' Gowda spoke quietly. He leaned back in his chair and peered at a corner of the wall.

Was he counting up to ten under his breath? Santosh

asked himself in amazement. What did I say that riled him so?

'A freak is someone who is a monster; an abnormally developed creature. A freak is someone with two heads or an extra limb. Do you understand? The sexual preference of a man or a woman doesn't make them freaks! Do you hear me?'

'Sir.' Santosh felt a cold finger run down his spine.

'When I was in college, I had a classmate. He was the nicest person I knew. But he was girlish in the way he walked, talked... His gestures were more female than male. Urmila, my friend, has a word for it. Camp. He was what you might call camp. He was teased mercilessly, but he had the gumption to put up with it. Until one day, a group who baited him all the time decided to teach the "freak", as they called him, a lesson. They beat him up and beat the spirit out of him. I don't think the physical abuse hurt him as much as what they did to his mind. He gave up. He probably thought this was how the rest of his life would be. He would be branded a freak and picked on by men who thought it was machismo to beat up someone who wasn't like them. He jumped in front of a moving train somewhere between City Station and Kengeri.'

'I am sorry, sir,' Santosh said in a low voice.

'You should be. I was like you. I was on the fringes of that group that hounded him to death. I haven't forgiven myself in all these years for what I did. My brutish intolerance is something I am ashamed of. Don't take on baggage you will never be rid of, Santosh.'

It was Gowda who broke the silence eventually.

'The earring. Let's get back to the earring. We can safely deduce Liaquat must have been in a scuffle that involved a woman. Right, now what kind of a person would someone like Liaquat be involved with? Thugs, prostitutes and their pimps ... but how would such a person wear such an earring?'

'Maybe it's imitation jewellery?' Santosh said. 'It looks tarnished.' He held the ziploc bag up to the light and gazed at it again.

'I would have thought so too. But for some strange reason, call it a hunch, I took it to a jeweller I know. He said it was a replica of an antique and had been buffed to look like an old piece. It is expensive.'

Santosh peered at Gowda, trying to read his expression.

He had heard about Gowda's instinct. Muni Reddy at Meenakshipalaya station had called it Gowda's sakaath sense. He had made it sound like an extra arm that allowed Gowda to hold a phone, a cup of hot fluids and write a report, all at the same time.

When the sakaath sense nudges him, you know the case is coming to an end. 'Deal time aagithe, sir,' Muni Reddy had said.

Head Constable Gajendra had referred to it as well. Only, he called it Gowda's super sakaath sense. 'You and I, sir, have only five senses. We can see, smell, touch, hear and taste. But he has a king sense. That makes him think differently. When the super sakaath sense is working, you can see it on his face. His eyes become like daggers, his jaw is like granite ... have you seen the Kudremukh hillside, that's what it looks like then. And you can hear a clock ticking in his head. Do you remember that famous Bina case?'

Santosh frowned. 'That airhostess?'

Gajendra nodded. 'She was clever, that one. She made sure the scene was staged so correctly that no one would suspect a thing. I mean, why would anyone suspect her? They were just engaged and, like any engaged couple seeking to be on their own, had gone for a drive. They went towards Bagalur. It is a deserted stretch and while they were there, three men came on a bike, robbed him and her, and stabbed him.

'She didn't know how to drive, she said, though she had a licence. So she had to wait until she was able to flag down a vehicle. A taxi was what came that way first and he was rushed to the hospital. Precisely what you would expect a fiancée to do ... so guess what got Gowda's super sakaath sense into action?'

Santosh shook his head. Gajendra grinned.

'She did it all right, except one thing. When she got into the car, she and the driver laid the fiancé down on the back seat. Now what would a fiancée do? She would sit in the back seat and place his head in her lap. She would cradle him to her ... this was her would-be, after all. Instead, this woman got into the front with the driver. That set Gowda thinking. That absence of grief...'

'It's just experience.' Santosh was dismissive.

'Experience is what helps take the super sakaath sense forward. But you are either born with it or not. Look at Dravid, look at Kumble... none of these new fellows have it, which is why they are getting their chaddis taken in England now... what a disaster. I don't even feel like switching the TV on to watch the cricket... One day soon, you'll see Gowda sir's super sakaath sense. Then you'll understand.' And then under his breath, he muttered, '*Kathegenu gothu kasturi parimala.*'

'What did you say?' Santosh demanded furiously. He had heard every syllable. He knew he had just been called a donkey who didn't have it in him to appreciate the fragrance of musk.

'Sir?' Head Constable Gajendra put on an innocent face. 'I didn't say anything.'

Santosh opened his mouth to voice a reprimand when Gajendra mumbled something about having to go to a layout nearby for police verification of a passport. 'Some friend of Gowda sir's,' he added quickly.

Santosh looked again to see if Gowda's eyes were sharpened knives and if his jaw bore the countenance of the Kudremukh slopes.

'What are you staring at my face for?' Gowda snapped.

'Nothing, sir.' Santosh shook his head. 'I was just suddenly struck by a thought.'

'Well, don't do your thinking staring at my face. I am not a chimpanzee in a zoo.'

'Sorry, sir,' Santosh mumbled. 'You were telling me about the earring.'

'Yes, you can see we have an expensive earring in the possession of a street element. The flames didn't get to it, so the earring was pretty much intact and the hospital orderly must have been honest, so it didn't get stolen. Which is how we have it with us.' Gowda paused dramatically. 'Remember that photo exhibition I was invited to inaugurate and the photo I was struck by...'

Santosh watched as Gowda laboriously moved the mouse to open his email account. Gowda, Santosh saw, wasn't very computer savvy. He could handle the essentials, but he still treated it like a beast that he didn't trust.

Gowda clicked the mouse impatiently. 'I asked them to send me a photograph and they sent it by email. The whole damn art exhibition.'

'Sir, may I?' Santosh asked, rising.

He set the slide show on. One by one the images appeared on the screen.

'That one,' Gowda said, poking his finger at the screen. Santosh winced.

He paused the slide show and opened the image to cover the full screen.

'See what I see?' Gowda asked.

Amidst a group of eunuchs was one who wasn't quite eunuch-like, but seemed more woman than many women he knew. Most of her face was in darkness, but he saw how the shadows accentuated her profile. In her ear was a replica of the earring that lay on the table.

'But how, sir?' Santosh stuttered.

'Exactly. A misfit,' Gowda said, peering at the screen again. 'So, this is what I want you to do.'

THURSDAY, 18 AUGUST

ACP Vidyaprasad examined himself in the mirror that hung in the corridor between his office and the station house. The police constables on duty pretended not to notice as the senior officer preened, looking at himself from various angles.

Gowda walked in and saluted. Everything in his being cried out at having to show respect to this ass of a man. But protocol had to be observed and this morning, he needed the ACP's acquiescence.

ACP Vidyaprasad saw Gowda reflected in the mirror. He frowned. Thanks to this idiot, his holiday had nearly been postponed. It irked him no end to see him here. 'What brings you here, Gowda?'

Gowda saw the constables' eyes glitter. 'I need to talk to you in private,' he murmured.

ACP Vidyaprasad frowned. 'That sounds ominous.'

'It may very well be, sir.' Gowda decided to be cryptic. Hopefully, that would entice his fool of a superior officer into his office.

The ACP nodded and walked into his room. Gowda followed.

'You know I am going on leave this evening, don't you? So I hope you haven't done anything that's going to upset me,' the ACP murmured, hoisting his foot onto the window sill. He flicked off with one finger an imaginary piece of lint that clung to the shiny brown leather. 'A reporter from *Bangalore Herald* is coming to see me in a few minutes. So hurry up and tell me whatever it is that seems to be so important to you.'

Gowda's eyes glazed for a moment. Just for a moment he imagined the ACP crouching in a corner while his boot made contact with that Gillette-smoothened, Fair and Lovely-ied, Cuticura-powdered face.

'Sit down, Gowda,' the ACP cut into his highly enjoyable reverie.

'Sir, it's these murders,' Gowda began.

'What murders?' The ACP's expression hardened. 'The CCB's taken that over. So how does it concern us?'

'I think we should conduct a parallel investigation.' Gowda stared back at the ACP, meeting his glare.

It was the ACP who dropped his gaze first, causing a small rumble of satisfaction in Gowda. 'You think so,' the ACP smirked. 'The big man thinks so!'

'Sir, it isn't just a series of random murders. There is something more. This is a serial murderer,' Gowda began. 'If you will let me explain…'

'Tell me, Gowda, how long have you been in service?'

'Twenty-four years, sir.'

'And you still haven't become an ACP. Ever wonder why?' the ACP asked softly.

Gowda retreated into silence.

'The problem with you, Gowda, is that you think you have a monopoly on righteousness. You think all others including me are idiots in uniforms and that you need to do our thinking for us. Which is why you end up pursuing cases that are destined to be B or C reports. Cases that are no cases. Files that are closed for lack of evidence. It doesn't look good on your record,' the ACP said. 'Think about it. Leave this set of murders to the CCB. If there is a serial murderer, they'll find him.'

'I don't think it is a him, sir,' Gowda burst out. 'That's why, you see, I wanted to...'

But the ACP wouldn't let him finish. 'Oh, that's your angle now. Turn this into a sensational case? You would like your face in the newspapers. Didn't you get your fill when you went after the minister's son in that kidnapping case four years ago? What an embarrassment it was for the department when the girl turned around and said she had eloped with the boy.'

Gowda clenched his fists around the arms of the chair. 'You know as well as I do that the minister bought the girl and her family's compliance.' He counted under his breath. 'Sir,' he began again, willing himself to not let either rage or frustration mark his voice.

'No, you listen to me. There's a lot happening in your station jurisdiction. Several Africans have made it their home. Some of them may have a drug connection. Check on that. A consortium of quarry owners have been sniffing around there. They would like us to look the other way. Police that. It'll do both you and me good. Leave all this serial murderer nonsense to the CCB.'

Gowda rose, defeated. If he were to go after this case, it would be on his own. With perhaps Santosh and Gajendra and the goodwill he had built over the years.

'Look at yourself, Gowda,' the ACP said. 'When did you last go to the gym? Officers have to set an example. An out-of-shape officer gives the service a bad name.'

Gowda sucked in his belly. He needed to go to the gym; he needed to work out. He needed to drink less and cut out smoking. He needed to change his lifestyle. In fact, he needed to learn to kiss ass and suck his superiors' dicks. Then, he would be a better man in the eyes of the world and the police force. But somehow Gowda didn't think he was going down that route.

'I remember how fit you were when I met you first... when you were stuck in that rat hole in Bowring Hospital. Get some exercise, Gowda,' the ACP said, and buried his head in what seemed suspiciously like a sheaf of tourism brochures.

And then something clicked in Gowda's head. Bowring Hospital.

Twelve years ago, Gowda had been shunted to the Bowring Hospital posting. Dowry deaths. Street fights. Road accidents. The mortuary and station records had seen so many unnatural deaths that after a while they seemed natural. Cases were booked, investigations conducted. Arrests had been made and criminals punished. Criminals who were acquitted. But Gowda was removed from all of that. He was merely the record keeper of the dead and dying brought to the hospital. At first, each case was unique. When did the apathy begin? When did the face morph into a case number and no more? Somewhere though, one part of his mind had kept tabs and it was this he remembered now.

An elderly man had been knocked down on the road. It had been booked as a case of rash and negligent driving. Only, the post-mortem revealed something else. His throat had been slit and it was a bleeding man who had stumbled onto the street into the path of a van. The van driver had slammed the brakes, but the elderly man had already been hit and tossed. In shock, the driver pressed the accelerator and, as horrified bystanders watched, the van wrapped itself around a tree, shattering the windshield. There was glass and blood. The driver had remained slumped on the steering wheel till a few people pulled him out. He had been too shocked to protest or even describe what had happened. The old man and he had been taken to the hospital in the same ambulance. One dead, the other unconscious.

The van driver wasn't drunk or on any medication. He had been driving at a sedate 30 kmph. 'The man walked into the van. What could I do?' he wept when he came out of sedation.

The government pathologist pointed out the cut-like wound in the neck. Long rather than deep. Spindle shaped. Clean-cut, well-defined and averted edges. 'Do you see this?' Dr Khan said, pointing to the skin. 'You would think a knife had been used. But I don't think so. I found particles of glass in the wound and on the victim's fingers. If a piece of glass was used to slash his throat, that would be the explanation for the particles in the throat wound. But what about the lacerations on the fingers?'

'There was glass from the shattered windshield,' Gowda said.

'Perhaps. But this seems like fine glass dust. In Hyderabad, where I grew up, we used glass dust like this to make the manja thread for our kites,' Dr Khan said. He looked at Gowda. 'There is something even more interesting. On examining his skull, I discovered that there was a depressed fracture. A roundish hard object had been used to inflict the blow. Just enough to disorient and maybe concuss if applied a few times, rigorously. So the idea was to get the victim disoriented. And then, see this...' He indicated a well-defined, slightly depressed mark on either side of the wound on the throat. 'Ligature marks.'

Dr Khan turned the body around. 'The ligature was tightened by pulling on the cross ends. Do you see this?' He pointed to the marks at different levels.

'And from this oblique marking, it appears that he was sitting down when the assailant applied the ligature standing from behind. Backwards and upward force. We know he was alive when he walked onto the road, but we would have known he was alive anyway by the bruising above and below the groove,' Dr Khan finished with a flourish. 'I have done my job.' Now it is up to you and your ilk to go after the assailant or ignore it, his stance said.

'You just gave what seemed like a sad accident a whole new angle.' Gowda's voice shook with excitement.

Gowda could see it in his mind: The elderly man, seated. An assailant creeping up behind him. The attack is swift: a hard blow on the head that stuns the victim. Then the ligature is used. A ligature that would slash even as it strangled. The victim struggles, tries to prise the ligature away. Perhaps someone walks in then. Perhaps the assailant isn't strong enough. But the victim manages to escape. In shock, in fear, in a desperate attempt to save himself, he stumbles onto the busy road and into the path of the van.

Gowda stepped out of the mortuary, the blood singing in his veins. He would have to take this up with a senior officer and start the investigations.

Gowda thought of the old man. His name was Ranganathan. Seventy-one years old. Gowda's grandfather was the same age. He had been wearing a white kurta and dhoti, and around his neck was a gold chain with a rudraksh bead. His chin was smooth and his hair combed back. He could have been Gowda's grandfather. Who would have wanted to kill him? And why?

Something akin to sorrow riddled him. If someone did this to his Aja, he would have broken his back first and then snapped his neck. He would want retribution.

In the corridor by the mortuary, a group of people waited. A woman in her thirties with a tear-stained face. The daughter or daughter-in-law, he presumed. A man stood by her, his arm around her as if to comfort her. One look was all it took for him to know that they were rich and probably well connected too. A couple of men dressed in safari suits stood with them. As Gowda watched, a police vehicle drove up and DCP Naresh stepped out and came towards him. Gowda sprang to attention and saluted. 'Sir,' he began.

'Gowda,' the DCP said, peering at Gowda's badge. 'If all the formalities are complete, please release the body. I know the family…'

The husband stepped forward. 'Naresh, do you know what happened?'

The DCP looked at Gowda's face, indicating he should

explain. Should he tell them what the pathologist had said?

'I hope the van driver has been arrested,' the woman, the daughter he realized now, cried.

'Madam, it wasn't the driver's fault. Your father stepped into moving traffic,' Gowda began.

'What?' The husband and wife's voices rang through the corridor.

The DCP stepped in neatly, 'Radhika, your father must have had one of his dizzy spells and in that disoriented state... you know...'

Gowda tried. Later, he would make peace with his conscience by telling himself that he had tried. 'Sir, I don't think...' he began.

'Just a minute, Gowda,' the DCP said softly, leading him aside.

'They are my friends. The old man is dead. And there are enough witnesses to prove the van driver is not guilty of negligent driving. Let it be. Whatever it was, nothing is going to change,' the DCP murmured.

'Sir, someone tried to kill him!' Gowda said.

'You are raking up mud, Gowda. Whatever you discover will only tarnish the old man's name. Why hurt the family? They are good people. Respectable people. Do you want to do this? The man was well known. Everyone's going to start speculating what happened if any of this comes out. It's best you look the other way, Gowda. Let's keep this an accident. A bizarre death no one was responsible for.'

'Sir, but there's a criminal out there who will think he has got away with murder!'

'The impact killed him,' the DCP said.

'Someone tried to strangle him; the ligature was covered

with glass. His throat was slit. He would have bled to death most probably,' Gowda said, willing his voice to stay even and moderate.

'Let it be, Gowda. There are so many criminals out there whom we haven't been able to do a thing about. He is part of that list now,' the DCP said, and walked back to the bereaved family.

Gowda stopped in his tracks. Would there still be any records of that case? Looking at it again seemed imperative. Was it the same assailant? If it was, why after all these years had he suddenly surfaced? Like a dormant virus, he had reappeared, many times more virulent, many times more dangerous, and seeking death rather than mere injury.

But first, there was something else that needed to be done. With a wicked grin, Gowda speed-dialled DCP Mirza. 'Sir, just wanted to clarify something. Since ACP Vidyaprasad is on leave from tomorrow, I suppose I could report any developments on the case to ACP Stanley Sagayaraj.'

Gowda's grin widened at the DCP's growl of anger.

'No sir, I wouldn't know ... I don't think he has cancelled his leave, at least that's the impression that I got.'

FRIDAY, 19 AUGUST

It was a little past 5 p.m. at Gujri Gunta. In a little teashop he had identified in the row of shops, Santosh sat biding his time. If you wait long enough, everything you want will come to you, his father often said. Santosh hoped that at least this time his father would be proved right.

The teashop was hot and stuffy. But it was perfectly located, just about 50 metres from the corporator's main gate and at an oblique angle. At 5 p.m., Head Constable Gajendra's watch would get over and it would be Santosh's turn. But first, Gajendra would join him at the teashop and brief him on what had transpired during his watch.

Santosh had worked out an elaborate plan. First a car, an old Maruti 800, had spluttered to a halt at about 2 p.m. Then Head Constable Gajendra had appeared in mufti, riding a moped. He was the mechanic trying to figure out what had caused the car to stall. 'There's nothing wrong with the car,' Santosh had briefed him. 'But if someone asks, say that it has engine trouble and if they're still persistent, you can add a dead battery too.'

'Who's going to ask?' Head Constable Gajendra asked. He stuck his little finger in his ear and shook it furiously.

'The watchman, perhaps. Or passers-by.' Santosh shrugged. 'You remember what you have to do, don't you?'

Head Constable Gajendra nodded. 'Yes, watch who is coming and going. But you do realize that it is a corporator's home. All kinds of people will walk in and out all day...'

Santosh's mouth twisted. It was a grimace he had acquired from Gowda. 'I do,' he said. The grimace said the rest.

Head Constable Gajendra looked at his face in amusement. 'Where did you get that from? Inspector Gowda? Ha! I hope you have picked up a few more things from him apart from that!'

Santosh turned on his heel and walked away fuming.

What was this? A station or a mad house? Every creature here was a specimen of some sort.

The corporator spotted the car a little past 3 p.m., when he stepped out into the balcony on a whim. The goddess had been not easy to appease that day. She seemed reluctant to bestow her powers on him. And Rupali and Nalini hadn't been able to come. They were both unwell, Akka had said, and instead two others had come. They were competent, but the goddess needed more than mere competence. She demanded brilliance. So when the puja was complete, he had felt a great urge to step out and draw in deep lungfuls of air. An iron band seemed to constrain his chest, and a certain weariness.

It was then that he saw the car. A mechanic was sitting beside it, deep in thought. The corporator went back in. He would take a little nap, he decided.

An hour later, the car was still there and so was the mechanic. He went in and called the watchman. 'What's wrong with that car?'

'I checked, Anna,' the watchman said. 'Something's wrong with the engine. The mechanic's waiting for a part, he said.'

The corporator nodded. He called King Kong. 'There's a car opposite our gate. It's been there for a while now. The mechanic claims he's waiting for a part. It's a Maruti 800, not a BMW. What part takes that long? Tell him to shift the car soon if it doesn't arrive,' he ordered.

A little past 5 p.m., when the corporator set out for a meeting in Jayamahal, the car was gone. But something rankled. Something wasn't in its place. He pulled out his cell phone and called the watchman. 'Don't let anyone park anywhere near our gates. And if you spot anything suspicious, call me...'

Chikka looked at his brother. 'What was that about?'

'Don't know why, but something tells me that the car parked by our gate this afternoon was no random occurrence. I think we are being watched.'

Chikka stiffened. 'Who could it be?'

The corporator's mouth spread in a mirthless smile. 'One thing I don't lack is enemies. It could be anybody. Jackie Kumar's men, Chicken Razak's men, some overenthusiastic newspaper reporter, the Crime Branch – I hear Ramachandra has made a complaint and asked for police protection after his dog was found with its throat slit ... so you see, it could be anybody. In the last week, I have added six more people to the list who would like to see me dead or behind bars at least!'

'Anna,' Chikka said, taking his brother's hand between his palms, 'maybe it's time to stop. Don't we have enough and more to keep us going? Do you need to live a life like this? Not knowing who's going to take a supari out on you.'

The corporator patted his brother's hand. 'You worry too much. No contract killer's going to get me.' He withdrew his hand from Chikka's clutch. 'Besides, there is no going back now. Once you are in, there is no way out. It was a choice the goddess guided me towards. She will watch out for me.'

Chikka looked down. He didn't dare talk to his brother when he was in this mood. What about me? he wanted to ask. Who's going to watch out for me?

Santosh took the glass tumbler of tea and blew into it noisily. 'I'll have one of those,' he said, gesturing to a bun encrusted with red and green bits of candied fruit.

He bit into the bun. It was stuffed with shredded coconut and sugar. He took a sip of tea. Something akin to contentment settled in him. Now, if only Gajendra would have something worthwhile to report.

Gajendra walked in, wiping his face with an enormous handkerchief. 'Why do we have to do this, sir?' he said wearily. 'The CCB is handling the case. Why do we need to get involved?'

'Sit down, Gajendra,' Santosh murmured. He turned to the teashop owner. 'One tea.' And then looking at Gajendra, he asked, 'Do you want a bun?'

'I want a bath,' Gajendra grumbled.

'And a bun.' Santosh gestured to the teashop owner.

'What happened?' Santosh asked, his eyes fixed on the corporator's gate.

'Nothing. The watchman wanted to know what was wrong. Then, an hour later, he said the corporator wanted the car moved. It is a no-parking zone apparently. All rubbish! As if I don't know whether it's a no parking zone or not...' Gajendra chewed on his bun hungrily. 'This is rather good. I haven't eaten it before.'

Santosh sighed. 'Did you make a list of everyone who came and went?'

Gajendra pulled out a sheet of paper. 'Here.'

Santosh scanned the list. He took a deep breath. 'Look, you need to be here for some more time. I'll be back at about half past six. Once it's dark, it will be easier for me to blend with the surroundings.'

'You want me to wait here,' Gajendra spluttered. A mouthful of crumbs landed on the table.

'This isn't a game, Gajendra.' Santosh stood up and drew himself to his full height. 'This is official. You are on surveillance duty. So...'

'Inspector Gowda...' Gajendra began.

'Don't even think about it. He knows. He is the one who ordered it in the first place. So if you think Inspector Gowda is going to let you go home, forget it.'

Santosh walked to the end of the road, deep in thought. His bike was parked in a by-lane.

Where was Gowda? There hadn't been a single call from him in the last one hour.

Gowda sat across from Urmila, sipping a mocktail in the piazza. He looked around him with interest. When she had mentioned that they could meet at UB City, he hadn't objected or suggested another venue. It was best they meet in a public place and no one from Gowda's world was likely to go to UB City. At least, not on a Friday evening.

'I'll be in the piazza,' Urmila had said on the phone.

'The what? Did you say pizza?' Gowda had waggled a finger in his ear.

'No, you nut,' Urmila had giggled. They were nineteen all over again. 'The piazza.'

'What's that?'

'It just means an open square... in Italian,' she said.

'Fine, I'll see you in pizza piazza whatever...'

And so here they were in the piazza, Urmila in a short white kurta and blue harem pants and wearing a strangely familiar-looking turquoise-blue bead necklace.

'Do you like it?' Urmila asked.

Gowda took a large sip of his Coco Colada. 'It would be better if there was a shot of white rum in it. This is plain pineapple juice.'

'I did ask you if you wanted a glass of white wine.'

'I can't drink while I am on duty,' he said.

She stirred her drink and peered at him. 'So you think this is duty?'

He looked away. Oh no, there she went again.

'Look, Urmila,' he said, 'I said I am still on police duty.'

She giggled. 'You are so easy to rile, Borei. I am just pulling your leg. Come on, lighten up. It's such a lovely evening!'

'It is,' Gowda said quietly. He should be enjoying this little sojourn into posh life. Lean back in his chair and watch the world pass by. Only, his world wasn't this and he couldn't stop wondering what Santosh and Gajendra had discovered during the course of their surveillance.

'Am I seriously out of shape?' he asked suddenly.

She narrowed her eyes. 'Nothing a few sessions at the gym won't sort out... and less of that chilli chicken and rum.'

Gowda sighed deeply.

'Come on,' Urmila said, standing up. 'I want to show you something. Leave that drink... you can have a proper one after seven p.m. You go off duty then, don't you?'

Gowda rose and walked with Urmila. He felt a few curious glances come their way. Urmila fitted in here amidst all the foreigners and upwardly mobile people. He stuck out. Then as now, he knew that no matter what Urmila claimed, they didn't belong together.

'Where are you taking me?' he asked.

'Do you remember this?' she said, tapping the bead necklace around her neck. 'You brought this for me from

Delhi when you went for the intercollegiate games. All those years ago, Borei. I never bought you a thing. Ever. So, now it's my turn.'

Gowda swallowed. They were standing outside the Montblanc showroom.

'But this is silly. It was so long ago and a trifle. I can't accept this,' Gowda growled. A Montblanc pen! If someone saw him with it, they would think he was on the take.

'But you collect pens, Borei!' Urmila tugged at his elbow.

'Not expensive pens,' Gowda said, pulling back. 'And I don't really collect in that sense.'

'Don't lie, Borei. Your son said you do. And Santosh said the one thing you do like is pens.'

'All rubbish.'

Her face fell. She squared her shoulders and turned on him furiously. 'Why won't you let me buy you a pen? What's the big deal? Or, are you worried that if you take something from me, you will be beholden?'

His phone rang. Gowda grabbed it with the fervour of a drowning man clutching at anything he can find. 'Yes, Santosh, tell me,' he said. He saw Urmila edge closer.

'Sir, nothing to report yet. The corporator and his brother left at about four forty-five p.m. Should we continue the surveillance now that they have gone?' Santosh's voice emerged tinny, flat and clearly audible.

'No, let the surveillance continue. Are you there?'

'No, I am at the commissioner's office. I thought I'll take a look at the SCRB and go back by six thirty.'

Gowda saw Urmila's eyes sparkle with interest. He glanced at his watch. 'Give me a call when you get there.'

'What's SCRB?' Urmila asked.

'State Crime Record Bureau,' Gowda said, slipping the

phone into his pocket. He shoved his fists into his pockets and took a deep breath. He cleared his throat.

'I need to go, Urmila. I am in the middle of a case. I'll call you,' he said firmly.

For a while he had thought he would have to abandon the evening's plan. He couldn't be seen going into the house. Then Bhuvana, or was it the goddess, sometimes they sounded alike, had whispered in his ear: Remember the other gate.

He had slipped back into the house by the side gate. Whoever was watching them hadn't thought of posting a man there.

'Do you think I look all right?' she asked.

'You look beautiful.' Akka smiled. 'What's with you today? I've never seen you like this. All fidgety and restless.'

'I don't know what you mean,' she said and leaned back in the chair. Then she looked at the elderly eunuch and said softly, 'Akka, I have to go out in a little while.'

Akka frowned. 'It's just a little past seven ... are you out of your mind?'

She shook her head. 'You think I don't know that? But I have to be somewhere by eight. It's important.'

The elderly eunuch frowned. 'What's going on? What are you up to?'

She tossed her head. 'Nothing's going on. Can't I go out on my own?'

'It's not safe...'

'I'll be careful. One hour is all I need. One hour and I'll be back,' she pleaded.

'I'll go with you,' the elderly eunuch said.

She nodded. 'Yes. But to a point. After that I have to go alone. I'll meet you at the Muthayalamma temple in one hour and we can return together.'

Santosh sat up as he saw two women leave the corporator's house. He narrowed his eyes to see better. The tall one was definitely a eunuch. Of the other he wasn't so sure. She looked like a real woman.

Santosh slapped a fifty-rupee note on the table and slid out of the teashop. 'I owe you only thirty-four rupees, but I don't have time to collect the change. I'll be back,' he told the bemused teashop owner as he hurried down the steps into the street.

Ahead of him, the eunuch and the young woman hurried towards Seppings Road. If they took an autorickshaw, he would be stuck. His bike was parked elsewhere. But he could follow them on foot if they continued to walk.

The eunuch paused and put her hand on her companion's shoulder, speaking earnestly. But the young woman seemed unwilling to listen. Was the eunuch a pimp? Santosh wondered. Was that what it was all about? Using the young woman to trap men and kill them to steal their possessions? He dismissed the thought almost instantly. That had been Gowda's first theory, but he seemed to have changed his mind.

Kothandaraman, the pharmacist, had been found with all his jewellery and money on him. The murder had a more sinister angle, Gowda had said.

Santosh waited in the shadows to see which way they would go. He still wasn't familiar with many parts of

Bangalore, but he would worry about that later. For now, he would tail them and see where they led him to. At a temple on Seppings Road, the eunuch and the woman paused again. Once again, it seemed to Santosh that the eunuch was pleading with the young woman, who just patted her hand and walked on.

Santosh sighed with relief when the eunuch entered the temple. He crossed the road and positioned himself by a shop and prepared to wait.

Gowda stared unseeingly at the TV. A tight close-up of a shrub, the narrator's drone, but Gowda couldn't focus on the life and times of Walking Stick Insect.

Last week, when Roshan was home, he had wanted him to watch something called *CSI*. 'It's all about how crime scene investigation is done in America, Appa,' Roshan had said, his eyes not straying for a moment from the screen as men and women worked with equipment that looked more space-labish than forensic. Do our forensic people even know about these techniques? Gowda wondered.

Gowda watched for a bit and then yawned.

'Appa, don't tell me you are bored,' Roshan had said.

'You don't really think all of this is true, do you?' Gowda asked, standing up.

'Of course it is!'

Just then, as if to vouch for Roshan's statute of faith, a CSI info bit came on: Did you know that *Crime Scene Investigation* has been marked as a problem for real-life crimes? It was dubbed as the 'CSI Effect' or 'CSI Syndrome' for raising the expectations from forensic science.

Gowda smirked.

'It's only because it's so realistic that criminals know what to do now,' Roshan defended his favourite TV show. Gowda looked down at his son and marvelled at his naivety.

'Perhaps,' he said. 'But you know something, we don't use the yellow tape to cordon off the crime scene area here, nor do we even put on gloves at times; we may not have such sophisticated equipment or methodology, our policemen are out of shape and mostly lazy, but the percentage of cases solved in India is far higher than in the West.'

'That's what you claim,' Roshan said, as the credits came on.

'It's the truth,' Gowda said, reclaiming the remote and switching channels. He paused as a programme on dolphins came on. Gowda dropped back into his chair.

Roshan stood up. 'I'm off to bed,' he said.

Gowda liked watching the nature programmes. He enjoyed picking up little nuggets of information; interesting facts about the world that these programmes were filled with. There were no untidy emotions to deal with; no chance word or thought that led his mind down alleys he wished to avoid. Nature was what you saw and knew. These shows merely enhanced knowledge.

'I really don't understand why you find these shows on animals and insects so fascinating,' Roshan called out from the door.

'Details, my boy, details and not drama. That's what gets me,' he said.

Tonight, too, it was a detail that niggled at him. He knew he ought to remember it, but it just wouldn't rise to the surface of his mind.

The case worried him more than any case had done in a long while. There was no such thing as a perfect murder, but it became one when no one was looking for the murderer. Gowda was certain that all four homicides, including Liaquat's, had been perpetrated by the same person. A serial murderer was at large. No one seemed to realize that. No one seemed to care. What would it take for things to hot up? The death of someone related to someone important? On his own, with just Santosh and Gajendra, he wouldn't get very far. What this needed was a full-scale investigation and a set of IOs who would use paranoia as a device, who would leave nothing unturned and examine every crevice and open end.

Gowda didn't think ACP Vidyaprasad was inclined to work this case. He would rather have Gowda in charge of the Evangelist meeting that was fixed for a week from now. 'Leave all this criminal investigation to the CCB. That's what they are there for,' he had admonished Gowda earlier that day.

DCP Mirza had made sure that ACP Vidyaprasad's leave was cancelled and the ACP was a furious man seeking to vent his ire on everything that came his way, most of all Inspector Gowda.

In the background, the narrator in that monotone so distinctive of nature programme voiceovers intoned: *In nature, to stand out is good only if one is a) poisonous or b) a predator. And even if a predator, blending in helps when stalking prey. The stick insect is a master of camouflage, giving itself away only when it moves. No wonder its name Phasmatodea is derived from the Greek phama, meaning phantom or apparition.*

Gowda watched the stick insect as it moved away from the habitat it had chosen to camouflage in. That was the key, he thought.

This predator too would have to be forced to make a move.

Her heart hammered in her chest. This was the first time she was seeing him after that first night. They had talked every night for a week now. She thought she knew everything there was to know about him. The cold, bare facts. Height, weight, education, family, his favourite colour, the vegetable he hated, his dog's name, the number of rooms in his family home, but when they met, he would be more than an assemblage of detail. He would be Sanjay. Her Sanju, as he said he was.

The autorickshaw spluttered to a halt near Komala Refreshments on Wheeler Road. He was seated on his bike outside the restaurant.

'I thought you weren't coming,' he said.

She smiled and moved into the shadows. Street lamps had a merciless eye, she knew. 'There was some extra work at office, so I had to stay back,' she said.

He smiled at the way she held herself back. The shy glance, the half smile, the shrinking… you hardly saw girls like her any more, he thought with infinite tenderness. Especially in Bangalore. Some of the girls he had seen on the street set his teeth on edge. The deep, deep necklines with half the breasts visible, the short skirts, the low-waisted jeans so when they sat on a chair or on a bike, the underwear could be seen. How could parents let their girls wander the streets dressed like that?

But Bhuvana, his Bhuvana, was not one of those sluts. Bhuvana was the kind of girl he knew his sisters to be. Shy, docile and traditional.

'I can't stay very long,' she said.

'Why? Chikka master keeping tabs on you?' Sanjay murmured.

'Yes.' She smiled and looked at her watch.

'I have to be back at my hostel by nine thirty.'

'Let's go in,' he said.

'No, not here,' she said quickly. 'Someone Chikka knows may see us. On the other side is another restaurant. Let's go there.'

'How do you know about the other place?' he asked curiously.

'Chikka told me about it. He said he was going to take me there as a treat.'

He nodded and pushed the bike off its stand. As they turned the corner, he asked, 'Have you had anything at all after lunch?'

She shook her head.

'Katthe,' he whispered. 'You shouldn't go hungry this long.'

She smiled. He had called her a donkey. But only if there was great feeling could there be such familiarity. 'I couldn't eat even if I wanted to,' she murmured.

'Why? Are you on some silly fast?' he said as he climbed the staircase.

'How could I eat when I knew I was going to see you?' she said quietly.

Sanjay smiled at her. He hummed a popular Kannada song, replacing the word Geetha with Bhuvana. '*Sanju mattu Bhuvana, serebeku antha, baredaagide indhu Brahmanu…*'

Bhuvana hid her smile. That Sanju and Bhuvana should belong to each other had been ordained by Brahma the creator himself…

Sanjay pushed open the restaurant doors and looked at the low lights and the little pools of intimate space it created. This place would certainly be more expensive than Komala Refreshments. But perhaps he could find a corner and hold her hand without shocking her out of her wits.

In the cover of darkness, girls even as demure as Bhuvana lost some of their timidity. A smile tugged at the corner of his lips.

She drank in his smile hungrily. Her heart felt as if it would explode with the weight of the love she felt for him.

He waited for her to slide into the bottle-green velvet sofa set against the wall. Instead of sitting across the table, he slid in beside her. She shrank into herself. He smiled at her tenderly and reached for her hand. 'Relax,' he murmured. 'I am not going to do anything to you even though…'

'Even though what?' she asked.

'Even though I want to… badly. Kiss you from head to toe … mmuwa mmuwa… till you ask me to stop.'

She smiled and hid her face in her hands. 'Oh Sanju,' she said, peering at him through a crack between her fingers.

He was a young man. Not older than twenty-six or twenty-seven. A nondescript young man working in a restaurant on the Outer Ring Road near Marathahalli, as a steward. The hours were long and the pay wasn't very good, but it was a place to start and he had grabbed his chance when a friend who supplied bottled water to the restaurant told him about it. 'Once you have some experience, I'll find you a place in a star hotel,' the friend had said. 'Or in the housekeeping section of one of the IT companies.'

Mohan liked his life the way it was just then. He had fled his little village near Kannur in Kerala, knowing that to live there was to be in a prison, trapped between his family's expectations and social compulsions. But in the anonymity of a big city like Bangalore, he was his own man and he could be anyone or anything. Free to wear the jeans that clung to his crotch like a second skin. Free to flirt with his customers. Free to find solace in the arms of whoever he chose. He liked them both: men and women. Different contours, different pleasures. 'You are just greedy,' a middle-aged schoolteacher with gaps in his teeth and a long curling tongue had told him a week ago. 'You want it all.'

Mohan smiled. He wanted it all. But he was also careful to not take any risks. He waited for them to come to him. He looked down at the man kneeling before him. The man had just given him one of the best blowjobs of his life and would pay him, too, for pleasuring him. 'That's why you like me so much,' he retorted.

But that evening, Mohan made a mistake. A customer at table number 8 had flirted with him even as he walked in. Darting glances his way, leaning forward as he ordered so his face was almost in Mohan's crotch. Calling him back to the table again and again. Chatting him up. What was he to make of it? Mohan liked what he saw; he was flattered by the obvious attention. When he brought the bill, he let his fingers slide over the customer's. And the man had sprung up from his table screaming, 'Get away from me, you bloody homo!'

Mohan had stood stricken.

The man flung the bill and its faux leather folder to the ground. He reached across and with one angry move swept the plate, dishes, cutlery, glass, water jug and the bud vase with a wilting-at-the-edge rosebud in it off the tablecloth. Over the din of smashing crockery, he hollered, 'Is this a restaurant or a pick-up joint?'

The other customers had looked up in shock. The chefs came to the kitchen doors. The other waiters stopped in their path. The manager came running. 'What's the problem, sir?'

'He made a pass at me. This fucking homo made a pass at me!' the man ranted. 'I came in here thinking this is a respectable place. But it's just a whorehouse for gays…'

'Sir, sir!' The manager plucked at his sleeve. 'Please, sir!' He gestured furiously to Mohan to get out of the man's sight.

The man was placated. The rest of the customers returned to their dinner. And Mohan was fired.

'I didn't do anything, sir,' Mohan pleaded.

But the manager was firm. 'This isn't like breaking a stack of plates or getting an order wrong. I don't want to know whether you were at fault or not. I just don't want you here. You can collect your salary and leave.'

And so, at half past nine, Mohan was out of work. As he left the restaurant for good, a violent rage coursed through him. An internal combustion that made him want to push himself to his limits. He wasn't a bloody homo, he wasn't one. He would find a woman, a whore if necessary, and fuck her brains out. He was a man; a proper red-blooded male.

He took a bus, not caring where it went. When it got to a traffic signal near Ramamurthy Nagar, he got out and began walking down the service road that ran alongside the Outer Ring Road. A can of diet Coke lay on its side. He kicked at it furiously. It sailed through the air and landed a few feet ahead, near an intersection where a small lane opened onto the service road. He walked towards it. A woman stepped out of the shadows and began walking alongside. 'Are you alone?' she asked softly.

Mohan muttered, 'We are all alone.'

'You are upset,' she said. 'I can see you are very disturbed.'

'What is it to you?' he snapped. 'Go away and leave me alone. You'll walk with me now and ten minutes later, you'll be screaming rape! Just go.'

'No, I won't,' she said. 'I can see you are hurting. I know how to make you feel better.'

In the pool of light from a street lamp, he turned to look at her. She wasn't bad looking at all. In fact, she was pretty. Then it struck him that something was amiss. What he saw was a man dressed as a woman. Well, if that was how he got his kicks, Mohan didn't mind. He just wanted to fuck and this creature before him was willing.

'Do you have a place to go to?' he asked.

She smiled. 'Of course.'

'Do you have a name?' he asked.

'Bhuvana.'

Santosh looked at his watch again. It was quarter past nine. The eunuch had been in there for almost two hours now. Didn't the temple close for the night?

Suddenly, the eunuch appeared at the doorway. She looked furious. Santosh shivered. He had never seen anyone or anything as menacing as this creature.

She walked down the road and flagged an autorickshaw.

Santosh felt his heart quicken. Where was she going? He saw an empty autorickshaw approaching. He stepped onto the road and waved it down. 'Follow that auto,' he said, jumping in. 'Don't lose it.'

The autorickshaw driver snapped, 'Who do you think you are? I am not chasing after any auto. Get out or I'll call the police.'

'I am the police,' Santosh said with a supreme sense of satisfaction. How many times had he heard this mouthed in the movies; now finally, he had said it. 'Go, go,' he urged.

The autorickshaw wound its way through the streets and soon, some of it became familiar. The Lingarajapuram flyover, down Kacharanakanahalli, across the Outer Ring Road strewn with barricades, earthmoving equipment and giant craters... this was almost their station jurisdiction area... and then Hennur Main Road. The autorickshaw turned into a by-lane and came to an abrupt halt.

The eunuch stepped out and knocked on the door of a rundown house.

'Stop,' Santosh said. The autorickshaw braked, nearly throwing him out of the seat. 'Mind it,' Santosh growled.

The door opened and the eunuch stepped in.

'A group of eunuchs live there,' the autorickshaw driver offered helpfully. 'It's a sort of mother house.'

'Mother house?' Santosh didn't even bother to hide his bafflement.

The autorickshaw driver flicked at his dashboard with a cloth. 'Like you and me and everyone else, even eunuchs need a place to go to. Since they don't have any ties with their real families, they create one of their own with an elderly eunuch or two being the mother and aunts...'

'How long have they lived here?'

'I don't know about that. But I've seen them here for almost ten years now. But why are you so interested in them?' The autorickshaw driver opened a packet of gutka and stuffed some into his cheek.

'None of your business,' Santosh said. 'Just park the auto where I ask you to, and wait.'

'For how long?'

The autorickshaw driver's questions annoyed Santosh. He was hungry, thirsty and tired. But he couldn't think about all that. 'As long as I want you to,' he snapped.

An hour later, all the lights in the house were switched off.

Santosh wondered what he should do. 'Sir, I have to get back,' the autorickshaw driver said, as if he had sensed Santosh's mood shift.

'Drop me back at Shivaji Nagar,' Santosh said. He would have to get his bike back and then ride all the way home. It would be midnight before he stumbled into bed. But he knew he wouldn't be able to sleep, weary though he was. Something had gone wrong this evening. But for the life of him, he couldn't figure out what.

'How much?' he asked as the autorickshaw paused at the mouth of the lane he had parked his bike in.

'You are going to pay me?' The autorickshaw driver craned his neck and peered out at the clear night sky.

'What are you doing?' Santosh asked curiously.

'Just checking if a crow's flying on its back and if the sun is shining at midnight. Such occurrences are known to happen when a policeman offers to pay!'

'You are a joker, aren't you?' Santosh said as he pulled two hundred-rupee notes out of his wallet.

It had been a wasted evening and it had cost him money for nothing. He wondered if he would be able to claim expenses.

SATURDAY, 20 AUGUST

The corporator ate his breakfast, watching his brother. He tore a piece of dosa, dipped it into a bowl of chutney and popped it into his mouth. Chikka, he noticed, was toying with his food.

'You look very preoccupied, Chikka,' the corporator said eventually. 'Something bothering you?'

Chikka looked up blankly. 'What?'

'I asked if something is worrying you,' the corporator said. 'You have not been yourself all morning. And you've hardly touched your breakfast.'

Chikka's head drooped.

'What's wrong? Tell your anna,' the corporator coaxed. It made him feel helpless to see Chikka so despondent.

'It's nothing. I have a bad headache.'

'Too much to drink last night, huh? You were out late?' Corporator laughed.

'I was home before you,' Chikka said defensively.

The corporator flushed. 'Did you see me come in?'

'No, but I heard you,' Chikka said, pushing his chair back. 'Where were you?'

The corporator followed Chikka to the washbasin. 'I had a few things to do,' he said, opening the tap and letting the water flow over his fingers.

'Like what? I know everything that's going on in your life. So I know there's nothing that should keep you out that late,' Chikka said, waiting his turn.

The corporator wiped his hands on a towel and slung it over his brother's shoulder. 'You think you know everything. That doesn't mean you do.'

Chikka washed his hands and wiped them on the towel. Then he carefully folded it and hung it on the towel ring so that the dry end was closest to hand.

He walked to the living room. The corporator was feeding his fish.

'Did you really mean that?' he asked baldly.

'What?' the corporator said absently as his fingers opened over the fish pond and let a fistful of fish food shower over the surface of the pond.

'That I don't know everything that's going on in your life.'

'It's my life, Chikka. I need my private time too,' the corporator said. He turned to look at Chikka. What he saw made his face harden. 'Some parts of my life are best kept secret. Knowing them will change things. It could even put your life in danger. So don't start snooping around. Do you hear me?'

Chikka said nothing.

Santosh was standing outside, speaking into his mobile, when Gowda rode into the police station on his Bullet.

Santosh ended his call in a hurry and rushed towards Gowda. He saluted and said, 'I've been trying to reach you since six this morning. But your phone kept ringing. I sent one of the constables to your house. He said the door was locked.'

Gowda frowned. At times, Santosh sounded almost like Mamtha.

'The bike needed some tweaking. I wanted to check the ignition points and timing,' Gowda said as he got off and parked the bike. 'There's a chap, Kumar. KK Garage at

Kammanahalli. He's a whiz!' He pulled the phone out of his pocket. It was on silent and the vibrator alert was off. 'My mistake. I should have remembered. What's wrong?'

'The control room reported a dead body near Nagawara Lake. There could be no connection. Or…'

'There could be,' Gowda finished for him. He glanced at his watch. It was a quarter to ten. 'It's not our station jurisdiction area. And the CCB's probably already there. But let's go anyway.'

The rush-hour traffic hadn't yet settled. At Hennur Junction, they were behind a lorry that seemed to suddenly develop engine trouble. Eventually, it took them almost an hour to arrive at the scene of crime. An ambulance drove away as PC David found a place to park.

The police had managed to cordon off the area with raised voices and glares. Gowda thought again of Roshan's *CSI* series. The IO and team were combing the area. The CCB men too seemed to have arrived. Stanley greeted Gowda with a scowl. 'I was waiting for you. What took you so long?'

Gowda grinned. 'Bike trouble!'

'You should have asked your sidekick to deal with it,' Stanley murmured, peering over Gowda's shoulder at Santosh, who was talking to one of the team.

'I don't let anyone ride my bike,' Gowda said.

Stanley made a face.

'I know what you are thinking,' Gowda said. '*It's a bike, not your wife*. Other people have said it behind my back.'

Stanley tried to hide his smile.

'You would never understand,' Gowda said firmly. 'Now tell me what you found.'

'It seems your murderer has been at it again,' Stanley said, showing Gowda the pictures he had shot of the body. He had used his digital camera well. No angle had been forgotten. Like all the others, this boy too had a slit throat; a ligature had severed as it strangled. And the wound on the cheek, as though someone had ground something hard into the tissue, tattering the skin and flesh and splintering the bone. Death was never easy on the eye. This one only enhanced the horrific nature of it.

'Anything else?' Gowda asked, chewing on his lip.

They walked towards the tree beneath which the body had been found.

'The cowherd who found the body was too scared to touch it. So nothing had been moved. Apart from the usual signs of death by strangulation, there was nothing strange. His legs were straight and his arms crossed on his chest. The assailant had very carefully arranged his limbs. He had taken his life, but didn't want to leave a messy body lying around.' Stanley sighed.

Gowda nodded, thinking of how Kiran's body had looked like it had been placed on the chair. And Kothandaraman's. A profile of the murderer was forming in his mind.

'There were tyre marks on the grass to show a car had driven up as far as it could go, and do you see this?' Stanley bent down and pointed out two strips of flattened grass that ran from the tyre markings to the foot of the tree.

'The body was dragged from the car to that spot,' Gowda said.

Stanley nodded.

'The body has already been sent to the mortuary for the post-mortem. The dog squad will be here any minute. The case is off your hands now, Gowda,' Stanley said as Gowda looked at the snaps all over again.

'Stanley, right from the beginning, something about this

serial murderer has had me puzzled,' Gowda said slowly, pretending not to have heard him.

'We don't know yet if it is a serial murderer,' Stanley said abruptly.

'Quit playing devil's advocate. You know it is as well as I do. The MO, the positioning of the body, all the victims are males... you know what they say, don't you?' Gowda turned his gaze to Stanley.

'Two times is a coincidence, three times is a pattern,' Stanley said.

'So what are we waiting for? A high-profile victim? Will that make it an important case?' Gowda's nostrils were pinched with rage.

Stanley rubbed his palms absently. 'That's unfair...'

Gowda scratched his forehead. 'I know. I apologize. But sometimes I feel like I am slamming my head against a wall. No one seems to be taking this seriously.'

From the road, there was an almost constant blare of horns and the hum of traffic. Gowda took a deep breath and stared into the distance. A cow with a crow perched on its back walked across the grass, oblivious to the goings-on in the adjoining field. A giant mound of garbage had been dumped by the path. A black plastic bag fluttered and rose from the heap and came to rest at Gowda's feet. He kicked at it viciously but it only tangled further into a clump of lantana. 'Bloody BBMP... can't they do something about this garbage-dumping business? This state is going to the dogs.'

'Have you had anything to eat?' Stanley asked suddenly.

'Why? And no...'

'That explains your mood. Get something to eat and I'll call you when the post-mortem report comes in.'

'I want to be there when the post-mortem is done,' Gowda said.

Stanley sighed. 'Fine. It'll be early evening. Get something to eat first, Gowda. You are useless and a bloody nuisance when you are like this!'

Gowda smiled. They went back a long way. Stanley could say things to Gowda that no one else would dare.

Gowda called for his vehicle. Santosh looked at Gowda's profile. He was deep in thought. 'You were outside the eunuch house up to what time?' Gowda asked suddenly.

'About eleven fifteen, sir,' Santosh said. 'There's only one door. I went back and checked this morning. So the eunuch was there as long as I was there.'

Gowda grunted.

'I don't understand.' Santosh's face was downcast. 'There was no way that the eunuch could have... I was there, tailing her all the time.'

'What about the companion?' Gowda asked.

'Oh, she left at about eight in the evening. She and the eunuch went to the temple and they separated there. You don't think it was her... How could it be?' Santosh spluttered. 'A woman! She seemed a timid woman at that!'

'I don't know, Santosh. But I think we'll know once we see what the post-mortem throws up.'

Gowda didn't speak as they drove. He motioned to PC David to stop at a Darshini. He didn't particularly care for these short-order restaurants that seemed to have a great ability to erase every dish of any distinct flavour or taste. Sameness ruled. But they were reasonably clean and you could be sure that they would serve you food from 6 a.m. to 10 p.m.

Santosh followed him into the restaurant. The tables were

being wiped clean by a boy in grey shorts and a shirt, with a cap on his head. The cloth in his hand was filthy with many wipings. Gowda glowered at the boy. 'That cloth looks older than your grandfather,' he said. 'Use a fresh one. Now.'

Santosh grinned to himself. He had overheard some of what Stanley had said to Gowda. The man's irritability was fun to watch as long as it was not directed towards him.

The boy rushed towards the kitchen and came back with a fresh wiping cloth. Through the serving hatch, faces peered. They saw the uniform and looked at each other. Policemen were always a nuisance. This one seemed to be even more so.

Santosh went to the counter and placed his order. Gowda had said he should eat as well.

Santosh came back with a tray heaped with food. Gowda said little as he ate alternately from his khara bath and kesari bath. He drank the tumbler of filter coffee in one gulp and then he gazed at Santosh and smiled. Santosh almost choked on a piece of oily uthappam he had just put into his mouth.

'You know something,' Gowda said. 'I think we need to break this into parts. Let's start looking at the deceased. Each one of them was a male but not of any specific age or type in terms of looks. The murderer was not looking for young men in particular. It seems to me that the murderer found them as and when. Alcohol and the promise of sex was probably how they were lured.'

Gowda's phone beeped. It was Stanley. Gowda finished the call and put down the phone. His face was grim.

'The dogs found a trail until the Ring Road and then it went cold.'

'Do you think the eunuch's companion is connected in some way?' Santosh's eyes glittered with excitement.

Gowda nodded. 'That's precisely what crossed my mind too.'

'But how? A woman? And she didn't even seem particularly strong.'

'Maybe she's not a woman.' Gowda's voice was even.

'How is that possible?' Santosh put his arms on the table, leaning almost into Gowda's face.

'A transvestite, perhaps?' Gowda shrugged. 'Men who like dressing up as women. And some of them are prettier than many women I know.'

'No wonder the eunuchs I talked to denied knowing anything about the one with the earring. She wasn't one of them.'

'Well,' Gowda said, taking a sip of water, 'even if they recognized her, they wouldn't admit to it. They are very loyal. Besides, you haven't been to the house in Hennur, have you? You need to speak to them as well...'

'So, where do we start looking for this criminal? It could be any man out there.'

'No, you forget we have some idea of what the murderer looks like. We have a photograph even if it is hazy and you have seen her, even if from a distance... I am going to have to tell Stanley. He'll be able to get a portrait drawn from what we have. We'll have more than just a shadowy image of the murderer.'

'And then?' Santosh asked curiously.

'And then, we'll have to see,' Gowda said, getting into the Bolero. Santosh followed, his mind buzzing.

What if he had followed the eunuch's companion? He would have apprehended the murderer before another murder had been committed.

For a moment Santosh fell into a reverie: of having his

photo in the newspapers as the man who had caught the murderer. He imagined the calls of congratulation. The adulation and ceremony. A promotion. More cases to solve. Of climbing up the ladder in giant leaps.

Gowda turned his head. 'Do you know the story of the egg seller who built castles in the air as she walked to the market? I'll sell my eggs and buy a chicken. I'll breed the chicken and sell them to buy a goat. Then a cow, then a house, then a husband. That's who you remind me of now. Remember what happened to her?'

Santosh felt broken eggs drip down his face. Look where you are going, the shards whispered, piercing his skin.

They sized him up. Santosh felt their eyes run over him, pause at every hair follicle and linger at each mole. Their gaze stripped him of every shred of clothing and probed the darkest recesses of his mind. Then they looked at each other and burst into laughter.

'So, Inspector sir, what can we do for you?' one of them asked, moving close to him. Santosh recoiled. He looked at Gajendra helplessly. They were mocking him. They knew that he was uneasy in their presence and wanted him to know they knew. Their resentment frightened him.

Gajendra opened a notebook and spoke sternly. 'Quit teasing him. One of these days he'll become a big shot in the police force and he'll flay your arse mercilessly.'

The eunuch giggled. 'If only...'

'Stop it, Ruku. We need to ask you a few questions. If you answer them quickly, we can go on with our lives and you with yours,' said Gajendra.

The eunuchs sat on a bench. 'Go on, ask us.' Sarita, the one sitting next to Ruku, batted her eyelashes.

Santosh looked away. 'Why can't we call them over?' he had demanded of Gajendra again as they drove to the mother house. Gowda had insisted Santosh go back in the afternoon before they headed to the mortuary.

Gajendra had shuddered. 'Are you mad? Bringing them into the station is inviting trouble. They'll pull their clothes off, scream and shout and make such a commotion that you would think they were being gang-raped. And you can be sure some human rights people will arrive on the spot, and on their heels, the media! No way! We'll go to them.'

'Last night,' Santosh said. 'Someone came here…'

'Someone?' Sarita opened her eyes wide and peered into his face. 'So many people come here.'

'One of you,' Santosh said helplessly. 'Tall, hefty, dark and elderly.'

He took a deep breath and said, 'She was wearing a dark-blue sari with a yellow border.'

'Akka!' Sarita laughed. 'Wait till she hears how you described her. Tall, hefty, dark and elderly. She will be livid.'

'What were you doing trailing her?' Ruku glared at him.

'None of your business,' Gajendra snapped.

'What do you want to know about her?' Ruku grimaced to show what she thought of them.

'What's her connection with Corporator Ravikumar?' Santosh's voice was silky.

'She's his housekeeper,' Ruku replied.

'That's unusual,' Gajendra said, frowning.

'Some years ago, he was beaten to an inch of his life and left near a railway track. Akka found him and nursed him back to health. When the corporator's mother died, he asked her to become their housekeeper,' Ruku said.

'Right,' Santosh said. 'There's something else.'

He held up a printout of the photograph from the exhibition.

'Do you know this wo... er... person?' he asked.

They looked at the printout. 'No,' they said in unison. 'We don't know who this is! Or any of the others.'

Ruku peered at it again. 'The thing is, we don't have to know every single hijra in town.'

'And sometimes they come from other places too,' Sarita added.

Santosh's stare hardened. 'I suppose your Akka will know.'

The eunuchs shrugged. 'Why don't you ask her?'

Santosh stomped out, furious with them and with himself for not being able to prise out of them what he was certain they knew: the identity of the woman with the earring.

They would have to bring in the elderly eunuch for questioning. There was no other way. He would leave it to Gowda to sort that out. ACP Stanley Sagayaraj seemed to be eating out of his hands anyway.

'Do you want to come in?' Gowda asked Santosh.

They were at the mortuary. Santosh hadn't forgotten his last visit here. Bile crawled up his mouth, but he swallowed it determinedly.

'I'd like to, sir,' he said.

Stanley looked away and smiled. He had seen it before. Gowda and his acolytes, who would walk to the ends of the world if they thought it would please him. The boy didn't look like he had the stomach to handle the sight of a body being cut open. He decided it would be prudent to stand behind Santosh, away from the trajectory of his vomit and in place to catch him if he were to faint.

The smell hit Gowda's nostrils even as he walked in. The smell of raw meat. After his first visit to the mortuary, Gowda had gone off meat for a while. He couldn't walk into the butcher's shop without wanting to throw up. Man or goat, we smell the same when slaughtered, he had thought. Mamtha had smiled when he said this and made sure that he never saw or smelt raw meat again. And slowly he began eating meat again. Now it didn't bother him at all.

'This is Dr N. Reddy,' Stanley introduced the surgeon to Gowda. 'I asked for him specifically. He's the best,' he said, patting the young doctor's arm in an avuncular manner.

Gowda nodded. The doctor looked abashed. Then he slipped on a pair of gloves. As he put on his mask, he paused. 'Perhaps you may like to put one of these on,' he suggested.

Santosh reached for a mask with relief. Some of that stench, the mixing of ether and putrefying flesh, the damp from sluiced floors and the chill of death would be less intense with a mask covering his nose and mouth. He watched Gowda and Stanley pull on masks too.

The body was placed on a stainless steel rectangular autopsy table.

The doctor began his external examination. Gowda and Stanley watched patiently. Dr Reddy was meticulous. Saliva swabs. Scrapings from the T-shirt and jeans the deceased was wearing. Samples of hair, both cut and pulled from six different areas of the scalp. Ten envelopes, one for each finger. Dr Reddy ran the apex of a twice-folded filter paper under each nail, holding the envelope under the finger.

Gowda glanced at Stanley.

'He is old-fashioned despite his youth and that makes him meticulous,' Stanley whispered.

Flakes of a beige material fell into the open mouth of the envelope. And something else that looked like lint from a soft rope. Dr Reddy used fine forceps to pull out tiny particles of glass dust from the tips of the fingers. Gowda and Stanley exchanged glances. So far the post-mortem had validated what they knew and had expected to see. Gowda caught Santosh's eye. He nodded briefly.

More notes. List of clothing, general condition of skin. Moles. Marks. Deformities.

Two of the mortuary attendants closed in on the body. They reeked of cheap liquor. 'Sir, shall we?' the shorter of the two men asked. He blinked as to if bring into focus the body that lay on the cold steel table and the service they were usually called upon to provide.

'We do it all the time,' the tall man with the face of a cadaver and bloodshot eyes mumbled. 'Why get your hands… and clothes dirty? Opening up a body is not for the faint-hearted.'

Santosh blanched.

'No, I'll do it,' the doctor said.

The two men looked at each other quizzically. Who was this character? No civil surgeon actually ever got his hands dirty. That's why there were men like them. To deal with the cutting and sawing, the blood and plasma, the piss and shit… they were so used to it that they didn't even hold their breath to stem the stench. And then there was the alcohol. It deadened the senses and calmed the nerve ends. When brandy sang in the veins, it helped them forget that this was who they were – butchers of a human abattoir. The slaughtering was done by someone else. No cries echoed in their ears. Instead, what they heard was a constant gurgling in their ears, blood gurgling even after death. But the brandy settled that too.

'Just wait here. I may need your help.' The doctor smiled at them.

They went into the shadows, puzzled. Who smiled in a mortuary? Was he a ghoul in human disguise? Or perhaps he was on drugs. They saw a great deal of that too.

'The body can reveal a great deal,' Dr Reddy said, rolling up his sleeves. He pulled out a smock he had brought in a plastic shopping bag. 'You just need to know where and how to look for it.'

Gowda rolled his eyes at Stanley to ask: Who is this enthu cutlet leaping out of the pan?

Dr Reddy looked at Stanley and Gowda. 'If you are squeamish, it would be best to leave now. What I have to do is not very pleasant.'

Gowda sighed. 'We realize that, doctor, please continue.'

More swabs. Anal and penile region. Pubic hair combed through. Samples taken. Dr Reddy was doing a textbook post-mortem, and slowly, as the evening turned to night, a picture emerged.

When Dr Reddy paused at the neck, Gowda moved closer. 'This is interesting,' the surgeon said, almost as if to himself. 'Do you see this?' He pointed to the edges of the wound. There were bruises, a reddish discolouration and blood dots around a gaping wound that opened like a smile on the neck.

'It's a cut-like wound. Look at this,' he said, pointing to the edges. 'It isn't a clean incision. This is a laceration. It seems to me that the ligature was used to saw through. See this, the irregular serrated edges of the wound. The epidermis is like an onion. It's built layer upon layer. The murder weapon sliced through the first layer.'

Dr Reddy looked up, his eyes glittering behind his

spectacles. 'The human body is amazing. The skin resists that initial attempt to cut through. It knows it has to protect what lies within. Do you know the epidermis has five layers in itself? But after a point, it opens onto the next layer and the next layer... The pressure was so great that it crushed the voice box and fractured it.'

The doctor probed the wound and then, using a pair of tweezers, pulled out shards of glass. 'This is interesting. Bits of glass...' Abruptly, the doctor turned the body over. He examined the skin around the neck. 'Fine, I understand it now.'

'What do you think the murder weapon could be?' Gowda asked.

'A ligature. This is classic ligature marking. See this...' He ran his finger just above the brown groove in the skin of the neck. 'It is transverse, completely encircling the neck.' Dr Reddy moved away and stood with his hands on his hips as Gowda and Stanley examined the bruising on the edges of the ligature mark.

'The victim was seated when the assailant tightened the ligature by pulling on the cross ends. Do you see this?' He pointed to the marks at different levels. 'This oblique marking is a definite indication that the assailant was behind him when applying the ligature. Backwards and upward force.'

Gowda felt a strange sense of déjà vu. Many years ago Dr Khan had said as much.

'Your murderer is a cautious creature. Let me explain to you. His ligature, made of soft rope, has also been encrusted with glass bits, almost as if it were a manja thread. It has been used to strangle, but with the pressure it also fractures the thyroid, larynx and trachea, and slices through the carotid artery. So, in a couple of minutes, the victim would lose consciousness because the brain has been deprived of oxygen. When the victim ceases to struggle, the assailant tightens the knots. So we will never know at what precise moment death occurred and if it was asphyxia or haemorrhage that finally caused it. Clever son of a bitch!'

Santosh, who had been listening carefully, leaned forward. 'How do you know it is a man?'

'In those one or two minutes before death occurs, the victim will struggle to free himself with an almost manic strength. Not many women would be able to retain their grip on the ligature while this happens. Look at this victim. He is a hundred and eighty-four centimetres tall and should weigh about seventy-two kilos at least. He wouldn't have been easy to handle in the last few minutes.'

'What if he had been struck on his head?' Gowda asked, thinking of Ranganathan and all the others.

'I was just getting there.' The doctor smiled with the affability of a TV chef putting final touches to a dish concocted in ten minutes. 'I was going to say, let's look to see if there is any evidence of that,' he said, moving back to the table.

He parted the hair and examined the scalp. 'I am going to have to shave the hair to give you a precise report. But for now, we can clearly see blunt force trauma. There are contusions,' he said, pointing to a side of the skull, 'and here is a depressed fracture.'

A wolfish smile of knowing.

'This, my friends, is called a fracture a la signature. Or the signature fracture in English. The pattern almost always resembles the weapon used. Something heavy, with a small striking surface, was used to inflict a tangential blow. It's a localized fracture. Enough to disorient a man. And then, in a matter of seconds, the ligature is used to slice and strangle.'

Gowda nodded. Dr Khan had said as much many years ago. Gowda peered at the scalp. 'Would you be able to indicate what the weapon could have been?'

'Something hard, small and rounded ... a hammer would splinter the surface differently. Imagine a coconut being swung against a man's head. But this isn't anything as big as a coconut. A ball of some sort is my initial reading...'

Gowda slipped off the mask. 'Thank you, doctor,' he said, beginning to move to the door.

'I am going to do the internal examination now. Don't you want to see what that throws up?'

'I need to step outside,' Gowda said. 'I need to make a few urgent phone calls.'

Gowda was still lost in thought when Stanley walked out a little later.

'What happened? Why did you leave?' Stanley asked curiously, watching Gowda light up.

'I needed to sort out my thoughts. There's something very obvious that I am not seeing and I know it's staring me in my face, but for the life of me, I can't seem to...' Gowda said, staring into the middle distance. He took a deep drag of his cigarette.

'The post-mortem report is going to be crucial,' Stanley said.

The sun had set and the veranda was wreathed in long shadows. Stanley glanced at Gowda and felt a great weariness. They had a bigger case to sort out. Counterfeit 1000-rupee notes were being unloaded in the state and they needed to be working on that. The impact it would have on the country's stability was frightening. Sure, there was a serial killer at work here. But this was, after all, a scum on scum murder.

Should he just leave it to Gowda? Stanley wondered. He would need to speak to his bosses first.

Dr Reddy stepped out into the veranda. 'You said he's from Kerala, didn't you?' he asked Stanley.

Stanley nodded.

'Can I bum a cigarette?' The doctor turned to Gowda with a sheepish smile.

'Sure,' Gowda said. He pulled out his pack of India Kings, flicked the top back and offered it. The doctor took a cigarette. Gowda turned to Stanley. 'C'mon, have a smoke. I can see you are dying for one.'

A wry smile lit up Stanley's face. 'I guess one cigarette's not going to kill me,' he said, pulling out a cigarette and tapping it against his palm.

Gowda lit a match and held the flame for both men to light up. He watched the two of them draw in the smoke with a hiss of satisfaction as the nicotine flooded their bloodstreams.

'Why did you ask if the deceased was from Kerala?' Gowda asked suddenly.

'I just had a look at his stomach contents,' Dr Reddy said, tapping ash into the ground. 'It looks like his last meal was from a Kerala restaurant. I could see bits of undigested food. Parota, and he probably had some meat with it. Which means, given the state of the stomach contents, his last meal was eaten at about ten p.m. and the estimated time of death would be between eleven and eleven thirty.'

A few minutes later, he added, 'One other thing. It will be in my report but I may as well tell you now. Your man liked to fuck in the ass. He's cleaned himself up after the act or his sexual partner did it for him, but I could still see some traces of faecal matter on his penis.'

'When will you be able to give us the final report?' Gowda asked.

'I'll pick it up from you first thing in the morning,' Stanley said, turning towards Dr Reddy. 'The forensic lab will take time to process the information, but your PM report will be enough for us to start giving direction to our investigations.'

Gowda's jaws clamped. He could see the case slipping away from him.

Later that night, Gowda and Stanley went back to Gowda's home. Gowda brought out a bottle of Old Monk rum and two glasses. 'Soda and ice or Coke?' he asked as he poured Stanley a double large.

'Jesus, Gowda, are you trying to get me drunk or what?' Stanley demanded at the sight of his near-full glass of raw spirit.

Gowda grinned.

'What about some touchings?' Stanley said, drinking deeply of his rum and Coke.

Gowda brought a plate of chakli and peanuts and settled back in his armchair.

'Shall we?' he asked.

'I thought this was a social call…' Stanley sniffed.

'We can socialize after we figure this out,' Gowda said.

'Fine.' Stanley sighed.

They got to work piecing together the murder. It began with a young man thrown out of his job.

Mohan must have left the restaurant at 9.30 p.m. He shared a small house with three other boys from Kerala in Kammanahalli. He didn't go back to his room however.

Someone saw him board a Volvo bus that went to Hebbal.

It was only logical to assume that he would have got off at either 80 Feet Road, Kalyan Nagar or Hennur Cross.

'The bus ride from Marathahalli to Hennur Cross takes forty-five minutes, give or take a few minutes,' Gowda said.

What had happened thereafter?

A call had come to the restaurant manager at a little past one. 'He is dead; Mohan's dead,' a voice had said. But the man woken out of sleep had slammed down the phone in disgust. The little cocksucker was now trying to make him feel guilty, he decided, turning over to sleep. The manager had revealed as much when he was picked up for questioning by the CCB men.

'In keeping with the calls that had been made to friends or family of the other targets. The murderer had a twisted sense of conscientiousness. It wasn't enough to merely murder, he felt the need to inform so that the body wouldn't remain untraced,' Stanley said.

'The estimated time of death is between eleven and eleven thirty. So we can assume that his last meal was eaten in the vicinity. Let's say, a radius of four kilometres,' Gowda said, circling a zone on the city map.

'How many restaurants do you have there that serve Kerala food?' Stanley asked.

Gowda shrugged. 'Quite a few!' He put his hand to his mouth and stifled a yawn.

Stanley looked thoughtfully at the diagram. 'So what are we looking at?' he asked.

'The first thing to do is to make a quick round of all the possible eating places and see if anyone remembers him,' Gowda said.

'I'll ask Santosh to take a couple of constables and a photo of the deceased. I'll ask them to go to every eating place that sells Kerala food within this zone,' he said, tracing the circle on the map, 'and ask around. Waiters. Cleaners. The manager. Parking attendants. Paanwallahs nearby. Let them check if he's been to any of those places. Who he was with, and for how long. This is going to pace up the investigation, Stanley.'

'Gowda, wait, I don't think Santosh should do this. I'll have to send my men,' Stanley said. 'You know this is technically our case now.'

'What do you mean?' Gowda growled.

Stanley shrugged. 'You know what I mean.'

Gowda looked away, too angry to speak. It was like that bloody story about the Arab and the camel all over again. He felt like the guileless Arab who had allowed the camel to stick its head through the flap of the tent so that it may keep itself warm. Before the Arab knew what was happening, the camel had taken over the tent and he was out shivering in the cold desert wind.

SUNDAY, 21 AUGUST

Gowda was in a little teashop in a shadowed alley that he didn't recognize. Urmila sat across the wooden table with a scarred white Formica top. Overhead, an old ceiling fan whirred slowly. He smiled at her. He watched as she smiled back, raised the chipped teacup and dropped it on the floor. The cup smashed into shards of white porcelain. The tea splashed his shoes and formed a puddle of milky brown. 'What the fuck, U?' Gowda began and felt his words escape him as Santosh and the corporator walked towards them.

Then, to his horror, Urmila reached for his cup brimming with tea and dropped it on the floor. The splintering sound of the cup filled his ears. All of them laughed at his consternation. The corporator, Santosh and Urmila, and was that Dr Reddy and his two ghoulish assistants behind them? Peals and peals of laughter that turned into a whickering note of mirth that drew closer and closer until it seemed to buzz through his ears. Gowda woke up, startled to hear the doorbell ringing through the house.

He sat up, feeling like he had trudged up a mountain. Breathless, his heart racing, his eyes clouding over. He glanced at his watch on the bedside table. Quarter to nine. Shanthi had asked for the day off. Had she changed her mind?

He ran his fingers through his hair and went to the door. 'I thought you said you wanted a day off,' he said as he opened the latch.

Urmila stood there with a grin. 'If Mohammed won't come to the mountain, the mountain … etc.'

He gaped.

'I dreamt of you,' he said nonplussed.

She stared at him. 'If anyone else had said that to me, I would have presumed that he was hitting on me. What were you dreaming of?'

He shook his head. 'It's complicated … sort of disjointed. What are you doing here?'

'I thought I'd surprise you. It's a Sunday and you said your maid had the day off. So…' The confidence in her voice seemed to be dipping by the syllable.

'Come in,' he said.

She followed him into the living room, which was a mess of dirty glasses, abandoned food and empty bottles. She wrinkled her nose. 'Late night?'

He grinned sheepishly. 'Stanley, do you remember him? Stanley Sagayaraj, the basketball captain ... he is in the police force too. He's with the CCB and we are working on a case and we decided to bring the discussion here...'

'And did it get anywhere?' she asked, picking up the glasses.

He stared at her for a moment. 'Not really,' he said, the grimness of his tone making her look up.

She put down the glasses and went to him. She placed her hand on his shoulder. 'Do you want to talk about it?'

He turned his head and, on an impulse, kissed her fingers. 'No ... but I am glad you are here.'

She smiled and nuzzled her cheek against his arm. 'Go take a shower. I'll make you some tea and something to eat.'

'A shower would be a good idea if it worked. Mine hasn't for god knows how long!'

She pushed him towards what she presumed was his bedroom. 'Go!'

Gowda stepped into the bathroom. He looked ruefully up at the shower. One of these days he would get around to sorting it out. All it needed was half an hour of a plumber's time and he could have long hot showers. In the meantime, he would have to make do with a bucket bath.

Gowda turned the tap on and adjusted the hot and cold streams. The water filled the bucket, splattering the silence of the house. He wondered what Urmila was doing. He hummed under his breath. He could hear his phone ring in the bedroom. He dipped the blue plastic mug into the bucket and threw water on himself. But the phone kept trilling, ruining the pleasure of water sluicing his skin. If he had been under a shower ... no matter what, he would get the shower fixed this week, he decided.

Urmila was making toast on the cast-iron griddle when he walked into the kitchen. 'You don't have a toaster,' she said. 'So it will have to be tawa toast for you...'

He saw that she had opened the cabinets and found the porcelain plates. At her home, perhaps only the help and the dogs ate off steel.

He shrugged. 'You shouldn't have gone to all this trouble. Shanthi must have left something in the fridge. Some food I can warm up...'

She didn't respond and continued to butter his toast. He watched, amused. 'I can butter my own bread,' he said.

She looked at him steadily. 'Really?'

He flushed.

'Good?' she asked, watching him eat.

He nodded. Her masala omelette melted in his mouth and the toast was precisely how he liked it: not too brown, but with a decided crunch and buttered liberally, so it flooded his mouth with an oozy, silky saltiness.

'Thank you,' he said, sipping his tea, strong and not too sweet, again just as he liked it.

'What now?' she asked. Unspoken questions hovered in the air.

'We are going to sit in adjoining chairs in the living room and read the newspapers. And when it's eleven, we'll open a couple of beers and then I am going to take care of some unfinished business with you.'

She frowned. 'What unfinished business?'

He laughed and reached for her. 'Actually the newspapers and beer can wait. What can't is this...'

She giggled against his chest. 'But you just had breakfast...'

'So?'

'So nothing,' she said.

He pulled her up towards him but it was she who found his mouth.

'You taste delicious,' she murmured. 'Of hot buttery toast.'

Gowda thought he had never heard anything more erotic in his life. Fuck, here he was wondering how he was going to make that first move and she was already taking him into some other realm of desire.

Her fingers crawled over his chest, snapping open the buttons on his shirt.

'Hey, that's what I should be doing...' he protested, grabbing her hand. 'Technically, the man ought to undress the woman first.'

'Fuck technicalities, Borei,' she murmured.

'Mmm ... the girl likes to talk dirty.' He grinned. 'One wouldn't have thought that of Lady Deviah.'

'Are we going to stand here talking all morning?' she said, leading him by the hand to his bedroom.

Who paused at the doorway? She or he?

Suddenly it didn't matter. The need to feel skin against skin overrode all other thought as he turned and, with an almost superhuman effort, lifted her in his arms and took her instead to the guest bedroom. Damn, he thought, as his breath whistled in his chest. How did those heroes in movies do it with such effortless ease?

So this was how love could be made, Gowda thought, as laughter punctuated the waves of passion. Joyous, glorious joy that edged the crest of pure sensation as her mouth found his again and again. As her caresses evoked in him a need to respond and raise her to abject surrender.

She wasn't shy; in fact, it was Gowda who felt as if he was the novice as she taught him all the ways in which he could pleasure her. She led him on a voyage of discovery of his own body and hers. When he poised himself above her, she pushed him down and straddled him, letting her breasts swing in his face. He watched her draw pleasure with an abandon that aroused him as much as her low throaty moans.

Suddenly she leaned forward and licked the sweat off his face.

Gowda groaned and gave himself up to her, to the rush of sensations that pumped through him, one after the other.

When Gowda opened his eyes, she was sitting at his side, watching him.

She touched the tattoo on his arm. 'I didn't ever think I would go to bed with a man who has a tattoo.' She smiled.

He smiled back. He didn't know what to say.

'Why didn't you wake me up?' he asked, trailing a finger down her arm.

'I had some unfinished business,' she said, echoing him from a while ago.

He frowned. 'What was that?'

'Come,' she said, pulling him up.

He rose unwillingly. 'Can't we just stay here?'

'We could. But I want you to see something.'

She led him into the bathroom of the master bedroom. 'Get under the shower,' she said.

'The shower doesn't work.' He made a face. 'I need to get it fixed.'

'I know,' she murmured, turning the faucet on. It came alive with silvery jets of water.

'What the fuck! What did you do?' he asked, as much in surprise as in delight, stepping under the spray of water.

'I had picked up a can of WD-40 from a friend last evening and it was still in the car. So I sprayed some around the shower head, removed it and put it in some warmy soapy water for a bit and then for the pores that didn't open, I used a safety pin from the outside and unclogged them. You could have done this yourself, Borei.'

Gowda soaped himself lazily. 'I could have. But what on earth is WD-40?'

'It's a wonder spray that loosens rusty nuts and bolts,' she began, but the words ebbed as she saw the look in his eyes.

'Get in here,' he said, his eyes narrowing with intent.

Urmila had left at seven. She had a dinner party to go to, she said. 'I would have got out of it if I could.'

Gowda had watched her leave, thinking, she didn't even ask me if I wanted to go with her. I wouldn't have. But she didn't ask.

Already it had begun, the gnawing loneliness, the relentless wondering: what was she doing? Who was she with?

Gowda pressed the side of his glass to his eyes. What am I doing? I am forty-nine and fucked. Unable to love the woman I am married to and furiously entangled with a woman I cannot even dream of a life with. Career in tatters and not a dream to propel me through this bleakness called the rest of my life. If he were to start life again, who could he be? Where would he begin? He was unemployable. He couldn't think of a single place that would have him.

Gowda looked at the time. It was almost midnight. He sat nursing a drink. He felt as if his mind had stalled. He tossed the drink down his throat, then poured himself another drink and took it to the veranda. Then another. And another. At some point, he crawled into bed in a drunken stupor.

MONDAY, 22 AUGUST

In the morning, Shanthi gave him a disapproving look. His eyes were bloodshot and his skin felt coarse and dry. A sledgehammer slammed in the back of his head and his mouth tasted of metal. When his hand reached for a cup of coffee, he saw it shake. Shanthi saw it too.

'It's not my place to say this to you, sir, but you drink too much.'

Gowda sipped the coffee. The hot fluid tasted like bitter dishwater in his mouth.

'We look up to people like you to look after us, sir. And so if you…' Shanthi concluded, walking into the kitchen.

Gowda made a face. He knew she was right. He drank too much. In the light of the day he could hide his insecurities behind a mask of diffidence. Nonchalance even. But as the day wore on, the mask crumbled. It felt more and more difficult to summon up that 'I don't give a shit' armour around himself. But when the first drink rolled down his throat and flooded his bloodstream, some of the inner resilience surfaced again. A light fuzziness that took the edge off every scathing remark. The innuendos and insults became less of a searing, open wound. A lifetime frittered away didn't seem so terrible after all. The rum fumes chased all such dragons away with an ease nothing else could match.

It was a pensive Gowda who went through the motions of eating his breakfast. Tear a piece of akki roti, dip in palya, chew. Tear. Dip. Chew. Tear. Dip. Chew.

He could sense Shanthi's affronted look. She had made him his favourite. And for what joy? It could very well have been the tablecloth he was eating.

At the station house, he was unable to wipe away the sense of dejection that weighed him down. A mountain of files waited to be dealt with. And the closing time of restaurants and bars had reared its head again.

The beat police had found a restaurant-bar in Kothanur that stayed open late into the night, much after the closing time of 11.30. Warnings had been issued, but the restaurant owner continued to keep his establishment open. 'Let them do what they want, I'll close my restaurant when I think it's time and not when they think it's time for me to,' he was reported to have said.

'You should have brought that idiot here and roughed him up a bit,' Gowda said wearily.

'But on what charges, sir?' PC Byrappa had mumbled.

'Don't throw the law at me,' Gowda frowned.

'No, sir, legally he hasn't done anything wrong,' the man protested. 'Each time we go there, the lights are off, shutters closed, etc., and he comes out looking innocent as a lamb and pretends he doesn't know what we are accusing him of. But I know for a fact that he's still serving drinks inside!'

'Raid the place,' Gowda said, flicking through the file. He glanced at his watch. Stanley would be here anytime now.

'We won't find a thing. He claims the back portion of the building is his home. And the men drinking there are friends!'

Gowda slammed the file shut. He would have to make a visit there himself today.

Stanley appeared in the doorway. Gowda stood up slowly.

'Have you been drinking all weekend?' Stanley said in greeting.

Gowda ran his fingers through his hair. He knew he looked a mess, a total wreck, in fact. But at least he had managed to shave, so he didn't seem a complete lout.

'Here,' Stanley said, throwing a file onto Gowda's table. 'The post-mortem report!'

'It's your case, why do you want me to read it?' Gowda couldn't help the note of petulance in his voice. Stanley stiffened.

'Look, Gowda,' he said, not bothering to hide his annoyance, 'I put myself out on the plank there for you to get this case back into your hands. Officially, you are to assist me with this. Unofficially, it's your baby. If you are going to make a hash of it…' Stanley reached for the file.

Gowda put his hand on it and held it back. 'No,' he said. He took a deep breath. 'I didn't mean … thanks, Stanley,' he said. 'I know you are sticking your neck out for me.'

'Well then, clean up. You are turning into a caricature of a man. A middle-aged drunk, a useless son-of-a-bitch masquerading as a police officer so no one realizes that he is a middle-aged, useless, son-of-a-bitch drunk.'

Gowda flinched. Stanley always went for the middle of

the abdomen. He knew how to knock the stuffing out of you without shedding a drop of blood. Blunt-force trauma, Gowda knew, wreaked more damage than a stab.

'I'll get Santosh to start questioning the Kerala restaurants in the area we demarcated on Saturday,' Gowda said.

'Keep me informed at every stage, Gowda. I need to know,' Stanley said, turning to leave.

'And what about you?' Stanley asked curiously from the door. 'What are you going to do?'

'I'm going home. I am going to switch off my phone and sleep till I wake up. When I return, I hope I will be less of a caricature,' Gowda muttered.

Stanley smiled. The last time he had ticked Gowda off, he had brought home the basketball championship for the college.

Santosh and Gajendra were tired and hungry. They had started trawling the Kerala restaurants in Banaswadi and Kammanahalli at a little past noon. One by one. But no one seemed to remember a thing. Santosh produced a photograph of the deceased. But all of them shook their heads.

'Besides, it was a busy time, sir,' one of them said. 'He looks familiar enough. But I could have seen him anywhere. So many people come and go, so unless there was something unusual, why would we remember them?'

Santosh looked at Gajendra helplessly. He had been certain that the glory of the day would be his, but it seemed they would have to return with nothing to report.

Gajendra cleared his throat. 'This young man, our victim, was not alone. He was with a woman,' he said.

The owner of Kerala Magic frowned. 'Here, let me take a look at the photo again.'

Santosh stared at Gajendra. Why hadn't he thought about asking that? He knew what Gajendra would say. He would raise a leg and delicately rub the back of his other leg with it and say, 'Experience, sir … nothing can duplicate experience!'

'So?' Gajendra asked.

The restaurateur peered at the photograph again and suddenly jabbed a finger at the photo card furiously. 'Yes, now I remember.' He turned and hollered, 'Gopal, come here!'

A young man hurried to their side. 'This is him, right? The son-of-a-whore and that bitch.'

Gopal peered at the photo. 'Yes, sir, this is him. I've kept the note aside in an envelope. I'll bring it.'

'We have a takeaway counter,' the man explained. 'So this man, boy actually, he couldn't be more than twenty-two, came four nights ago. He ordered eight Kerala parotas, a plate of mutton curry and two pieces of fried fish. The bill was three hundred and ten rupees. The woman with him offered to pay and produced a thousand-rupee note. We gave them change, they collected the food parcel and left. Next morning, my accountant said the note was fake.'

'How do you know that it was the young man's?' Santosh asked curiously.

'We have two separate cash counters. One for the restaurant, one for the takeaway section. Friday night, the takeaway counter had received only three thousand-rupee notes. The other two are my regular customers,' the man said.

'When is the police going to do something about these counterfeit notes?' he demanded abruptly.

Santosh held up the note and looked at it carefully. 'Soon.

The Crime Branch is working on it,' he said absently. He hoped they were. But what else could he say?

'Did you see where he went?'

The owner shook his head. 'It was a busy night.'

Gopal piped up suddenly. 'I saw them walk towards the auto stand.'

Santosh glanced at his watch. It was almost two. 'Since we are here, we might as well eat lunch,' he said.

Gajendra smiled. He didn't particularly care if they caught the murderer. But he did what he was asked to. Gowda raged at him for his apathy but Gajendra didn't care. This was just a job and would never be more than that. Gowda would have been rushing to the auto stand by now. This one was more human, he decided as they waited for the food to arrive.

None of the auto drivers remembered the young man. Just as Santosh and Gajendra were turning to go, another man arrived. Santosh watched him laugh and talk to the auto drivers. He was a gregarious man who seemed to be on best terms with the world and everyone.

One of the older auto drivers said, 'Sir, you should ask him too. He occasionally drives his friend's auto. I think he was here four nights ago.'

He would clutch at any straw now, Santosh thought as he beckoned the man and showed him the photo card.

The man peered at it and said instantly. 'I remember him. He and a woman. I dropped them off near a factory-like building near Narayanapura. The woman said her house was at the end of the alley and the road was all dug up.'

Santosh's eyes lit up. His hand shook with excitement as he thrust the card into a folder. 'You remember the place, don't you?' he asked quickly.

'I am not sure.' The man grinned sheepishly. 'It was dark and I was in a hurry to get home, so I didn't really look at what was nearby. Maybe if I went that side again.'

'Well then, come along,' Santosh said firmly, walking towards the cheetah motorbike.

The man looked at the spotted sides of the motorbike. 'On this?' he asked hopefully. A sub-inspector wearing a jacket that proclaimed 'POLICE' on its back driving him on his bike!

'No,' Santosh said. 'Gajendra and you lead the way in an autorickshaw. I'll follow.'

Three hours later, when they returned to the station, they saw Gowda walk into his room. Santosh followed him, unable to contain his excitement.

'Sir,' he said, 'your hunch about the corporator's involvement is right.'

Gowda turned around.

'We found the factory. There are no houses nearby. Just a few abandoned sheds. Apparently, it used to be a garment factory many years ago. It was shut down and has been lying vacant for some time now.'

'So what's the link to the corporator?' Gowda asked. He raised his arms above his head and stretched. The nap had done him good. He felt ready to take on the world and the corporator.

'Sir, I made some enquiries. The building belongs to the corporator. He bought it a few months ago.'

Gowda looked thoughtful.

'If we can get a search warrant,' Santosh spoke slowly.

Gowda nodded. 'The counterfeit note ... where is it?'

'I was going to keep it in the evidence box,' Santosh said.

Gowda looked at Santosh. 'I know how to get the search warrant.'

He picked up his phone. 'Stanley,' he said carefully. 'Something has come up. We need to talk.'

Stanley thumbed the 1000-rupee note. There was no doubt at all. It was counterfeit.

'Can you spot the difference?' Stanley asked, pulling out a 1000-rupee note from his wallet. 'Sometimes it is hard to know which is which. So I always keep a note in my pocket.'

He held up both notes. Santosh leaned forward. 'May I?'

Stanley smiled and placed both notes on the table, jumbling them this way and that.

Santosh held up one note, then the other. He looked at both carefully.

'What are you looking for?' Stanley's voice was smug.

'The security thread. I was told fake currency doesn't have that,' Santosh said. 'But both these notes seem to have it. So...' He put the notes back on the table, puzzled.

'Not any more. The new ones, the ISI-produced notes, are very hard to distinguish from the real ones.'

Stanley leaned forward and held up both notes. 'See this, the security thread and the RBI logo are distinct. But this one is hazy. The counterfeit ones can't get that absolutely right!'

'There is a whole list of directives. Like the hazy security thread. The three watermarks – the Ashoka pillar, the denomination and RBI – are prominent on the real ones and not so prominent on the counterfeit. See this, the alignment of the register on the left side of the watermark. Those bloody fellows didn't even spare the Mahatma. His eyes and spectacles are thicker in size. And the sprinkled dots are visible when you hold it up in UV light. The fake ones won't show that ... the RBI wallahs have more specifics. Like the size and alignment of the series prefix and distinctive numbers are smaller in the fake ones, not in line, unlike in the original ones. And the paper used, that's made of wood pulp.'

Santosh looked dazzled by Stanley's revelations.

'And I am only talking about what the D Company, that is, Dawood Ibrahim's people, produce and smuggle into India. Those bastards use our own people to bring it back.'

Gowda frowned. 'What do you mean?'

'Hyderabad has been the receiving port. There are workers from Nizamabad, Kadappa, Karimnagar who go to the Gulf on work, so they are used as conduits. These chaps are so grateful for a free ticket that they don't mind bringing back a suitcase packed with perfume, clothes, etc., not knowing that the counterfeit currency is packed in carbon paper beneath. Or in a photo album...' Stanley sighed. 'We are doing our best, although now the racket's shifted to Bangalore and it's coming by road. But I know all of this anyway.'

'Well, what you don't is that the woman who was with Mohan, the murdered boy, was the one who paid with this note,' Gowda said.

'But there's no knowing where she got it from,' Stanley said, frowning at what seemed like Gowda's almost childish glee.

'No, we don't. But we could ask her. There is something I have to tell you, but don't blow your top, okay?' Gowda said, darting a glance at Santosh.

'On a whim, last Friday, Santosh had gone to Shivaji Nagar. He ended up near Gujri Gunta. And somehow ended up near Corporator Ravikumar's house,' Gowda began.

Stanley's mouth tightened into a thin line. 'And?'

'You don't look very pleased?' Gowda said, surprised at Stanley's reaction.

'I'll get to that later. Now tell me what you have to say.'

'Well, Santosh saw two people leave the place in the evening. One, a eunuch, and the other who seemed like a regular female. Since we have been wondering about a possible eunuch connection, Santosh followed them. He managed a good look at the woman: weight, size, colour of clothes. Unfortunately, he stuck close to the eunuch and had to let the other one go when they separated. Now, the restaurant people and the auto driver both mentioned a woman who seems to be the one who was with the eunuch. And the auto driver said he dropped the woman and Mohan near an abandoned factory, which we discover is the corporator's.'

'I should charge-sheet you for this, Gowda. You had no business mounting a surveillance on the corporator without clearing it with me.' Stanley's face was grim.

'What surveillance?' Gowda said, hoping the injured note in his voice sounded genuine enough.

'Don't fuck with me, Gowda,' Stanley muttered.

'Sir, I was looking for a spare part for my bike,' Santosh piped up. 'I happened to be...'

Stanley silenced him with a glare.

'You are missing the forest for the trees,' Gowda said, inspecting his nails.

'And don't throw literature at me,' Stanley snapped. 'I did *Macbeth* in college too.'

'No, Stanley. Listen to me, I think the corporator's involved in some way. The serial murders and the counterfeit currency seem to have him as a common denominator. One other thing. The eunuch who was with the woman is his housekeeper. I don't know if there is a real link, or if he's a link to the link.'

Stanley sniffed. 'That's precisely why I am not going to take any action. But Gowda, you are on a very slippery slope here. Do you hear me? And what you would do good to remember is, you take me with you when you go down. You have to clear everything you do with me. On this case, I am your senior officer ... do you understand?'

Gowda nodded. He could feel that familiar hopelessness settle in him. Stanley was driven by the need to bust the counterfeit ring. The murders were a by-the-way sort of a case. He would do nothing to jeopardize the primary case. A warrant or bringing in the eunuch for questioning would alert the corporator and probably ruin Stanley's plans. Meanwhile, the murderer, whoever he or she was, would be free to continue.

'There's something else,' Gowda said, trying to formulate the thought as it occurred to him. 'The first victim, who we presume was the first victim, was targeted about a month ago. The next one, three weeks after that. But the one after that, a week after. And this one a week ago. So the murderer seems to have accelerated. Almost as if he or she can't stop. We have little less than four days before another young man is killed. Are we just going to wait and watch?'

Stanley stared across the room.

'And, sir,' Santosh spoke up. 'I don't know if this is of any relevance, but the old factory was sold to the corporator only two months ago. It may mean nothing...'

'Or everything,' Gowda finished for him.

Stanley slumped into a chair. He reached for the glass paperweight on the table and placed it on the palm of his hand. Gowda and Santosh watched Stanley stare into it as though it held the answer he was searching for.

Gowda cleared his throat. 'We could tell him that we need to search the factory for a case that went back, say, six months ago. And if there's something there, we can take it to the next step.'

Santosh felt as if his chest would burst with the pressure of the air trapped within. He didn't dare exhale. What if it changed the tide of Stanley's peregrinations? What if it collided with Gowda's star and was pushed off its path? What if it got Gowda's goat? Gowda had snarled at him for lesser offences.

Stanley considered the glass paperweight once again. 'We don't see too many of these any more,' he said, holding it up to the light.

Gowda clenched his jaw, reached forward and took the paperweight away. 'I'll arrange for a truckload of these if you like it so much.'

'I don't, actually.' Stanley smiled.

'So?' Gowda prodded.

'So I'm going to arrange twenty-four-hour surveillance of his house. In the meantime, you can have the warrant to search the factory premises. Only the factory premises. We'll take it from there.'

Santosh's breath exploded in his chest.

Mamtha called. When was he coming to Hassan next, she asked.

Gowda felt the skin on his forehead pleat into a frown. 'I am in the middle of a case,' he said. 'You can't expect me to keep coming to Hassan every second week.'

What was going on? she demanded to know.

What was going on? he thundered back.

'Roshan talks of art shows and dinner parties. Places you took him to. All the people he met. You seem to have time for all of that now that you are alone. When I was there, it was always work, work, work.'

Gowda grunted. 'This was work too.'

'Who is this Urmila? You seem to be spending a lot of time with her.'

Gowda felt his heart sink.

'Mamtha, what's wrong with you? She is a college friend who's back in Bangalore.' Gowda spoke the truth as it were, knowing that sometimes the truth can conceal much more than any lie could.

'Oh.' Mamtha retreated into a silence.

Gowda could sense her embarrassment.

'So, how was your day?' he asked, affecting a heartiness he didn't feel.

When Mamtha had finished describing her long tedious day, Gowda waited for her to ask him about his. But Mamtha had to go and then the phone rang again.

It was Urmila. Gowda held his breath. Something akin to guilt washed over him. This friendship, this whatever-it-was with Urmila, wasn't doing right by Mamtha. And yet it felt so good, so right.

'How was your day, Borei?' Urmila asked.

Gowda studied his fingernails. How was it the woman who was your wife, the one who was supposed to be companion and soul mate, didn't even feel inclined to ask about his day? While another woman, whose role in his life was tenuous, was so interested in the warp and weft of his daily life.

'Rather strange,' he said. Mamtha seemed to have clamped his tongue.

'You sound distracted. What's wrong?' Her voice felt like a caress on his brow.

But Gowda couldn't speak. He was too churned up inside. The many loose ends danced in the periphery of his mind. Loose ends he may not even be allowed to tie up because it was his case only unofficially.

Gowda mouthed a platitude into the phone and ended the call.

TUESDAY, 23 AUGUST

'I've had a strange feeling since morning,' the corporator said, scratching Tiger's head.

'What kind of strange feeling?' Chikka asked, looking up from the statement of accounts Anna had asked him to check.

'I have this feeling that someone is watching me. I had my men check, but they said the street was clear.' The corporator stood up and went to the window. He peered out and then pulled the heavy curtains back in place.

'Are you sure you are not imagining it?' Chikka asked slowly.

'I don't imagine things,' the corporator said, rubbing his chin with the heel of his palm.

He looked at Chikka for a long moment and said quietly, 'There are days when I wonder if all this is worth it. There are days when I want to escape and start life again as someone else.'

The corporator stared at the man in dismay. He ran his fingers through his hair and asked slowly, 'You are sure? You are really sure?'

The man nodded. 'My source is reliable, Anna. He wouldn't lie about a thing like this.'

He watched Anna pace. He had never seen him look so agitated, so out of control. You couldn't flap Anna, no matter what. If you were to tell him that the sky was falling, he would merely smile that slow smile of his and say, 'So, let it fall. I'll find someone up there who'll know how to stop it falling! Everyone has a price, you see!'

But not this morning. Anna was behaving just like anyone else would if they knew they were being watched by the police.

'I'm cleaning up the whole business, you know that, don't you?' The corporator stopped near the window, parted the drapes and looked outside. There was nothing on the street. What had he expected anyway? They were getting better and better at it and now they could access mobile phone records as well.

The man cleared his throat. 'I heard.'

'It's not worth the risk. But I still have one last consignment to take to Kerala. What happened to the man you were going to bring?' The corporator drew the drapes and picked up the tumbler of coffee he had been drinking when Ibrahim had arrived, asking to speak to him urgently. The coffee was tepid and a skin had formed on its top. The corporator made a face and slammed the tumbler down.

'Since morning, it's been one thing or the other. Whose face did I see when I woke up?'

Ibrahim looked at the floor as if to say 'not mine! Who did you sleep with last night?' There were all kinds of rumours about Anna but none of them paid any attention to what they heard. Anna was their big brother, and sometimes when one's big brother does something strange, you look away.

'Have you found someone suitable yet?' Anna asked again. He leaned towards the wall and pressed a switch. Somewhere within the house a bell rang.

'There's a boy,' Ibrahim began.

'No children. I told you that.'

A woman slid into the room. Ibrahim looked at her in surprise. So it was true after all, what he had heard. Anna had a bunch of chhakkas in his house.

'Akka,' the corporator said, 'I need some coffee. And some tea for him.' He gestured at Ibrahim. 'And if there's any naastha left, bring it over.'

The eunuch's eyes raked Ibrahim. Anna didn't extend hospitality to any of his minions. What had brought this on? Tea and tiffin! What next?

Ibrahim licked his lips. What had come over Anna? In all these years, not once had he offered him a glass of water and suddenly he was being given tea and nibbles.

Anna wasn't a kanjoos. In fact, he was generous to a fault. New clothes, sweets and an envelope of cash for the Hindus for Diwali, and for the Muslims at Eid. Sometimes a gift box would arrive at their homes for no real reason. Anna had an open palm, but he didn't open his home to anyone who worked for him or with him. So why was he suddenly being so hospitable? He really must be perturbed.

'No, Anna, I'm fasting,' Ibrahim burst out. 'Thanks very much, Anna, but no, no, please, I don't need anything.'

He saw the eunuch try and hide a smile. The eunuch had seemed as surprised by Anna's sudden burst of hospitality.

Anna made a sweeping move of his arm. Whatever.

'He's not a child, Anna,' Ibrahim said. 'A young man in his late twenties. Looks like the son everyone would want to have. Well-built, soft-spoken. No one will suspect him at all.'

'Where did you find him?'

Ibrahim flushed. Then, with an almost coy grin, he said, 'At Boobi ma's.'

Anna's eyebrows rose. Boobi ma ran a whorehouse in Tannery Road area. Or used to. He thought she had retired. 'She's still around?'

'Boobi ma's too old. Though some of her old customers still come to her. But her daughter's young and there are a few other young women.' Ibrahim's expression softened at the thought of the pretty girl with her turned-up nose. He was going to ask for her the next time. 'Boobi ma's son introduced him to me. The new boy and I got talking and he seemed perfect for what we had in mind.'

'You trust him?' The corporator rubbed his left temple with his index finger to relieve the pressure building up there.

'I handpicked him myself. He is trustworthy. But is anyone fully trustworthy? I don't know ... but we have to take our chances.'

The corporator pressed one nostril shut and drew in air noisily. 'My sinuses are all clogged,' he said in explanation.

'Steam inhalation helps,' Ibrahim said.

The corporator nodded. 'And you have briefed him already.'

'I have told him what is expected of him. Not the details. We'll keep that for the last minute.' Ibrahim lowered his voice. 'Especially as the police seem to be moving in.'

The eunuch appeared with a tumbler of coffee on a tray. Silver, Ibrahim noticed. The gossip was Anna's dog had a silver water bowl and Anna shat in a gold pan.

'Akka, your phone...' The corporator stretched his hand out. The eunuch looked nonplussed. Then, from deep inside her blouse, she pulled out a phone.

'I'm going to have to use your number for a while, Akka. Here, Ibrahim, take this down. You call me on this to inform me about anything confidential. But don't forget to call once in a while on my number. I don't want them to know I know.'

Ibrahim grinned.

'I'll call you later this evening or tomorrow. I need to meet this boy. See for myself if he is all that you say he is.' Anna sipped his coffee with a loud slurp.

Ibrahim turned to go.

'One more thing,' Anna called. 'I don't want anyone coming here for a few days. Pass the word around.'

The eunuch watched Ibrahim leave. She licked her lips, unable to make up her mind. 'Ruku called this morning.'

The corporator waited for her to continue.

'The police were at the mother house, wanting to know about me and what my role in your home is. Do you think I should go away for a few days?'

'You are not going anywhere, Akka,' the corporator said. 'Besides, the police have set up shop outside our gate anyway. We just have to be careful.'

The eunuch stared. 'What are we going to do?' A whisper.

'Nothing. As long as we do nothing, we'll be safe. It'll give me time to plan how to go forward. For now, we just sit on our arses and wait.'

'My boys just called in with their report,' Stanley said. 'They didn't see any unusual comings and goings. The phone calls too haven't revealed anything that would interest you.'

'Tell me,' Gowda whispered into the phone. 'Has the surveillance thrown up anything that has anything to do with the counterfeit currency?'

'Hmmm...' Stanley mumbled. 'Early evening, a man called Ibrahim arrived. We've had our eyes on him for a while. After he left, the corporator's phone went significantly slow.'

'So?'

'So, I think one of ours is on the corporator's payroll and he's passed the word on about the surveillance.'

'Can you get Ibrahim?' Gowda asked.

'What?'

'I said, can you get Ibrahim picked up?'

'Listen, Borei, these fellows won't squeal no matter what. And they come in mouthing the Human Right Commission's guidelines. I don't want trouble.'

Gowda laughed. 'We can make him talk without inflicting a single bruise on him. Or, at least, Gajendra will. He's the expert. I am still learning from him...'

'What do you mean?' Stanley couldn't hide his curiosity.

'You'll see. Trust me. But we have to grab Ibrahim asap. Once Ramzan's over, it will be difficult...'

'What's the connection with Ramzan?' Stanley asked.

'I can't explain now but Ramzan is part of the process … it will make everything that much easier. Trust me, Stanley, he will talk.'

WEDNESDAY, 24 AUGUST

The factory was in the middle of a field. On the other side of the road they were driving down was a quarry. A thin veil of grey dust hung over it as stone was cut and crushed to form gravel. Gowda's eyes narrowed at the sight of the ravaged landscape. Deep gouges, mountains of gravel and the constant whirr of the crusher as it reduced sheets of rock into pea-sized bits.

'The factory stopped functioning almost fifteen years ago,' Santosh said, as they turned towards the building. 'The woman told the auto driver that her house was at the end of this alley and the road is all dug up.'

The road was dug up. In fact, it was a sea of mud. It had rained the night before and the road had turned into a stretch of puddles and slippery slopes. Beyond it was nothing but an abandoned vineyard with cement posts standing in sentinel rows under the open skies. Further away was a row of gnarled trees, a few broken-down buildings and a derelict temple. But no houses of any sort.

'What is this place?' Gowda asked curiously.

'The owner was a bit of a nut case, I heard. I've been making some enquiries. He ran a garment factory here. Long before the IT companies started doing it, he would bring the employees in a bus. Alongside the factory was this vineyard. All of this, thirty acres in all, was his and he came here every day till he died. The family put an end to everything after his death and the corporator bought it off them,' Santosh replied, waiting for the man lurking outside the gate to open the padlock and chain.

The police vehicle drove up the gravelled pathway towards the main door.

The man pushed the gates back in place and ran to open the door. 'Anna said you would be coming. I have been waiting here for you all morning,' he said in explanation for his presence.

Gowda raised an eyebrow. Santosh leaned forward. 'Anna?'

'Corporator Ravikumar. We call him Anna! He is our big brother...'

He turned back to the door and slid a key into the giant lock. He pushed the bolt back and the door swung back quickly and easily.

'So Anna comes here often?' Gowda's tone was bland.

The man cocked his head. 'Hardly. There's nothing here but some broken bits and pieces of old sewing machines. Anna's going to turn this into a dairy farm. And there will also be an orphanage and old-age home...'

'Did you say your Anna's name is Mohandas Karamchand Gandhi?' Gowda asked carefully. Santosh muffled a laugh.

The man shook his head, refusing to take umbrage. 'He could very well be another Gandhi.'

Santosh decided to step in before the man clammed up. 'Tell me, Manjunath, that's your name, right? Tell me, Manjunath, what about the quarry? Won't it be a nuisance? The noise, the dust...'

The man smiled. 'You see, the beauty of it is that the quarry belongs to Anna too. Once everything's functional here, he'll close it down.'

Gowda could see the beauty of it. As long as the quarry worked, no one would buy the factory and the land. The owners must have gone down on bended knees to thank the corporator when he made them the offer. He must have got it for almost nothing, the bastard, Gowda thought, surveying the acreage from the doorway.

He followed the man into a veranda from which a warren of rooms opened. Once, it must have housed the administrative part of the business. A thick sheath of dust covered the floor. The whine of the stone crusher filled the room. Dust rose as the man opened a window. Gowda coughed. He pulled out his handkerchief and covered his nose. The man led the way through a central corridor onto the factory floor.

The false ceiling beneath the asbestos roofing was broken in parts. Remnants of ceiling lights were still attached to beams rigged expressly for that purpose. The windows were latched shut and there was an odour of mustiness and rodent urine. Manjunath pushed open a window. A rat scuttled from a pile of rubbish and disappeared into what was once a built-in rack system.

Gowda looked around him.

It was empty except for a lone sewing machine and a heap of wooden planks, a broken chair and parts of sewing machines.

'There used to be three hundred workers in this room,' Manjunath said. 'Imagine!'

Gowda shuddered. Three hundred workers in a room that could hold two hundred. No wonder he had chosen to locate his factory so far away. It had been a sweat shop.

Probably the sweat from one brow running down to the arm of another. How had they borne it?

'What happened to the machinery?' Santosh asked curiously.

'The daughter sold it after her father's death,' Manjunath said. 'If it had been a son, he would have continued his father's business. What can a daughter do?'

Gowda hid his smile. If Urmila were to hear him, she would probably impale him on a spike with a sternly spoken 'this is what daughters can do, you sexist oaf!'

On the other side of the factory floor was a door that led to the packing and dispatch section. 'And this was the office room,' Manjunath said, leading them to a room with sheet glass for a wall.

Gowda frowned. The rest of the factory was wreathed in dust and giant cobwebs. But this room was clean. There was a table and two chairs, and an old maroon-coloured Rexine sofa-cum-bed.

'Where does the door lead to?'

'To the car park. The owner didn't like using the main entrance. He had his own entrance,' Manjunath said.

'There, that's him.' He pointed to a series of framed photographs mounted on the wall.

Gowda moved closer to peer at them. In one, the man was in a suit in a busy street in some foreign city. In another, he was shaking hands with Venkatasubbiah Pendekante, governor of Karnataka. In the last one, he sat flanked by his family on either side. Daughter. Son-in-law. Grandchildren.

'I think his name was Ranganathan,' Manjunath said.

Gowda didn't respond. He stared at the photograph, again remembering the body on the mortuary table; the grieving daughter, the son-in-law and his important connections.

'You know something, sir,' Manjunath said. 'Anna's father used to work here as a watchman. And Anna used to come here as a boy with his father. Isn't it destiny that a mere worker's son is now lord and master of all this?'

Gowda stared at the man unseeingly. He reached across and pulled at the cord. The Venetian blind clacked down smoothly, shutting the factory floor out. Gowda looked around the room again.

Someone came here regularly, no matter what Manjunath claimed. Someone who used the side entrance door. Someone who had wiped the dust off surfaces, opened and closed the blind. 'Where's the key to the door?' he asked.

'I think Anna has it. Have you seen what you wanted to?' Manjunath asked, glancing at his watch.

'Not yet...' Gowda began and paused. From the corner of his eye, something had caught his attention. In the crevice between the sofa back and seat was a pale-brown fleck attached to a small line of black. He bent down and used his handkerchief to extract it.

A hairslide and, attached to it, a withered jasmine. Gowda wrapped his handkerchief around it and slid it into his pocket thoughtfully. Someone had been here a few nights ago.

He stood gazing at the photographs again.

'So did you find what you were looking for?'

Gowda turned around abruptly. The corporator stood before him and, as always, a few steps behind was his runt of a brother. When had they crept in here? But Gowda was adept at camouflaging his feelings and retorted in a clipped voice, 'It depends!'

The corporator nodded as though that was the answer he would have expected anyway. Gowda saw the younger brother's eyes narrow. He was very protective of his anna, Gowda had heard.

'I have had this place only for two months now, Inspector. You can hardly hold me responsible for what happened here before that...' the corporator said with a smile. A disarming smile, if I didn't know better, Gowda told himself.

'But you know this place well enough,' Gowda said quietly.

'What are you insinuating, Inspector?' It was the brother who spoke up.

Gowda looked at him in surprise. The boy had spoken in English, unlike his older brother, who could speak only Kannada, Tamil and Dakhani Urdu.

'Ramesh went to college,' the corporator said, throwing a fond look at his sibling, who seemed to be bristling on his behalf. 'I never went beyond the fifth standard. But he is an MA, the first in our family. And he has a black belt in karate. Are you a postgraduate, Inspector?'

Gowda held up his hand to stem the corporator's eulogy of his brother. 'Enough,' he snapped. 'I didn't ask for your brother's bio-data. All I asked was if you were familiar with this factory.'

'We both are,' Chikka said. 'Our father used to work as a watchman here. We came here when we were children. So we know this place well.' He went to stand by his brother.

'When did you come here last?' Gowda asked.

The corporator frowned. 'A week ago, I think. The engineer who's going to help convert this factory into a dairy farm came with me. Why?'

'I hear you have grand plans for this place. An old-age home, an orphanage...'

The corporator met his brother's glance. 'Someone's been talking, I can see!'

'I told you, Anna, there was no need for you to discuss your plans with Manjunath. He has a mouth like a pot without a bottom,' Chikka muttered.

'Is it wrong to help the destitute, Inspector?' The corporator smiled again, opening his hands out in a gesture of not knowing.

Gowda ignored the corporator and turned to the younger brother. 'So Mr Postgraduate, tell me about all those Ravi Varma prints in that mansion you two live in.'

Santosh stared at Gowda, amazed. What was he doing?

The young man bit his lip as if to control his fury. Then he spoke carefully, imitating, it seemed, his older brother's silken tones. 'Is it a crime to hang up Ravi Varma prints?'

'Did I say that? I was just curious.'

'Well then, I like them. I like art, Inspector, and Anna gave me a free hand to choose what to put up on the walls. Does that satisfy you, Inspector?'

Santosh hissed. Gowda grinned. 'I like you, Chikka.'

'I don't think I can reciprocate the emotion,' Chikka snarled. 'I don't like men like you. Full of yourself. Full of how superior you are to the rest of us. Full of answers even if you don't know an ant from an arsehole.'

'Hush, Chikka.' The corporator put his hand on the young man's arm. 'What is all this about?'

'Hot-headed, is he?' Gowda asked, putting on a concerned expression. 'Not good at all. You must advise him.'

'What do you want, Inspector? What is it you are looking for?'

'I would hardly tell you, would I, Caddy Ravi?' Gowda

walked to the door. 'Did you think I wouldn't find out your street name?'

'That was a long time ago, Inspector. We don't always stay in our past.' The corporator's eyes alone gave away the extent of his fury.

'I can see that,' Gowda said, his gaze falling on the car parked outside. A brand-new Honda CRV. In the sunlight, its whiteness gleamed. Leaning against it, with his arms crossed, was a boulder of a man. Anna's driver and bodyguard. He had a name. Godzilla? No, it came to him now. King Kong.

People like the corporator made him furious. It seemed to him that they knew precisely how to work the system to their advantage. They knew which holes to plug and which knots to untie so the system worked for their benefit alone. People like the corporator made Gowda feel even more like a loser.

Not this time though. Gowda was getting tired of being the loser.

'So that was a dead end,' Santosh stated as they drove back. 'I don't understand this case at all, sir. It seems all in bits and pieces with nothing to hold it together.'

Gowda took his handkerchief out and laid it open. 'See this,' he said, gesturing with his chin to the hairslide and withered flower.

'The corporator claims he was there a week ago. This flower is not that old. Besides, why would he or his engineer have a hairslide or flowers on them? Someone else was in there. Someone with flowers in her hair. Someone who could be our murderer. And that someone is connected to our corporator's household one way or the other,' Gowda said, tucking the handkerchief back in his pocket. 'Stanley will have to process this. I'll call him. You will have to take it to the forensic lab right away,' he added.

'If only we could haul in the old eunuch and start the interrogation,' Santosh said.

'If only,' Gowda agreed. 'But Stanley won't allow it.' He retreated into his thoughts again. If he didn't push it too hard, it would come to him. The missing link.

In the world of informers, no one is above a price. Information can always be bought. The only difference is in the coinage. One man's price may not be another's, but every man has a price. And when that is placed before him, he'll sing as sweetly as a pet mynah. This is the fundamental premise of working with informers.

As Ibrahim walked down Tannery Road towards the butcher's shop he liked to buy from, a Tata Sumo drew to a halt near him, almost running him off the road into the ditch alongside the road.

'Maa ki choot,' Ibrahim shouted in a rage, shaking a fist.

Two men stepped out of the vehicle. Ibrahim walked towards them, glaring. 'Where the fuck do you think you are going?' he shouted. His heart still beat in his ears.

The two men looked at each other.

Then they strode towards him wordlessly, grabbed him by his arms from either side and pushed him towards the car.

At first, Ibrahim was too astonished to even scream. Then he tried to pull his arms out of their vice-like grip. 'Let go, you lund ke baal. Who the fuck are you? Let me go. What do you think you are doing?' A torrent of abuse followed.

A few people turned and looked. But something about the men, their impassive faces, their short hair, muscular bodies and their silence unnerved them. They turned their heads away and hurried down the street.

'Shut up,' one of the men finally barked out. The menace in the words sent a shiver running down Ibrahim's spine. He shut up. Who were these men? Nanoo's? Or Shabir's? A scramble of names in his head. But there was no reason for any of the gang lords to pick him up. Anna had made sure of that. Anna's omnipotence made that possible. Some of the Bombay men were moving in here, he had heard. But why would they wait to pick him up? He wasn't anyone important.

He allowed them to push him into the rear seat of the car and watched as they sat on either side, hemming him in. He saw the almost opaque tinted windows slide up, cutting him off from the rest of the world.

'Who are you?' he asked, injecting a note of deference into his voice. 'What do you want?'

The man on his left snarled, 'Good. That's the tone we approve of.' He stuck his little finger in his ear and wiggled it.

The other man, the one on the right with a birthmark the shape of India on his jaw, smiled. 'Why? You've run out of abuse, have you?'

They didn't speak after that. Ibrahim felt a knot of fear grow in him as the minutes sped by. Then, abruptly, the car braked to a halt.

Ibrahim tried to resist as they led him up a flight of steps into what seemed like a newly built bungalow. He tried to shake off their grip but they merely yanked his arms behind him, almost pulling them off their sockets, and pushed him forward. He yelped in pain. 'Where are you taking me?' he whimpered in fright, suddenly seeing his life dangle at the end of a snub-nosed revolver pointed at him.

India on the jaw sniggered. 'Afraid, are you?'

Ibrahim bit down an angry retort.

Itchy ears knocked on the door. After a long pause, the door opened and a clone of the two men stood within. Ibrahim stumbled as they thrust him in.

'C'mon, take it easy. He isn't a criminal, just someone we want to chat with,' a voice spoke from the end of the room.

Ibrahim blinked. He searched for the source of the voice. A tall man, middle-aged and veering towards burly, sat on a sofa. There were flecks of grey in his short hair.

India on the jaw loosened his grip and suddenly let go. Itchy ears hawked as if in disgust.

'Come here, Ibrahim,' the tall man said. 'Sit down. There's nothing to be afraid of.' He spoke Dakhani Urdu while the others had spoken in Kannada.

Ibrahim continued to stand. He drew himself in. He had heard enough about this good guy–bad guy routine from some of the boys on the street who had been taken in.

'Mamu, one arsehole will pretend to be your friend while another arsehole will pretend to be the tough type, out to pull the hair off your balls one by one,' Soup Sayeed had said only a few days ago. 'And they'll play with you in such a way that you'll end up telling them everything including your sister's menstruation dates. Motherfuckers!'

They were the police. Ibrahim realized that now. If they took VRS and left the force, they could rent themselves out to one of the gang lords. Thugs, each one of them. The only difference was that these had a uniform and a pension when they retired.

The tall man's fingers played on the sofa arm as if to rein in his impatience. He stood up abruptly and thrust his hands into the pockets of his trousers. This must be the senior man, Ibrahim decided.

'I must apologize, Ibrahim,' he said. 'My men deal with criminals all the time. In their eyes everyone brought in is either a criminal or one in the making.'

'So I am free to go,' Ibrahim demanded.

'Yes, of course. But you need to answer a few of my questions before that. Think of it as a casual chat and no more.' The voice was silky, the tone pitched between a steely firmness and easy joviality. 'Here,' the tall man said, walking towards a dining table and pulling out a chair. 'Sit down.'

Ibrahim looked at the oval-shaped table and the six chairs. Once, in another life, Ibrahim had been a carpenter; a man who made furniture. A man who went to sleep every night and slept through the night.

Rubbish, factory-produced furniture, he thought as he pulled out a chair. Overpriced too. 'What did this cost?' he asked, unable to help himself.

The tall man stared at him blankly. 'What?' he asked. Then catching on, he shrugged. 'I don't know. Does it matter?'

Ibrahim shrugged. 'I was making casual chit-chat. Isn't that what you wanted?'

Ibrahim could see that the tall man would have liked to lean across the table, haul him up by his collar and snarl, 'Don't fuck with me!'

But he held himself back. Only the drumming of his fingers on the table bespoke his agitation.

India on the jaw emerged from his side. He shoved Ibrahim against the wall. 'You are too soft, sir. Let me deal with this bastard...'

'No, I'll handle this.'

'What do you want, sir?' Ibrahim spoke to the tall man. 'What is it you want to know?'

The tall man peered at his watch. The room was wreathed in shadows. It was almost six. He raised his hand to a panel on the wall and switched on an overhead lamp. The little pool of light on the table turned it into an interrogation room. Or, at least, like those Ibrahim had seen in the movies. He swallowed. A lump of saliva that made a plop as it slid down his throat. His eyes met the tall man's fleetingly. He dropped his gaze.

'Do you want a drink?' the man asked.

Ibrahim shook his head. 'I don't drink.'

'Don't lie, Ibrahim. I know you do ... a small one?'

Ibrahim shook his head again. 'No, I am fasting. It's Ramzan, you know. Once a year I try to be all I should be for the rest of the year. A good Muslim!'

The tall man nodded. He leaned forward, his eyes gleaming, and said, 'So you will be honest with me. Isn't that part of being a good Muslim? No lies or games!'

Ibrahim licked his lips.

'What's your connection with the corporator?'

Ibrahim's heart skipped a beat. 'Which corporator? Shamima Bibi? I used to know her as a child. But now she's the corporator of my ward...'

'Not Shamima Bibi. I am talking about Ravikumar. Caddy Ravi, as he used to be called.'

'Sir, I made some furniture for Anna. Then he asked me to work for him. I do some plumbing and electrical work too. So he asked me to become a kind of manager of his properties. Make sure everything's working, etc.' Ibrahim spread his arms in an all-encompassing sweep.

'That's all there is...'

'That's all, sir. I swear by all I hold precious that I am his employee, a lowly employee.' Ibrahim leaned forward and folded his palms in supplication.

The tall man stood up and moved into the shadows.

'Who else is there at his home?'

'His younger brother. Their parents died some years ago. Anna hasn't married yet, though he has been searching for a bride for the last ten years now, and this may sound strange, but the house is run by an elderly chhakka called Akka.' Ibrahim's voice dropped to a whisper.

'Why hasn't he married yet?'

'I don't know for sure, but the talk is Anna got a certificate saying he belongs to a scheduled caste and he stood for the elections under the SC quota. Now none of his caste people will marry their daughters to him; they think he has lost his claim on the caste he was born into ... I don't know the truth, but this is what everyone says.'

'No one else lives there?'

'No one else, unless you take into account all the people who come and go. Anna's sisters visit once in a while. And oh, the corporator has a special puja every Friday. A group of eunuchs come to help, and sometimes stay over. I don't understand why the chhakkas have to be there ... some strange ritual associated with the goddess they worship ... no one else.'

Ibrahim's stomach growled. Soon it would be time for the maghrib prayer. What would Khadija cook tonight? He had set out to buy the meat when these arselickers had grabbed him.

'As part of your job, you fetch and carry little packets for him?' a disembodied voice demanded.

Ibrahim took a deep breath. 'Sometimes, sir. Sometimes Anna tells me to do it if the driver has to do something else.'

'No outstation trips?'

Ibrahim's heart hammered in his chest. 'A few times. But I don't like leaving home...'

'Ever checked on the contents?'

'No, sir. I presume it's printed material. A relative of his runs a small press. Anna subsidized it, so he takes a great interest in the business.'

'And you were never curious?' His interrogator suddenly moved into his line of vision. 'You have absolutely no idea what it could be...'

'Anna is a good employer. Why would I risk my job?' Ibrahim snapped, unable to help himself. He was weary and irritable. All through the day, his thoughts were hinged to the evening prayer. When the maghrib was over, there would be food. He could hold on until then. Not any longer.

'So, tell me again, how did your association with Ravikumar begin?'

Ibrahim blinked. Was the man an idiot? 'I just told you...' he said furiously.

'So, tell us again...' India on the jaw appeared out of the shadows.

Ibrahim looked at his fingernails. 'Even if you break every bone in my body, I will have nothing new to say...'

'Just tell us how you began your association with Ravikumar,' the tall man spoke up now.

'Like I said, I made some furniture.'

Two hours later, Ibrahim was faint with hunger. But he still clung to his story of caretaker, occasional courier and absolute ignorance.

The tall man stood up. 'Seeing that he has been so cooperative, give him some biriyani,' he said.

India on the jaw grinned. Through his hunger-crazed eyes Ibrahim wondered what the grin meant. And if finally his ordeal was over.

It was close to midnight when they dropped him back. They opened the car door and shoved him out, like one might a sack of rubbish, onto the street they had picked him up from. He stumbled, then straightened himself and glared at them. Motherfuckers! he cursed under his breath.

Itchy ears wiggled his little finger in his ear once again. 'You asked for it!' he said lazily, pulling his finger out and searching its end as though he expected to see an elephant perched on his nail. 'You could have saved us and yourself all that trouble!'

India on the jaw leaned across his companion and called out, 'In the end, you did bleat like the goat in the biriyani!'

Ibrahim hawked and spat a gob of saliva in their direction.

Itchy ears narrowed his eyes and turned to India on the jaw. 'Are you sure it really was a goat in the biriyani?'

'What do you mean?' Ibrahim asked with growing horror.

'Well, the constable I sent picked up the biriyani in Johnson Market. I read something in the newspapers the other day that goat is too expensive. So it could very well have been bow bow biriyani!' Itchy ears spoke slowly.

India on the jaw yelped in laughter. The door slammed shut and the car sped away. Ibrahim leaned over, retching...

He had been kept waiting at the dining table for another half hour after the tall man, whose name he subsequently discovered was Inspector Gowda, left. Itchy ears came in and asked, 'Do you want to use the lavatory?'

Ibrahim didn't understand the word. 'What?' he asked.

Itchy ears' mouth twisted. 'Kakoos?'

Ibrahim nodded.

The toilet was tiny but it had a washbasin. Ibrahim peed, washed himself and decided he may as well as do the wudu he should have done before the maghrib. He would have at least fulfilled one of the prerequisites, of cleansing himself before formal prayers, as his religion advocated.

He sluiced his hands up to his wrist three times. Then he rinsed his mouth out three times. Then the nostrils, the face, the arms up to the elbows three times again. He wetted his hands and wiped his head and then cleaned the insides of his ears with his index finger and the back of the ears with his thumbs. He took his handkerchief, held it under the water and wiped the back of his neck. All that was left was his feet. He filled a plastic mug and poured it over his feet. Once. Twice. Thrice.

Itchy ears called out, 'Hey, what are you doing in there? Bathing?'

Ibrahim opened the door. Itchy ears saw the wet floor and sighed. 'What did you do? Pee on the floor?'

Ibrahim glowered, but didn't speak.

A newspaper-wrapped parcel sat on the table. Ibrahim tore open the wrapping and fell on the biriyani. What would Khadija and the children eat? Someone would send them food. That was certain. But there was no knowing when he would have his next meal. These bastards would keep him here through the night, he knew.

Ibrahim hiccupped. A glass of water had been placed on the table. He drank from it and shovelled more of the biriyani into his mouth. He realized the game they were playing. Being good cop again: We're friends. We don't want to hurt you. Just tell us. Ibrahim would have to be born again before he became such a haraami. You can call me anything, but I'll never be a snitch.

Ibrahim belched. He would kill for a Suleimani, he thought. A lime-flavoured tea from Bombay Tea House. The best in the world. After the maghrib and the fast-breaking meal, he had taken to wandering towards Shivaji Nagar. There was always a Bombay to Goa auto available for the ride back home.

Ibrahim's lips rose at the corners. Those autos starting from Shivaji Nagar going up to Nagawara via Tannery Road were a bloody rollercoaster ride. Packed with at least eight people, the auto would trundle, truckle, leaping over every pothole and hump, so one man's nose was in another's armpit for a bit and in someone's neck the next moment. But no one complained. It was all part of the celebratory mood, like being at a carnival. You even relished the pushing, pulling, brushing of skin, the fug of body smells, attar and breath.

'Since you are having such a good time, here's another packet of biriyani.' India on the jaw thrust a packet before him.

Ibrahim frowned. They were really pushing the good cop routine. 'No, it's fine. I don't want it. I am not hungry any more.'

India on the jaw pushed Ibrahim down on the chair. 'Did I ask you if you were hungry? Eat it!'

'I can't.' Ibrahim shook his head.

'You'd better, Ibrahim. Do you want me to force it down your throat?'

Ibrahim opened the parcel wordlessly. He began

shovelling the food into his mouth. Halfway through, he couldn't eat a morsel any more. He pushed the parcel away.

'Eat it up, Ibrahim. Every last grain of rice,' India on the jaw spoke softly.

What was this new game? Ibrahim felt his throat constrict. He reached for the parcel and fed himself the biriyani slowly. At some point he gagged, but he continued to eat. Grain by grain. Till all that was left on the butter paper were two pieces of meat, three cloves and a piece of cinnamon. He licked his fingers one by one and glared at India on the jaw. No one was going to get the better of Ibrahim!

'Get up,' India on the jaw said from the doorway. Ibrahim followed the man into what looked like a storeroom. Ibrahim hesitated at the doorway. What now?

'Stand here,' he was told.

So Ibrahim stood. The meal hung heavy in his intestines. His chest constricted with the grease and spice. A faint queasiness filled his mouth. He was sleepy and ached to lie down. There was just enough room for him to stretch out. He lowered himself on the floor. But India on the jaw came to the doorway, barking, 'Stand up. No lying down, no sitting, do you hear me? What do you think this place is? Your mother-in-law's mansion, for you to stuff yourself and snore!'

Ibrahim paced in the narrow space. Four steps this way, four steps that. Hot air filled his ears, he was beginning to feel nauseous. He stopped and leaned against the shelf. The hands of a giant clock crawled in his head. A second. How slowly a second moved to the next!

An eternity later, India on the jaw appeared at the doorway.

'Come with me,' he said, leading the way back to the dining room.

Ibrahim's eyes lit up. Perhaps the man called Gowda had

returned. He hurried after the man. Then his feet stilled. On the dining table was yet another packet of biriyani. A wave of nausea gushed up his throat. He clamped his lips shut.

'Time to eat!' India on the jaw jeered, gesturing at the parcel.

Ibrahim continued to stand at the door.

'You have a choice. Tell us what you know or we'll keep stuffing biriyani down your throat every hour. It is all in your hands. Or should I say, all in your mouth. Speak or swallow!'

Ibrahim didn't know when he felt his will break. Was it after the fourth or fifth packet of biriyani? Was it when he couldn't take any more the ache in his legs, the pain in the small of his back, the pressing need to lie down, to rush to the kakoos and shit what seemed to be a mountain of turds building in him? All he knew was he held up his hand and croaked, 'Enough. I'll tell you what I know.'

She stared at the phone, unable to make up her mind. He had called thrice already and she had let it ring, unwilling to press the reject button, unable to take the call and speak to him. She sat with others who didn't know that she existed. She sat with others who wouldn't understand anyway.

'I don't like this,' he had said. Her Sanjay.

'I don't like meeting you in stealth. We are both young and unmarried. So what are you afraid of?' he had said last Friday, taking her hand in his. 'You have such pretty hands,' he murmured, caressing it. 'Such soft skin, like a bird's wing.'

Her heart was a trapped bird in her chest. The fluttering of wings filled her ears. What could she say? She had been rash and foolish to take it this far. She slid her hand out of his.

'Now that I am staying at the hostel, I don't have vessels to scrub or clothes to wash. So my hands would be soft.' She tried to inject the flatness of everyday into the sibilance of his sweet nothings.

'I have to go,' she said abruptly.

'I'll drop you at the hostel,' he said. And then at the gate, 'there's a new film releasing next week. Shall we go for it?'

She had nodded, knowing that she would have to find an excuse when the time came.

And here he was, calling again and again, to ask her to go with him on Friday evening.

She would have sold her soul to do any of those things women of her age did with little thought or planning. To sit on the back of a motorbike clinging to him. To walk in a park with him. To step into the light and let him see her untouched by the shadows. Maybe, one day she could. There were operations that would allow her to be herself. But what would she do until then, trapped within a man's body?

And Sanjay, would he accept her once he knew the truth? He had put her on a pedestal and all it would take was one long look to dislodge her from it.

The mobile trilled again.

THURSDAY, 25 AUGUST

The corporator frowned. He had taken to standing at the window of an upper room from where he had a clear view of the gate. The house was built like a fortress. No one could get in by scaling the walls. But the gate was an opening and since he was the corporator of a ward, there were always people coming in to see him with a petition, a complaint, a request, a bribe.

Ibrahim's whisper of surveillance had spooked him. He had been careful all along. It was one thing to evade the eyes of the Lok Ayukta and its fierce guardian, Justice Santosh Hegde. He had made sure that all his amassed property was in the names of Chikka and his two sisters. If there was a raid, all they would come up with would be the expected. There would be some things for them to find. To keep himself completely clean would make Hegde smell a rat. And he was very good at sniffing out rats, the corporator knew. If there was a raid, there would be a minor scandal, some rubbish in the media and then time would spread a cloak of forgetting ... but the Crime Branch mounting a surveillance was something else. If they found out what was really going on, everything that he had worked so hard for would come to an end. So, to see Ibrahim at the gate in less than forty-eight hours was a matter of concern.

The corporator rushed down.

'They grabbed me,' Ibrahim stated baldly. 'They grabbed me last evening.'

'And?' The corporator sat in his chair, betraying no evidence of fear or anger.

Ibrahim swallowed. 'I resisted. I resisted for as long as I could. They wanted to know about our association. I did what we had talked about all along. I told them the truth. But they didn't buy that.'

Ibrahim paused. His throat constricted. What would Anna say when he knew?

'Once upon a time those bastards would have tried to beat

the confession out of me. I would have been able to handle that. I would have passed out … but this … this was inhuman torture. Which shaitan mind could have thought it up?'

The corporator listened without interrupting.

'In the end, I broke down, Anna, I didn't have the will to go on, hold on … so…'

'So?'

'So, I had to give them a name. I said I knew nothing but there was someone who did. Someone who knew about the entire operation. I gave them the new boy's name. He is the only one who won't squeal because he knows nothing. All the others will,' Ibrahim said. 'Which means we will have to wait a bit to send out the next consignment. Another pigeon has to be found.'

Anna nodded thoughtfully, but didn't speak.

'I had no option, Anna…'

'Where is he?'

'He's gone to Mysore on some work. He has a job. He's a certified AC mechanic attached to a service centre.'

Anna looked at his fingernails. 'We have to make sure that he disappears.'

'But it would still come back to you if something happened to him.'

'Not if it's made to look like one of the others got to him first. A pawn in a gang war. That would divert their attention elsewhere.'

Ibrahim nodded. He knew what must be done. He had to make amends and sometimes that involved an offering. God had intervened and provided that other Ibrahim a ram instead of his son Ishmael as the sacrificial animal. But no one had intervened for the ram. And so it would be for the new boy.

It was almost eight in the evening when Gowda stumbled home. It had been a long day of routine police work that didn't allow him to sit quietly with the scattered findings of the case. To try and put it together, he needed to map it in his mind. But how was a man to do that when his desk was piled with nonsense like the stray cattle menace, a burglary at a construction site nearby from where a load of metal rods had gone missing, a complaint about a wedding hall that routinely played loud music. In the end Gowda had decided to deal with those petty cases before he set his mind to work on what seemed to him to be no case at all.

Gowda kicked his shoes off in the veranda. He peeled away his socks and flung them on top of the shoes. Eventually, he would have to put the shoes away on the shoe rack and carry the socks to the laundry basket in the work area adjacent to the kitchen. Or they would stay there till morning, till Shanthi arrived to bring order into his home and life. And he didn't like her doing that. She did enough already. Gowda stared at his shoes and socks. Then, with a sigh, he bent and put the shoes on the rack. He opened the door and walked in, holding his balled socks.

The house was airless and smelt a little like unwashed socks. Gowda uttered an expletive under his breath. It bounced off the walls and came back at him. He opened the windows. The breeze wafted in, bringing with it the fragrance of jasmine. At one end of the veranda, Shanthi had planted a jasmine creeper. It had finally begun to bloom. Gowda breathed in the fragrance. And it came to him again, that hairslide with the withered jasmine attached to it. It probably had been part of a string of jasmines. The string had fallen off or had been cleared to leave no evidence, and only this had slid into the fold of the sofa-cum-bed.

Gowda went around the house switching on lights and the geyser. First a bath and then the rest, he told himself, taking a bottle of water from the fridge and drinking deeply from it.

A man was entitled to a few minutes with himself.

He stood under the hot shower, feeling his fatigue drain away. He peered at the showerhead, feeling the spray sting his upturned face. If it wasn't for Urmila ... He hadn't been able to speak to her all day. She must be furious. He heard the phone ring. No, he wasn't going to rush for it, he told himself as he ran the towel between each toe. He put on track pants and a T-shirt, splashed some cologne on himself and combed his hair carefully. Where are you off to? He smiled at himself. All spruced up like a bridegroom!

Gowda poured himself a rum and topped it with Coke. He carried the drink and phone to the veranda, sat down in his chair and only then allowed himself to take a look at the phone. Three missed calls.

Two from Santosh and one from Urmila. She had sent three messages as well:

Tried calling u. Call back.

Where are u?

???

Gowda looked at his phone thoughtfully.

He sipped his drink. He walked to the edge of the veranda and plucked a jasmine. He held it to his nose and inhaled the fragrance.

First the call to Urmila. He heard out her tirade patiently. There was little he could say to defend himself except that he was in the middle of a case.

'You always are, Borei.' She sounded cross. 'Why couldn't I have fallen in love with a bank clerk? Someone who finishes work at half past five and isn't preoccupied with work even when he is with me.'

Gowda frowned. There it was. The L-word again. He twirled the jasmine by its stalk. 'You knew I am a policeman…'

'Is there something I can do to help?'

'Not really.'

'Is it those murders?' she asked. 'You still don't have a suspect?'

Gowda grunted.

'My neighbour in Sussex, a behavioural psychologist, used to help the police there with criminal profiling. Do you want me to write to him? He could help you. The human mind must be the same, no matter where it is located,' Urmila offered.

He could hear soft tinkly music playing in the background. He imagined her sitting in her living room, holding the phone in her hand, her legs elegantly crossed at the ankles. She would have the table lamps on and perhaps a glass of wine by the laptop on the table. What was he doing with a woman like her? Or, more accurately, what was she doing with a man like him!

'What?' Gowda asked.

Urmila told him again. 'Give it a shot. You are groping in the dark as it is. He is very good, Borei,' she added, her voice soft as satin in his ears.

'How old is he?' Gowda asked suddenly. Who was this doctor? What did he mean to her?

'He must be sixty,' Urmila murmured. 'Why? How does it matter?'

'I was just curious.'

'I'll write to him now and tell him you will be in touch,' she said. 'So when do I see you?'

'Soon.'

Mamtha's call had shaken him. Yet he was unwilling to let Urmila go. He didn't want to lose her but didn't know where to take their relationship. One of these days she would demand that he make a decision. What then?

'Soon, Urmila,' he said again. 'Let me just catch my breath. Give me the doctor's email id.'

One more call. Santosh. Gowda's mind was a sodden sponge, heavy and incapable of absorbing anything more. He decided to ignore Santosh's call. If it was truly urgent, Santosh would land up at his doorstep, he told himself.

The night was still. The breeze had stopped. A dog howled in the distance.

The couple upstairs had gone away for a week. To Goa for a holiday, they had said. The dog had been put into a boarding kennel for that period. Gowda made a face. He was actually missing its high-pitched bark and the sound of its scampering overhead.

Gowda finished his drink and went back in.

A solitary dinner, a dreamless night. That was all he wanted now.

FRIDAY, 26 AUGUST

Stanley was still at work when Pradeep came in. He looked up at his assistant, who stood hesitating by the door.

Pradeep touched the birthmark on his jaw. A brown birthmark that looked like the shape of India. 'I have some bad news, sir.'

Stanley raised an eyebrow.

'The man Ibrahim told us about...'

Stanley waited, and then asked, 'Yes, what's happened to him? Fled the place, has he?'

'No, sir. He's dead,' Pradeep mumbled.

'What?' Stanley's voice cracked.

'We went to pick him up yesterday. But his roommate said he'd gone to Mysore and was expected this evening. So we went back. He had been hacked to death in his room.'

'So, the corporator got to him,' Stanley said grimly.

'Sir, I don't think the corporator had anything to do with it. Looks like he was also involved with the sand mafia in some way. You could make out that it was Nepali Ricki's work.'

'Kukri?'

'Yes, thrust into the abdomen and turned. Triangle-shaped wounds. The intestines were hanging out and his signature: the right wrist chopped off. It was gruesome.'

'I thought Nepali Ricki had retired,' Stanley said, wiping his brow with his handkerchief.

'Who knows with these fellows, sir?' Pradeep ran his fingers through his hair, trying hard not to reveal his disappointment. All those days of work had come to naught. They would have to start all over again. 'What about the surveillance, sir?'

'We'll keep it going for another forty-eight hours. And then we'll see.' Stanley began walking to the door. 'Let's go. I might as well see the crime spot.'

She stared at her phone again. Where was he? She messaged him again, but he wasn't responding. Was he angry with her for not taking his calls on Wednesday night? But she had explained it to him later that night, saying it wouldn't be possible for them to go to the movie. And he had seemed to understand. They had arranged to meet on Friday night as usual.

'You have to make up for my disappointment,' he said.

'I'll buy you an ice-cream.' She smiled.

'I am not six years old to be appeased by an ice-cream or a balloon,' he whispered in her ear. She shivered.

'What else can I give you? I don't have too much money ... maybe when I get my salary!'

'You can give me something. It won't cost you anything, but will mean everything to me,' he murmured.

'What is that?'

'A kiss...'

'Oh Sanju ... you shouldn't talk to me like this,' she protested.

'Well, that is the only thing that is going to make up for not going to the movie with me...'

It was quarter to eight. He hadn't called all day. There had been an early morning text, but nothing after that.

What if he'd had an accident? He rode the bike too fast, she had told him. But he had said he was in control. 'And I am careful, Bhuvana. Would I risk my life after having met someone like you?'

Or had he given up on her? Why bother with someone like her? Someone who seemed to have so many terms and conditions about how to manage their relationship when he could find himself a girl who was more compliant?

She sank her head in her palms. She couldn't think of a life without him.

Where was he? When were they going to meet?

Akka stood at the door. 'The girls want to go out.'

She stared at Akka wordlessly.

'Are you still waiting for him to call?' Akka asked.

She didn't have to answer. Akka could read her face.

'You should be more careful next time,' Akka said, looking at her distraught face.

'But Sanjay is a good man.'

'Is that his name?' Akka walked away.

Men, they were all the same. Akka was right. In the end she was left with nothing but the taste of ashes in her mouth. She wasn't going to sit here waiting for him. He can go fuck himself, she told herself. If he didn't want her, she didn't want him either.

There were others who wanted her. A soft giggle escaped her mouth. In their arms, she would once again be Bhuvana, the beautiful one.

SATURDAY, 27 AUGUST

Chikka sipped his coffee and watched Anna. He had never seen him scour the newspapers so carefully. What was he looking for? The sheet crackled with his impatience as he flipped it. He saw Anna pause at each page. He saw him scrutinize the page carefully.

'What is it?' Chikka asked. The morning had dawned cool and grey. Almost every evening the clouds gathered into a grey mass and then the skies opened up. A stinging sheet of rain that filled up the drains, turned roads into streams and held up the traffic.

'Here,' Anna said, thrusting the newspaper towards him. 'I can't find it. You look for it. It's a murder report involving Nepali Ricki.'

Chikka frowned. He knew better than to ask his brother questions.

'I just need to make sure that Ibrahim kept his word,' Anna said, yawning. 'The fool got caught by the crime branch.'

Chikka's eyes widened. 'And...'

'He had the good sense to give them a name. A new recruit. And so, to divert attention, the new boy had to be dealt with.'

Chikka scanned the newspaper carefully. The Kannada broadsheet his brother favoured had almost a quarter page, including a small photograph of the crime scene, devoted to the news item.

'SAND MAFIA CLAIMS ONE MORE'

Staff Reporter

The police say the prime suspect, Nepali Ricki of Banaswadi, is absconding

Bangalore: Last evening a young man was found hacked to death in his lodge room in Banaswadi area. Senior police officials don't rule out the possibility of the sand mafia's role in the murder.

With the construction boom back in full swing in the city, sand suppliers have been doing brisk business over the last few months. The young man, Sanjay Patil, reportedly muscled into the sand mafia's territory, which was being controlled by another career criminal, whom the police refused to name as it could be detrimental to their investigation.

Sanjay appears to have provoked the mafia when he began extracting hafta from sand suppliers, preliminary investigations have revealed.

The city police have formed

a special team to track down the suspects. The team comprises officials from Central Crime Branch (CCB) and several police stations from the east division.

'So far no arrests have been made,' said Assistant Commissioner of Police Stanley Sagayaraj (Crime).

'We have sent our teams to neighbouring districts and also alerted our counterparts in neighbouring States,' a CCB officer told this reporter.

The people staying near the scene of crime are feigning ignorance about the murder.

Two things occurred to Gowda almost at the same instant. One, that Dr Robert King was very good at what he did. Two, that there definitely had been something going on between the two of them.

Call me Robert, he had said in his email in response to Gowda's, which Santosh had keyed in and sent for him. In his mind, the phrase struck. Call me Robert had studied the case notes and written again. In a strange way, all he had done was arrive at the same conclusion that Gowda had, but he had done so in a cohesive fashion, attributing whys and wherefores and making it seem much more plausible. There were charts and graphs and examples cited of casual grimy horror that made it seem less like speculation and conjecture and resonated with the authority of actual findings.

Gowda thought of his high-school maths master, a thin man with a narrow face and a pair of spectacles perched on his bony nose. 'Show the workings, Borei,' he'd admonish Gowda. 'I need to see how you arrived at the answer. I know your answer's right, but I need to see how you found it. The workings are very important. That's what will convince the examiner.'

Gowda had never been able to do the workings. Then or now. Which was why his instinct was suspect, while Call me Robert's analysis was being read with great attention by Stanley.

He watched Stanley's eyes scan the printout. Word for word.

Gowda chewed his lip. He thought of the last paragraph of the email: *And how's U? Do tell my dear friend that the English summer isn't as spectacular without her gracing the horizon.*

You could put that down to affection. But there had been a photograph as well. Of Urmila and Call me Robert in a garden, each wearing what looked to Gowda like soppy smiles. Call me Robert was marking territory, Gowda realized. What was going on between the two of them? Gowda chewed his lip some more.

Stanley looked up. Gowda, it seemed, was devouring most of his lower lip. He was oblivious to the goings-on at the station house. Outside, he could hear a woman wailing. Someone was trying to comfort her. Through the window he saw Gajendra stride towards them. Gajendra was the kind of man who gave policemen a bad name. Arrogant, foul-mouthed and certain that he inhabited an upper echelon in the universe that allowed no questioning of its authority. But he was unswervingly loyal and matchless at defusing situations. Through the window, he saw Gajendra glower down at the woman and then turn to the man. Gajendra stuck his little finger in his ear and wiggled it. Then he said something to the man, who stared at the policeman, mouth open in astonishment. Or was it horror? Hard to tell. The next thing they knew, the man and woman were scuttling away! Stanley smiled.

'Borei,' he said, turning his attention to Gowda, whose lip must be mash by now, he thought.

Gowda looked up. 'What do you think?'

'He's corroborating what you've been saying all along.' Stanley flipped the sheets of paper.

Gowda shrugged. 'The assailant's a man; there is no doubt about it. That kind of injury necessitates some strength. If the victims were drunk or drugged, they wouldn't have fought back. But that wasn't the case. However, the earring, and the statements of the parking attendant at the theatre, the restaurant owner and the auto driver indicate a woman's presence. So either it's a eunuch or a man dressed up as a woman. Nothing has been stolen. And apart from Roopesh, whose body was too decomposed for us to discover anything, all the other victims seem to have had sex. So the assailant's motive is not material effects but sexual gain. But why kill them? That's what I couldn't understand. And Dr King seems to point us there.'

Stanley's eyes settled on a paragraph. Childhood trauma. Low self-esteem. Power hungry. The desperate need to feel in control and hence the use of the ligature. The phrases leapt off the page. And something else. In most serial killers, there is a trigger that sets off the killing spree.

'And you think you know what the trigger is?' Stanley frowned. 'These are all suppositions, Borei.'

'I am not certain, but if you continue the surveillance on the corporator's house, I will know for sure,' Gowda said, playing with the paperweight.

Stanley's phone erupted to life. He peered at the screen and then picked it up. 'Tell me,' he said. A couple of minutes later, he put the phone down thoughtfully.

'The boy, Sanjay, he was killed yesterday,' Stanley said.

Gowda nodded.

'I heard,' Gowda said. 'Ibrahim must have told them that he had given us the boy's name.'

'That's what I thought too. But his death had nothing to do with Ibrahim. Nepali Ricki's the one. And he's in hiding. No, the boys have been going through the deceased's phone. The contacts list had been completely deleted. But there were a few draft messages. All to someone called Bhuvana. Nothing extraordinary about it. The only thing is the number belongs to a set of SIMs that the corporator has in his name,' Stanley said. 'So, I am keeping the surveillance on.'

Gowda doodled on the pad. Bhuvana. Who could she be? Why would the corporator's SIM be with her?

'Shall we bring the eunuch in for questioning?' Gowda asked.

Stanley shook his head. 'Not yet.'

SUNDAY, 28 AUGUST

Gowda and Santosh walked into the Country Club Resort on Doddaballapur Road. 'You are certain he is here, sir,' Santosh asked.

Gowda nodded.

As they entered the lobby, curious glances darted their way. They were not in uniform, but something about them suggested these were men with a purpose other than recreation on their minds.

'Where do you think he is?' Santosh asked, his eyes

drinking in the details of the resort. The potted plants and deep cane sofas with bluish-green cushions. The nature studies on the walls and plate-glass windows that overlooked green lawns. A giant ponytail palm rose towards the sky in the middle of the atrium, and a whole wall was a bank of creepers.

'Let's look around. He must be either by the pool or in the bar,' Gowda said absently.

He must bring his father here one Sunday. He would like it. The expanse of green, the conspicuous luxury, the notion of his son taking him to an expensive place. He would protest about the cost of everything and say, 'You must be taking bribes, how else can you afford to bring me here?' Saying which, he would go on to enjoy himself thoroughly.

Maybe he would ask Urmila to go with them. He would claim she had a membership and they were her guests. He would ask Michael along too just to even the numbers and so his father didn't suspect a rat.

He was certain Urmila would be game. She would like it too. That he was weaving her into his everyday and his small deceptions as much as he could.

They found him by the pool with a blue-and-white towel wrapped around his hips. He was wearing sunglasses and was stretched out on a sun lounger under an umbrella. A fat gold chain with a pendant of a goddess studded with rubies nestled on his bare chest.

They watched a steward place on the table alongside, two glasses of something cold, decorated with a cherry and a slice of lime.

They waited for the steward to leave before padding their way to his side. He was napping.

'Good morning, Corporator sir,' Gowda said.

The corporator woke up startled. He pulled the sunglasses off his face and sat up frowning. 'Now what? This is harassment...'

Gowda frowned. 'What makes you so frightened of us? Someone invited us to come over. And when we spotted you, we thought we'd come by and say hello.'

Gowda dragged up a lounger and sat on it. 'But now that we've met, let me ask you what I needed to ask you anyway.'

The corporator's mouth tightened into a line. 'What is it, Gowda?'

'Where is the eunuch who lives in your home?'

The corporator frowned.

'We have been looking for her since yesterday evening but she seems to have gone missing,' Gowda said.

'I don't know where Akka is. She is a free agent and can come and go as she pleases,' the corporator bit out.

'In which case, you can tell us this. Who is Bhuvana?'

'Who?'

'Precisely my question. Who is Bhuvana? A young man was found murdered a couple of days ago. In his phone were messages to someone called Bhuvana. The number, we discovered, belongs to a SIM that is in your name.'

Gowda reached across, took the corporator's drink and sipped from it. It was fresh lime soda.

The corporator stiffened. 'I don't know any Bhuvana. It must be a mistake. I tell you there is no one called Bhuvana in my family. My sisters are called Jayanthi and Saraswati. Their daughters are Ammu and Ratna.'

'What about the eunuch? Would she know?' Santosh asked.

The corporator glared at him. 'Akka runs my house for me. But she doesn't run my life.'

'Perhaps one of her friends has been using your number,' Santosh suggested.

'That is highly unlikely.' The corporator dropped his gaze.

'You are hiding something from us,' Gowda said. 'It is strange that you didn't ask us who the young man who died was. Something tells me you know already.'

'What's going on here, Gowda?' ACP Vidyaprasad stood behind them, glaring, taking in the scene.

'Are you here in an official capacity?' the ACP demanded.

Gowda shrugged.

'If you are not, please leave my guest alone.'

Gowda slammed his drink down on the table, spilling its contents and causing the other glass to topple. 'Enjoy your Sunday!'

On the way out, Gowda spotted the ACP's new Honda City parked to a side. It gave him immense pleasure to run his key along its side from bonnet to boot.

'Sir, what are you doing?' Santosh's horrified voice asked.

'Are you here in an official capacity?' Gowda mimicked his senior officer's tone. 'If not, please leave me alone.'

They got him that night as he rode back from SR Wines, a little after Kothanur. He had run out of rum and had stepped out at half past eight. When he turned off the main road onto the small road that led towards Greenview Residency, where his house was, a Scorpio came out of the shadows and nearly ran into him. Gowda went off the road and into the ditch. 'What the fuck…'

'Borei, what's happening?' Urmila's voice rang through the night as he sought to gain control of the heavy Bullet.

He had been talking to Urmila on the Bluetooth as he rode back, telling her about the resort.

But before he could answer, he saw the SUV stop.

From where he was he saw the man called King Kong step out. But he stayed by the car and three others walked towards him.

Gowda had just about enough time to get off the Bullet before they descended on him. Through the haze of pain from that first blow, Gowda heard the splintering of glass. The headlight of his bike. He hoped to god they would leave his Bullet alone. Nothing was said as they slapped him around, kicking his shins, punching him in his gut. One of the punches landed on his face, breaking his nose.

Gowda felt his knees give way. But even as he tottered and slid into a heap on the ground, he realized the corporator had a secret he was trying to safeguard.

MONDAY, 29 AUGUST

When he opened his eyes, it felt as though someone had taken a hammer to his head and to the rest of his body. Every inch of it ached. He touched his face gingerly. It seemed like someone else's face. A bandage seemed to hold his nose in place.

Curtains had been drawn to keep the light out. The room seemed both familiar and strange. For a moment, he wondered where he was. Then he realized he was in his own bedroom. But how had he got here?

Urmila walked into the room. 'How are you feeling?' she asked.

He tried to shrug, but even that seemed to unleash a giant wave of pain.

'In the scuffle, your phone slipped out of your pocket but your Bluetooth device stayed fastened to your ear. I heard every single blow and punch...'

'Did I scream?' he asked, holding her gaze.

'No, you didn't.'

There was a moment of silence. Then Urmila continued, 'I thought they were going to kill you. I was getting into my car when I remembered I had Santosh's number. I called him. Gajendra and he got there before they did serious damage. I reached in time to take you to the hospital.'

'What is the verdict?'

'Concussion, two bruised ribs and a broken nose. You should be able to move around in a couple of days. But you need to stay in bed until then.'

Gowda stared at the ceiling. 'What time is it?'

'Six in the evening. You were under sedation, Borei.' Suddenly her voice broke. 'I almost died, Borei, on the drive here, not knowing what they had done to you ... if you were alive or dead. Who were they?'

Gowda turned his head towards her and reached for her hand. 'I am here.'

'Yes, you are here...'

'Mamtha?' Gowda whispered.

She held his gaze as she spoke. 'I said there was no need to inform Mamtha. Why worry her? I told Santosh it would be best to not mention this to anyone. Both Gajendra and he have told everyone at the station and your senior officers that your bike skidded and you fell.'

Gowda smiled. 'Maybe you should take over my job as well. You probably would do it better than I seem to be doing it.'

She leaned over and murmured, 'When the swelling goes down, your new nose is going to make you look very sexy. Like a decadent Roman emperor!'

TUESDAY, 30 AUGUST

Gowda was awake when Santosh came to see him. It was a little past eight and he was sitting up in bed, propped up against pillows.

Gowda was bored and restless. He'd had a field day with the telemarketing people. To one, he had said he wouldn't be able to go ahead with a balance transfer as his mother wouldn't like it.

'What?' the woman at the other end had yelped.

'Yes,' Gowda said in an aggrieved tone. 'My mother is very strict. She won't agree. Why don't you speak to her?'

With another man offering a loan, Gowda had introduced an eager note into his voice. 'Yes, I really need a loan. Actually I need twelve loans. One each for a house, a car, my dog, my broken nose…'

The man had hung up on him.

'How are you feeling, sir?' Santosh asked, trying hard not to stare at Gowda's swollen face.

'Did you see who they were?' Gowda asked by way of greeting.

'Not really, sir. Did you?'

Gowda nodded. 'It was the corporator's men.'

'They broke your bike's headlight.'

Gowda winced.

'Anything else?' he asked slowly.

'No, they probably thought it wasn't worth the effort. To them, it's just an old bike. What should we do?'

'Nothing as of now. Let me get back on my feet.' Gowda's face gave nothing away.

'I saw the tattoo on your arm. It's really interesting…'

Gowda glared at him. Santosh flinched.

Then, as if unable to help himself, he said, 'Sir, one more body has been found. Same MO. A man again. He was identified as a jewellery showroom assistant. Married, but his family lives in Anantapur. One of his colleagues received a call alerting him about his death. ACP Stanley said he would drop by tomorrow and brief you on it. He said you should be allowed to rest or you would jump up and rush to the crime scene. That's why I didn't tell you as soon as I heard it from the control room. And, sir, there were couple of reporters at the crime scene, so it will be in the newspapers.'

Urmila walked into the bedroom with tea and porridge on a tray.

'What's this?' Gowda asked suspiciously, looking at what seemed like Fevicol into which chopped-up cockroaches had been sprinkled.

'Oats with dates. It's good for you,' she said, throwing a smile Santosh's way. 'Some tea for you, Santosh?'

'No, madam.'

Gowda wondered what Santosh made of his unorthodox home set-up. He was yet to meet Mamtha, but as of now he seemed smitten by this madam's charm.

'If it weren't for madam's presence of mind to call me, sir … those thugs would have hurt you very badly,' Santosh said.

In Urmila's presence, Santosh seemed to have transformed into a little puppy wagging its tail and beaming love, loyalty and eternal devotion.

Urmila seemed to have won over Shanthi as well. She had come in at least half a dozen times to tell him how fortunate he was to have Urmila take him to the hospital, nurse him, be there for him – unlike Mamtha, though the words were never voiced. At the best of times, Shanthi and Mamtha tolerated each other. When Mamtha moved to Hassan, Shanthi had been relieved. With Urmila, though, Shanthi seemed to have pledged her troth in blood.

Gowda felt a twinge of discomfort every time he inhaled. He didn't know if it was the result of the beating he had received or at the thought of how easily Mamtha had been cast aside.

THURSDAY, 1 SEPTEMBER

Stanley Sagayaraj, old boy from St Joseph's, didn't bat an eye when he saw Urmila, old girl from St Joseph's, at Gowda's home.

'You remember Urmila from college, don't you?' Gowda said, as if it was the most normal thing to have your college sweetheart play nurse at your bedside.

Stanley smiled. 'Yes, of course. But I thought you lived in the UK.'

'I do.' Urmila smiled. 'But I am in Bangalore for a few months. I heard about Gowda's accident from Michael Hunt ... I have been pitching in as Borei is all alone here.'

Stanley nodded. Gowda watched her, amazed at the casual ease with which she had bent the truth to make it seem so plausible.

Stanley waited for Urmila to leave the room before snapping, 'What the fuck were you doing, Gowda, pulling a stunt like this?'

Gowda opened his eyes wide, as much as the swelling on his face would allow him to, and murmured artlessly, 'What stunt? The bike skidded...'

'If you choose to do wheelies on your bike, it is your business. I am referring to the visit you paid to the Country Club Resort. ACP Vidyaprasad complained to me that you had scratched his new car on purpose. I didn't pay any particular attention to that. If I had known, I would have asked you to add a scratch on my behalf. But he said something else. He used words like harassment. You cannot question the corporator without my permission. You broke protocol and jeopardized my team's efforts.'

'Do you know that the eunuch in his house has disappeared?'

Stanley frowned.

'I sent Byrappa across in mufti on Saturday evening and the watchman told him she went out on Friday evening and hasn't been seen since.'

Stanley scratched his forehead as if unable to decide.

'The corporator's hiding something, Stanley. It may or may not have anything to do with the counterfeit currency, but it certainly has something to do with Bhuvana, the mystery woman.'

Stanley rose and went to stand by the window of the room. 'Why do you say that?'

'Look at me...' Gowda said.

Stanley turned in surprise.

'I didn't fall off my bike. The corporator had his men do this to me.'

'What?'

Gowda smiled. A grim smile. 'It was a warning of sorts to keep away. ACP Vidyaprasad must have told him I have nothing to do with this case. He must have seen my questioning as nosiness that needed to be dealt with.'

Stanley returned to the chair and slumped in it wearily. 'We found another body.'

'Santosh told me and I read about it in this morning's papers. We won't be able to keep it quiet very much longer...'

Stanley nodded. 'The commissioner has called for a meeting this evening. Are you up to it?'

Gowda placed his feet on the ground carefully and stood up. He winced with the effort, but he said, 'I will be.'

She lay curled up on the bed, her cheek digging deep into the pillow, which was damp with the tears she had shed.

It was a clammy afternoon. It had rained all morning and then suddenly and fiercely the sun had come out, drying up the moisture in the air. And then again the clouds had gathered. Pressing down upon the city, squeezing the wind out of the narrow alleys and choked lanes. She turned on her stomach and cradled her face in her arms. Her eyes felt hot and heavy and in the back of her head, a little imp sat pounding at the insides of her brain with a malevolent fury.

Would it ever stop? Would this ache in her heart ever heal? The fan whirred overhead.

Outside, the pandal was filling up with people.

They were all like that. Men. Taking what they wanted without ever once thinking of what they might destroy in the process. Every man she had known had that streak of self-absorption. As long as their needs were appeased, their hides protected, they didn't care about the damage caused. Every man was the same. Ruthless. Selfish. Brutal.

You think you can forgive them but you never do. You just pretend you have. And then, one day, it comes back to you. Even more vivid in remembrance than in actual life.

He was nine years old when his mother took him to the block of flats on Palace Cross Road where she worked as a cleaner. He was nine years old when the nice old Mr Ranganathan in 3B asked him in to show him his pet squirrel.

'It's shy, a very shy creature,' nice Mr Ranganathan said, closing the door and leading him to the veranda.

All his life he had wanted a pet. But his father in a drunken fit had kicked the pup he had brought home. Kicked it so hard that it flew into the street. He would never forget the sickening crunch of flesh and bone as a minivan ran over the puppy. A neighbour had offered to bring him another pup, but he refused. His father would get drunk again, he knew.

Now the little boy felt a skip of delight leap in him. A squirrel! Something to touch and hold. Something warm and live to love and cherish even if he couldn't keep. The little boy smiled.

The veranda was hung with bamboo blinds. Amidst several potted plants, some almost as big as trees, were a chair and a table. 'This is where I spend most of my time when I am home,' the old man said. 'And so this is where my squirrel hides.'

The little boy's eyes darted around. Where was it? 'Does it have a name?' he whispered.

'You can call it what you want. It'll answer to anything you call it.'

He licked his lips and whispered, 'Juicy ... Juicy!'

The old man cocked his head at an angle and smiled. 'What a lovely name! Juicy. I like it. I think he'll like it. But Juicy won't come if you call him like that. Come here, I'll show you what to do.'

He went to the old man and let himself be picked up and perched on the old man's knee. He let the old man take his hands in his gnarled and stiff fingers. 'Here,' he said, thrusting the boy's hand into the folds of his dhoti. 'Stroke it, slowly ... yes, slowly and soon it will wake up.'

He let his fingers glide over the squirrel. How small it was! So small and defenceless. 'Juicy,' he said softly, 'Juicy ... Juicy.'

He felt it rouse itself and looked up in excitement. 'Uncle,' he cried.

But the old man seemed to have turned deaf. His face was clenched and there was a drop of spittle at the corner of his open mouth. He let go of the squirrel in fear. The old man grabbed his hand and fastened it back on the squirrel. 'Hold him, boy ... don't lose him. Hold Juicy!'

And so he fondled it again and again and felt within him a warmth that gathered and gathered ... and so over the next two months till school began, he sought Ranganathan with the same fervour with which the old man waited for him to arrive.

He had just turned nine when he made the acquaintance

of Juicy who lived in Ranganathan's lap. Juicy who came to life with his touch, and juicy whose nose he kissed. And then a few months later Juicy crawled into his mouth and spat his heart into it. He was ten years old when he discovered the truth about himself. Ranganathan became his benefactor. And so the family's.

School fees, books and everything he needed. A job for his drunk of a father in Ranganathan's garment factory. Occasional loans for his mother. 'He reminds me of my little brother when we were boys,' Ranganathan said, stroking his cheek absently as he handed over the boy's school fees to his mother.

After a while, no one thought about it. Like his father's drunkenness on Saturdays. Everyone knew that he went to visit the old man twice a week.

When he turned twelve, Ranganathan decided to take him to Madras. He was going to meet with a few buyers in Madras. He was driving down, Ranganathan told his mother. 'I want him to see the beach,' Ranganathan said. 'And it will be good to have someone in the car with me.'

His spirit soared at the sight of the sea. The blue expanse that went on and on. Nothing in life until then had prepared him for this. And later, when Ranganathan took him into his bed, he felt as if he was riding the waves.

When they returned from Madras, Ranganathan decided the apartment was too much of a risk. His daughter lived in the adjacent apartment and had a key. What if she walked in on them?

So he moved their trysts to the garment unit. It was all perfectly legitimate. He would come in Ranganathan's car just as the workers were leaving. Mr Ranganathan would help him with some lessons and, on the way to the club, would drop him off at the corner of the street on which he lived.

Only they knew, Ranganathan and he. How, when the motorized treads ground to a halt and the sound of the sewing machines settled into silence, there, in the factory surrounded by the mute machinery, Ranganathan stirred in him countless variations of pleasure.

Perhaps Ranganathan grew careless. Or was it he who grew greedy, but on an evening he shouldn't have been there, he went to see the old man. 'What a surprise, dear boy,' Ranganathan said, looking up from a file.

He didn't speak. Instead, he put his school satchel down and walked to the glass wall of the cubicle and pulled the blinds down. The old man watched him. And then putting down his file, he stood up, murmuring, 'You are turning into a little slut, aren't you?'

Ranganathan undressed him carefully and laid him on the maroon Rexine sofa. He trailed his tongue down his spine, then caressed his buttocks and slapped the flesh suddenly. A hot tight slap that sent a wave of desire coursing through him. His nerve ends tingled and he giggled; a high girlish giggle of glee.

And then suddenly someone flung open the door of the room. His head turned of its own volition to look at the intruder. He felt a bucket of cold shock wash over him. What was he going to do?

'You missed lunch. Why haven't you eaten all day?' The voice came from the doorway.

'I am not hungry,' she said, not bothering to hide the petulance striating her tone.

'Why?' Akka asked, heedless. 'What's with you? You

look a sight ... I go away for three days and everything is awry here.'

'Leave me alone.' A muffled sob emerged from the pillow she had sunk her face into.

Akka went towards the bed. 'Tell me. Akka will make it better. You know Akka can!'

A tear-stained face turned to Akka. 'But even you, Akka, can't breathe life into what is dead.'

Akka frowned. 'What died?'

'All I had with Sanjay...'

'Sanjay? What do you mean?' Akka asked slowly. She reached out and took the woebegone creature on the bed in her arms. 'Oh ... him! What can I say? I told you, darling, didn't I? That it would end in grief. Men like him are not for us...'

The front yard of the corporator's mansion had been converted into a festival ground. Serial lights ran up and down the length of the street and all over the building. Gaily patterned shamianas were strung up and festooned with flowers. The poles were covered with floral garlands and at one end was a raised platform on which sat a painted six-foot-tall Ganesha. A priest stood before the idol, chanting prayers, and for once the gates were flung wide open, so anyone who wished to could be part of the celebrations. Several plastic chairs had been placed and vats of food were kept, so all who came were offered a paper plate laden with sweets and savouries. The loudspeaker blared out devotional songs and in the evening a live orchestra had been arranged to play music.

'Make sure it's only melodies,' King Kong had warned the orchestra manager.

Anna stood in his balcony, watching the hustle and bustle at the pandal. Chikka stood listlessly at his side. After a while, he said, 'I don't know why we need to do this year after year ... it's all so pointless.'

Anna frowned at Chikka. 'We do it because it is expected of us...'

'I am tired of doing only what is expected of me ... what about me? Don't I have any dreams and desires of my own? Am I not allowed to have them? Why do we have to do everything your way?' Chikka's voice turned shrill with emotion before he stopped abruptly. He turned on his heel and went back inside.

Akka came to the door. 'Anna ... I heard voices. What's wrong?'

He turned. 'Did you want something?'

'They want you at the pandal. It's time to start the puja.'

The corporator sighed.

'Is there something on your mind?'

He shrugged. Then he turned and asked, 'Is Chikka involved with someone?'

'Why? Did you hear or see something?'

'No.' The corporator's fingers tightened around the balustrade to suppress his irritation. 'I just had a feeling and wondered if you had sensed anything?'

'Who knows, Anna ... a young man of his age. It's quite natural,' Akka said.

'I don't like it. I have other plans for him. And all this nonsense is just adding to my stress levels. Don't I do everything for each one of you? What need is there to go seeking someone else? She may not be right for our family. As if I don't have enough troubles to deal with. Do you know that the police are breathing down my neck, trying to sniff out my activities. God knows what he has been saying to her. He kept prattling on about his dreams and desires. If I had thought the same, would we have had any of this?'

'Maybe you should take him away for a few days. Put some distance between him and whatever is on his mind.'

The corporator looked at the eunuch and smiled. 'Now, why didn't I think of that … I'll take Chikka with me. We'll go visit our sisters. I haven't seen them for some time now. Akka, I would suggest you too stay away while we are gone. I don't want them troubling you when I am not around. We'll leave this afternoon. Will you tell him to get everything ready?'

Akka smiled thinly, wondering what Chikka would say.

TUESDAY, 6 SEPTEMBER

It was almost half past nine at night when they reached home. They had stayed away longer than they had intended to. There were so many relatives to visit, so many things that needed to be done. 'You hardly come here and so when you do, we have to make the most of it,' a second cousin said, heaping food on a banana-leaf plate for them. 'Have you visited Govindaswamy yet? He's been ailing for the last six months…' a brother-in-law said. 'He'll be comforted that you called on him.'

He tossed and turned in his bed, unable to sleep. At a little past eleven, he got up and went to the terrace. From the storeroom there, he pulled out a cardboard carton in which he kept the things he needed.

First the cord. A strong white cord that was about half an inch thick. He used a razor blade to cut the length he required. About 30 inches long. Then he knotted both ends and hitched one end to the window grille. He was humming as he worked.

Next, he rolled out the inner tube of a bicycle tyre and cut a narrow strip. He placed it on the inner end of the cord and swiftly and firmly wound the rubber tubing on the cord for about six inches from the knot. Then he looped the end of the tube strip and snipped the end. He unhitched the cord and replicated the same at the other end.

He held the cord by its rubber grips and tugged at it. The cord tautened with tension. He smiled, satisfied.

On a newspaper, he laid out tiny shards of glass. He wound cloth around his hands and, with a rolling pin, he ground the glass into fine particles. He opened a jar of glue and smeared it all over the open cord. He laid the cord over the glass dust and rolled it this way and that, until the surface was coated with a layer of fine glass. The cord shimmered and sparkled.

While he waited for it to dry, he put away the remaining cord, tubing, glue and glass. This was all he needed to construct his ligature.

He liked to use a fresh one each time. The thought of using a ligature into which someone had bled nauseated him. And it didn't work as effectively as the first time it was used. He had realized that with the frooter Liaquat in the alley. The ligature hadn't done the job it was expected to. Which is why he had been alive when they burnt him. Motherfucker. It was all his fault that things had got so messy.

He ran his finger along the glass-encrusted cord. To his immense satisfaction, a thin line of red appeared on his skin almost instantly.

He sucked on his bleeding finger as he switched off the light and went back to his room, dangling the cord from the other hand. It had taken him less than forty-five minutes to create his weapon.

THURSDAY, 8 SEPTEMBER

4.21 p.m.

Gowda stood near the police point at the Basilica. Santosh had posted himself at the end of the Gujri Gunta. He said he had a perfect view from there.

Nine days ago the flag had been hoisted at St Mary's Basilica by the archbishop. God knows where they came from, but they did: countless men and women dressed in saffron. Everywhere one turned, there were people. On rooftops, thronging the roads, perched on walls. Some were merely curious onlookers. The rest were all devotees, each with a need in the heart and a prayer on their lips. Some held babies, who too were dressed in saffron. Mother Mary had to be thanked for blessing them with a child.

The evening sky was not the blue of September. Late in the afternoon, masses of clouds had been gathering to form a grey wool blanket that stifled the air. When a few drops of rain fell, the devotees stared at the skies in dismay. Not everyone had brought an umbrella. Besides, holding an umbrella aloft while following the car procession would be almost impossible.

'There has hardly been any movement,' Santosh had said in the morning.

Gowda nodded. At the meeting, it had been decided to keep up the surveillance and start a serious manhunt (or woman hunt as ACP Stanley Sagayaraj corrected himself) for the killer before it escalated into something beyond their control. Gowda had officially been brought into the investigation on ACP Stanley Sagayaraj's request.

'The corporator is well informed about everything we do ... and his household will be in on it as well. So, everyone will lie low for a while.'

Gowda's eyes lit on the wall calendar. 8 September. What was the significance? There was something, he knew. And then it came to him. St Mary's Feast. He thought of the crowds that would fill the streets. Even if Bhuvana, whoever she was, had decided to ease up for a while, she would step out this evening, certain that no one would notice her in the sea of saffron-clad humanity that would take over the streets.

'There will be,' Gowda said, cryptically.

Santosh stared at him, puzzled. 'How do you know that, sir?'

'This evening, St Mary's Basilica will hold its car festival and she will come out knowing that she won't be visible.'

'She, sir?' Santosh held his breath.

'Bhuvana. That's what she calls herself.'

'It could be a eunuch,' Santosh asserted.

'It could be.' Gowda put his hands on the table and stared at the lines on his palms. What did they signify? What did the lines on the palms of the killer look like? Would they whorl in a way different from his? Would they twist and turn in some inexplicable fashion that translated a murderous thought into action?

'Trust me, something tells me we'll know this evening.'

Santosh nodded. He would see for himself if the sakaath sense attributed to Gowda was for real or one more of Gajendra's fabrications.

'Find a place on that street somewhere, by about four. And Santosh, you'll be in mufti. Wear a saffron-colour shirt. Buy it if you don't have one.'

Santosh was puzzled. But he understood once he arrived in Shivaji Nagar.

4.27 p.m.

Everywhere, saffron reigned. Shirts, saris, kurtas. It was the perfect cover for a policeman on surveillance duty.

Santosh found the CCB team in their room that was part of a cluster of offices above a wholesale timber merchant's. The CCB had grabbed a room some months ago when they started this operation, setting themselves up amidst brokerage firms, marketing consultants, and even a dentist.

The room sat four floors up, looming over the adjoining building, with almost a direct view of the corporator's street and his home.

They grinned, looking at him. Inspector Pradeep fingered the fabric of his shirt. The material hissed as he rubbed it between his fingers. 'New, is it?' He laughed.

Santosh flushed. 'Thought it would be the best way to blend with the crowds,' he said, then added as an afterthought, 'Inspector Gowda asked me to.'

'It's a waste of time. The corporator knows that we are watching him. He's being extra careful.'

Santosh gaped. 'But how?'

'A loose word, a paper carelessly left. Who knows? But Ibrahim seemed to indicate that the corporator had been warned...' Pradeep spoke softly. 'Did you want something?'

'No.' Santosh flushed. 'I just wanted to check if something had come up.'

Pradeep shrugged.

'I'd better get going,' Santosh said.

'Have fun,' Pradeep threw at him as Santosh went down the narrow stairs.

4.42 p.m.

Santosh had walked up and down the street, eaten a stick of pink cotton candy, drunk a cup of tea and had finally found a group seated on the steps of a shop diagonally across from the gate. A group of saffron-clad men and women. They had beckoned him over. 'It'll only start at five, sir,' one of the men said. 'Sit when you can. Once the chariot starts moving, you will be swept along.'

Santosh squeezed in. A woman with tightly plaited grey hair smiled at him. 'Is this your first time?'

He nodded, wondering how she knew.

'I've been coming here for twenty-five years. I missed it only once, when my brother died. So I can tell when it is a person's first time.'

Santosh smiled. Were all seasoned pilgrims the same, he wondered. The fervour, the need to initiate the new to the ways and nuances of the pilgrimage, the inability to stop a practice once they had been doing it a few years. Last year, he had been to Sabarimala. And he had seen it there as well.

'It's a rather special sight, the chariot!' the elderly woman spoke.

'Don't spoil it for him, Nirmala Jessy amma. Let him feel the grace for himself,' one of the men smiled.

The skies were dark. A streak of lightning flashed. Santosh flinched.

'Trust me, it won't rain,' Nirmala Jessy said. 'Mother Mary won't allow her children to be drenched.'

'Did you go towards the Basilica?' someone else asked.

Santosh shook his head.

'It's a splendid sight. The tall illuminated cross on the steeple. Against this sky, it will be spectacular. We can take a quick walk there and get back here in time before the procession begins,' the young man offered.

Nirmala Jessy looked up and her arm on the young man's tightened. 'No, don't go.'

'Don't fuss, Mummy.' He shrugged her arm off and stood up.

Santosh glanced at his watch. 'How long will it take?'

'Ten minutes, bro. We'll take the alley route. The main roads will be choked up.'

Ignatious Arul, that was his name he said, led the way through a maze of alleys. 'My mother believes I was born only because Mother Mary blessed her. She brought me here as an infant and, ever since, has insisted that I come with her.' He smiled.

Suddenly they were in front of the Basilica. Santosh saw the sight he had been promised. The steeple rose high into the sky and its apex was the illuminated cross. 'One hundred and seventy-two feet high,' Ignatious murmured, enjoying the look in Santosh's eye.

Santosh saw something else. Gowda, leaning against a police vehicle, his eyes lazily surveying the crowds.

Santosh swallowed.

'We'd better get back,' he said, turning.

The street had filled up in the time they were gone. Pilgrims with candles and flowers, and a few vendors selling balloons, cotton candy and plastic toys. A roar seemed to emanate from the crowd. 'The procession has started,' Nirmala Jessy's animated voice cried out and she stood up, unable to help herself.

'Relax, Mummy,' Ignatious said. 'It'll take a while before it gets here.'

They could hear the sound of singing from the distance. The old woman wrung her hands. 'Next year, Ignatious, we must find a place closer to the Basilica. This is too far away. I want to join in when they sing Ava Maria.'

'You can sing it when the chariot comes this way,' Ignatious Arul said, throwing Santosh a wry look.

The corporator had set up a long table outside his gate. Four round-bellied terracotta pots were placed on it. Two men manned the table, offering water and buttermilk in plastic cups to anyone who wandered in that direction. Santosh watched the gate lazily. Gowda's sakaath sense wasn't working this evening, he thought. The table was placed in front of the gates so no one could enter or leave.

'He's a good man, the corporator,' Nirmala Jessy said.

Santosh stared at her.

'Every year he organizes water and buttermilk for the pilgrims. Long before he became corporator or had this house or all that he has now,' Nirmala Jessy said.

Ignatious Arul nodded. 'He made a hefty donation to St Mary's Association in Lingarajapuram. That's where we are from. He said all mother goddesses have to be venerated.'

Santosh's phone trilled. Gowda.

'Sir,' he murmured into the phone.

'How's it going?'

'It's very crowded. And very hot. Luckily Corporator Ravikumar has set up a table in front of his gate, offering water and buttermilk.'

'There's another gate.'

'Oh.'

'Yes, I thought you wouldn't know. A small gate on the other side opens onto a street that's a dead end. Keep an eye on it.'

'I will, sir.'

'Call me the moment you spot anything or anyone.'

Santosh put his phone back thoughtfully. He saw Ignatious look at him. 'My landlord,' he said in explanation. 'He'll be joining me, he said. I'd better go and meet him. He said he'll come to the end of the road.'

Nirmala Jessy nodded. 'That's how it should be. What did you say your name is?'

'Santosh.'

'And your church name? Didn't they give you a Christian name when they baptized you?'

Santosh's eyes flashed wildly. Christian name. Suddenly he remembered the fish shop on Hennur Road.

'Jonah!' he said.

'Are you with the police?' Ignatious asked.

'No, why do you ask?' Santosh mumbled, remembering to switch on a puzzled look.

'Something about you ... the hair,' he said with a grin, and then added slyly, 'the way you stand, with your chest puffed out, your shoulders pulled back and your arms behind you, surveying the world as though you own it.'

Santosh flushed. Fuck!

Nirmala Jessy smiled. 'He wants to join the police ... that's his dream. Why don't you write the test too?'

Santosh heaved himself up. If he hung around here any longer, she would find him a bride and plan his pension fund as well. 'I should be going,' he said.

5.12 p.m.

All afternoon they came, each seeking to lay their dreams at the feet of a goddess and hoping for succour.

She lay on the bed, staring at the fan. The sound of the crowds intensified. Akka had walked in briefly to say, 'The pilgrims will fill up the entire place in a little while. There won't be a square inch left.'

At night she couldn't sleep. Each time she closed her eyes, memories pressed down upon her, making her want to flee to some distant place.

Everything that had been beautiful in her life had been corrupted. Everything was tainted and ugly. All of it had been ruined. Again and again.

But she wasn't that boy any more. She would never again be that powerless, frightened creature. She would never again allow anyone to decide the course of her life. Over the years, she had learnt how to wrest control into her hands and keep it there.

She sat up suddenly and hugged her knees.

Something tugged at her. A need to get out. A need to be

someone else. Only that would cease the ache in her. Only that would allow her to forget, at least for a bit.

Bhuvana giggled. A snickering sound of girlish glee at what she had planned. A little laugh that demanded: What are you waiting for?

She switched on the series of light bulbs that circled the mirror and opened the make-up kit and started working quickly, smiling shyly at her reflection in the mirror.

Then she drew out her six vials of attar. This evening she didn't even bother with sniffing at the mouth of the vial.

It would be her favourite Jannat ul firdous.

And saffron, so she would blend in.

From one of the drawers, she pulled out a petticoat and blouse. Then the padded bra and the matching panty. She was still humming as she adjusted the blouse and pinned the sari so it hung low, showing off her waist.

From the shelf on top, she chose a wig of shoulder-length hair.

She fastened her pearl earrings that had just come back from the jeweller. In the mirror she saw herself and shook her head in delight.

I am the most beautiful woman I know. Where were you until now, Bhuvana? When you went away, Bhuvana, I was lost.

On the heel of that thought came another. Without Sanjay there would be no Bhuvana.

Once, this had been for him. But none of it remained. A tear grew in her eye. For him. For her. For the end of a dream.

And then a voice whispered: look up.

She did. In the mirror was someone else.

Kamakshi, with twice as much spirit and power. It was Kamakshi who placed the tip of her finger against her glossy lip and murmured. Tonight, tonight ... She gazed at herself in the mirror and struck a pose, placing her hand on her hip and thrusting her hip to a side. What a slut you are, Kamakshi!

She touched the topaz in her navel. She imagined a tongue probing her navel. She shivered.

Kamakshi, the wanton-eyed, who knew how to make it all possible.

5.48 p.m.

It was a small lane with a line of houses running into each other on one side and the corporator's wall on the other. A goat was tethered to a stake. Washing flapped on a roof. There was a corporation tap and children on the road, playing. Women sat on the doorsteps cleaning rice, braiding flowers or doing whatever it was women seemed to need a doorstep to do it on. A line of granite stacks barred traffic from entering the road. A two-wheeler could squeeze through, but nothing wider than that. Some of the pilgrims had spilled over into this lane as well.

The street lights came on, flooding the lane and casting pools of shadow. Santosh leaned against the wall.

'Aren't you coming?' a pilgrim called out to Santosh, hastening to the mouth of the lane. 'The chariot's almost here!'

Santosh straightened up and walked slowly towards the granite stacks. In the distance he could see a sea of people moving ahead in waves. As he watched, he saw a glowing object enter his line of vision. A ripple of sounds and singing as people entered the street.

'The procession will stop before it turns at the corner,'

someone called out. Elbows dug into his side as the pilgrims tried to push past him in their haste to reach the chariot.

Without wanting to, Santosh found himself near the chariot, ablaze with light. Within the chariot was the six-foot statue of Mother Mary clad in a saffron sari, standing holding Infant Jesus. 'Amma, amma...' the voices called around him as they threw flowers and held up candles.

The chariot tilted dangerously. Would it topple? Santosh worried. The cross on top seemed too big. All that was needed to start a stampede was one panicked pilgrim. Santosh tried to extricate himself from the crowds and push back into the lane. As he turned, he saw a movement near the gate.

Through the little gate, someone emerged. Santosh pushed through the people around him, to move closer. For a moment the shadows swallowed the figure. Then he saw a woman emerge into a pool of light. A woman dressed in a saffron sari.

Bhuvana. This must be the Bhuvana Gowda had mentioned. And suddenly Santosh knew something else. This was also the woman he had seen with the eunuch.

He followed the woman with his eyes, walking towards her even as he speed-dialled Gowda. 'Sir,' he said.

Gowda held the phone away from his ear. Santosh's voice would perforate his ear drum, he thought. In the background, he could hear the crowd noises – people talking, the blare of horns, music playing, 'Yes, Santosh,' Gowda said. 'What is it?'

'Sir, I think I saw the woman.' Santosh's voice quivered in excitement.

6.10 p.m.

Gowda looked at his watch. It was a little past six. Evening had disappeared without a trace into night. A few drops of rain fell. He raised his face to the sky, to the raindrops.

'Sir,' one of the policemen called out. 'You'll get wet. Why don't you sit in the vehicle?'

Gowda nodded and walked towards the Bolero. How far had Santosh got tailing Bhuvana? Something akin to disquiet washed over him. Would the boy be safe? He was young, inexperienced and eager to make a mark – just the combination to make him take risks he shouldn't. Rain thudded above him noisily. Gowda peered at the cross above the steeple and murmured a prayer: Mother, keep him safe.

6.24 p.m.

Santosh had managed to not lose her despite the crowds. She wasn't in a hurry anyway. She seemed lost in thought as she glided through the streets. Gowda had told him to follow her, but had he realized that Bhuvana was the woman with the eunuch? The one they were certain was the killer. Though it seemed impossible when you looked at her. She was small and fragile-looking.

The rain had begun to fall heavily now. He saw her duck into the canopied doorway of a shop. There were a few other pilgrims jostling for space. Santosh stepped in and joined them.

He stood right behind her. She was small. So small that she came only up to his chest. And he was only 5'8" in his socks.

Every follicle of his skin sensed her. He smelt jasmine. Was it her perfume or the flowers she wore in her hair?

She gathered the end of the sari around herself and Santosh noticed the earrings she wore. The breath snagged in his throat. It was an exact replica of the one that had been found on Liaquat. But how? There was someone else, Santosh decided. The actual killer was someone else. She was merely the bait to lure the victims. And that was when Santosh decided what he must do next.

She felt the warmth of his gaze on the nape of her neck. She felt his eyes wander and rove over her. It wasn't the animal lust that men's eyes seemed to emanate. This was a gentler gaze; of a man curious, a man attracted, a man gathering a memory by the moment.

She shifted her stance so he could see her better. She brushed a lock of hair away from her face and tucked it behind her ear. This was how it had begun with Sanjay too. The warmth of a glance.

A sob rose in her throat. Her Sanjay.

Stabbed and stabbed again. His intestines falling out of the wound. She thought of a rat she had seen; lying on its side with its intestines spilling out while a crow feasted on it with a hop, skip and a tilt of its head. Her insides heaved. Her head whirled. She felt the ground rush towards her.

Santosh felt rather than saw her slide towards the floor. Instinctively, he reached out and gathered her into his arms. She weighed almost nothing.

A moment later, she recovered. 'I'm sorry,' she said hastily as others turned towards them.

'Anything wrong?' a man asked.

'No, I am all right,' she said.

'She's with me. All the crowd pressing in ... nothing serious,' Santosh said and turned to her. 'Are you all right?'

She nodded. 'Thank you,' she said.

'You shouldn't have stepped out while it was so crowded,' Santosh said and almost bit his tongue. What was he saying?

'I had to be here.'

'Were you going somewhere?'

She glanced up at him and tightened her lips. Then she threw him a piercing look. 'Why? Why do you want to know?'

'Sorry,' he said stiffly. 'It's none of my business.'

'No, no, I didn't mean it that way.' She spoke urgently as if to bridge the distance he had wrought between them.

'I am just so confused. I don't know what I am saying.' She turned to him with imploring eyes.

'Look, do you want me to take you home? I can drop you wherever you want me to,' he said.

She looked at him again.

He didn't understand the purport of that gaze. His heart was beating too hard for him to try and figure it out. What would she say?

In the end, they were all the same. Seeking merely to gratify their egos and their pricks. Everything else was an act. For a moment there, she had thought he was different. Like she had thought her Sanjay was.

But even Sanjay had turned out to be a sham. Masquerading as a prince when he was a villain within. His life had been as shadowed by darkness as hers was. And she had thought he was untouched by all that constituted her life. She had thought that here was sweetness, here was perhaps even true love. In the end, he too would have wanted of her what the others did.

She turned to him, her unlikely saviour. Her eyes narrowed as she took him in. The way he stood with his fingers hooked to the waistband of his trousers. His saffron shirt open at the neck. The short hair. The clean-shaven jaw. The glint in his eye. And she realized why he seemed so familiar. She had seen him before. He had accompanied Inspector Gowda. So he was on the prowl, was he? Well, well, well...

Kamakshi smiled at him.

7.04 p.m.

Gowda glanced at his phone every few minutes but it stayed resolutely silent. Where was Santosh, he wondered. Why wasn't he reporting in?

The rain wasn't deterring the crowd. Policemen hated evenings like this when even the weather seemed to conspire against them. Every moment was a potential threat to peace. So many lives. So many random acts. A purse snatched. A breast grabbed. A toe stamped upon. An earring lost. Nothing planned or premeditated. Nothing anyone went seeking.

The wireless crackled. A report of an elderly couple found dead in their Koramangala bungalow ... a boy missing ... a building collapse in Beggars Colony...

Gowda stepped out of the vehicle. The rain had quietened down to a drizzle. 'I need to leave,' he told the SI, holding a hand over his head.

'Sir, we can't move for another hour at least ... the traffic, as you can see...' the man apologized.

Gowda nodded. He had used the police vehicle to get here. Downright stupid of him. He should have brought his bike and parked it nearby. He could hardly go looking for Santosh on foot.

7.23 p.m.

She seemed to know the way through the maze that was Shivaji Nagar. Santosh followed her, not daring to ask her where they were going.

'Do you come for the car procession every year?' she asked. The rain had cooled the night. Santosh wished he had brought his jacket.

'It's my first time. And you?' He stepped around a puddle carefully.

'Ever since I was four.' She dimpled at him.

He still hadn't managed to look at her properly. But even in the patchy light he could see she was pretty. What was her connection with the corporator's household?

'Are you going to drop me to an auto stand or all the way?' she asked suddenly.

'All the way. I don't like the look of these streets at night,' he said, taking in the narrow lanes speckled with rubbish and people, mostly men. He saw a man by the side of the street watching them. A toothpick dangled from his mouth. The man adjusted his crotch and murmured something.

'It's not safe for a woman,' Santosh added.

'Actually, this is the safest place for a woman to be,' she said. 'It's crowded any time of the day or night and if a woman makes even one sound of distress, there will be at least ten men wanting to know what's wrong...'

'Rowdies, all of them.'

'You sound like a policeman.' She darted a look at him.

'I am a … er,' he began and then changed it to, 'I am a man. I know how men think!'

Santosh glanced at his watch. He hadn't been able to text or call Gowda. He must be furious.

'I need a smoke,' he said abruptly. 'Do you mind?'

She paused while he ducked into a petty shop. 'One India Kings,' he said, remembering the brand Gowda smoked. As the man pulled out a cigarette, Santosh took his phone out to text Gowda: *Following B. At Shivaji Nagar now.*

Sensing her at his side, he pressed send and put his phone in his pocket.

He took the cigarette, tapped it against his chin and said, 'Actually, I'll smoke it later … I am trying to quit!'

She smiled.

She asked him to find them an autorickshaw. Her house was some distance away. She would direct the driver, she said.

'You are new to Bangalore, aren't you?' she asked.

He smiled wryly. 'Is it so obvious?'

And then with a certain slyness, he added, 'Only new to the city!'

She smiled at him and drew her sari pallu around her. She enjoyed this part of the game. The flirtation, the banter. The innuendo. The sidelong glances. The cat-and-mouse game.

In the autorickshaw, their shoulders touched. Sometimes it threw them against each other when it entered or exited a dug-up road. And one time, when it caused their hands to brush, she felt him take hers in his.

'Do you mind?' he asked.

Meaning, do you want to fuck?

Yes, she wanted to.

She shook her head shyly. That was part of the game. The kind of men who went for someone like her wanted that. A touch of shyness. A downcast face. A virgin even if she had been fucked silly before. In the end, all men were the same.

7.47 p.m.

Gowda walked up Jumma Masjid Road, weaving through the traffic, and cut into Commercial Street. The shops were all ablaze with light.

If Mamtha saw him now. All these years, he had never accompanied Mamtha any time she had asked him to go with her to Commercial Street. She did her annual shopping before Ugadi and he had always pleaded work as an excuse to extricate himself from what it entailed trailing her from shop to shop, looking for the same item in six different shops, the dithering, the pointless discussions on merits and faults. And yet, here he was, his eyes seeking every face and shop front: Was Santosh here?

He called Santosh again. Not reachable, an electronic voice declared.

Gowda would have to call Urmila.

He would ask her to drive him. She would be game, he knew. Here is your chance to be part of my working life. So don't ever complain I don't tell you anything, he would joke.

He could imagine the smile that would appear on her face. He could see her even dress the part. Pulling on jeans and a shirt, slipping her feet into sneakers that had never known a scuff mark. Choosing to take the Scorpio rather than the Audi A4 she drove. This was police work after all.

How much of their relationship was role-playing, he

wondered. This thing with him. Was it like slipping into another role? The one that went with meeting an old flame?

He clenched his jaw. He wouldn't allow his mind to go down that road.

Instead, he began walking towards Kamaraj Road. He would tell her to meet him at the mouth of Commercial Street.

'What's wrong?' Urmila asked a little later.

Gowda shook his head. 'Nothing, really.' He shrugged. Then he changed his mind and said, 'Santosh hasn't been in contact for the last two hours. And I can't get through to him.'

'He is a grown man, Borei.' Her lips twitched.

'But an inexperienced investigator. I asked him to trail someone. I shouldn't have. He could be in trouble.' Gowda leaned against the dashboard and knocked his head against it gently again and again.

'Don't do that. Your nose will start bleeding again. Borei, he'll be fine. This is Bangalore, after all…' she said quietly.

'We were investigating a murder. I should have told Stanley what we were planning. I had no right dragging Santosh into it. And now he's gone missing,' Gowda said, still with his head against the dashboard.

'Where do we go now?'

Gowda straightened. 'Keep driving. I'll tell you. I'm going on a mere hunch, you see…'

The road was crowded. All the diverted traffic and the rain hadn't helped. As they inched their way towards Wheeler Road, in the narrowest part of the road where Sabapathi Lane intersected Kamaraj Road, a small truck laden beyond capacity braked abruptly. One of its back tyres had burst.

There was no room to pull out, so Gowda and Urmila sat in silence while people gathered, scratched their heads and decided what had to be done.

Gowda tried Santosh's number again. Unreachable.

8.21 p.m.

Santosh felt the breeze whip at his face. Where were they going?

'You haven't told me your name,' he said.

'Neither have you,' she replied, throwing him one more of those sidelong glances she specialized in.

'Santosh Ignatious,' he improvised.

'Kamakshi,' she said.

He frowned. Gowda had said her name was Bhuvana. So she was making up a name as he had. Was he being reckless? If she could lie so easily, she would be capable of anything. Then he saw her finger twist a hanky. And he relaxed. Maybe she was called Kamakshi at home.

'How far is your home, Kamakshi?' he asked.

'Yes, madam, where are we going?' the auto driver chipped in.

'Keep going. When you get to Nagawara, I'll tell you,' she said.

'It's not my home. I live with my brother and his family,' she said, turning to Santosh. And then, after a pause, 'You know how that is…'

He nodded.

Gowda was completely wrong about her, he decided.

'They didn't want me to come to the car festival, but I didn't want to break what I had begun … so many years ago,' she said, and then to the auto driver, 'turn left.'

The autorickshaw turned into a narrow alley of shops. A huge apartment block loomed above the rest of the buildings in the street.

A pack of dogs stood beside a rubbish bin. Two of them stared at the autorickshaw and chased after it, barking.

'Bloody nuisance, these dogs!' the auto driver growled. 'If you had told me you were coming this far, I wouldn't have taken the trip!'

'Stop complaining,' Santosh snapped. 'It's your job!'

'All very well for you to say that! I am the one who has to return all the way back with an empty backseat!'

'I'll take a ride back till the Ring Road. That satisfy you?' Santosh said, and watched with surprise as she shook her head.

'But you can't go. I want you to meet my brother,' she said.

Santosh hid his smile. This was getting interesting.

Suddenly, he was struck by a thought. What if it was the brother? But why? The murders had been random and not for gain. Could there be a deeper, darker motive? Organ robbery? But all the victims had their kidneys and livers in place...

Santosh remembered Gajendra talking to him of Umesh Reddy. They had been looking at a criminal case together. Of a man whose hands had been hacked by a rowdy. That's when Gajendra mentioned Jack the Ripper. That was the name the media had given the serial killer. His victims were mostly lower-class women. Robbing their homes after the act was simply his way of misleading the police. He was sick in his head. 'Pure psychopath. He killed for the sheer pleasure of it. Those are the ones we should fear,' Gajendra had added as Santosh stared at him in amazement.

Santosh decided he would ask the auto driver to stay. It was also time to let Gowda know where he was.

He pulled his phone out. He saw that his message was still in the outbox. Gowda would be frothing at the mouth, he thought unhappily.

He tried calling Gowda but it wouldn't go through. It was a low-signal zone. He sent the message again and decided he would key in another one quickly, the moment they reached their destination, wherever that was.

The auto turned another curve and Santosh realized that they had reached the garment factory from the other side.

In the darkness, it stood like a brooding monster from hell. His mouth went dry.

'Is this where you stay?' he asked quietly.

'Don't be silly. It's at the end of the lane. My brother's the watchman.'

'Who? Manjunath?'

She looked at him curiously. But her tone was flat when she spoke. 'So you know him.'

'I met him once,' Santosh said, cursing under his breath. 'I came here with the contractor,' he added.

'So, you've been here before?'

He nodded.

'Stop,' she told the auto driver. He obliged with a screech of brakes.

'I'll take care of it,' Santosh said.

He got out and waited for her.

'Here,' he said, drawing a hundred-rupee note from his wallet. 'I'll pay you a hundred when I get back as waiting charge. Just fifteen minutes. I'll be back before that.'

The auto driver looked at the note. He took it between two fingers. 'Fifteen minutes.'

She led the way. He followed, punching the keys on his phone. *Garment factory*.

She turned and smiled. 'This is a no-signal zone ... you'll have to wait to get back to the main road for your phone to work.'

Santosh saw the message had gone. So he smiled and said nothing. He couldn't have even if he wanted to. His tongue seemed to be stuck to the roof of his mouth.

She knew he had been here before. She knew he had recognized the factory. She knew he was walking behind her, reining in his fear. This was a new thing. Usually, the fear factor came at the end, when they knew what she had decided for them. But this was even better. Fear from the start.

Had he known from the moment he had seen her and had he been playing along? Or had he realized only now? She would ask him in a bit. He would tell her. Fear would prod his mouth open and form the words. Fear made people do many things.

She opened a gate and led him in. 'I don't think anyone's home,' she said. 'I wonder where they went...'

He didn't speak. She could sense the way he held himself, in readiness for whatever swung in to attack him.

'Listen, I have the key to the side room in the factory. If we go in, I can switch the lights on. I could wait there till my brother comes. You can leave. No point in keeping the auto waiting,' she said.

'Here,' she continued, fishing out a key from her bag and handing it to him.

She held up the phone so he could see the keyhole in its light.

She watched him wrestle with the lock. It took only ten

seconds to pull the sock-wrapped ball from her bag and another ten seconds to swing it at his skull.

A fierce crack, a soft thud, the perfect note of a ball struck.

He crumpled to the floor.

9.10 p.m.

Gowda's phone beeped. He stared at the screen. 'Just as I thought,' he said. 'He's with her.'

'But where did they go?' Urmila asked, negotiating yet another speed breaker on the road.

The rattle of metal against metal. Gowda craned his neck curiously. 'What's in the back?'

Urmila's mouth twitched, 'My golf kit. I played at the BGC this morning.'

'Good game?' Gowda asked. He didn't know a thing about golf and didn't even know if it was appropriate to use the word 'game'.

'All right ... my usual caddy was unwell so I had an old relic. Ijas. He wouldn't stop talking. According to him, he was not just caddy, but conscience keeper too, to everyone who is anyone in this city.'

'What does a caddy do? Doesn't he just lug the clubs around?' Gowda's eyes were on the traffic as he spoke.

'That he does ... but he is also someone who has insights about the course and can tell me how to play it best, given my handicap.'

Gowda licked his lips. He didn't understand a word of what she was saying.

'By the way, he said something very interesting. Did you know that your Corporator Ravikumar used to be a caddy at the BGC? Ijas took him in as an apprentice.'

Gowda felt his head spin. Everything around him seemed to slip away.

The missing bit in the jigsaw. There before him all along and he hadn't seen it. He had known that Corporator Ravikumar had once been called Caddy Ravi but he hadn't ever asked why.

The eunuchs in the house. The pearl earring. The Scorpio parked at the corporator's home. The Ravi Varma prints. The counterfeit currency. The old factory. The fractured skulls. Ranganathan many years ago, and then the more recent victims. What had Dr Khan said? And later Dr Reddy?

The pattern almost always resembles the weapon used. Something heavy, with a small striking surface, was used to inflict a tangential blow. It's a localized fracture. Enough to disorient a man. Something hard, small and rounded ... a hammer would splinter the surface differently. Imagine a coconut being swung against a man's head. But this isn't anything as big as a coconut. A ball of some sort is my initial reading...

A golf ball as a cosh. Someone who knew the exact force required to inflict injury. A weapon that could be easily hidden in a handbag when the murderer set out seeking her victim.

The corporator would never pass as a woman, no matter how much he tried. At best, he would be a mannish woman. But his younger brother. That little runt with his smooth cheeks, dainty steps and diamond earrings. He would make an alluring woman. The educated brother who saw himself as one of the women in the Ravi Varma prints he favoured. The pearl earrings were his. That was who Bhuvana was: small, lethal and perfectly trained to throw a man twice his height and weight.

Fuck, fuck, fuck ... why hadn't he seen it? Fucking rum had addled his brains. He was never going to drink again. And Santosh was with her now, god knows where. He had to find the boy before she...

His phone beeped again. He stared at the message and said, 'Fuck!'

'What?' Urmila asked.

'Can you make this go any faster? That bloody fool's with her at the factory. God knows what she'll do to him before we get there...'

Urmila pressed her big toe down on the accelerator. The speedometer swung up. 'Faster?' she asked.

'Faster,' he said.

9.19 p.m.

When Santosh regained consciousness, she was sitting by his side. He tried to raise his head and a streak of excruciating pain seared through him.

'It hurts less if you don't move,' she said.

He lay back on the Rexine sofa. 'You bitch,' he said, even though it hurt to even speak the words.

'What did you think, Sub-inspector Santosh?' she asked. 'Did you think I am a fool?'

He closed his eyes.

'All you men are the same. All you men. You think you are smarter than us women?'

He opened his eyes and said, 'But you are not a woman, are you? Much as you may think you are.'

She slapped him. A man's blow.

'I'm better than any woman,' she said, furiously. 'Do you want me to give you a blowjob? What my tongue can do to your cock will make you forget any woman. No woman will suck you off like I could. No woman will let you fuck her like I could let you.'

He stared at the half-crazed creature pacing the room. As long as he kept her talking, she wouldn't do to him whatever she had planned. Would the auto driver come looking for him? Would Gowda come in the meantime? He had to keep her talking.

'That still doesn't make you a woman,' he murmured. She stopped and slapped him again. 'Don't say that,' she snarled and began her furious pacing.

Santosh reached for the mobile in his trouser pocket. The last person he had called was Gowda. His fingers fumbled. He began punching the keys.

She stopped mid-stride and said, 'You think you are very smart!'

She groped in his pocket, drew out the mobile and flung it on the table.

'My brother's the same,' she said. 'He thinks I am a silly performing animal who can be taught tricks but isn't capable of a single independent thought.'

She propped him up so he was sitting straight. Then she took a length of cord and tied his legs and arms. 'There, let's see what you can do with your hands and legs tied.' She giggled, peering down at him.

A chill went down his spine as he stared at her through a haze of pain. Suddenly it fell into place.

He saw that she had seen realization dawn in his eyes.

'You are,' he croaked but she wouldn't let him speak further.

She walked behind him. She didn't like looking at them. She didn't like the thought that they would see how it made her feel. Pleasure had to be private, for oneself rather than to be shared. All that kicking and writhing, screaming and struggling turned it into a disorderly thing. This was how she liked them. Powerless, acquiescent and hers to do with as she pleased.

She hadn't thought she would find so much pleasure in it that first time. To slip the ligature round the neck and let it do its work while she just tugged and tightened. It felt a little like flying a kite but with better results. In that last moment, as life ebbed out, she was the kite. Soaring above the world. Queen of the moment.

Santosh felt a cord tighten around his neck, glass slice into his throat. And as he felt blood spurt, he struggled.

Through the fear and the pain, he heard a voice. 'What the fuck's going on here?'

She turned and the ligature slipped out of her hands.

'Why is it you always walk in just when I am beginning to enjoy myself?' she demanded furiously.

'What? Who?' The corporator walked in, brandishing a gun. He stopped abruptly, unable to believe what he was seeing.

'Yes, Anna, it's me,' Chikka said.

The corporator stared at the unconscious man bleeding almost certainly to death; at his brother in the guise of a woman. He had heard that sometimes someone came to the factory at night. A woman had been spotted. Chikka was the only other person who had access to the key. When the call came a little earlier, he had decided to investigate for himself. Was that little idiot taking his slut there to fuck her?

What bizarre madness was this?

'Where's the ape? King Kong? Your loyal arselicker ...

you thought he was your brother from another mother…' Chikka asked.

The corporator slumped on a chair. He threw the gun on the table. King Kong was still at the bar near Kothanur where they had been when the call came. 'You were the one using this place. What is this, Chikka? What's going on?' He sank his head into his arms. 'What madness is this?'

'You,' Chikka said. 'You started it all.'

'What?' he asked.

'Didn't I beg and plead with you to not buy the factory? But you wanted it. And you brought back the past. My past that I so wanted to forget. Did you know Ranganathan would fuck me here? I liked it. I liked being fucked by him. I liked being able to pleasure him. Till you walked in on us. And the look I saw in your eyes … the disgust … something in me died, do you know that?'

Anna saw in his mind again the old man's open mouth, the desire in his eyes; he saw his little brother on the sofa, almost naked, and how his fingers were curled into a fist.

Chikka closed his eyes, seeing again the anger and disgust in his brother's eyes.

Everything came back in a rush. Ranganathan falling to his knees. The sound of glass breaking. The tearing of fabric. The clang of metal hitting the ground. Ranganathan groaning, and Anna screaming, 'You dirty old man, is this what all your niceness was for? You bastard.'

Chikka heard the sound of slaps … flesh against flesh. He curled into a ball when Anna drew close to him. 'I … I didn't…' Chikka whispered.

'Don't … it's not your fault … don't worry, I am here, your Anna is here to deal with it … punish him for what he did,' Anna's voice had whispered as he pulled Chikka up and helped him dress. 'Come, Chikka,' Anna said gently, furiously. 'This scum will never hurt you again.'

Chikka let himself be led away. He felt numb and sickened at the disgust he had seen in his brother's eyes. How could something that felt so good be so wrong?

It suited Anna and everyone else at home to have Chikka as the victim of an old man's perverse lust. It suited Chikka to believe it. Anything else would make him want to seek that wonder he had found in Ranganathan's clutch. That spiralling wonder that made him forget all his fears and shrug off his demons ... but what if Anna found out? Chikka shuddered at the thought of what he would encounter in his brother's eyes.

Chikka, or was it Bhuvana, or was it Kamakshi ... she didn't know any more who she was ... peered into Anna's face. Anna had said you can forget. All you need to do is decide to forget. She had. She had taught herself to forget.

It had begun with killing Ranganathan. The old man had waylaid him a couple of times and they had gone back to the factory. Chikka couldn't say no to him, much as he wanted to.

Anna heard about a car picking up Chikka from school. 'Amma said you went to a friend's house in his car. Which friend is that?'

'Sailesh,' Chikka lied. 'His father has a used-car business. So we went in this car he was taking to a customer.'

Anna nodded but Chikka was afraid. If he never saw Ranganathan again, it would be over, he decided. He planned it carefully, using Anna's own speciality – the golf ball in a sock, and some more. A ligature like no one had ever seen before. He had seen how the kites with manja thread sliced the kite strings of rival kites. He had ground the glass himself and mixed it in with Fevicol and applied it to the string, leaving it to dry on the roof of the house, away from everyone else's gaze.

'I was young and not strong enough. He escaped me and was run over when crossing the street. And I thought it had come to an end. I was free. But then you had to do this, didn't you? If you hadn't bought this damn factory, none of it would have come back to me. And then you dragged me here to view it. I saw how your face tightened when you saw this sofa.' Chikka kicked the side of the sofa on which Santosh was slumped.

'I knew you were thinking of what had happened here ... and I knew it too. The stillness of the factory. The silence. Ecstasy followed by guilt. I wanted that pleasure. Even more than before. Then the goddess came to me. You thought that only you could summon the goddess, didn't you? Well, I can too. She comes to me on her own. She seeks me out because she knows that I am twice as strong as you are. She showed me the way. She taught me how to dress and who to be. And she leads me to them.

'They are everywhere. Jaded men. Eager boys. I find them or they find me. Our need is the same, you see. But when it's over, I see it again ... that disgust in your eye ... it haunts me. The goddess said all I have to do is erase that memory. So I kill them ... Because, like you said that night, Anna, it's not my fault. They made me do it! And so they have to be punished for it!'

The corporator shook his head, unable to believe his ears or eyes.

'What are you saying, Chikka?' he asked weakly.

'You can't believe this about me. You think only you have it in you to play god, to bless or punish. Like you did with my Sanjay! You took my Sanjay's life without a second thought. God didn't decide that Sanjay's time on earth had come to an end. You did. And simply because Sanjay may have posed a threat.'

'Sanjay?' The corporator raised his head.

'My Sanjay loved me. Do you hear that? But you took him away as well. And you don't even know his name. Everything to you is dispensable ... everything!'

The corporator heard the click first.

Chikka had the gun in his hands.

'How does it feel, Anna, to know that you are powerless? How does it feel to know that your life is not in your control? How does it feel to be Chikka?'

'I...' the corporator began. The bullet made only a soft plop as it pierced his heart.

9.36 p.m.

Gowda and Urmila saw an auto drive away as they turned into the lane the factory was in.

Gowda had called the control room and asked for reinforcements to be sent to the factory. 'It's an emergency, send a patrol vehicle immediately,' he had hollered, hoping a Hoysala would get there in time. He had then called Gajendra and asked him to rush to the factory.

Gowda frowned as Urmila drove into the factory yard. Where was the Hoysala? Only the corporator's white Honda CRV. Urmila parked behind it.

Gowda rushed in, unheeding of Urmila's call for caution.

On the sofa Santosh was slumped with his throat cut. On the chair sat the corporator with a look of stupefaction on his dead face.

On the floor sat his younger brother, his chin on his knees. A gun lay on the ground. And further along, a puddle of clothes. A woman's sari and a wig.

Chikka raised his tear-stained face to Gowda. 'I had to kill him. It was Anna, sir, it was him all along. All those murders. But I was too late to save your colleague...'

Gowda stared, unable to believe what he saw.

A Hoysala vehicle arrived. A team of policemen trooped in. Gowda gestured to them, and one of the policemen stepped forward to take the corporator's younger brother away.

Gowda watched him as he turned and gazed at his dead brother and into the darkness that was the factory floor. There was a remarkable calm in his gaze. Gowda frowned. What had happened here?

Then he saw Santosh's mobile on the table.

He picked it up. It seemed to have been recording something. He clicked shut the phone and slipped it into his pocket. He would look at it later.

A police van arrived to take the dead corporator. The CCB men were on their way, Head Constable Gajendra said, walking in.

'Santosh, sir?' he asked, unable to finish the sentence.

Gowda nodded. He walked towards Santosh and looked down at the boy. Guilt tussled with regret. How transient life was. This was the first time he had lost a colleague, he realized. And he had been responsible for it. He shouldn't have let Santosh go into this on his own. He was only a boy ... a few years older than his son. Gowda closed his eyes. Then he heard a faint groan.

'He's alive,' Gowda shouted. 'He's alive. We need to get him to a hospital. Immediately. Now.'

Gajendra leapt forward, calling for assistance to take Santosh to the hospital.

Gowda followed them as they carried Santosh into the van. A first-aid box was opened and a wad of cotton wool plugged into the wound. Gajendra, who seemed to have lost his habitual apathy, was making sure that Santosh was laid on his belly. He grabbed a bunch of files and placed it beneath Santosh's chest so that his head inclined downwards. He turned Santosh's head to a side and prised his mouth open so he didn't choke on his own blood. 'I'll go with him, sir,' Gajendra told Gowda as they slammed shut the van doors.

Gowda turned to look at the factory once again.

He would ask Urmila, who was waiting for him in the Scorpio, to follow the police van to the hospital. He would bully the doctors, the staff, make sure Santosh had the best medical attention to drag him back to life.

And when Santosh woke up, Gowda would be there, waiting for him.

BIBLIOGRAPHY AND REFERENCE MATERIAL

Books and Journals

Narayan, K.S. Dr, *The Essentials of Forensic Medicine and Toxicology* (XI edition)

Banerjee, A.K., *Police Diaries* (1993)

Rakesh P., 'Setting Tongues Loose', *Deccan Herald*, Sunday, 4 January 2004

Police Manual [http://www.ksp.gov.in/home/policemanual/index.php]

Websites

http://www.hindu.com/2011/01/19/stories/2011011963810300.htm

http://www.cidap.gov.in/documents/FAKE%20CURRENCY.pdf

ACKNOWLEDGEMENTS

I began work on this book in May 2010 on a whim. A page later, I realized that it was going to need more than just bookish research. There are several people I would like to thank for their help in making each aspect of information gathering that much easier and bringing this book to completion, foremost among them Mr Nizammudin, Former Director General and Inspector General of Police, Bangalore, and P.K. Hormis Tharakan, Former Director General of the Kerala Police. Several officers of the Karnataka State Police offered suggestions and inputs that made all the difference. However, for reasons most obvious, they do not wish to be named. Thank you, gentlemen, you know who you are!

Dr P.K. Sunil for first leading me into the possibilities a forensic textbook can offer to the imagination of a writer, and then offering me the title; Dr Rajamani MD, Forensic Medicine, for answering my questions with patience and great humour; and Dr Naresh Shetty, Medical Director, MS Ramaiah Hospital, and his team at Ramaiah Medical College for taking me through the intricacies of a post-mortem.

Naseer Ahmed for taking me on that marvellous night-time walk through Shivaji Nagar in Bangalore and opening my senses to a world that I didn't know existed.

Jayant Kodkani, this time for not just being my first reader, but also for taking the time out to pen memories of a Bangalore in the 1970s.

Sunil Koliyot for being such a great buddy and a useful one at that, and especially for providing me the know-how on how to clean stubborn shower heads.

Pradeep Menon of Dark Arts The Tattoo Studio, Bangalore, for generously sharing information on tattoos.

Chetan Krishnaswamy, for countless tit-bits and trivia, insights and information, and weeding out errors of incomprehension. (And for all the beer, chilli chicken and laughs.)

And Junoo Simon, old friend and sty mate for all the fun times, and then for designing a knock-out cover!

And as always, this book wouldn't be what it is were it not for V.K. Karthika, who shares my vision for every book I have written and with unflagging faith nurtures the light and passion.

Shantanu Ray Chaudhuri, who with quiet and great efficiency saw the book through to its final form.

Camilla Ferrier and the team at The Marsh Agency for their sustained support.

Mini Kuruvilla for continued back-up.

Sukhita Aiyer, Madhu Ambat, Sumentha and Franklin Bell, Francesca Diano, Leela Kalyanraman, Gita Krishnankutty, Achuthan Kudallur, Carmen Lavin, Dimpy and Suresh Menon, S. Prasannarajan, Rajesh M.B., Sunita Shankar, Abhijeet Shetty, Navtej Singh, Rajani Sunil, Jayapriya Vasudevan and Patrick Wilson – friends who make most days so much easier to deal with in countless ways.

The cornerstones of my life: my parents, Soumini and Bhaskaran; and Unni, Maitreya and Sugar for being there for me. Always.

CHAIN OF CUSTODY

Anita Nair

'The only thing necessary for the triumph of evil is for good men to do nothing.'

– Edmund Burke

1

It's a smell I recognize. Grime, sweat and the unwashed smell of a body covered by soiled clothes that are threadbare in patches and unravelling at the edges. The reek of desperation. For I've lived with it.

Inside the crowded general compartment of train number 18463 Prashanthi Express, scheduled to reach Bangalore City Junction at 12.05 p.m., the pong of desperation hangs like a low cloud; the collective breath of creatures occupying every seat and aisle.

I look around. It's a mixed group as always. About ninety people packed into a compartment meant to hold seventy-two. There's barely room to move. The ticket collector will make a cursory visit and seldom go beyond the door. The stench from the bathrooms and from the clogged pores of the vacant-eyed hollow-cheeked passengers will deter even the bravest man. Once in a while he will pounce on a hapless face and demand, 'Tickets! Tickets!'

Sometimes, a tiny runnel of luck will slip into the cloud of desperation and, even if he doesn't have one, his neighbour or someone else from the aisle will pass him one. And such would be the impact of that jet of luck that the ticket checker will not ask the neighbour for his ticket. Such happenstances occur in the general compartment.

Sometimes, though, a face gives itself away. A shifty look, beads of sweat on the upper lip. The ticket checker is not an idiot. He sees the owner of that face for what he is. Class: vermin. Category: vagrant. And with the glee of a dog sniffing out a nest of rat babies, he will pounce on the itinerant. Ready to toss him out onto the next platform with a growl and a threat, 'Do you want me to call the railway police?'

It is here that I appear. Krishna. Holding a sheaf of tickets in my pocket. Wedging my way through the heaving mass of perspiration and fear till I reach the group I know is certain to have no tickets and no knowledge of what lies next.

I lean against one of the seats. The boys avoid looking at me. They stare out of the window or at the floor. Look at me, I want to tell them.

I repeat in my head the words Pujari said to me the first time and several times thereafter. '*Quavi by esa guna mayi mama maya duratyaya*; *mam era ye prapadyante mayam etam taranti te.*' My mysterious cloud of appearance is hard to pass beyond; but those who in truth come to me go beyond the world of shadows. For I am Krishna and this is what is said in the Bhagavad Gita, Chapter 7, verse 14.

I boarded the train at Dhone junction at 3.08 a.m. It's an hour when no one notices anything. Sleep weighs heavily on the eyelids and turns thoughts into a murky sluggish stream. At 4.30 a.m., we will be at Guntakal with the possibility of the ticket checker looming. I have a few minutes to make the boys my own.

They sit leaning against each other. Three of them are dressed in T-shirts and track pants. Each of them has a thread around his neck with a little silver charm. The boys are clutching a plastic bag each. It must hold all their possessions: a few worn-out clothes and a worthless gewgaw that each will fight viciously to keep. Their feet are bare and only a little dirtier than their faces. I am Krishna and I know it all. For I was once them.

They have two bottles of water between them. One of the boys raises a bottle to his lips. His eyes meet mine.

'*Tame kouthu asicha*?' I mumble in Odiya, hiding a yawn behind my hand.

His eyes widen and he mumbles something to the boy next to him. This one is the leader of the group. He frowns and then replies to my query after a pause.

'Satpada,' he says. 'And you?'

'Puri,' I say. That is always my stock answer. And if someone probes, my house is in one of the lanes by the temple. I imagine the lane. A dirty smelly narrow strip of land crowded with people and animals, rickshaws and vendors. Pujari said that's how it is. But no one ever asked me.

'I've been to Lake Chilika,' I say.

There's a gleam in the boy's eye. Is it the relief of meeting someone who knows his home?

'Do you have tickets?' I ask.

The boy's brow furrows again. But he speaks firmly. 'Yes, yes.'

He's lying. How easily they give themselves away.

'Well then, it's fine. The ticket checker will come in at the next station and the ticketless rats, as he calls them, will be thrown to the platform where the railway police will drag them to their jail. A black hole filled with real rats and thrashings thrice a day instead of food. But you don't have to worry. Since you have your tickets, just sit tight and watch the fun!' I wink at him.

I hold onto the metal railing and let my face rest against the crook of my upturned elbow. I count under my breath. At the count of seven, I hear his low voice. 'Dada.'

I shift my gaze to meet his. 'Yes,' I say slowly. My voice takes on a sonorous tone of the big brother for he has anointed me thus.

'We don't have tickets. What do we do?'

I frown. 'That's a problem and ...'

Before I can finish, he blurts out, 'Please help us.'

I scratch my head thoughtfully. 'Three of my friends were to have joined me. But their boss didn't let them travel. So we'll just pretend that you three are the friends I bought the tickets for.'

I smile at them. My best Krishna smile that Pujari said could light a street, melt ice and open locks. How can these tribal boys from the middle of nowhere resist it? The tightness around the boys' mouth dissolves. They will go with me to the end of the world, I know.

There's something else you must be prepared for, I tell them. Their eyes widen.

I explain what lies ahead. Pujari had taught me to do so. 'You are Krishna, the charioteer. It's your dharma to guide and lead so the others may know what to expect.' It made sense then. It makes sense now. Pujari says I have an ancient soul. I know instinctively what others must spend a whole lifetime trying to understand.

'You can call me Dada, but for all other purpose, all of us have a thekedar we owe everything to.'

The boys stare uncomprehendingly. They don't know the word and I can't remember the exact equivalent in Odiya for contractor.

'You'll do as I say. I'll be able to help only if I have your faith and obedience.'

My voice is firm. The boys nod.

'Start with your names,' I tell them. 'And the names of

your parents. Actually, it doesn't matter. The names of your parents will be what I tell you, and don't forget a word of what I'm going to tell you now.'

They make room for me and I huddle with them. Most of the other travellers are asleep, lulled by the rocking of the train and their fatigue into a place where conscious thought has no room. But my boys are wide awake.

They listen.

'Bangalore is not the city you think it is...' I begin. I see the fear in their eyes, in their clenched fists, in the tautness of their bodies. Fear is good. Fear allows me to take control. Fear allows me to rule.

Rekha cannot decide on what she must tell her parents. Nowadays, no parent believes in the myth of combined study. And it's not just her parents she must convince. Suraj, her brother, can be just as difficult. 'Wat do I say @ home?' she Whatsapps Sid.

'Try cmbnd study!' The phone beeps.

'De won't buy it.' Her fingers race over the touch screen.

Her face lights up, seeing the reply. 'Gender studies sem @ NLS.'

That would work. NLS is some distance away. She can say she would sleep over at Priya, her friend's home. Priya would understand if she said she was going away with Sid for a long cosy date. Priya's parents wouldn't mind if Sid dropped her back by about eleven. And the next morning, if Suraj picked her up from Priya's, nobody would know a thing. Except Sid and I. She smiles at the thought.

'Why are you smiling at the wall?' Suraj says from the doorway.

'Su, I need a favour. I need to go for a seminar at NLS,' she says on a whim.

'Who are you going with?'

'Priya, a few of my classmates and some seniors.'

'So what's the problem?' he asks as he turns to leave.

'Wait Su. It's in the evening, so I'll need to stay back at Priya's. But I'm not sure if the parents will agree. Will you persuade them?'

Suraj gives her a long look. 'You're not involved with some silly idiot, are you?'

Rekha makes a face. 'Do you want to speak to Priya?' she tosses back a question, holding her phone out to him.

Suraj backs off as she knows he will. Suraj has a crush on Priya and the thought of speaking to her is as daunting a prospect as, probably, piercing his ear.

She pulls on a pair of black leggings and a long tunic-like green kurta in white paisley and goes looking for her mother, who is counting a stack of dosas on a plate. 'Are you ready to eat?' her mother asks.

Rekha nods. 'Amma, I have a seminar this evening.'

Her mother frowns. She doesn't like the sound of it.

'It's at NLS. So I think I'll stay at Priya's house tonight. Better than coming back late,' Rekha finishes in a rush.

Her mother shakes her head. 'I don't know if your father will agree...'

'But it's important I go,' Rekha says as she takes a plate and helps herself to a dosa. She isn't hungry but her mother won't let her go to college on an empty stomach.

In the end it's Suraj who settles it for her. He tells their parents that he'll pick her up at 6.30 in the morning and, besides, Priya has been Rekha's friend since Class VI.

Her mother eyes her clothes. 'I like this top,' she says. 'It's smart and decent. Some of the clothes these young girls wear make me want to grab a dupatta and swaddle them in it.'

Rekha hides a smile. In her bag is a little red top with a plunging neckline, cropped waist-high. Once she steps out of the college gates, Sid will take her to a mall and she'll change there.

Sid said it was part of the game: 'You have to look sexy and good enough to eat. These guys can't get it up, so you don't have to worry. And you're going to get paid serious bucks just to chit-chat. C'mon, Rex, no harm done. Would I ask you to do it if I thought it involved any touchy-feely? You know how possessive I am.'

She snuggled deeper into his side and said, 'Mmm.' They were in a multiplex watching a movie. But mostly it was about canoodling under a dupatta while his hands played with her breasts and he coaxed her to touch his erection.

Sid and she will be together till about 7 p.m. Then three hours of chit-chat with the client who has an international flight to catch and nothing to do between 7 and 10 p.m. Sid has promised to sit somewhere in the lounge or restaurant to keep an eye on her and make sure she is safe.

But first someone called Pujari is going to tell Sid where they have to go. Rekha eats her dosa quietly. Is she making a mistake, she wonders? A cloud of yellow butterflies flutter their wings in the pit of her belly that suddenly feels hollow.

Moina stares at the ceiling. She doesn't know if there's one. But she has to imagine it, for only that will allow her to believe that one day this will end. The thought of an eternity condemned to this hell with no hope of escape ever, would make her growl and scream; claw her nails through her client's skin and pound her fists on his chest and kick his shins. The guards wouldn't like that. And their punishment goes beyond a mere thrashing. So she says nothing and lies there, seeing in her mind a ceiling and, far beyond that, a sky with a blazing sun. She has forgotten what the sun looks like. Or the clouds. Or the trees. Or the feel of a breeze.

The client is drunk. That's all she can smell. The stale smell of alcohol and his foetid breath; of a body drying from within. It cuts through the all-pervasive odour that hangs around her, above her and wafts from her – sex, sweat, filth and hopelessness.

When did she have a bath last? She can't remember. Has it been three days or five? They gave her a small bucket of water to clean herself with. It was left in the corner of the cubicle. There was also the perfume spray she was asked to douse herself with. And a tin of talc. 'The clients don't care what your face looks like when they fuck you. But each one comes here thinking he's having you first ... so don't let them smell another man on you,' Daulat Ali, the big guard, said that first day she became a khanki. A slut. A whore.

Client. Her eyes widened. Ten men had fucked her one after the other. Who or what was a client?

'What?' he asked, seeing her look of puzzlement. He spoke some Bengali and so it was he who told her what she must and mustn't do.

'Gaard, who is a client?' Moina asked.

'Mokkel.' He used the Bengali word. 'That's all the men who fuck you. It doesn't matter who he is. Black or fair, tall or short, fat or thin ... they are all clients and you address them, if you must, as bava.'

'Bava?'

'Lover, husband, man, I don't know what the word is

in Telugu ... Does it matter?' Daulat Khan said snarlingly, reaching across and slapping her so hard that she fell against the wall. End of conversation.

Moina huddled in her cubicle, too afraid to speak. Daulat Ali and two other guards she never saw again had dealt with her in those first few days when she had been brought in. What did it matter, as the Gaard had said. She would call them whatever she was asked to. Bava. Sharukh Khan. Sachin Tendulkar. The memory still made her freeze. On top of her, the client feels the muscles clench around him. He grunts as he collapses on her, flooding her with a wetness that she has stopped sensing except as a stickiness on the insides of her thighs.

The client rises, fumbles with his clothes and leaves. She lies there on her back for a while, cradling her head on an arm. With the other she reaches for a rag beneath the bed and wipes herself dry. Then she turns on her side and curls into a ball. She sucks on her thumb slowly. Ma, she says. Ma, where are you?

There is a scuffling sound outside the plywood partition that is hers. Another client is on the way. Moina is on the verge of emitting a scream.

There's a knock on the partition. In five minutes a man will appear. The smaller of the guards, Muniraju, is a local. He speaks some Hindi and doesn't meet her eye. But it's he who keeps the ledger. A long notebook, in which he meticulously keeps accounts. The clients' names, the time spent and the amount received. Once, just once, on the second day, when Moina still had some fight left in her, she had padded her way to the open space beyond the four plywood partitions, all empty apart from hers, and fumbled at the ledger. The script was beyond her comprehension but she could read the numbers. She had been fucked by twenty men until then and each fuck cost Rs 1000 each. On top of each page was a squiggle. She had seen it only outside temples. It was a swastika.

Daulat Ali had slapped her hard for it and allowed her no food. 'That's our thekedar's book of accounts. How dare you touch it?' he said as he dragged her by her hair to her little hole and hurled her into it. Then he took his belt to her and said, 'You will not step outside this room unless I say you can.' The belt slashed her skin. Later that day he gave her some cream to put on the welts.

Two more girls seem to have arrived. She knows by the sound of voices and amidst it a low husky voice. That must be the thekedar, she realizes, hearing the note of deference in Daulat Ali's voice. Then two other male voices she doesn't recognize; one of them calls the low husky-voiced man Pujari.

The second knock. Muniraju telling her to get ready. A client is here.

Her mouth is stale and her gudh is painful and sore. In the past few weeks, she has not once thought about her vagina. But now she does; that's all she can think about. The soreness, the spasms of pain, the violation of her insides. She sits up and hooks the clasp of the bra at her back. Then she goes to the bucket on the floor and squats. She cups some water in her palm and washes herself. The water feels cold; it soothes the stinging ache. She pulls the ends of the lehenga down to her ankles and adjusts her blouse. She reaches for the deodorant and sprays herself again.

Does she have time for a pee? It's excruciatingly painful each time she needs to go and her body clenches. Only when she coaxes her body to let go does the urine trickle and then each second feels as if a million razor blades have slashed the passage through which it flows. But clients can't be kept waiting.

Dr Amar Rathore glances at his watch. It's ten past seven. His next appointment is in five minutes. He frowns. He hopes the man will be on time. He doesn't like to be kept waiting. This next appointment isn't even a client. Merely a middle man, a land broker, who has promised him access to the owners of the land one of his clients is interested in acquiring.

The clock strikes the quarter hour. He had sought to intimidate the broker by asking him to be there at 6.15. He had seen that in a movie on a flight. He didn't remember much about the film or the trip. After a while, all international flights, destinations and movies seem alike. But this had coded itself firmly in the hippocampus part of his brain. He dislikes sloppiness and when people say silly things like, keep a memory in your heart, he is much inclined to shake them rudely and say, 'The heart holds no memories. It's just an organ that serves as a pump. Memories are received and stored in the brain.'

He remembers Maggie Smith, the actress. His son in London, a great Harry Potter fan, had made him watch the film on the flight and has referred to her as Professor Minerva McGonagall. Maggie Smith who, as Miss Brodie, said: 'She thinks to intimidate me by the use of the quarter hours?'

He loved that. Corporate law is a war game and he seeks for his arsenal weapons of intimidation hitherto unused. An appointment at the quarter hour is a brilliant manoeuvre. No one will ever manage to arrive at the precise time and he will have the moral advantage of having been kept waiting to set the tone of the meeting. And he needs a decided advantage for this next meeting.

Land brokers are vicious as sharks with the tenacity of an octopus, and are as hard to budge as a sea urchin and as slimy as seaweed. Dr Amar Rathore grins at himself in the ornamental hallway mirror. He likes the neatness of his thought; of how he stayed within the ocean as he listed out metaphors for a land broker.

His eyes swoop on the table in front of the mirror. The stone Khmer Buddha he picked up in Cambodia has been moved from its place by two inches, skewing the arrangement. He shifts it back into place. Then he peers at himself once again and twirls the hair at the arch of his eyebrow.

He's a good-looking man with a strong face of planes and shadows. His eyebrows are heavy and, as if to compensate for them, he keeps his face clean shaven. A greenish shadow appears by dusk and some days, Dr Amar Rathore shaves twice. He plays squash two times a week and swims fifteen laps every day. He is considering joining a Krav Maga class to enhance his combat strength.

He knows the impression he makes: good-looking, strong, fit and on the go. There is just one thing he can do nothing about. He is short. At 5'4" in his socks, he feels at a disadvantage if the man in front of him is taller.

The bell rings. He switches on the intercom.

'Who is it?'

There is a pause and then a low husky voice enunciates in clear unaccented English, 'Dr Rathore, this is Pujari. I'm here about the five acres in Hoskote.'

They reach just a few minutes before the temple closes after the morning puja. He apologized all the way from the house to the temple until she had put her hand on his arm and murmured, 'It's fine. We can always come back another day.'

'No, it's not fine,' he says, his mouth twisting into a grimace. 'I know you had a reason for wanting to go there this morning and I shouldn't have cluttered the hour with appointments.'

'Husband, shut up,' she says softly.

He looks at her and smiles. 'Yes, wife!'

She squeezes his arm gently. They met at school when they were both eight years old. She, the village priest's daughter, and he, the schoolmaster's son at a little village near Latur. They have been together since then, through school and college. He went on to study further while she waited at home working on her trousseau until he came to claim her.

There was never anyone else anyway. When they were eighteen, they sneaked out for a bike ride to the Kharosa caves. An oil spill on the road caused the bike to skid; he escaped with minor injuries, she was paralysed waist down. Any opposition her family may have had dissolved when he took full responsibility for the accident and her life.

They moved to Bangalore a year after they were married. Thirty-two years of marriage and forty-seven years of togetherness. She thinks she knows how the hair in each pore of his grows. She thinks he must feel the same way. And that worries her.

'Aren't you ever tired of this?' she asks.

'What makes you say that?' His hands clench the steering wheel. 'Do I give you that impression?'

'How can anyone be as compassionate as you are? Every day, and it is the truth, almost every day I ask myself if I have ruined your life, your happiness...'

'I'm the happiest man on this earth. You and our children are all I ever wanted. So stop this silliness,' he says with a mock growl. He wooed her with that mock growl when they were eight. He the prowling lion, she the lost deer.

He parks near the entrance of the temple. Then he lifts her into his arms carefully and carries her. There's hardly anyone else there but the priest is waiting.

He sits her down on the floor against a wall and goes back to the car to fetch the offerings.

'Who is he?' one of the devotees asks.

The other man shrugs. 'Somebody very rich. Why else do you think the temple is open until now? I have seen him and his wife a few times here. I think his name is Pujari.'

He comes back with a platter laden with fruits and flowers, a coconut and a small wad of money. The priest's eyes widen. Whatever is on the 'archana' plate is for him to take. There must be at least a thousand rupees there, he thinks, unable to help his joy from showing.

The priest takes the platter from the man. The woman says to the priest, 'Please do the archana in the name of Sharad Pujari, Revati nakshatra, Bharadwaj gotra.'

The priest lights the lamps and rings the bell. He raises the lamp to the deity and begins chanting her 108 names as he circles the figurine with the lit lamp. Divine powers being invoked to keep Sharad Pujari able, well, prosperous and content.

'Happy?' he asks her as they drive back home.

'When am I not, husband?' She smiles back at him. 'As long as you are with me...'

Later, when they've had their breakfast and he has settled

her in bed, he goes downstairs to his study. He switches on the laptop and mobile phone and waits for the barrage of mails in his inbox and the log of missed calls on his phone.

The phone trills. He glances at it and presses the answer key.

'I don't want any excuses and explanations. Just give me the report for yesterday,' he says, his low husky voice not rising a decibel higher than the voice he reserved for his wife.

The man at the other end of the line feels the hair at the nape of his neck rise at the menace in the tone.

ABOUT THE AUTHOR

Anita Nair is one of India's most acclaimed authors whose oeuvre ranges from literary fiction to noir to poetry to children's literature to translation. Her books have been translated into thirty-two languages around the world and have been adapted for audio, the stage and the screen. She is the recipient of several prizes and honours including the Central Sahitya Akademi award, the Crossword Prize and the National Film Award.

Founder of the creative writing mentorship programme Anita's Attic which has mentored over 125 writers, Anita Nair is also a High-Profile Supporter of the UNHCR.

Anita Nair's new novel is *Hot Stage*, third in the Borei Gowda noir series.

ALSO IN THE SERIES

CHAIN OF CUSTODY

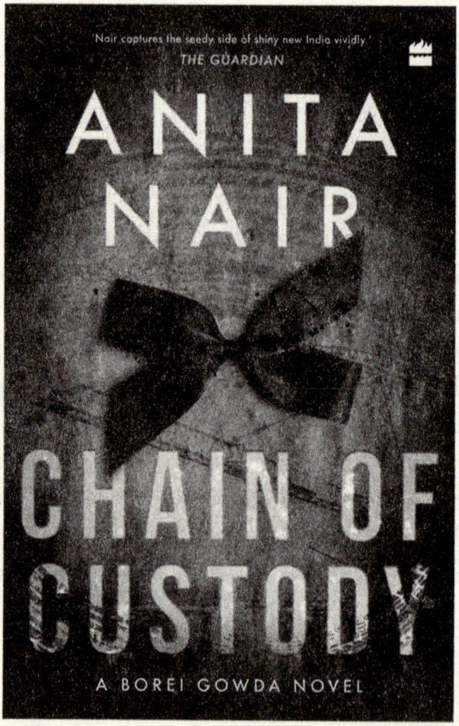

Moina had handed her a sliver of soap. Wash yourself, she had mimed. Nandita's hand shook as she ran the soap on herself. It was the first bath she had been allowed after the day she was brought to this place.

The blisters on her legs had burned on contact with the soap. Her legs had trembled. The filthy hole they called a bathroom had smelled of stale urine. The walls were grey and damp. She had thought she would throw up as the water caused the stink from the floor to rise. A dry retching sound had escaped the throat.

'Ssh …' Moina had held a finger to her lips. 'Jaldi,' she had murmured. 'Hurry up.'

Nandita had been given a rag to dry herself with. Moina had handed her some clothes. A skirt that reached her knees and a frilly top. There were no underclothes. Not even a slip, she had realized. Nandita had blanched in horror. 'What's this?' she had protested, peering at the older girl through the sheer fabric. Moina hadn't replied. Nandita had wondered who she was. Moina, it seemed, was her only ally … Nandita had pulled the top on and the skirt. She didn't feel safe without her school uniform. She had tugged at the top so it went over the skirt, offering some modicum of cover. She crossed her arms over her chest to hide her breasts and hunched her shoulders as she walked back with Moina to the cubicle that she had been allotted.

Nandita stood up and peered outside the cubicle. She didn't know what to expect. She knew, though, that she was in a bad place. And that the beatings, the starvation, the strange clothes, the isolation were only a preparation for what would come next.

She trembled again. It was as if she couldn't stop trembling. She knew that she had no one to blame but herself. She had been worried about the exams. There was a lot riding on how well she did. A scholarship had been announced and her mother had decided that she had to win it. Nandita didn't think she could.

One of the girls at school said she should go to the Infant Jesus church at Vivek Nagar. 'If you go every Thursday for six weeks and light a candle there, your wish will be granted. I swear by it,' Selvi had said. But Nandita didn't think that her mother would allow it.

'Jesus will not write the scholarship exam. You have to do it, and for that you need to study. Not moon around in front of the mirror or watch TV all the time,' Shanthi would have snapped.

Her mother seemed to snap and snarl all the time. Selvi had suggested the Basilica then. 'Well, what about the St Mary's Basilica at Shivaji Nagar? She is the mother of Jesus and will do for one candle what Baby Jesus needs six candles for.'

Nandita had thought that was doable. It had seemed very simple when she thought it through. Sneak out early from the exam hall. Catch a bus to Hennur depot. And a bus from there to Shivaji Nagar. The bus stand was by the Basilica. She would light a candle to Mother Mary, offer her prayers, make a vow of some sort, and catch a bus back to the depot. It would take her less than two hours and she would be home at the usual time. A few extra minutes wouldn't perturb her mother. Nandita had never given her mother any cause for worry until now.

It had all gone according to plan until she had reached the Basilica. She had stood helplessly at the doorway of the church, not knowing what to do.

'Are you alone here, baby?' a voice had asked in Kannada.

She had turned to see a middle-aged woman in a white sari with small blue flowers, the pallu pulled over her hair, standing a few feet behind her. She looked tired, her face etched with lines, her mouth drooping at the corners, her eyes dull. She could have been her mother, right down to the side parting.

'Yes,' she said.

'And you want to make a special prayer to our Mother?' the woman asked.

Nandita nodded.

'Mother Mary isn't inside the church. We need to go to the shrine outside. Come with me,' the woman said.

'What's your name, Aunty?' Nandita asked.

'Mary,' the woman said.

Nandita felt her heart thud. Mother Mary was said to appear to those who sought her with ardent prayer. Was this woman Our Lady in disguise? The woman helped her light the candle she had brought with her. She knelt with Nandita and they prayed together.

'You are too young to be out on your own,' the woman said when Nandita thanked her.

'I should go now,' Nandita said reluctantly.

'Where is your home?' the woman asked.

'Kothanur area.'

'Where is that?' The woman laughed. 'Never heard of the place!'

'Beyond Hennur, Aunty,' Nandita said, flushing. Her father shouted at her mother every second day for having dragged him to a village for a piece of asbestos over their heads. She looked at the crowded street outside the Basilica, fearful someone her parents knew would choose to pass that way.

'Hmm …' the lady said. 'I need to go as far as Tannery Road.

And I am taking an auto. Why don't you come with me? I'll put you on a bus to Hennur and you can continue to Kothanur from there.' She waved at an autorickshaw.

Nandita clambered in quickly. Now that she had made her petition to Mother Mary, she wanted to go home to her mother.

But she hadn't. She didn't remember much after Aunty had offered her a juice from a bag. She had felt unable to talk or resist and had watched in a sort of stupefied horror as she was taken through roads and alleys she didn't recognize.

The auto had stopped outside an unplastered building. On the ground level were two shops. One had a couple of stacks of tyres and a boy stood beside them. The other had paint tins and cement sacks spilling out of the entrance. Two other shops had their shutters drawn.

She had felt her legs grow heavy and her eyes droop even as the woman dragged her out.

She had felt herself being pushed up a flight of stairs and then they were in a room and she had thought all she wanted to do was lie down. She had tried to curl her tongue around the word 'Aunty' but it had refused to move. She had felt herself slipping away into a grey space where everything turned into shadows.

She had no idea how long she stayed there. Or if she had woken and slipped back into the space. She had visions of prising the bindi off her forehead and sticking it on the door as she usually did, and of her mother holding a glass of water to her dry lips.

When she became fully conscious, she stood up on shaking legs and looked for a way out. A tall burly man had slapped her hard, hurling her against a wall. She had been dragged to this cubicle and left here till Moina was sent to her. How had she reached here? She had no recollection at all.

HOT STAGE

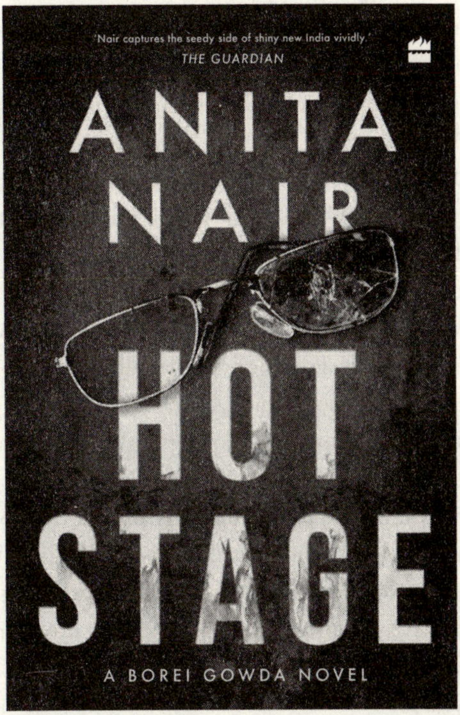

27 November 2012, 3 p.m.

A grimy nylon string dangled from a hook in the ceiling that was once the colour of ivory but was now an indeterminate brown. The man standing inside the bar-counter cage grabbed a piece of newspaper from the bunch of squares shoved onto a nail on the wall.

The punter tossed his first cutting of Old Admiral brandy down his throat as he watched the bar attendant hold aloft a boiled egg on a piece of paper and use the string to slice the egg so that it burst into bloom. He marvelled, as he always did, at the artistry. The egg was no longer an egg but a frangipani flower with fat white petals and a yellow heart. He watched the man sprinkle onto it a mixture of pepper and salt from a greasy blue plastic bottle.

Gulping his second cutting, the punter took the paper plate heaped with the sliced egg. He ate it slowly, relishing each bite. The egg-flower followed the Old Admiral into a happy place inside him.

He gestured for a refill. This time a 90 ml, he indicated with his thumb and forefinger. The brandy sloshed against the glass as he walked to the island of tables at the centre of the bar. He plonked himself down in a chair. He had had a good day and had decided to treat himself to an afternoon of pleasure. He looked up, still flushed with a sense of well-being, at the man seated opposite him.

'Namaskara,' the punter said, jumping to his feet and joining his palms together to indicate his total subservience. He gave the man a nervous smile as he took his glass and himself to one of the counters that ran alongside the wall of the dark, dingy bar.

He stared at the brandy in his glass and told himself that he was lucky to have got away without having his nose broken or his teeth on the floor. No one sat at Oil Mill Jaggi's table. Not unless he invited you to.

There was a time when Oil Mill Road was just a road. No one knew it by name. People coming in from the city took it to get to the newly built Jal Vayu Vihar, an apartment complex for naval and air force officers. The military, not to be left out, had set up Sena Vihar across the road, soon turning Kammnahalli into this bustling area with people from different parts of India and foreign countries. It was difficult to walk through this stretch without running into Arabs, Africans, Koreans and God knows who else, the punter thought. Not that it bothered him one bit. He liked crowded places.

But Oil Mill Road was still his territory. He knew most of the shop owners by name and could even squeeze them for a 'temporary loan; return guaranteed'. The punter felt like he belonged there. Usually. But not this afternoon. The presence of Oil Mill Jaggi had unnerved him and made it seem as if he was trespassing on an area he should have steered clear of.

The curtains parted and a man walked in. Even though it was three in the afternoon and the sharp light of the November sun blazed in the street outside, the punter felt a chill down his spine. He recognized the man by face. He wasn't a regular at this bar or at any other. But the punter knew him; knew of him. He was called Military. He didn't speak much but you knew when Military was in a good mood. For he would sponsor a quarter for anyone who caught his eye. You also knew when Military was in a bad mood. The punter had seen him smash an argumentative drunk's face into the wall and drag it against the surface, all without a bead of sweat popping up on his brow.

Military walked to Oil Mill Jaggi's table and sat across him. He gestured to the man in the cage.

'Jaggi,' the man said. 'What are you doing here?'

Oil Mill Jaggi shrugged. 'Do I need to state the obvious?'

'Don't forget . . . it's a big day—the day after tomorrow. This isn't when you drink yourself into a state where you don't know your elbow from your knee.'

Oil Mill Jaggi narrowed his eyes, and then, as if he had changed his mind, ignored the presence of the glass with some alcohol in it and said blithely, 'Chill, Military. I haven't been drinking. This is where I come to think.'

The man frowned. 'My boss won't like it.'

'Your boss and I go back a long way. Long before you started calling him boss.' Oil Mill Jaggi yawned loudly and stretched. 'Relax and have a quarter, Military. Why are you getting so worked up? Or is it that you don't trust me anymore?'

'It's big stakes, Jaggi. I can't relax. I have a lot riding on this,' the man said, pulling out a chair.

'You will be a rich man and so will I,' Oil Mill Jaggi said and pushed the plate of mudde and mutton curry from the next-door Naidu restaurant towards him. 'Or we will be fucked. It can go only two ways, so why stress?'

Military looked at the ragi balls as if they were pieces of dog turd and said, 'I just had lunch. Besides, how can you eat this? It gets stuck in the throat.'

Oil Mill Jaggi flexed his enormous biceps at Military. 'Mudde is what began this and mudde is what keeps it going.' He tore a piece off the purplish brown ball, daubed it in the mutton curry, forked a piece of meat with his fingers and popped all of it into his mouth, almost defiantly. Then he swallowed it with a convulsive movement of his throat.

The punter would have liked the mudde. He looked at it hungrily. And without thinking, he let his gaze wander to Military.

For a fleeting moment, their eyes met. His two cuttings dissipated into a thin vapour of fear.

The punter took his glass and moved to the farthest end of the counter. Any further and he would be in the toilet. But it was best to keep his distance from those two, he decided. He didn't want to be accused of listening in. Or get caught in between if the two of them broke into a fight. The punter wondered at their power equation. It was hard to tell who feared whom and who would survive if they got into a fistfight.

He saw Military toss his rum down his throat and leave the bar, squeezing Oil Mill Jaggi's shoulder on his way out. A little later, Oil Mill Jaggi followed. The punter heaved a sigh of relief and finished his drink in one gulp. What a waste of money! He had treated himself to a better brand instead of his usual Silver Cup. It felt like he had drunk one quarter of rasam rather than brandy. 'Thoo, bosadi magane,' he swore, spat into his hand and wiped it on his shirtsleeve. There was something immensely satisfying about calling those two men sons of a whore. It didn't make up for the wasted afternoon but it was some compensation, he told himself.

Then, because it was prudent to do so, the punter drew out a brand-new razorblade still in its sleeve from beneath the multiple red threads wound tight around his right wrist. He took the blade out and popped it into his mouth. It would buy him enough time to escape and flee if either of them decided to pounce on him for being in the bar when they were there.

The punter chewed on the blade as he walked on to Oil Mill Road with the furtive step of a rat on the prowl.

HarperCollins *Publishers* India

At HarperCollins India, we believe in telling the best stories and finding the widest readership for our books in every format possible. We started publishing in 1992; a great deal has changed since then, but what has remained constant is the passion with which our authors write their books, the love with which readers receive them, and the sheer joy and excitement that we as publishers feel in being a part of the publishing process.

Over the years, we've had the pleasure of publishing some of the finest writing from the subcontinent and around the world, including several award-winning titles and some of the biggest bestsellers in India's publishing history. But nothing has meant more to us than the fact that millions of people have read the books we published, and that somewhere, a book of ours might have made a difference.

As we look to the future, we go back to that one word—a word which has been a driving force for us all these years.

Read.

Harper Collins

HARPER PERENNIAL

HARPER BUSINESS

HARPER BLACK

हार्पर हिन्दी

HarperCollins *Children'sBooks*

HARPER DESIGN

HARPER VANTAGE

Harper Sport